Zachary Hill

The

Lost

Promise

Book 1 in the Path of
Light Series

Published by White Feather Press, LLC

ISBN 978-1-61808-123-0

Printed in the United States of America

Back/front cover knight photo ©iStockphoto.com/Diana Hirsch

Front cover Castle photo ©iStockphoto.com/windowseat

White Feather Press

Reaffirming Faith in God, Family, and Country!

To my wife, the reason I breathe.

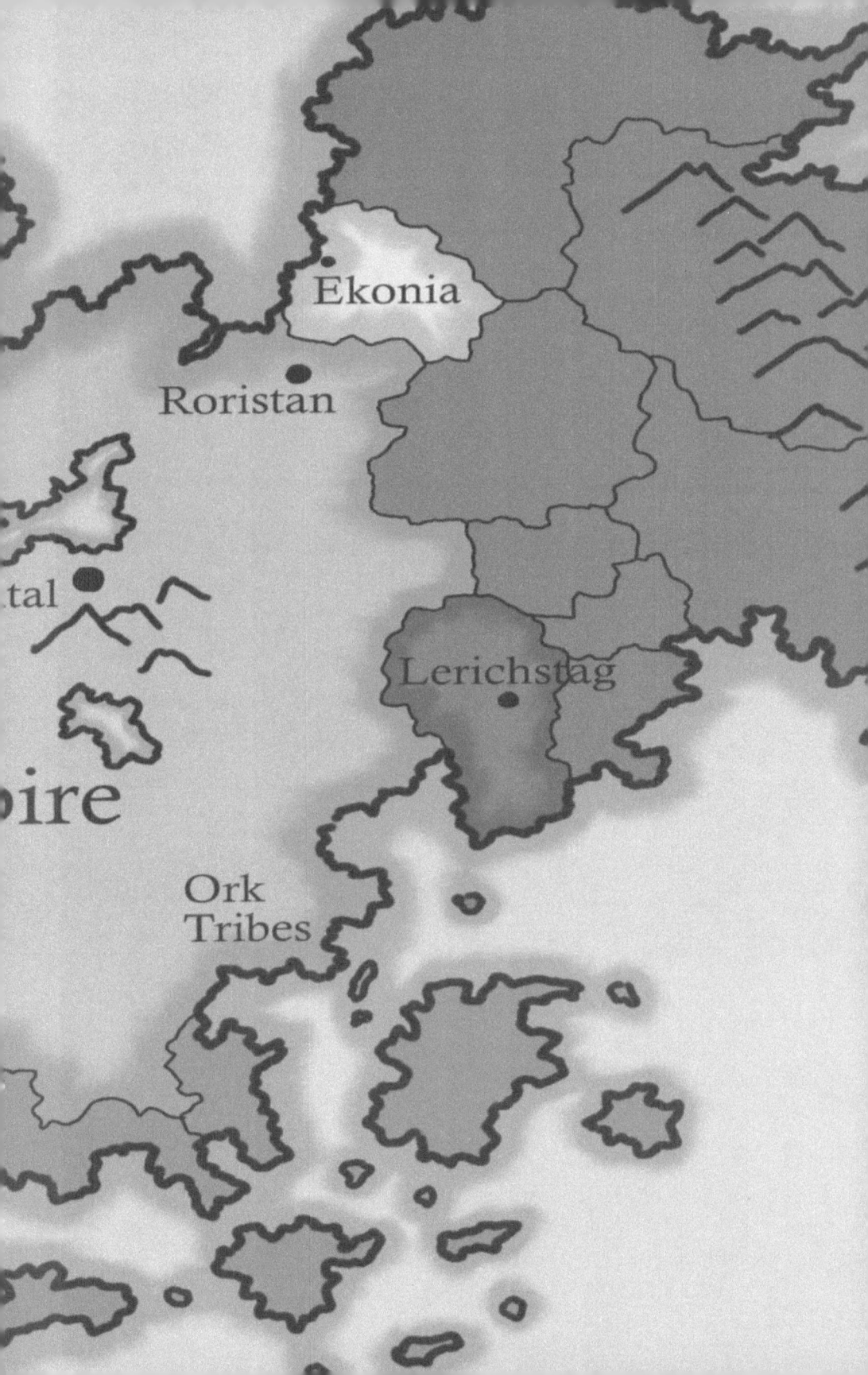

Chapter One

GREZA PRAYED FOR FORGIVENESS FOR THE life she was about to take. Every morning she prayed that she wouldn't have to kill anyone. That desire wouldn't be answered this day but another one would be. It was a wish she hadn't dared think of for a long time.

After tonight she would be free, but she had to survive this fight first. That was the only thing she had to focus on. That and nothing else even though she knew that upstairs, Erinad her was dying.

The sun was setting when she heard a knock at her door.

"Yes?"

"Greza, the masters have ordered you to prepare to entertain tonight. They will call you within the hour. Go get ready," the muffled female voice said through the wooden door.

"Yes."

She always spoke with simple words to the others, especially her masters. If they suspected that she had a fraction of the learning she did have, they'd punish her and possibly Erinad as well. It was illegal for a slave to read and have religion and because of him she had both.

She got up off her knees, grabbed her armor and left her small room. It was time for her preparation ritual. She'd use this time to get her mind ready for what she had to do.

She walked through the slaves' quarters and past other slaves that were busy running around doing mindless chores. She was like them but wasn't one of them. She was a slave but didn't do the menial tasks they did. She was the Masters' prized fighter.

She'd give anything if she only had to scrub floors. Countless times she asked Erinad if the Divine Lights would forgive her for killing.

"What do you think will happen if you refuse to fight?" The old Dark Elf would ask.

His bony finger would point at her and shake as if to punctuate his sentence.

"The masters will hurt me," she would say.

"They'd do that and more. I can protect you from the worst of their treatment because I've claimed you as my 'privilege,' but if you fail them I won't be able to protect you from that."

"So, I have to fight."

"To save yourself, yes. And you are worth saving, Greza. Far more than you know."

They had had that same conversation many times over the years and each time she needed to hear him say it. She needed to know that she wasn't sinning in the eyes of the Divine Lights. But lately she felt her sin was becoming something else, the sin of not feeling.

She came to the door that led to the rest of the mansion. Slaves were only allowed there if they had work to do or were summoned. The guards were used to her coming and going as she was always going up to Erinad's room where he would teach her about history, philosophy and the Path of Light.

She looked out into the mansion proper and looked over the polished wood room for signs of the master's sons. Every time they saw her they'd taunt her about Erinad because they assumed they were lovers.

Only a guard was standing by so she made sure to keep her eyes down and shoulders slumped as she walked past him not too slow to look lazy and not too fast to look suspicious.

As she shuffled past she eyed the matchlock the guard held in his hands. Would that gun be fired at her tonight as she escaped? How good of a shot was this guard?

No, she couldn't think about that. She had to focus on the fight. Once she won that, the rest was clear. Erinad had everything set up so she wouldn't have to worry about it.

Not yet, anyways.

The room had a giant tapestry with the family's crest on it hanging above the empty fireplace. The Master was always bragging how his family could be traced back to the founding of the Empire and had distant ties to the Therosian Dynasty of Dark Elf Emperors. It was something they bragged about to everyone they met.

She made her way to the servants' room where maids and butlers were. Two slave girls were brought in to get Greza ready for the fight. It was the same preparation each time.

It was the usual Satyr and Human girl. Good, they new the routine and wouldn't make her late.

She stripped down while two girl slaves rubbed oil all over her slender and scar covered body. Some of the scars were from training and fights, but most were from the lash. When she failed to perform to their impossible expectations she would be flogged, though that didn't happen nearly as often now and she suspected they did it just to remind her of her place. She hadn't lost a single fight in the past two years since she was officially put on the roll of gladiators.

Greza wondered what the two slave girls thought of her. Did they only see a brutish Ork? She had the black hair, greenish skin and sharp teeth of an Ork, but she was a runt. She was smaller and scrawnier than most Orks, but that made her deceptively strong. An Ork was about ten times stronger than a Human of the same size. She was at least twice as strong as a large man. Maybe stronger.

Then the girls wrapped her chest with a simple, tan cloth and another cloth around her loins. Modesty was not a high priority to nobles and she felt exposed for everyone to see. The cloth around the chest was customary to keep women's breasts from interfering. She did not have much to worry about and wrapping them made little difference. Then they braided her long, thick hair in intricate designs with ribbons weaved into it and strapped armor onto her shins and arms.

The last thing they put on were her archaic weapons; the cestus. A cestus was a gauntlet designed to enhance a punch to lethal levels. Out of all the weapons she had ever used, even more so than the sword or ax, the cestus was her favorite. Nothing else came close to their effectiveness.

Now, armed and ready she pushed everything out of her mind. She had to focus. Distraction leads to death. She couldn't think about Erinad or what was to come later that night. All of that had to be shoved out of her mind.

She could hear the music and laughter from the party through the closed door. They were probably bragging about each other's gladiators and making bets. It was a custom of theirs when visiting to pit their gladiator pets against each other.

Already she could feel the rush of her blood and anticipation. A part of her, a part she was ashamed of, actually enjoyed the thrill. It was a sin but she loved the challenge and never felt more alive than when she fought. Her body craved the rush of all her senses heightened to new levels.

She also hated it. She hated watching her opponents die in front of her and even more she hated the cheers from the nobles. Most of all she hated knowing that she was the cause of the other's death.

She stretched her muscles and limbered up. Like Erinad said, she couldn't die or get injured. An injury would slow her down and she had to make it to the border by sunrise.

The estate was near the border of the Empire and close to the divided kingdoms that did nothing more than war with each other over petty differences. The entire continent had been one massive empire long ago, now the Empire was a shadow of its self with the eastern half and the southern parts of the continent independent kingdoms and republics. To the west was a narrow strip of land that led to a vast, uninhabitable wasteland.

It was to the east that she would run.

As she waited for the match to begin she couldn't help but think of Erinad. He was dying upstairs and she wouldn't even be able to see him. He had called her to his room that morning and told her everything.

"You're not going to like what I have to say, Greza."

Sometimes she wished he wouldn't be so blunt. All of the other Dark Elf nobles spoke in such allegoric terms that their subtlety was hard to understand. Erinad spoke with the bluntness of a blacksmith's hammer.

She took a deep breath and prepared for the worst.

"Greza, I'm dying. I know it and you know it."

"You don't know that."

He looked up at her and furrowed his brows like he always did when he scolded her.

"Have you learned nothing? There is no use in denying the truth that is plain before you. We have to accept and adapt. That is how we grow. My time for growing is at an end and now I can only hope that that growth has been enough."

"Of course it will," she said.

"Greza, I'm not a perfect man. I've made more than my share of mistakes."

She inhaled to prepare to speak, but nothing came to her lips. What was she supposed to say to that? This was the man who rescued and protected her. She hadn't seen anything but generosity and kindness from him.

But then he told her what she had not expected. She knew he was dying and had feared it for a long while. This was something else.

"Tonight you will fight in a match. It is my nephew's birthday and to celebrate, it will be a fight to the death."

She straightened her spine at that news. Fights to the death were only for special holidays and events and each one had the possibility that she would be killed or that she would kill the other. Neither was a choice she liked.

"But you must win, Greza, and you must not be wounded. You'll need your strength. Tonight I will die and that will cause a commotion. There will be many things to do and people to send out on tasks. During the confusion is your time to escape. I've hidden a pack in the cellar behind the wine racks. It has supplies and a change of clothes. Use it to leave this place."

"You can't leave me like this."

"No, I can't. That's why you have to run. Without me to protect you they will destroy you and you have a great work to do. My death will mean your freedom."

Then his eyes closed and he went to sleep and those were the last words she would ever hear from him. She would never be scolded for mispronouncing a word or sloppy handwriting. She would never hear his lectures about the history of the Empire or hear his readings of the great philosophers.

She hadn't even told him that she loved him.

He would die tonight and she would run. She had seen what happened to slaves that had been caught trying to escape. The first time they were flogged almost to death, the second time they were hung and fed to the pigs.

She prayed to the Divine Lights that they would receive Erinad in their arms.

Then the door opened and it was time.

Chapter Two

GREZA TOOK A DEEP BREATH WALKED OUT into the dinning hall where the banners of all the attending nobles hung. Her bare feet padded along the red marble floor and the smell of fried food and fresh bread filled her stomach. She never ate before a fight and she hadn't eaten all day. Thoughts of Erinad washed away her appetite. Flower decorations hung from the rafters and musicians played a loud and chaotic song. The young duke's son sat in the place of honor surrounded by all his noble friends. The teenagers watched her enter and she could hear some of their comments. It seemed getting women into their beds was all they cared about. The adults sat off to the side having their adult conversations about the qualities of a gladiator and the price of good slaves.

Some pointed and cheered at her entrance. Others, mostly the women, didn't seem to notice.

She looked around for her opponent but didn't see him.

Then one of the young nobles, the birthday boy's older brother, stood up and raised his voice.

"Attention, attention! Here we have the representative of House Roristan. Our gladiator fights in the ancient method of the Second Empire. Though old, it is not to be discounted as this slave has fought ten battles this year with no losses. She will be a difficult opponent for our guests."

The party clapped.

Then a young nobleman she didn't recognize stood up. He was a Pale Elf with long silver hair.

"Attention, attention! I am pleased to introduce to you, the representative of House Tilefaria."

The doors on the other side of the hall opened. A large human entered. He was the size of an Ork with large and toned muscles. He had a shaved head and fully armored arms and legs. He carried a round shield with a spike jutting out of it and a short sword with a spiked pommel.

The crowd 'oohed' and 'awed.' He was an intimidating specimen.

But what the soft nobles didn't understand was that this fight wasn't really about size. In fact, Greza hoped that it would work to her benefit. This man would see a scrawny Ork girl in front of him. He would underestimate her to a large degree.

However, she couldn't underestimate him either. This was a dangerous man and she couldn't play with him and prolong the fight for the amusement of the audience. This was a fight to the death. She had to end it as quickly as she could. There was no other option if she wanted to live and Erinad had told her that she must.

Thinking of escaping sent a cold shiver down her back and she had to block it out of her mind. Distractions lead to death.

"But, it's a young girl against that brute?" One of the noblewomen asked. "Hardly seems sporting."

"She's a trained killer," a man sitting next to her said.

"She doesn't even have a sword!"

"Won't need one."

She watched from the corner of her eyes as they all began placing the bets. The nobles in their brightly colored coats and silk shirts looked ridiculous and she wondered if they had any idea how out of harmony with the real world they were. The world was dancing to one tune and they were dancing to another that only they heard.

This wasn't how the Divine Lights wished people to live. They didn't want a small group of entitled people to have complete control over everyone else and no accountability. It was a disgrace.

But when the Promised Victor was lost, so was their faith and their decency. The Path of Light had forbidden slavery and when the Church fell, so did its beliefs.

"Gladiators, this fight is to honor the birthday of Sir Ferulu. As such, to properly honor his sixteenth year, this fight will be to the death as is the custom. Gladiators, the match begins…now!"

The enormous man stepped forward and beat his sword against his shield.

"This isn't even a real fight!" The human shouted to the audience. A smile formed on his lips. He then turned to her. "I'm going to break you in half, little girl."

Greza said nothing. She never wasted her breath and energy in boasting.

Unlike most boasting though, this man seemed to believe every word of it.

She stretched her arms and wiggled her fingers to loosen them up.

Greza looked around for something to throw. She was within arm's reach of a serving table where the kitchen kept extra plates and goblets handy.

As the man took his first step she reached for the table and grabbed a bowl. In one smooth motion she threw the bowl at the man. As she predicted the man raised his shield to block. This blinded him for a crucial moment.

She took that moment to rush forward as fast as she could. She was halfway there by the time the bowl clanged off his shield. And when the man had eyes on her again she was already on top of him.

Greza grabbed the man's shield and yanked it to the left, pulling him off balance, exposing his side and getting herself out of reach of his sword. The man was quick and was already preparing a swing to backhand her with his shield but before he could, she kicked him in the knee. It was more like a quick stomp that she put all her weight into.

No matter how big and tough a person was, if they lost their knee, they were immobilized.

Her foot smashed into his knee and it crumbled to the side in an unnatural way.

He howled in pain and fell to his good knee.

The audience made a collective gasp. They were shocked at her speed and power.

The spectacle of a girl fighting a man twice her size had to be amusing to the languid nobles. She was half this man's weight at least, but just as strong.

The man was on the ground but she couldn't stop there. As a gladiator she'd been trained to prolong a fight for entertainment, but she could not play with this man. Not this time.

Greza moved behind him to get into a position to choke him but he thrust his sword at her face. Her left arm came up to block the sword and with her right hand she smashed the back of the man's head where the spine met the base of the skull.

She heard the sickening crunch of broken bone and felt the warm gush of blood run over her hand.

"I'm sorry," she whispered.

At least it had been quick.

The man fell to the ground and she stood up, breathing hard.

The audience was silent. The fight had lasted maybe twenty seconds at most.

"It's over?" One particularly stupid woman asked.

Then the cheering and booing began. The head servant nodded toward the door and she left to the sounds of arguing and laughing. Money was being exchanged and the man's body was left where it fell.

"That was...quite a fight," one of the women slaves said. She held a platter of food and stared at her with wide eyes.

One of her trainers, a retired human gladiator walked in. Harok used to be a gladiator years ago before they became slaves. He had the scars to prove it. He was a man with an incredibly broad chest and little compassion. At one time he used to be as fit as the man she had just killed but retirement had made him soft in the middle.

"I think they wanted you to put on more of a show," Harok said.

He was frowning. He usually reserved frowns for when she made a mistake in training.

"It was to the death and he was too dangerous."

Harok shrugged.

"You're lucky our masters sound pleased. I guess that's all that matters."

He folded his arms and leaned against the wall.

At first he had been hard on her, almost cruel. But after a few years and discovering that she could destroy him he backed off and let her do as she pleased. She seldom saw him anymore. He simply had nothing to teach her anymore.

With her heart still pounding and the adrenaline still rushing through her system she walked back to her room and began cleaning her body.

She took off the armored cestus and found that her right hand was covered in blood. It reeked of it.

Did this make her wicked? She wondered if it counted as self defense. She could have refused. Was her life any better than that man's?

But Erinad had told her she must live and so she had done what it took to live.

Now that the fight was over her mind cleared. She thought back to Erinad and everything he had said to her.

Now all she had to do was wait for news of his death.

It was torture.

Greza stayed awake and listened for the commotion that would mark his passing. She couldn't go up and be with him for his last moments. She wouldn't be able to mourn him or cry. No, he would die knowing that she would gain her freedom from it. That would have to be enough.

They were both running off the assumption that she would make it. The possibility of being caught was very real and she didn't want to imagine the consequences.

Sometime around midnight she heard commotion in the halls. People began running around and speaking in hurried voices. Greza got up and looked out into the hall. She saw two of the women servants still wearing their nightgowns.

They noticed her and stopped.

"Lord Erinad has died. There's so much do."

Then the servants rushed off in different directions.

This was the time. Her father had given her this opportunity and she had to take it.

She grabbed her cestus, knife and candle and walked with calm, deliberate strides to the cellar. No one noticed her. The few people she saw were running around in agitation.

She opened the door to the cellar when no one was around and went in. It was cold and damp and the walls were thick, white stone. Barrels and crates of supplies filled the basement but left a path to the wooden wine racks. Behind the rack of wine was a brown backpack and inside were dried meats, fruits and cheeses. Clothing, lots of money and a pair of boots. There was also a note.

Greza, do not feel sad for me. Go live your life. Find freedom, love and happiness. Remember that you are watched over by Divine Lights. They know you and will protect you. I will be with you as well.
Erinad.

A single sob escaped her mouth and she covered it with her hand so no one would hear. She didn't have time for that. She had twenty miles to go. *Distraction is death.* She took off her slave dress and began putting on the tight, black pants, shirt, hooded jacket, scarf and boots. She had never worn pants before and they felt restrictive.

Simply by taking off the slave dress and putting on these black clothes she was breaking the law. It was illegal for a slave to dress in the clothing of a citizen and if caught she'd get at least twenty lashes.

She tried to do all of this as quietly as she could so she could listen. Nobody came but she did hear a great deal of commotion above her.

The cellar had a door that led outside and she went to it and opened it a crack. Lanterns were coming on everywhere in the house and she checked to make sure no one was looking.

Once she was sure the way was clear, she shouldered the backpack and ran for the woods. She had to cover a lot of distance. She ran past the slave quarters, the well, the cow pen, the chicken pen and over a vast field of wheat.

Normally there were guards or servants about and few slaves could make it to the distant woods without being spotted. But she was faster and they were distracted. She could do this.

Greza ran as fast as she could over the dried fields and didn't look back. She couldn't waste time. If they saw her she'd hear it.

Only when she reached the woods did she spare a glance back at the distant manor.

No one was coming after her. She saw more lights coming on in the manor and shapes running around inside, but no one was coming after her.

This was far more dangerous than any match she had ever fought. If they found her they'd torture her in front of the other slaves as an example. When they got bored then they'd get around to killing her.

Erinad.

He was gone. It hadn't sunk in that she'd never see him again. Even if she stayed he wouldn't be there. The manor was her prison but it was all she knew. She had food, a bed and sometimes a fire on winter nights.

But she couldn't stay. Without him there she'd be exposed for any noble that wanted her. She had seen it happen to other gladiators. After their match the winner or whoever bid the most would get to take the gladiator to their bed.

Greza was still a virgin and that was thanks to Erinad. He had saved her from horrible things that she couldn't imagine.

She felt the tears well up in her eyes and this time she let them. She ran as she cried and didn't look back again.

Her eyes could see in the dark fairly well. As she understood it, Humans, Pale Elves and some other races had difficulty seeing in the dark.

She had no trouble at all and she ran through the woods, jumping over logs, dodging branches and avoiding holes.

When she came to a stream she would run down a ways in the water to lose any scent or footprints. She had heard about how they used dogs to track people and game and had read all about it.

Greza continued to run until she grew tired and then ran some more. Her muscles ached and her lungs cried for a break but she knew she couldn't give them the rest they demanded.

Eventually woods ended and she found herself running through grass covered rolling hills. Large boulders lay about as if tossed by giants. The horizon was turning purple and red. She had been running for at least six hours, maybe more. It had to be twenty miles by now.

Greza slowed to a walk and as she struggled to catch her breath she leaned against a boulder.

She was alive. She had done it. Even if they caught up with her eventually, she was free now.

She kept walking as her body struggled to stay upright. In training she had had to run around the manor grounds several times but never had she ran like that. She had had no idea that her body was capable of it.

By the time the sky started turning light purple she was stumbling and if she didn't stop she could fall and risk breaking something she couldn't afford to break.

Without thinking anything more she lay on the ground, positioned her backpack as a pillow and fell asleep without trying. Her mind was running around but her body was too exhausted to care.

She didn't sleep long. The sun and her own mind prevented it. It had been maybe two or three hours at most.

Digging out an apple from the backpack she continued on, though at a fast walk instead of a run. Her body ached all over and her muscles were tight and stiff.

She wondered where she was. There were no villages, roads or farms. She had never learned much about this place. She knew the country was the Danata Kingdom. Though she could tell you the history of the kingdom she couldn't say anything about the people here. The Danata Kingdom was only an ally of the Empire and they spoke Haran like all Imperials, or at least some of them did. Maybe. She wasn't sure.

Now that she had time to think she began to wonder what exactly she was going to do.

She had her freedom now but no way to get food and shelter. In the outside world people worked for money. All she knew how to do was fight.

All her favorite heroes from the histories and stories were soldiers. Like her they knew the cost of taking a life. Only they took lives to protect others.

The problem was that she couldn't join the Imperial Army. They'd know she was an escaped slave and she'd be brought back to her masters. She had to go outside the Empire to the smaller, less civilized kingdoms.

Greza tried to remember the map of the world in her head. She was heading east and past Danata there was the Kingdom of Ekonia. She had read about Ekonia. It was a tiny, warlike dukedom that prided itself on the quality of their soldiers. The warlike dukedom was also new. The sell sword band called the Chimera Company had saved a king's daughter from kidnappers. The price had been half the kingdom. It was either five or six years ago. She remembered because Erinad thought that remaking the maps was a fun thing to do in his leisure time.

The problem was that mercenaries weren't honorable. She wanted to be like the heroes of old. None of them were sell-swords. She didn't want to kill for money. If she joined them, she'd be fighting other people's battles regardless of who was right or wrong.

But she had to think about this rationally. Like the philosopher Sarnalitus said: *"Always put your heart aside when making a decision. Think through the issue with reason and intellect. Then, after seeing the facts for what they are, bring in the heart to judge the decision."*

So, she thought it through rationally.

If she didn't join the ex-mercenary dukedom she would be forced to be a hired worker or worse. She'd be paid very little and without connections she simply wouldn't make it without compromising her values further. She knew very well what happened to poor girls without a place to turn to. The stories were full of impoverished women turning to prostitution. She'd die before she did that. The Path would not allow such a degradation.

On the other hand, if she joined a mercenary country, she could fight, earn a decent living and maybe rise in rank to something respectable. Perhaps she could even do some good while she was there.

Ekonia it was. She'd keep walking until she saw the black flag with the Chimera symbol on it. The books said that they accepted anyone that could prove their worth.

Who else would possibly accept her?

Chapter Three

GREZA AVOIDED THE SMALLER TOWNS WHERE she'd stand out. She kept to the main roads and covered her face with her scarf and kept her hood up. There was hopefully nothing about her to draw attention.

She kept her head down but her eyes open. No one would see her long, pointy ears or her sharp teeth. She was just a traveler passing through.

Her backpack had a few days of food but when she opened the purse she had found more money than she had ever imagined. A hundred gold Imperials. She wasn't sure exactly how much that really was, but she knew a small farm might cost as little as eighty Imperials.

But nobody would sell an escaped slave a house. The scars on her body, her mannerisms and her lack of knowledge of the outside world would be like signs pointing to her, telling the world about who and what she was.

The further she walked the more convinced she was that she had no other real option than Ekonia.

She had time now to mourn Erinad in her own, silent way. She walked for days over grassy fields, rolling hills and sprawling woods. The weather was growing colder and she had counted a week of freedom so far. Every night she would pray for Erinad's spirit to reach his Reward and sit among the gods.

Erinad used to have a necklace he kept hidden under his robes. It was the symbol for the Divine Lights. A circle with a starburst in the middle. She had always wanted one but didn't want to be caught with it.

Now that she was free she'd make one herself. She also needed a copy of the Path of Light. She had always read Erinad's copy in his room and it was her comfort and release from the world. She'd read a chapter and then Erinad would discuss it with her. The old man had had the entire book practically memorized and could quote it without pausing.

This new life was certainly unusual. She could stop whenever she wanted to, eat when she chose to and sleep in if she wanted. She was alone but she was free to do as she chose.

On the tenth day she woke up to the sound of horses. She looked out from behind the bushes where she was sleeping and saw eight riders coming down the road. They and their horses wore black armor with white trimming. One of them carried a banner that had a black background and what looked like a silver lion on it.

They wore heavy breastplates, full helmets with rectangle slits for eyes, two triangular holes for a nose and vertical slits for the mouth. They reminded her of skulls. Their thighs and hands were armored but the rest was black leather. They carried short matchlocks in scabbards and numerous pistols along their chest, hips and saddles.

But as they came closer she saw that it wasn't a lion but a chimera. It had a goat head beside the lion one and a snake for a tail.

She snatched up her backpack and walked out next to the road to meet them. She saw the lead rider's hand inch closer to his pistol. She made sure her scarf still covered her face. If hunters asked these men she didn't want to put them in the position to have to lie for her; assuming they would in the first place.

As they drew closer she raised her hand in greeting.

The lead rider spurred his horse ahead and came to a stop in front of her.

"Good day," she said.

"Do you have business with us?" The man asked with a voice that sounded metallic through the fully enclosed helmet.

"I go to Ekonia to join the army," she said.

"Do you now? What makes you think they'll take you?"

"I can fight."

"Of course.

Then the other riders caught up.

"What do we have here?" The rider holding the banner asked.

"A peasant girl that wants to join the company, sir."

The banner holder looked at her for a few, long moments. Then he took off his helmet revealing a human man with a scar down one side of his face and a dead eye.

"Girl, we don't take underfed castaways. You have to know how to fight or at least show you can learn to fight. It doesn't look like you could pull a bow string."

"I can fight," Greza said.

"You said that before," the lead rider said. "She isn't much of a talker, either."

"We don't have time for games, Den. Keep moving," the banner man said. "Right."

Then the lead rider made to push her away with his foot.

She grabbed his foot with both hands bolted forward, pushing him out of his saddle. He landed in the road with a dull 'thud' and the sound of banged metal.

Greza moved back with her hands up, ready to defend herself, but instead she saw that the other men were laughing.

"She told you she could fight, Den!" One of the men called out.

"Shoulda listened to her," another one said.

The banner man laughed and rode up to her.

"What's your name, girl?"

"Greza."

"Just Greza, eh? Well, Greza, maybe you got some fire in you. You're a five day walk to Ekonia and another one to our headquarters. Stick to the main roads. There are signs so you can't miss it. Take this."

He tossed her a small, silver coin. It was heavier than most and had a boars head on it.

"When you get to the castle gate, tell them Richkurk said you were alright."

"Thank you," she said.

"Get off the ground, Den. It's just your pride that's hurt."

When he got back on his horse she saw that even Den was smiling.

"You got some strength there, lass," Den said before riding off.

She watched them go and stood there with the man's coin in her hand. So, those were soldiers of the Chimera Company of Ekonia. She wondered if she'd get to wear that black and white armor and ride a horse. She'd never ridden a horse before.

After meeting them she picked up her pace and took fewer breaks. She paused in the towns long enough to buy food and moved on.

The buildings were different in this flat part of the world. Instead of wooden tiles they had thatch roofs and windows with a dozen smaller panes instead of a single large one. The food also tasted more of wild herbs.

Around noon of the fifth day she came to a sign that marked the border to Ekonia. A small, rocky river marked the boundary between the Empire and Ekonia. She paused long enough to say a quick prayer of thanks.

As she walked that day she saw that Ekonia was one massive, rock filled field with stunted, scrabbly looking weeds. A plow had never touched this land before. Scattered among the fields were bogs and marshes. She began to wonder if the king had given the Chimera Company the half of the kingdom he didn't want anyways.

A few dead, scraggly trees dotted the bleak landscape and what were either large crows or small vultures rested in their tortured branches. She couldn't tell from the distance but she was sure they were watching her.

Nothing in her histories or stories mentioned lands as dreadful as this. It didn't look as if anything important ever happened here or could happen here. Even farmers would avoid this place.

She slept on the side of the road with no cover or hint of shelter. When she woke in the morning the sky had turned grey and heavy and she knew it was going to rain. She ate the last of her carrots and continued down the long road.

An hour later it began raining. It was a cold rain that seeped into her bones and made her breath visible. All she could do was button her coat and put her hood up. It wasn't long before the road was nothing but mud.

Eventually she came to a fork in the road with a faded sign. One way pointed to a town called "Lerak" and the other pointed to "Chimera Fortress." She went left, toward the fortress.

Half way between noon and sunset she saw a dark shape in the distance. It was a small dot that rose up above the featureless bogs. She kept walking and a half hour later she came to the foot of a hill with a squat, stony fortress on top. It didn't look anything like an Imperial building. There was no elegance, sophistication or ornamentation to it. It was bare, stone walls that rose up to battlements and round towers that rose a little higher than the walls. It was hard to tell with stone but the place felt enormously old.

The giant wooden gates were closed. She could make out the shapes of soldiers standing on top of the gatehouse.

She moved to put up her scarf but remembered that she didn't want to hide from these people.

Greza took a deep breath and steeled herself. She hated how she talked. She spoke like a simpleton. Her mind spoke in eloquent, verbose language but none of that translated to her speech. The past eight years she had trained herself to speak as a slave and now that she no longer needed to she found that she couldn't do anything else.

She approached the gate and knocked. She waited but nothing happened.

Just before she was about to knock again a hatch opened up in the door and a man's face appeared.

"Who are you and what do you want?" The man asked.

She moved in closer because she knew her voice didn't carry. Years of speaking quietly hadn't developed a strong speaking voice.

"I'm Greza. I came to join the company."

The man smiled as if she had just told a joke.

"We don't need any washerwomen."

"I'm here to fight." She held up the silver coin. "Richkurk said I was alright."

"Richkurk? He said that?"

He grumbled something that she couldn't make out and then she heard the sound of the gate's bolts being unlatched.

The gate swung open just enough for her to squeeze in and then it closed behind her with a thunderous 'clang.'

Four soldiers stood there eyeing her up. She didn't know what to say so she held up the coin.

"I can't tell if Richkurk is mad or a genius," one of the soldiers said.

"He aint never been wrong before."

"What are you, girl? You're either the ugliest green Elf I've ever seen or the scrawniest Ork."

"Never mind him, 'mam," a soldier in the back said. He stepped forward. He was a young human with only stubble for hair. "What's your name?"

"Greza."

"Well, Greza, welcome to Chimera Fortress. I'll take you to see the chief. He'll sort you out and figure what to do with you."

She had made it. Her feet and back ached and she was shivering, but she had made it. If she could get a job here, any job, then she'd have a living. She'd be free. Now she didn't have to look over her shoulder for slave catchers.

Greza followed the soldier into the courtyard of the fortress. Everywhere she looked she saw soldiers training. Some were practicing marksmanship, others were practicing with swords or pikes in formation. She also saw shields and clubs, which was peculiar because no current army used clubs or shields.

Their uniforms were black but resembled some of the clothing she had seen in the nearby towns. They wore long shirts that went to the knee, high boots, elbow length gloves and round hats with flaps for the ears. A few wore archaic chainmail as well as heavy breastplates.

The matchlock men also carried tall axes with one long, curved blade and they'd rest the barrels of the guns on the top of the axes to steady their aim.

The courtyard was paved with wide stones, now covered in mud from soldiers coming in and out. Pipes led to barrels that collected rain water and the whole place smelled like dirt and sweat. There was a sharper, bitter smell behind everything that she couldn't identify until a gunner fired at a target. The smell of gunpowder.

All this she took in a glance as she was led to a side door of the courtyard. Inside was a cold, dark, stone room with a lantern that was dim from filthy glass and a wooden desk with splinters and exposed nails. Maps of all kinds hung from the wall as well as a few posters asking for recruits. A one armed man sat behind the desk. He had a white beard that went to his waist.

"We got a new recruit here," the escorting soldier said.

The bearded man looked up from his papers and looked her over. He then waived the soldier away. After the door closed the man tapped the table and then picked up his quill pen.

"What are you here for?" The man asked.

"I want to join."

"Why?"

"To fight."

"Why?"

"Because I'm good at it."

"Of course you are. Parents?"

"My mother is dead and I don't know my father."

"When was the last time you had sexual activity?"

"Never. I'm a virgin."

"A virgin? I've seen more unicorns than virgins. That aint no joke either."

"It's true."

She didn't want to explain how she remained so. It hurt just to think about father.

"Have they explained terms of service and pay?" He asked.

She shook her head.

"You sign a contract for two years. At the end of those two years you can choose to sign back up for another two. You will get ten Imperials a month not counting hazard pay or any other pay from circumstances. We have rules here. Don't break them. I don't know what you've heard about us, but we're a professional army. Act accordingly. That means act like a soldier and don't do anything stupid."

She nodded that she understood.

"Where you come from?" He asked.

She didn't want to say. If anyone came looking for her they would find her quickly just by looking at the log book.

"Be honest, girl. We won't return you to your masters."

So, it was indeed obvious.

"The Duchy Roristan. In the Empire."

"I know where Roristan is. How long ago you escape?"

"Two weeks."

"And you came straight here?"

"Yes."

"You think you can fight?"

"I do."

"We get a lot of people that think that. What, you get into a few fist fights with your fellow slaves?"

"Gladiator."

"Gladiator? Well I'll be tossed down a well and pissed on. You're an entertainer that thinks they can fight. Very cute."

The man stood up with the help of his good arm and hobbled over to a trunk that was covered in the black uniform shirts of the Company.

"You're a small size so..." He said as he dug through the pile of clothing. Then he tossed a shirt and pants at her. "Try those on and tell me how they fit."

She looked around and didn't see a place to change for privacy. She had read about this. Soldiers didn't get privacy. She wasn't used to privacy either, so, she began to strip off her wet clothes right there.

The man laughed.

"Damn, girl. I was going to at least turn around."

He turned around and waited while she changed. The shirt felt enormous and the pants felt too tight.

"Finished," she said.

He turned back around and looked her up and down.

"Sit down there and we'll fit you for boots."

She sat down on the trunk and he went through three pairs of boots before finding one that fit right. They felt stiff and constricting.

"You got bigger feet than I expected," he said.

She wondered if that was good or bad.

He had her get up and walk around a bit before making her sign a paper with everything she'd been given. He took her wet clothes and everything else and threw them in a basket.

"You'll get those back when you finish training one way or another. If you fail out, we can always use more cooks."

She did not escape and come all this way to be a cook. Father said she had a great destiny ahead of her and she was going to make that come true.

He then handed her a bag and put in doubles of everything she had already received.

"The rest of your gear will be given to you by your training platoon," he said. "Now, do you swear to obey your superiors?"

"I do."

"Swear to uphold the honor of the Dukedom of Ekonia and always act within guidelines?"

"I do."

"Swear to not steal, cheat, hurt or dishonor your fellow soldiers?"

"I do."

He then shoved a few more papers at her that she had to sign. She signed in her curving Dark Elf script and handed them back.

"Well, Greza, welcome to the Chimera Fortress. You're not a member of the Company until you finish training. Once that happens you'll be sworn in officially. I hope your stay is longer than most. Your training sergeant will explain all the rest."

Then she was pushed out of the room and back out into the cold courtyard. He waved down one of the soldiers that was idly smoking a pipe. It was a human with a short beard and messy dark hair.

"Take this new recruit to barracks R-1," the one-armed man said.

The solider rolled his eyes and stood up.

"Follow me," he said.

Greza held her bag with both arms and followed close behind him. He weaved through the different units until he came to a door at the far side of the courtyard. That opened to a staircase that led down below the ground and then a long hallway with several doors spread far apart.

It felt as if she were entering a new world, maybe the underworld from the Sanctified Scrolls. For the first time she began to wonder if she was making the right decision.

At the very end of the hall was a door marked "R1." The man opened the door and stuck his head in.

"Hey, Vick. We got a new one for you," the soldier said.

And then without ceremony he pushed her inside.

She found herself face to face with a room full of men and a few women. They wore black uniforms like she was now wearing and were sitting around playing cards, dice, talking or laughing.

An older, rugged Human, stepped forward. His uniform had silver stripes, badges and patches.

"What little runt do we have here?"

Chapter Four

GREZA LOOKED UP AT THE GIANT HUMAN who had his arms folded and one eyebrow raised.

"Greza. New recruit," she said.

"Greza...Sergeant," he shouted with what she guessed to be as loud as he could. "The last thing out of your pig sucking mouth will be 'sergeant.' You understand?"

"I understand, sergeant."

If he was trying to intimidate her, it wasn't working. She had been yelled at all her life. It would be odd if they didn't yell.

"Who let you in here? I don't take any worthless stray off the street."

She fished in her bag and held up the silver coin.

"Richkurk said I was alright, sergeant."

She noticed his hesitation. Whoever Richkurk was, he was a highly respected person.

"Well, you're not alright. You're far from alright! You have to prove yourself to me before I consider you worthy to shine my boots." He then turned his back to her and began walking away. "Follow me, maggot puss."

She followed him to the back of the room where there was a doorway with a curtain.

"This is the female area. Pick out a bunk. We'll start training in a half hour."

Then the giant sergeant left.

She looked around the room. It had six beds lined up in rows along the walls with trunks at the foot of each bed. Four of the beds had boots by the trunks and equipment hanging from pegs.

The curtain parted and a human woman with long brown hair done up in two braids entered. She had an oval face with freckles and round, brown eyes.

"New recruit, eh? Where you from?" The woman asked in an accent she didn't recognize.

"Roristan, in the Empire."

"Never heard of it. Name's Nika."

"Greza."

The woman held out her hand and at first Greza wondered if the woman was asking for something. But then she remembered that Dark Elves don't shake hands. It was a human custom so Greza took it.

"Peace and fortune," Nika said.

"Peace and fortune," Greza repeated, though she had never heard that greeting before.

"We've been here over a week so you have a little catching up to do, but we'll help you out. So far, all we've been doing is marching around in formations, learning rules of the Company, getting yelled at and doing a lot of exercise."

She didn't see how marching in formation was so difficult that it would warrant several days of practice.

Nika helped her put her things in her trunk and then took her out to the main room where everyone else was. A few waved, a few smiled and some didn't look as if they cared. She did a quick count. Thirty seven recruits. Most were human. There was one Elf female, three Elf males, a Dark Elf male, a male Hobgoblin and a male Satyr. No other Orks. Not surprising. Orks tended to stay in the south and didn't venture this far north. At least that was what her books told her.

"This is Greza from Roristan," Nika said.

"Have a seat," one of the male card players said.

He pointed to a small stool beside the table where three others sat.

Greza sat down, not sure at all what to do. What did people do in a situation like this?

"So, Greza, why'd you come all the way out here? This is dangerous work and it doesn't look like you've even pushed a plow."

"I came to fight."

"Fighting isn't for girls. Maybe they can teach you to shoot a gun, but don't expect to win in hand to hand."

The man spoke with an expression that said he thought he knew everything. It was the same expression her masters had worn. He didn't know everything. He not only misjudged her but he had been there for only a week.

Some of the nearby men nodded in agreement but she didn't respond. There would be no point. Whatever she said wouldn't be believed.

"You're an Ork?" One of the men asked.

"That's a dumb question," someone else said.

"It's not dumb."

"Why ask? She's obviously an Ork. That's like asking, hey Beno, you Human?"

There was some laughter.

The man who had invited her to sit down looked up from his cards.

"You don't talk much," he said.

"Don't need to."

"What did you do before coming here?" He asked.

She saw how little regard was shown to gladiators so she had to think of something else.

"Worked at a manor," she said.

"A maid?" Nika asked.

That was an even worse answer.

"Yes."

Some of the men laughed.

"A maid wants to play soldier?" The card man asked.

"She can play with my soldier," the Satyr said.

"She could be good for morale," another recruit said.

"Shut up," Nika said.

That just made them laugh louder.

"You came for the men, right? You wanna be surrounded by a bunch of lonely men?" A human asked.

Greza didn't like the implications at all. She was no "branch seller." She knew the Divine Lights taught purity in mind and body and was about to retort with a quote of scripture, but she held her tongue. No one would care. It was a religion that few still believed and she doubted these men were religious on any account.

The men and women continued to throw jokes at each other, some of them very crude. For some reason they thought they had to be rude to be funny. It didn't make sense.

She ignored them until the sergeant returned and yelled at them to hurry outside and get into formation. She ran out with the others into the courtyard that was now empty of training soldiers.

They lined up in neat rows and she was placed at the very end of the front rank. She copied the stiff way the others stood.

The sergeant began to walk up and down the ranks, glaring at recruits' faces and uniforms.

"That was slow," the Sergeant said. "If it's that slow again we'll be out here all night practicing."

Then the Sergeant came and stopped in front of her.

"The damn new girl holds herself better than any of you," the Sergeant said.

The rest of the day was spent marching around the courtyard in different formations. It was all easy and she didn't understand why some people had a problem with it.

But too many turned left when they were supposed to turn right and the next thing she knew they were all doing pushups.

She did feel sorry for the humans though. They really seemed to struggle with it. They were out of breath by the end of it. She didn't have any problem at all. She wasn't even breathing hard when they finished.

When they went to dinner they entered a large room with dozens of tables. Other units of soldiers were already seated. They formed a line and were served bowls of soup and bread.

She had never had so much soup at one time before. And the bread was much larger and far tastier than the slave food she had eaten back in Roristan.

"This stuff isn't fit for pigs," one of the men said.

"Dogs, maybe."

"That would have to be one hungry dog."

After her belly was full, she didn't remember the last time that happened, they went back out to the courtyard where the Sergeant sat them all down and taught them about personal hygiene.

Everything he said was more than obvious. She cleaned herself every day. Her Dark Elf masters hated smelly slaves and would beat any slave they found to be dirty.

Then the Sergeant explained about fornication. His explanations were very crude but he essentially told them to avoid it because it spread all sorts of diseases and caused personnel problems within the unit.

"So, if you do have to charge with your pike, don't advance toward a friendly unit. The last thing a unit needs is a bunch of emotional kids crying about their girlfriends cheating on them and then having that girlfriend watch their back in a fight. I'm serious, recruits. Don't do it. If you're caught sleeping with someone in your unit, you will be disciplined."

By the wincing reactions of the other recruits, Greza guessed that being "disciplined" was not a pleasant experience. She must have missed that lecture.

The Sergeant's class didn't end until well after dark. Then they were released to go back to their barracks.

While the others stayed up, laughing and talking about the day's events, she lay in her bed and put her hands behind her head.

This felt very strange. The mattress was more comfortable than she was used to. She had a warm blanket, hot food and she was equal to everyone else. She knew there were hardships to come, but for now it was very agreeable.

Perhaps she was meant to come here after all. She was warm, fed and free. She didn't need anything more than that. She gave thanks to the Divine Lights and her Father who was watching over her.

★★★★

GREZA WOKE UP TO THE SOUND OF A HORN BLOWING. She had become used to the harsh sound but that didn't slow her down at all. It had been two weeks and all they had been learning was marching, physical fitness and discipline. Immediate obedience was always demanded. That was what she was used to but it seemed that many others had a problem with it.

She sat up, threw back her covers and began putting on her uniform and boots. As soon as she was finished she turned around and made her bed like they had taught her to do.

When she looked up she saw that she had actually beaten the other females. In the Company they weren't women or girls, they were always "females."

When she walked out into the main room where the males were, she noticed that they were all excited about something. There was more play fighting and joking than usual.

She wanted to ask but they'd just respond with a rude or useless joke.

When they formed up in the biting cold out in the courtyard Sergeant Drakan walked up and down their ranks, inspecting each recruit. He seemed to scowl more than usual.

"Recruits! Listen up. Today we begin combat training," Sergeant Draken said.

He glared around just asking for one of the recruits to say something so they could be punished.

"You'll be sparring against your fellow recruits today in an evaluation to determine your skill level: beginner, intermediary and advanced. For the most part, you will spar against other recruits of your same skill level, but this will not always be the case. In war, you cannot choose your opponent or their ability. You must be prepared for anything."

He stopped pacing and pointed to the first man in formation.

"We'll start here and work our way down. You will spar the man behind you."

There were four ranks so it was even, but she was on the end and no one was behind her. She wanted to show her skill so the males would stop calling her a 'scrawny maid.'

For once they were doing something interesting, something she knew she could do.

"You will be using padded staves for now. First two, step out of formation and take positions on either side of the field."

The "field" was a roped in pen covered in straw. The male human and hobgoblin walked out into the pen and stood at rest to await further instruction.

"Now, pick up a stave and wait for my order. When I say, attack. Do not purposefully harm the other recruit. Understood? Accidents will happen but if I see that you did it on purpose, I'll make sure you regret it. That said, there are no rules. You do what you must to win."

They had already lost one recruit for thievery. He had been tied to a stake and lashed before being thrown out of the fortress. That was incentive enough.

She knew exactly what it felt like to be lashed. Her back bore the marks of the lash and her torso, legs and arms bore the marks of countless fights. She always bathed when no one else was around, to avoid questions.

Greza didn't want them to know she had been a slave. They were always using the term 'slave' as an insult and it made her wince every time she heard it.

It was humiliating.

She looked up as the match began. The two men held their staves in an awkward manner. She could see by the placement of their feet that neither of them knew what they were doing.

As they attacked, they did so in halting movements as if they weren't sure what they were doing. It was somewhat painful to watch.

The fight burst into a spastic series of clumsy swinging until one of them was hit more than the other.

They were both put into "intermediary." What would it take to be put into beginner? Lying on the ground and crying?

Two by two they went into the "field" and fought. Most went into beginner or intermediary. Only a few went into advanced. She didn't see how any of these people could be a threat.

Finally, it was her turn. Sergeant Drakan stepped in front of her.

"It's just you, recruit Greza. I'll let you choose which skill level you want to fight."

"Advanced."

There was some snickering from the other recruits. Sgt. Drakan chose to ignore it.

"Alright, Greza wishes to fight an advanced student. Hyrin, step forward."

Hyrin was the card player from her first night. He was strong for a Human and had been a guard of some kind back in his hometown.

She walked into the "field" and over to the rack of staves. She picked it up and felt the weight in her hands and tested the balance.

Greza turned around and watched Hyrin as he stood there with his stave. He was relaxed and not alert at all.

She took a breath and waited for Sgt. Drakan's signal.

"Go!" Drakan said.

As soon as Drakan said it, she threw her stave right at Hyrin's head. He did two things. He raised his stave to block the projectile and he tried to dodge at the same time.

She bolted at him as soon as the stave left her hands. She plowed into Hyrin and grabbed his arm. Greza yanked him down, almost to the ground. Then she moved behind him, grabbed hold of his stave and pulled it in to begin choking him.

Then the whistle blew to end the fight and she instantly let go and stepped away. Hyrin fell to the ground, coughing. The fight had only taken a few seconds. After every fight people clapped but when she looked over she saw that they all stood there in silence.

Sgt. Drakan walked up and looked down at her.

"Where did you learn to fight like that, recruit?"

"I was a gladiator, sergeant," she whispered so only he would hear.

This drew some murmurs from the other recruits but she couldn't tell if this was good or bad.

"I see your skill level is a little higher than the other recruits. I want to see how much higher. I'm your next opponent."

She kept her eyes to the ground as Sgt. Drakan took off his coat and picked up a wooden practice sword. Fighting another recruit was expected, but she couldn't fight a sergeant. She'd be punished. The leaders will find out and throw her out of the fortress like they did the thief.

She put her padded stave back in the rack and also picked up a practice sword.

Sgt. Drakan walked up and stood before her.

"Greza, don't hold back. Don't be afraid to hurt me, because I will not hold back. Understood?"

She nodded.

Raising a hand against a superior would normally be death, but now she had to. It was just another exhibition fight against a trainer. Nothing different.

Sgt. Drakan readied himself.

"Fight!"

She knew he'd come at her with everything he had. He was a veteran and knew what a real fight was. Clever tricks wouldn't work on him.

With her wooden sword in her off hand, she charged at the sergeant. As he moved he kept his balance. He was good and knew what he was doing.

As she got within striking distance she made an obvious attack with her left hand sword. It was a distraction for the real attack.

Drakan raised his sword to block. He was fast for a human. His instincts were good. He saw the sword and didn't think, he just reacted.

But then Greza's leg shot out and kicked the side of Drakan's knee. She pulled it but the blow still crumbled that leg and brought him down to his knee.

Again she struck with the sword. He blocked it and was preparing for a strike inside her guard that was definitely aimed for her head.

But her real attack was already going.

Her right fist slammed into the side of Drakan's head and knocked him into the dirt. She had pulled the blow to avoid killing him. If she had been armed with her cestus, she would have cracked his skull right open.

Again, there was only silence.

Then Sgt. Drakan slowly got to his feet. Blood was coming down the side of his head where she had struck him.

Now that she had time to think she wondered how she could do such a thing. She wasn't allowed to hurt her superiors, even in training. She was in big trouble and she dropped her sword.

Then Sgt. Drakan began laughing.

"Girl, you pack a punch like a swinging log. Well done." Then he turned to the other recruits. "Recruits, listen up. Recruit Greza has demonstrated how to fight. You use deception, strength and skill. You do whatever it takes to win. She is far above any of your skill levels and she will not be participating in your daily combat training for this quarter."

Then he turned to her.

"Greza, I have something special for you."

Chapter Five

AFTER THE FIGHT WITH **S**ERGEANT **D**RAKAN the other recruits were very quiet for the rest of the day. It wasn't until dinner that anyone spoke to her.

Nika sat down across from her with her tray and she was followed by Yuro a man with a reputation for being smelly and another female, Bosha who always complained that people were stealing her stuff and then found whatever was lost a few minutes later.

"That was amazing, Grez," Nika said.

"Yeah, I can't believe you're that tough," Bosha said.

She thought they would have been angry that she was better than them.

"Though I don't think you made friends with some of the males," Bosha said.

Bosha pointed over to the far table where Hyrin and some of the other males sat. They were whispering and casting glares at her.

"You were really a gladiator?" Yuro asked.

Greza nodded.

"You fought? Did you kill anyone?" Yuro asked.

Greza nodded.

"Yuro!" Nika said. "Don't ask her questions like that."

"Why not?"

"Just don't."

After dinner they marched back to their barracks and she hurried to the female quarters to avoid any confrontation with the other recruits. Having been around males she knew they were always struggling to prove they were on top of the pile. Her victories today would be a challenge.

She took out of her footlocker a knife and a piece of wood. During time off like this she often spent it carving a necklace like the one Erinad had. She wanted a symbol for the faith and a reminder of everything Erinad had given her.

Nika came in a while later and sat at the foot of Greza's bunk.

"What you got there?" Nika asked.

"It will be a necklace."

Nika leaned over to get a look.

"I've seen that symbol before. Isn't that some religion no one believes in anymore? That's right. The Lost Victor."

"I believe in it."

"The Promised Victor was killed. Those gods can't protect us. If they couldn't protect their own Promised Child, then what good are they?"

"The Promise hasn't been broken yet. And on each side he shall be flanked by his trusted companions, a mighty Bull and a Storm Raven."

"What was that?"

"A passage from the Revelation Cycle of Therin Aldus."

Nika's eyes went wide.

"You're educated."

Greza nodded.

Nika leaned back onto her elbows and her eyes stared out at nothing.

"They wouldn't let us learn to read. Our lords said peasants didn't need to know how to read."

"You're from the empire, yes?"

"Farmers. Hundreds of generations of farmers. My father was a pig farmer. I hate the smelly things."

"You run away?"

"Kind of. I told them I was leaving and they didn't stop me. You did, didn't you?"

"They all realize I was a slave?"

"I don't think so. I only know because we had a noble stop by our farm to water his horses and he had a gladiator with him. He was a large man covered in scars. We heard the noble talking. You have any scars?"

Greza pushed up the sleeve of her shirt to show off the three large scars on her shoulder and bicep. Nika grimaced.

She knew if the others found out, they'd mock her even more.

"Please don't tell anyone," Greza said.

"Of course."

In the morning she was ignored by most of the men. The females all sat at her table now but the men wouldn't joke with her anymore.

After breakfast they went out for morning formation. Sergeant Drakan had the others fall out and go over to the "field" for training but he kept Greza off to the side. He said he had "something different" for her.

Once he had the other recruits situated he told Greza to follow him. He didn't say where they were going and she wasn't about to ask.

He took her inside the fort and up some stairs. This part of the fort had more decorations and comforts. There were rugs on the floor, weapons hanging on the walls and fireplaces that kept out the morning chill.

They passed by older soldiers who were relaxing and talking of old times. None of them paid her a second glance.

Then they came to a room with a larger than usual door with iron bands and a decorated knocker in the shape of a lion's head. Sergeant Drakan shouldered it open and waved her in.

Inside were several soldiers in padded training armor. They were practicing with wooden swords and hand to hand.

One of the trainees walked up to Sergeant Drakan.

"This the recruit you told us about?" The human with a pointed beard asked.

"It is, sir."

Sir? That meant this man was an officer. She was in a room full of officers. In the Empire only nobles could be officers and she wondered if it was the same here.

She did not want to fight for the amusement of officers. If they were nobles they'd have nothing but disdain for her no matter what she did. She didn't want to waste her time amusing more nobles. Never again.

The man with the pointy beard looked her over.

"She doesn't look like much," he finally said.

"She beat me easily, sir."

This raised an eyebrow from the man.

"Very well, sergeant. I'll take your word on this."

Greza still had no idea what she was doing here.

The officer walked away and began calling his fellow officers together. Drakan turned to her.

"Greza, I want you to teach these officers how to fight like you do."

"Train nobles?"

"They're not nobles. Some of them are, but not all and the ones that are don't have lands anymore. Right now, think of them as your students. When you teach, you're in charge. I'll be here to help you, but the show's yours."

Greza turned to face the now assembled group of officers. Talking was not one of her strong abilities and talking down to nobles even less so.

She closed her eyes and tried to think of what to say.

She thought back to her first days of training. She remembered the beatings and the harsh discipline but she waved all that aside and tried to remember what her trainer had said.

"When you fight you have to destroy your opponent with ruthless, sudden and deceptive violence. You must not show mercy," Greza quoted. "Mercy will cause hesitation. Hesitation will kill you. Do not give your opponent a moment to size you up. Attack and take them off guard."

"How about a demonstration?" One of the female officers asked.

"A match?"

"Yes! Show us what you mean so we can understand it better," an Elf officer said.

"You just volunteered then," the man with the pointy beard said.

The officers laughed but the Elf stood and walked up to her.

"Choose whatever weapon you like," Greza said.

The man chose a sword. Swords gave the wielder reach, but that was it. Once she closed the distance all their advantage was gone.

The fight lasted only a few seconds. She came in, tackled him in the waist, knocked him to the ground and brought her fist within inches of his face.

She fought two more matches to show exactly what she was capable of and that winning so quickly was no fluke.

After that they were much more inclined to hear what she had to say. She stuttered and spoke in halting, quotes from her former trainer, but after two hours she had them in basic drills that she remembered doing for days.

Sergeant Drakan had left somewhere along the way; probably to go check on the recruits.

By dinner the officers were exhausted and were covered in sweat and bruises.

The pointy beard man came up and put a hand on her shoulder.

"That was most educational," he said. "You must return tomorrow and teach us more."

"Yes, sir."

"Excellent job. No, go on back to your unit, soldier."

Soldier? Did they not know she was a recruit?

Still, she was glad that she hadn't embarrassed herself. They seemed to be learning a lot. It was strange to have her superiors listening to her. She knew she didn't speak well and stumbled over the clumsy words she used.

Speaking in front of important people was something she would never get used to or be good at.

Greza trained with the officers every day after that. They learned fast and most of them were eager.

Every day she wore her newly carved symbol of Light under her shirt. It was like having her father with her at all times.

"They stole it!" Bosha said as she began to frantically search through her footlocker.

"No one stole it, whatever it is," Vertia said.

"Well, it aint where I put it."

"Doesn't mean they stole it."

"Someone took it. It didn't fly off."

Today was their one day of rest a week. They were to clean their clothes, clean their barracks and rest their bodies. The night before they had done a five mile run. Many of the recruits weren't used to such activity and were now complaining of soreness. She couldn't help but wonder how the humans became a dominant race.

She knew of course. They came to the continent two thousand years ago with steel armor and weapons. Their pike formations and heavy armor were unstoppable. If their numbers had been greater they would have conquered the entire continent. As it was they "only" founded the First Empire.

While Nika played cards with one of the other females Greza took her towel and went to the bathroom down the hall. No other female would be taking a bath at this time.

She pulled the cord which lowered a tube and water came down. She filled her bucket and sat on a stool beside it. As she scrubbed she thought about where her life was now. It was hard to imagine that she wasn't a slave anymore. She still had to obey and do as she was told so she still felt like a slave, but what was different was that she could leave at any time. Once she graduated and gained more freedom she wouldn't have the illusion of being a slave and she wondered how she'd accept that.

Then the bathroom door opened and Nika came in.

"I thought I'd join you Grez. I..." Then Nika's eyes fell on Greza's back and Greza ducked into the water. "What happened?"

Greza's back was covered in scars from numerous beatings and whippings. Her shoulders and legs were covered in training and battle scars. The explanations would bring up humiliating memories she did not wish to think about.

She also worried if Nika and the others would think less of her. Would all her skill at fighting mean nothing if she was just an escaped slave?

Nika came over took a stool in front of her. Her large brown eyes looked right at her and Greza kept her gaze on the ground.

"Grez, speak to me."

"It's nothing."

"Nothing? But..."

"It's nothing, I said. I was a slave. Slaves get beaten. There's nothing to say."

"I'm sorry."

They both fell silent for a while. Then Nika spoke up again.

"I thought pig farming was bad."

"Pig farming is bad."

This got a small chuckle from Nika.

Nika stripped down and began washing herself as well.

"So, tell me, Grez, why believe in a dead religion?"

"It's not dead."

"Well, it will be soon. Only a few fanatics still believe in it."

"I'm not a fanatic."

"Exactly. So why do you?"

"I was taught and I believed."

"You need to work on your conversational skills."

"I am beginner skill level."

Nika laughed.

"That you are."

"Have you seen Duke Verin?"

She had been here for two weeks and so far she had yet to see the young duke that had made it into the history books already. He started this mercenary company and had won this kingdom. She was curious to see how the stories matched with the man.

"No. I think he's away from the fort making alliances for the summer or something."

Neither of them mentioned the scars again.

The next day they fell into formation as they always did. It was cold enough to see their breath and it was raining. Their rain ponchos weren't helping very much.

"Good morning recruits. Lovely weather, isn't it? Today we won't be doing weapons practice. Instead we have an obstacle course to test your strength, endurance and problem solving."

He led them out of the gate and over to the west side of the fortress. There she saw a "figure 8" track covered in walls, ropes and other obstacles she'd need to get a closer look at before understanding.

They marched to the start of the course and listened while Sergeant Drakan went over the rules and told them all to be safe. Everywhere they went there were rules and warnings about safety.

The course was run one person at a time but with only a minute in between so it was possible to be overtaken by the next person. The order was by whoever the Sergeant saw first so she wasn't last this time. It didn't really matter. If this course was designed for humans then she'd have no difficulty. Some of her fellow recruits were worried, but they were humans, Satyrs and Elves.

When it was her turn she took off running and climbed over the first wall without a problem. Then she climbed a rope, walked across a beam and down a rope again. She crawled under barbed posts, up and down a small tower and hopped from one post to another. All of it was too easy and she passed by two of the others as they struggled to climb over a wooden wall.

Then she came to a tunnel filled with water and she stopped and stared. It was a hole in the ground that she had to go in and come out the other side. But it was filled with water.

Water meant death. If she went in there she would die. Every particle of her brain screamed against going in the water. Orks couldn't swim. They sunk like stones. She read in a book of science that due to the denser muscle mass of Ork muscle tissue, it meant they weren't buoyant and were instinctively afraid of water.

She had never tried to swim before but her instincts were freezing her in place. Knowing the science wasn't helping the irrational fear that was causing her hands to shake. Just the thought of being trapped in that watery tunnel was enough to make her want to run away.

Then Yuro came up behind her.

"What's wrong, Grez? Jump in and get moving,"

"I can't."

"Can't swim?"

"No."

"Don't need to. Just pull yourself along the way. It's easy."

He climbed in, took a deep breath and went under. A few seconds later he came out the other side and continued on without pause.

Then she saw Sergeant Drakan walking towards her. He was going to ask why she was standing there and force her to go in. He would be angry with her and wouldn't trust or respect her. She had to do it.

If she didn't go in she'd let him and her fellow recruits down. They expected more from her. Drakan would be ashamed of her.

It felt as though everyone was looking at her.

Perhaps some of them would feel fear like this before a battle. It was a soldier's duty to move past such fear. If she couldn't beat this then she couldn't be a soldier.

She had to go now before she thought about it more. Greza climbed in the muddy water. It came up to her waist.

Just pull yourself along, distraction is death, she thought over and over again.

She took a deep breath and plunged down.

Blind, she groped for the sides of the tunnel and felt the wood beams. It wasn't a tight squeeze and she could get good hand holds. Frantic, of being buried by water, she began to scramble down the tunnel. Her hands clawed for anything and her feet kicked as fast as she could.

She felt her air running out and the water crushing down on her. She saw herself drowning and sinking down into an endless abyss. Every second that passed was one closer to death, like the water was reaching around her and crushing her.

But then her head broke the surface and she gasped for air. Greza climbed out of the pool and lay on the ground gasping for air. Her hands and entire body were shaking now.

Then she felt strong hands lift her up to her feet.

It was Sergeant Drakan.

"I can't believe you did that," he said.

"Did what, sergeant?" She asked with a quivering voice.

"I've never seen anyone with Ork blood go into the water."

"But you ordered us through the course. I had to."

For the first time she saw him smile.

"I was coming over to say that you could go around. I forgot to tell you at the beginning," he said and then paused to look at her. "You alright to continue?"

"I will continue," she said with a voice that didn't sound 'alright.'

He patted her on the back and walked away.

She finished the course though not nearly as fast as she had been. When she came to the end she walked over to where the other finished recruits were and collapsed on the ground. The hot breaths came up in clouds of steam and despite the cold morning she saw that some looked like they were trying to cool down.

"You alright, Grez?" Nika asked.

Greza nodded.

"You sure? You're shaking."

"It's nothing."

Nika eyed her as if looking for the truth.

Chapter Six

GREZA STOOD AT ATTENTION WITH THE REST of the recruits as Lieutenant Daren walked up and down their ranks. He was a tall, thin man with blond hair. He walked with precise movements and he said very little.

The officer's silence was more frightening than Sergeant Drakan's shouting.

"Recruits, today you will begin your basic marksmanship training," the lieutenant said. "Over the next three weeks we will test and score you on every weapon in our inventory. How you perform will determine where we put you once you join our ranks. If you score high with the hand to hand weapons, you will be made a targeteer. If you excel in physical training and survival you will be a scout. If you're a good marksman, you will be one of our gunners."

They were split into groups and her group would be training with the matchlock for the next few days.

She knew how to kill up close but she had never killed at a distance. It seemed that if she could end the fight before getting close then that would be a better way of doing it.

The instructor, a veteran soldier, showed them how to load and fire. The matchlock was a large, heavy thing and at first it felt awkward but as she learned how to hold it and use it properly it became almost natural.

As Greza began loading her matchlock she heard shouting coming from the gatehouse. Everyone stopped and turned to see what was going on.

The portcullis opened and a column of horsemen came riding in. They were fully armored with visored helmets, banners and dragoon matchlocks in scabbards. There were a few people on foot including the largest man she had ever seen. He was as tall as a man and wore some kind of frightening horned helmet.

Then her eyes fell on one rider in particular. He was wearing a fur coat over his black armor and his helmet hung from his saddle. He was a young man but with ancient eyes. He had stubble on his face and head and no special adornments, banners or anything else to mark him as separate, but she knew at a glance that this was Duke Verin.

As Duke Verin glanced around the courtyard she saw a small glimmer of pleasure but mostly she saw sadness. This was a troubled man. Like her, he knew what it was like to take a life. To become such a famous warrior at a young age he must have started early.

One thing the history books never mentioned was where he came from. He showed up on the records eight years ago at the head of a small mercenary band and in two years time had built a large and successful company. Before that his life was completely unknown.

They rode into the middle of the courtyard and dismounted. Men came out and took their horses and his companions walked up to him. The enormous man with the horns walked up and took off his helmet. When he did she saw that it wasn't the helmet that had horns, but the man.

It was a Minotaur. She had only ever read about them. Now that she had a chance, she took a closer look and saw that he had hooves and a head that only superficially resembled a bull's. He was covered in hair and had sharp teeth in his short snout.

The other person that approached Duke Verin was a small woman with shiny black hair that hung to her waist. She was pale with dark eyes that were constantly on the move. She slumped as she walked and kept rubbing her slender hands together like she was cold. She had a loose robe over her armor that billowed out on either side of her like wings.

Duke Verin's companions stood on either side of him and for a moment Greza stood immobile. The moment froze and Greza knew there was meaning behind this. The others were watching because it was their duke, returned home at last, but Greza saw something else entirely.

She saw a hero with a bull and a raven at his side.

It was an image of what the Promised Victor was supposed to be. Perhaps she was having a vision of what might have been. He was a natural leader and seemed to appear from nowhere. At his side were a bull-man and a woman all in black with jet black hair like a raven's.

But then the moment passed and the duke turned and entered the keep with his companions.

It can't be. The Promised Victor?

She had always heard the story and believed it, but facing the possibility of the prophecy in the face was stunning.

"That was Duke Verin, everyone. I've never fought under a better man," the veteran trainer said.

Greza turned toward him.

"Why?" She asked.

"He brings us victory."

"That all?"

The veteran shook his shaved head.

"If that were all, he'd get my respect. Duke Verin gets my life and honor."

Greza was about to ask why but the veteran began barking out more orders to load their guns.

They continued on with the day of matchlock training. She managed to focus, but in breaks in training she'd look up at the keep and wonder why she saw him as the Lost Victor. A Minotaur wasn't a bull and the small woman with black hair and black eyes wasn't a raven. Besides, the Victor was dead: murdered by cultists.

But her mind wouldn't leave the thought behind and she went to bed thinking about little else.

By the end of the week they were hitting their targets almost every time.

"Good work everyone. Tomorrow we'll double the distance to usual combat range and see how you do from there."

She enjoyed shooting the matchlock. She was a little quicker on loading than most but she hadn't been the best shot from her group. Still, it was something that she'd want to hone and become proficient at even if she wasn't assigned as a gunner. She wanted to learn all weapons because sometimes you didn't get to chose what you fought with.

Greza lay in bed unable to sleep. Duke Verin kept entering her mind. It meant something. A message of some sort.

She held her Symbol of Light as she drifted off into sleep.

The next morning they went back to the range for more target practice. During a break she took the opportunity to speak to the instructor.

"Sir?"

"Yes, recruit?"

"Where did Duke Verin come from?"

"From a mother that bedded a man, just like everyone else."

"No, that's not what I meant."

The veteran soldier looked around and then motioned for her to sit down on the block of hay next to him. She took her seat beside him.

"You'd learn sooner or later so I might as well be the one. Someone else would tell you some pigswill and get it wrong. Listen to the story and decide if you could follow such a man. I swear that you'll find none better."

This didn't sound like it was going to be a pleasant story.

"Our Duke didn't start off to a life of privilege. He was born a parentless slave."

That couldn't be right. The duke, the ruler of this country had been a slave like her? Slaves couldn't rule. They'd always have the stigma against them.

"Verin escaped from his masters, killing a few of them in the process, and joined a mercenary company when he was fourteen. He didn't fight at first but he kept his eyes and ears open. Then during a battle their positions were being overrun. He grabbed a sword from the blacksmith's tent and fought to protect the camp. After that he rose through the ranks like a horse on fire."

He stopped and looked at her.

"You seem surprised," he said.

"Confused, maybe."

"Why? Because you were a slave?"

"How did..."

"You have the same look in your eyes that he has. I've seen other escaped slaves come here. You carry yourself like one. Even now you won't look me in the eyes."

"Is it that obvious?"

"Only to someone who knows what to look for."

A slave like her. It didn't feel possible. Slaves had no rights and no ability to lead. Where did Verin's confidence come from?

After three weeks of weapons training, tactics and strategy, they were ready for their first mock battle. Greza stood in the front line next to her fellow recruits. Across the marshy field was an equal sized force made up of Chimera soldiers. Everyone wore armor and helmets.

She was a targeteer. In her hands was a large, rectangular shield that could supposedly stop bullets and a pistol in her hand. Four more pistols were on a bandolier across her chest. None of them were loaded with ball, just powder to make a 'bang' sound. She wore a thick coat with a chain mail shirt that had metal plates attached to it. It was heavy and would slow her down and she didn't see what good it would do against a gun.

Judges were along with each army to decide who lived and who died. Sergeant Drakan was their leader and she was in charge of a squad of five other recruits. Yuro was the only one she really knew in her squad of targeteers.

They all had their shields and pistols ready. A wooden short sword was on her hip but if it came down to hand to hand, she doubted that she'd need it.

The gunners were behind them with their matchlocks resting on the tops of their axes and the pike men were on the flanks, ready to move in if there was trouble.

"Well, look at that," Drakan said in almost a whisper.

She looked to where he was looking and saw Duke Verin and his two companions riding up to the field.

"They've come to see how amazing we are," Hyrin said from somewhere behind her.

Again he was flanked by the bull and raven. None of them spoke a word; they just watched from their saddles.

She turned back to the unit of veterans across the field from her. They had been told to go easy on them, but she wondered how easy it was really going to be. She knew all too well the difference between a fighter who was trained or untrained.

Greza tightened the grip on her shield and looked over the "enemy." Chances were that these were men and women she'd be fighting along side once she joined the company. She had to impress them.

Unfortunately raw fighting ability wouldn't do it. She had to show them that she could work in a unit and follow orders.

The metal helmet with the padding was hot even in the cold air of the approaching winter and the chain mail weighed her down. Sergeant Drakan said that once a person got used to it they wouldn't notice they were wearing it. That day couldn't come soon enough. She was used to fighting in significantly less.

Then the whistle blew and the battle started. She listened for the horn calls of their orders.

A single long note from a horn sounded telling them to advance at walking pace. The tall grass was damp from the morning dew and the bottom of her jacket, near the tops of her boots was getting soaked.

Focus, Greza. Distraction was death.

Two short blasts from the horn told them to stop. When they stopped she waved her squad to take a knee and plant their shields to form a wall to protect the gunners.

Behind her the gunners opened fire. The light charges in their matchlocks didn't have the sudden, sharp violence a real gunshot had.

The veteran squad fired a second later and judges began running back and forth tying red cloth to "casualties." Orders were being shouted and guns were firing. She aimed her pistol and fired.

One of her squad went down with a red cloth tied around their arm creating a gap in the gunners shield wall.

"Close the hole!" Greza called out.

They probably didn't hear her over all the noise, but they saw her hand gestures and moved in closer.

Then the veteran squad charged with their targeteers in front and axes in back.

"Hold position!" She shouted out.

Their pike men moved up and counter charged.

Suddenly everything was chaos. The enemy was right on top of them and she had a man with a padded axe banging away at her shield. The shield was huge and awkward and she couldn't get a hit on him with her pistol.

So, she dropped the pistol and shield rammed the man, knocking him up and off his feet.

Without pausing she kicked another enemy soldier to her side and hurried back into relative position.

One of the recruit axe men was tangled up with an enemy targeteer and she kicked the enemy in the back of the knee which brought him to the ground.

Then an axe blade caught her shield and pulled hard, almost yanking the shield out of her hands. She yanked back and pulled the man right up to her. That was right where she wanted an enemy.

She grabbed the man by his chain mail with her free hand and pushed him back into the men behind him. He fell off balance and collided with his men.

When she looked around next she was surrounded by enemy. They had pushed her men back and she was alone.

She could either make a hasty retreat and hope to make it without getting shot or fight to the last. She made a quick glance behind her and saw an axe man ready to take a swing. She wasn't getting out without a fight.

There was nothing else to think about.

Greza threw her shield at the axe man and charged. He sidestepped the shield and was ready for her charge. He swung with a wide overhead swing. This man wasn't holding back. Even with the padding, that blow would cause serious pain if it connected.

But she didn't let the blow connect. She dodged to the side just enough to avoid it and came in to tackle him in the waist. He had thrown himself off balance with his vicious swing and left himself wide open. Wrapping both arms around him she heaved with her legs and lifted him off the ground. Then she slammed him into the ground on his back.

He lay there stunned while she snatched the axe out of his hand and turned to face the enemy.

There were three matchlocks pointed at her. An officer stood behind them. She recognized him as one of the officers she helped train.

"You're too dangerous to let loose," the officer said.

The three guns fired and she felt a judge tie a red cloth around her arm.

She sighed and dropped the axe. The veterans were looking at her but she couldn't tell what they saw. Had she disappointed them or did they not care?

When she looked for her unit she saw they were all lying on the ground with red cloth on their arms.

They had been beaten that quickly? How embarrassing.

The veterans withdrew and left the recruits to themselves. The veterans were laughing and patting themselves on the back as they walked back to the fortress.

"How'd you do?" Nika asked as she sat down next to her.

She shrugged.

"Not good, huh?" Nika asked.

"I guess not."

Then Duke Verin got down from his horse and approached their group. They all stood and saluted with fists to their chests. He waved them all and motioned for them to take their seats again.

He stood there with his hands resting on his pistol belt. He was very relaxed and held himself with a subtle confidence that she admired. This man knew he could kill most people he met. But he also looked like someone who wouldn't want to.

"You just got your first taste of what a battle is like," Duke Verin said. "Let me assure you that the real thing is much worse. Instead of wet grass you'll be slipping on your friends' blood. Those men went easy on you today. It's different when the man in front of you is trying his hardest to kill you.

"You never had a chance to win this battle. I want you to know what you're up against. I also wanted to show you what you can become. In a week's time you will graduate from recruit to a soldier in my army. If you wish to succeed then you must learn discipline and integrity. I don't care what you've

47

heard. We are not brigands and cut-throats. We are professional soldiers. That said, we will also destroy whatever enemy we face. We do not hold back until the fighting is done."

She listened to every word he said. His voice was like a calm music ready to burst into a powerful explosion of sound. Behind each word was a book full of meaning. He was also the most handsome man she had ever seen.

She knew at that moment that this was a man worthy of her respect. She would gladly serve him in any way possible.

When he finished speaking, Duke Verin gave them a relaxed salute and mounted back up on his horse. Wordlessly they rode back to the fortress.

Sergeant Drakan stood up in front of them.

"That was our Duke. Listen to him and you can't go wrong. Now, let's go over today's action."

She barely listened to the report of their performance. The Duke's words still sang through her mind and she was lost in thought until she heard her name.

"Greza?"

"Here!"

There was some laughing.

"Good work today. You kept the formation as long as you could and then fought like a manticore until you were overwhelmed. Let that be a lesson to all of you. No one, no matter how tough, can survive on their own. That is why you must all keep together or the whole thing falls apart."

But his words faded away as the sound of the Duke's voice filled her memory once again.

Chapter Seven

THE EARLY MORNING WATCH WAS ALWAYS THE coldest and no matter how many layers she wore she never could get warm enough.

She had finally graduated into the ranks of the army, but not as a scout like she wanted, but as a simple front-line targeteer. All they saw of her was her brute strength and not her mind.

Greza stood on the top of the fortress's outer wall and walked up and down its length. She had a matchlock cradled in her arms and the helmet was starting to feel heavy.

The winter wind found every opening in her clothing and sliced at her. Only her eyes were uncovered and she wished she had some way to cover those.

And she had volunteered for this. It was some kind of holiday for the Ekonians and a few other countries nearby. She had never heard of this holiday but it apparently revolved around too much eating and drinking.

If there was one thing she didn't like, it was being around drunken people. She valued intelligence and wine and ale only served to make people into idiots.

She looked out over the gray, flat landscape as the cold moon rose above the frozen marshes. There were no fires allowed up on the walls because it would prevent the guards from seeing in the dark.

"Who goes there?" A friendly voice said.

She looked over to see a large man walking towards her.

"Ox?"

She was relieved it was only him. Unlike most alpha dogs after being beaten, in arm wrestling, Ox actually befriended her. That had been unexpected but very much appreciated.

"I got tricked into volunteering. How'd they get you?" Ox asked.

"I don't drink."

He laughed.

"No, I guess I've never seen you drink."

He came over and looked out over the marshes beside her.

"Not what you thought mercenary life would be when you signed up, right?"

"I didn't know what to expect."

"Still, never heard you complain."

She shrugged.

"You don't come from a comfortable life, do you?" He asked.

She didn't answer.

"You can tell the ones that know what actual suffering is. This ..." he waved a hand around, "isn't so bad once you get used to it."

"It's cold."

"Very cold. But things will be different once the campaigning season starts. Then things will be so much better and so much worse."

"How?"

"Better because we'll be doing things and getting more money. Worse because some of us will die and there will be hardships. Did you know that most armies retreat after taking only ten percent casualties? It's true. Let's say we only take five percent each battle. How many battles will it take to eventually get to you? Try doing that math in your head this summer."

"How long have you been in the Company?"

"Three years, four months and six days."

"Long time."

"Gladiator, huh?"

"Yes."

"I heard things about gladiators."

She didn't want to hear what horrible things he'd heard. They'd only bring up memories she wished to keep buried.

He just grunted and leaned on the battlements.

"Once campaign season comes, you may look back on these cold nights with fondness. At least we're safe here," he said.

They didn't talk much for the rest of their three hours, but it was nice to walk with someone.

When she got back to her bunk she kicked her boots off and fell right asleep. She had the morning off and wasn't going to worry about breakfast. She wanted sleep more.

She was awakened by people singing in the male barracks area. It was some drunken song devoid of real meaning or beauty. They all seemed to think it was funny though.

Since sleep wasn't going to happen anymore, she took out her scriptures and began reading. Word had spread that she was a follower of the path of light and people mocked her behind her back. "Zealot" was the most popular name for her at the moment.

Then she sat up when she saw what this particular chapter was about.

The Promised Victor.

The prophets said that he would be born amid fiery devastation that would kill his family yet he would be spared. That had happened when the baby was found in the smoking remains of his family's house. It spoke how he would rise up and lead the people to victory against a terrible threat from the west. She never could find out what this threat was.

The ancient prophets were never specific.

But then she had to remember what had happened. The child had been found and was being brought to the Imperial capital when they were ambushed by men wearing red and black. The child was taken and a week later his severed finger was sent as proof of his death.

But the prophecy had to be fulfilled. Was there another child somewhere that fit the criteria of the prophecy? A second plan in case the first plan went wrong?

Seems logical.

After lunch it was back to work. Luckily the Lieutenant wasn't around. It was just Sergeant Deran. He liked to keep his classes informal and they just gathered in the barracks.

Greza took a seat in the back like she usually did.

"Alright soldiers, let's begin," Sergeant Deran said. "What's the most important piece of equipment you have to take care of on a long march?"

"Matchlock," someone said.

"No," Sergeant Deran said.

"Sword in case of ambush," another soldier said.

"No."

"Map?"

"No."

"Boots and socks," Greza said.

Some of the soldiers laughed.

"Stop laughing," Deran said. "She's right. Your socks. Blisters, rot foot and rashes can all make a soldier a casualty just as easily as a gun. Now, next question: how do we win wars?"

That was a broad question, but one she knew the answer to. If she answered this one, they might resent her so she kept her mouth closed this time.

"Bravery."

"Skill."

"Tactics."

All of the answers were wrong.

"Logistics," Deran said.

She knew this from reading. Every great general knew that an army couldn't march on an empty stomach or fight without equipment. Beans, blades and blankets.

"The art of war is getting enough people with enough weapons and enough food to the right place at the right time," Deran said.

"Wait, what about fighting, courage and soldiers?" One of the men asked.

"Important, but they're just a part of the equation. Sure, better soldiers may win a battle, but it takes logistics to win a war."

They spent the rest of the two-hour class using cups, shoes and knives to represent military units on a battlefield and went over all the strategies the Company used.

"It's important for the common soldier to understand your place in the battle. It cuts down on confusion and confusion is lethal."

Distraction was death.

She could think of several examples from history where misunderstood orders cost an army the battle.

Everything he went over she had read about, but it was interesting to see someone with experience talk about them. It made the battles make more sense. Yes, she had read many books but experience was a very different thing and she paid attention.

She wanted to learn everything she could about the art of war. She wanted to know everything from how the supply wagons were organized to how the men formed up on the field.

She wanted to become the best soldier she could be.

****

Greza strapped on her breastplate over her chain mail and then put her helmet on. A chain mail veil hung down from the sides and back of the conical helmet. It was all very different than the armor from the Empire.

The last thing she put on were her old Cestus. There was no rule against wearing them and she could still hold her shield and other weapons.

"You look like a real soldier," Burana said.

Greza went over and helped Burana strap her armor on. She was a mess and needed some help.

"We're going to have to do this every day?" Burana asked.

"While on campaign, I'd imagine so."

"Is it wrong to look forward to battle?"

"Depends why," Greza said.

"To test myself."

"You're religion?"

"I don't know if my religion would approve of such a test."

Then they heard the sergeants shouting from the other room.

"Time to go," Burana said.

They all hurried out to the courtyard where other units were forming up. Half the Army was participating in today's training.

"There you are, little sister," Ox said and slapped her on the shoulder as she ran by.

They got into formation and went to attention. A few minutes later Lieutenant Tezana came out. By all accounts she was an ugly woman and not in the best of shape. Her armor bulged out in the middle too much.

Her small eyes looked them up and down before she began shaking her head.

"Pathetic," Lieutenant Tezana said. "I've seen recruits do a better formation. I watched you and you're slow. You're sloppy and your armor isn't polished."

Greza glanced around and saw that everyone's clothing and armor were clean. If the lieutenant was trying to motivate them to perform better, she was going about it in a very poor way. If she actually believed what she said then she was even worse.

Lieutenant Tezana sneered at them before turning to face the 1st Company's captain. They did roll call and then the captain stepped forward to address the 1st company. The other companies' captains were doing the same. Five out of ten companies of five platoons each were participating. That was a lot of soldiers.

She had never seen so many gathered together. It was an impressive sight and it had to be intimidating for an enemy to see marching at them.

The captain began telling them about the day's exercises. Mainly, they were to practice large unit movements and unit cohesion. Sounded like this was mainly practice for the sergeants and officers.

As the captain talked on and on about the importance of the day's exercise, she saw movement coming from the right. She looked only with her eyes and saw Duke Verin and his entourage enter the courtyard. They were all mounted except the giant Minotaur who was in full armor. The small, dark haired woman rode beside Verin. They were talking but they were too far away to hear.

She couldn't take her eyes off the Duke. He was an intelligent man. She could see by the way he examined everything around him and always paused to think before speaking. He was handsome, but it was so much more than that. He was powerful, but not in a physical way.

She couldn't explain it but she couldn't stop looking at him. She did make sure to keep her head facing forward, at least.

She wanted to get to know the Duke and find out who he really was, but she was just a grunt. Maybe if she did something spectacular she'd meet him long enough for him to pin a medal on her chest, but that was about it. She knew that those in charge avoided the common people the same way they avoided pigs.

Unless they wanted something. Then they'd just take and it never ended well for the pigs.

She wondered if Duke Verin was that kind of man. She hoped not.

Then the lieutenant barked orders to the sergeants and they began to march out of the fortress. They went by order of company and platoon.

They spent the day marching around and getting into position as quickly and accurately as possible. Then they'd have to turn the entire army without breaking rank. Most of the work seemed to fall on the lieutenants and sergeants to keep everyone together.

By the end of the day the soldiers knew what to do without much instruction. Some of the newer human recruits complained about sore feet. She wondered what it would be like to be so weak. She felt sorry for them.

Perhaps there was a way to help them. Maybe during the marches she could carry some of their things in her own pack.

At sunset all the units went back to the fortress for supper. There was a long line and most people ate out in the courtyard because the cafeteria wasn't made to take everyone at once.

She got her tray and went outside to sit beside Burana. She just sat on the ground with her back against the stone wall.

"That was a lot of marching," Burana said.

"It was good practice."

"For parades to impress the Duke."

"No, for battle."

"I don't think battle will be anything like that."

"The basics, yes."

Then Ox came over and sat down beside her.

"What'd you think of all that?" Burana asked.

"It's important, Bur," Ox said.

Burana rolled her eyes and went back to her meal.

"You get the hang of it?" Ox asked.

"I've read about these formations, but being in them is different."

"You can only learn so much from your books."

"I'm starting to see that."

"Where'd you learn to read, Grez?" Burana asked.

"My father taught me."

"I can't read. My pa can't read. His pa couldn't read," Burana said.

"I read a little," Ox said.

"I can teach you," Greza said. "There's nothing more enjoyable than a good book."

"I can think of a few," Burana said.

"I thought you guys were about suffering," Ox said.

Burana shrugged.

"None of us are perfect."

After they ate, Ox went off to participate in some wrestling contest another platoon was holding. Burana and she went back to the barracks. They stripped off their boots and armor and lay down. Burana rubbed her feet.

"They hurt?" Greza asked.

"Yeah, they do! Marching around all day kills me."

"Sorry."

"Grez, how come you don't speak more?"

"Huh?"

"You're obviously educated and smart, but you don't show it. You hiding it?"

She didn't want to hide it. If she could have shown it she might have ended up as a scout or something besides a targeteer. A front line brute.

There'd be little chance for her to prove herself capable of more. She was good at fighting and that's all she'd be able to do.

Chapter Eight

THE WINTER PASSED IN SLOW DAYS FULL OF gray skies and cold nights. The others complained of it being painfully boring but Greza had actually enjoyed it. Except the cold. She could have done without freezing every night on guard duty. But she had learned so much from her fellow soldiers and officers and she had read several books, each one a treasure of knowledge.

But now that spring was starting to show, it was time to leave. Rumors about where they were going and who they were fighting differed depending on who one asked and everyone asked everyone.

The simple truth was that no one knew and if they did it was buried in the sea of rumors.

Everyday they did inventory, counting flints, balls, powder, spare parts for the guns, oil, boots, gloves and everything else they'd be bringing with them. All training ceased as every unit inventoried what they had and began assembling individuals' specific kits.

Burana was cleaning the matchlock she'd be taking with her as her assigned gun. Greza was cleaning the scabbard of her battle knife so the blade wouldn't rust in the sheath.

"I hope we go south. I'd like to go somewhere warm by the ocean. I've never seen the ocean," Burana said.

"Me neither."

The ocean sounded beautiful. Every description she had ever read made her want to see it more than ever. Orks were from the south so she wondered if she'd be able to take the heat better than she handled the cold.

The only place she didn't want to go was back to her masters' homeland. She didn't want their scorn. She didn't want them trying to get her back. She didn't want revenge either. She just wanted to never see them again.

"I heard the ocean's only fifty miles to the west of us," Greza said.

She knew it from the maps she liked to study. Maps contained such stories apart from their aesthetic beauty.

"But I heard they're cold and rocky. No one wants to go to them," Burana said.

She thought they sounded lovely, but she answered with a shrug.

"My mother said she'd been to the ocean when she was a little girl. She always talked about it," Burana said.

Mother never talked about her life before she was captured as a slave. From what little she could remember mother had lived in a swamp with her tribe of Orks. It didn't sound very pleasant.

She finished cleaning her weapons and laid everything she'd been issued on her bunk. It was a lot of stuff.

"And to think, we're going to be issued more stuff," Burana said. "Don't worry though. Each squad will have a pack mule. Hey, you want to share a tent?"

Greza nodded. There was no one else she'd want to share with. Burana accepted her faith and her history without all the annoying questions that the others were always asking.

"Great. We'll be battle companions. I watch your back, you watch mine. That doesn't just go for the battlefield you know. If I get into a fight, you got to jump in and help."

"Try not to get into fights."

Burana laughed.

"Of course not, but just in case, you know?"

Greza nodded.

Now that she was finished with her personal inventory, for today, she went up to the library to decide on which books to bring on campaign. She had a waterproof bag just for this occasion that she bought on her one trip to town.

One book would obviously be the scriptures. There was no way she was marching into the lion's mouth without her copy of "The Divine Path."

She got to the library and began looking through the shelves. She didn't want to take anything that looked valuable or irreplaceable.

As she was searching through the history section she heard someone else come in. She had always been the only one in the library.

Greza peered around the shelf to peek at who had entered.

It was Duke Verin. He was wearing a fur coat and was thumbing through a book. He wore no hat and his stubble head was recognizable from miles away.

He looked so sad for some reason.

But then the thought of actually meeting him made her duck back. What would she say to a duke? She had never spoken to a nobleman before except Erinad, but he was eccentric and unique in every way.

Maybe she could sneak out without being noticed.

"Alethia? That you?" Duke Verin asked.

Oh, no.

She tried to think of what to do. If she ran for it, he might see her and order her to stop and then she'd look suspicious because she ran. If she stayed, she would have to speak to him and she didn't even know how to speak to a duke. She had been ordered by dukes, barons and even a prince, but never had she spoken back except to say "yes, lord," or "no, lord."

"Who are you?" Duke Verin asked right beside her.

She jumped and almost tripped backwards.

"Duke Verin, I..."

He held up his gloved hand.

"Relax, soldier. What's your name?"

"Greza, sir...I mean, Duke."

"Greza," he said as if thinking about the name. He leaned on the book case and scratched his chin. "An Ork name, but I can't remember what it means."

"I didn't know it had a meaning, my Duke."

That was stupid of her to say. Now he was going to think she was a dumb brute like everyone else. What normal person didn't know the meaning of their own name?

"It does and one I've heard before. I'll remember it eventually. So, you came to my library to read?"

His library? Was this not open for everyone?

Fear struck her like a wave. She couldn't be accused of theft. It would ruin her. Her reputation would be destroyed, no one would trust her and she'd be kicked out of the Company.

"Yes, my Duke. I came to read," she managed to get out.

"What are you reading?"

"Path of Light, my Duke," she blurted out before thinking.

He raised an eyebrow.

"A dead religion's book? What for?"

"It's not dead, my Duke. I believe in it."

She knew saying such a thing would make her look like an idiot. She wanted to run away and hide.

He smiled and then looked around.

"I'm afraid this library doesn't get used as much as I'd like. It seems soldiers would prefer to gamble and drink."

"I don't drink or gamble, my Duke."

"Because you're busy reading."

"It's against my faith."

"I see. You're from the Empire. I can tell by your accent. You came a long way, Greza. I hope we don't disappoint you."

With that he gave a slight nod and left.

She stood there, wondering how big of an idiot she had looked.

GREZA STOOD IN FORMATION IN THE EARLY MORNING and watched as the sky turned from dark purple to a dull red. The mornings were still bitterly cold and frost covered everything that had been left outside.

All units except for the ones staying for garrison were lined up in their order of march. All around her soldiers, horses and carts were crammed in a spiral that would uncoil as the Company marched out of the courtyard.

They were waiting for the Duke.

"Taking his time with his breakfast?" Someone said behind her.

"Making sure the padding on his saddle is comfortable enough," another soldier said.

"Quiet, you two," Greza said without turning her head.

Her retort was answered with snickering. Half these men still acted like children. Maybe because they had been allowed to be children. Her childhood was serving her masters: running around delivering things, sweeping, cleaning and feeding animals. The only time she had had to herself was at nighttime when she went to bed. Then she'd look out the window and wonder what was beyond the woods.

Finally the Duke rode out on his horse. He was in full armor and held his helmet in his lap.

"Company!" The captains shouted in unison.

"Platoon!" The lieutenants shouted in unison.

"Attention!" The Duke called out. He didn't shout like the other officers, but his voice was still loud and clear.

Verin rode to the front where the gate was and took a moment to look over his army.

"Today we leave the comfort of our fort and march many miles over strange roads," Duke Verin said. "Our march will take us south and east. The numerous kingdoms there are engaging in a vicious war between themselves and the pirates that plague their shores. King Emeron has invited us to assist him in bringing order and peace to the area and we will be doing that. Soldiers, you're the best out there. Don't forget that. We will kill and tread under our boots anyone who opposes us."

This got a cheer from the army and even she couldn't resist throwing her armored fist in the air.

"Men, women, when the time comes that we face our enemy across the field of battle, I know you will not hesitate. Kill them before they kill you. Stay alert at all times. Watch each other's back. Remember that you are all Chimera Company. Maintain our honor and maintain the fear they have for us."

With that, Duke Verin turned his horse and rode out the gate. The officers and sergeants shouted out orders and the army was on the move.

It was great to finally be leaving. She was on her way with the army surrounding her. They'd be going to lands she'd never seen and gain victories.

Greza didn't care about the glory, but she did like the honor. They would end a war between several countries so that people could get back to their normal lives.

Also, this was her chance to see what she could really do. She knew she could win almost any one-on-one fight, but this would be different. There was so much more to being a soldier than a gladiator. Before she just had to focus on the one thing, defeating the person in front of her. Now she had to worry about everyone behind and beside her, the numerous enemies in front of her, her water, her ammunition, the commands of her officers and the ground at her feet.

She was going to be the best. She would rise through the ranks and prove to everyone that she wasn't an idiotic, brutish slave.

As they marched the sun rose up over the flat, marshy land. No wonder the king gave Verin this land for payment. No one else wanted it. It did have a stark kind of beauty that she actually enjoyed, but there was little anyone could do with it.

At first there was singing and conversation, but after the first few hours it was just silent marching. She looked around and tried to read the expressions on her fellow soldiers' faces. Most were unreadable. Some were smiling and others didn't look happy at all. She wondered if they were nervous or afraid.

Some were probably excited to finally be on the march like her.

But then her readings came back to her. She remembered ancient poets lamenting about the horrors and uselessness of war. They spoke of friends dying cruel deaths and innocents being caught up in battles. They spoke of worse things that she didn't want to think about.

In any war, horrible things happened to innocents and she knew some of the soldiers in the Ekonian army would also do these horrible things. She would do all she could to stop them from looting and raping. She would guard their souls as well as their physical bodies.

She couldn't imagine what such a barbaric thing was like. Erinad had saved her from the cruel hands of her masters and for that, if nothing else, she'd be eternally grateful. She'd listened as it happened to other slaves and every time she knew it could have been her.

No, she would not allow that to happen with her people.

It was amazing how different her life would have been if Erinad hadn't stepped in and saved her. She hoped his spirit was watching her from Paradise. She wanted him to know that she was doing well.

They stopped around mid-day for lunch and a brief rest. She rested up against a wagon that was carrying some sort of siege machine. Burana sat down beside her with her hard bread and dried pork.

"This isn't so bad," Burana said.

"This is just the first day and we have nice weather," Greza said.

"Strength through suffering," she said and shrugged.

She must have had a gift for prophecy because the next day it started raining. The roads turned to mud which slowed the entire army down and everyone was drenched head to toe.

Now instead of faces she saw hooded rain coats. When a breeze kicked up, their oiled rain coats would flutter and flap. That, coupled with the slogging of their feet in the mud were the only sounds she heard. The sound of rain faded out into the background and she had to actively listen for it to hear it anymore.

She liked the feel of the rain on her face. The rain wasn't so cold and once she accepted that everything was wet, it stopped bothering her.

At night they built many fires and circled the tents around the fires. No one really dried off, but if they couldn't be warm and dry at least they could be warm.

She lay in her tent reading her scriptures. This all wasn't so bad. The food wasn't good and even her feet were starting to get tired of marching, but as a whole, she was safe, she was fed, she was relatively warm, and she was free.

Burana was carving on a large stick while whistling a tune.

"You have any boyfriends back home?" Burana asked.

"No. Don't want any."

"Why not."

"None of them interested me."

Burana stopped whistling.

"What? You don't like boys then?"

"Never thought about them."

"But they must have approached you."

She hadn't been popular back home. The other slaves didn't like her for her slightly more pampered status as a gladiator and she guessed none of them thought Orks were attractive.

It didn't make sense. Orks were relatives of elves, just green, stronger and with pronounced canines. It was probably the Pale and Dark Elves that came up with the current ideas of 'beauty.'

"Nope," Greza said.

"What about Ox. You like him, right?"

"Of course I like him."

"No, I mean, you like him...in a 'special way' as my mam used to say."

"Romantically?"

"Yeah."

"No."

"Well..."

Burana thought for a moment but then rolled back over and continued carving.

On the third day they crossed the border and left Ekonia. The land changed from wet marshes to dry prairie and what few trees there were, were tall and thin with most of the leaves up top.

"Isn't this an invasion? How come no one's here to stop us?" Burana asked as they trudged through the mud.

"They make deals with the countries they pass through," Greza said.

"They just let them?"

"They all rely on mercenaries so they all agree to it ... unless they're the country they're fighting."

"Odd."

The rain finally stopped a few hours before sundown and everyone cheered. She didn't because she liked the rain. Duke Verin decided to stop early for the day and everyone celebrated as they dried out.

Greza hung her raincoat up and walked over to sit beside the fire next to Ox. Someone had brought a lute and was playing while others sang along.

"These are the nights you're going to look back on," Ox said in a hushed voice. "Most of them don't realize it and won't remember this night."

"I will."

"See that you do. They won't come often. I think that's why we stopped."

"Why we stopped?"

"Because I think Duke Verin knows we have to celebrate every little thing. Because once we get into war, little sister, there won't be much smiling."

Chapter Nine

THE FIRST TOWN THEY CAME TO ON THE SIXTH day had a high wall with towers and at first she thought it was a fortress. She wasn't very knowledgeable about the history of this region so she could only guess that war was common here.

The army stopped a half mile from the town and the Duke and his escort went to the town to negotiate.

"They won't let us all into the town," Ox said.

"Too many of us?" Greza asked.

"Even cities don't like letting us all in. Small groups, sure. People that want to do business will come out to us."

That was sort of disappointing. She had been hoping to see the far off cities of the world.

As Ox said, only the supply sergeants were let in to purchase necessary provisions. But, Ox was also right because some of the town's people came out to do business. One farmer was trying to sell goats and Greza didn't know why anyone would buy a goat on the march. Many others were selling beer, ale and wine and some were selling what looked like useless trinkets.

Then she saw a group of brightly dressed women come out. They weren't holding anything.

"Whores," Burana said with disgust.

She had never seen a prostitute before and couldn't believe that they'd be so brazen to come out in the middle of the day.

The army camped there that night and there was more singing and drinking. Female soldiers snuck off into the tents of male soldiers and Greza tried to ignore it. Years ago most of these people would have been Followers of Light. And now they had abandoned those beliefs and morality.

They moved on the next day and the land kept getting drier and rockier. If this kept up, they'd be in a desert before too long. The days were also getting warmer. Mornings and nights were still cold, but in the day she had to take off her outer jacket.

The tent she shared with Burana was small but at night time they'd have long conversations. Mostly Burana spoke. She liked to talk about the farm and village she came from and though she hated tending to pigs, Greza could tell that a part of her missed that simple life.

That night, she had guard duty so conversation was cut short. She went to bed and was awakened by one of the guards when it was her turn. She put on her coat, helmet and bandolier of pistols. She lit the wicks just in case and began patrolling the camp.

Times like these were lonely. There were no other guards to talk to because they had to be spread out. Even if Ox or Burana were here, she had trouble talking to them about her deeper thoughts. For whatever reason she couldn't be herself completely around them. It was like she always had armor on over her heart.

She missed Erinad.

Greza straightened her back because Erinad would probably have scolded her on her poor posture. He'd know everything about this region and be able to tell her of kings and battles.

Then she heard something. Movement in the grass. She turned and scanned the direction of the noise. If it was an animal she couldn't have it digging around in the army's provisions.

Greza adjusted her cestus and walked toward the source of the noise.

"Who's there?" She called out.

A moment later a man stood up out of the tall grass. At first she thought it was a town's person coming in to steal something, but then she saw the uniform. He was a young man and from what she could see of his shadowed face, he looked frightened. He kept glancing around and he held his head ducked down.

"What are you doing, sneaking around here?" Greza asked; glad that she wouldn't have to shoot anyone.

"I'm leaving. Please let me go," the man whispered.

In the silence of night his whisper carried almost like a shout.

"You signed a contract."

"Damn the contract! I've had enough. I didn't sign up for this. All we do is march all day and get yelled at."

"It's a tough life, but you have to get used to it. Now, turn around and march back to your tent."

"I can't. I won't."

This man was weak, but it wasn't because he was human. His was a weakness of the will. He was not used to hardships and discipline. She wondered what this man's life had been like to expect anything else.

But she also pitied the man. She knew what it was like to be trapped somewhere, forced to work all day and do things she didn't want to do. Perhaps this man felt like a slave and wanted to escape. Could she possibly blame him for that?

"Please," he begged.

"No."

The man straightened his shoulders and looked her in the eye. Then he bolted off running as fast as he could.

At that moment she had a choice.

She could let him run and be free of a life he didn't want. That was exactly what she had done. That desire still lived inside her.

Or she could do her duty to the Company and stop this man. She had sworn an oath to obey.

So had this man. This man had sworn to serve at least two years in the Company. He had given his word. That was the difference between him and a slave. He had agreed to this. So had she. Because she had sworn, it was her duty to stop him. If she didn't, she'd be breaking her oath.

She took off running after the man. He was slow and she caught up in no time. The man barely had time to turn before he realized she was on top of him. She tackled him to the ground and pinned him to the dirt.

"You're going back. I'm sorry," she said.

"Please!"

She picked him up and held an arm behind his back as she marched him back to the camp.

"Where's your officer?" She asked.

When he didn't answer she pushed up on his arm, making him grunt in pain.

"Artillery Company. First platoon."

She knew where every unit was by position and quickly found the flag of the artillery corp. The red and green background with a gold cannon wasn't hard to miss.

Reluctantly the soldier directed her to his lieutenant's tent. She was stopped by a guard and the guard went to wake up the lieutenant.

The lieutenant was an Elf and he came out of his tent rubbing his eyes and scowling. His long hair was a mess and his uniform was crinkled from sleeping in it.

"Is this important?" The lieutenant asked.

"Yes, sir. I found this man attempting to run away," Greza said.

The Elf paused and then looked over to her captive.

"Karuno? This true?" The Elf lieutenant asked.

The man only nodded.

"That's the sixth time this month. If you don't man up and ..." then he looked back to Greza. "I apologize about this, soldier. He runs off all the time and always comes back in the morning. He's an indecisive little puke."

Greza didn't see how this officer wasn't mad. The man had tried to run off. He should be punished.

"Thank you, soldier. That will be all. I'll take it from here," the Elf said.

Greza nodded and went back to her post.

That had been a waste of effort and time. The man was a weak willed worm and wasn't going to be punished. He'd never learn until... Until what? Until he got a few stripes on his back like she had?

Is that what she would have done?

She could still feel the sting of the lash on her own back. How could she ever allow that to happen to anyone else?

Right and wrong were no longer clear and that was endlessly frustrating.

15th day of the march.

GREZA NOTICED COMMOTION UP AHEAD IN THE FORmation. They continued to march but she strained to get a look at what was happening up front. Officers on horses were gathering and talking. They gestured wildly and were practically shouting. She could hear them from a distance but couldn't make out what they were saying.

"What's going on?" Ox asked.

"You tell me," Greza said.

He was the veteran after all. Ox was also a good head taller than most people around them and had a good view.

"I don't know. It looks like trouble though," he said.

A few minutes later all the officers, even platoon leaders were called in a massive group over on the side. The Duke and his entourage were there. She tried to keep an eye on him as she walked past. His face was an unreadable statue. Some of the other officers had scowling faces and others had closed mouths and wide eyes.

Ox was correct. It did look like trouble.

Then the assembled officers called a halt to the march and everyone stopped. Some took out their canteens and others began whispering about what was going on.

A few minutes later the conclave of officers broke up and came back to their units. Lieutenant Tezana rushed up to the front of their platoon.

"Platoon, listen up!" She barked. "Drop your packs and carry only your battle kit. The capital city of Lerichstag is under siege and we move to support them. The enemy army is camped outside the walls and is aware of our presence. Expect battle."

The platoon burst into excited shouts, questions, complaints and cursing. The quietest ones were the veterans. She looked to the veterans to see how they acted and tried to act the same.

She couldn't help but feel nervous. A part of her was excited and wanted to prove herself in battle, but the larger part knew this could end up being very terrible.

This was why she was here. This was her chance to prove herself. She had to show them – she had to show the Duke what she was capable of.

She put on her cestus and lit the wicks on her pistols.

The army then moved out. It was going to be five miles to the battle. The support units were staying behind to guard their things and set up a base camp.

The march was quick but not so fast that they'd be worn out before they arrived. Soldiers spoke of what they'd accomplish; boasting before the battle even began.

The forest opened up and a vast plain opened up before them. Farms spread out from the city and the sky was blue with scattered white clouds. A walled city with tall towers and a blocky castle with square towers stood in the middle. An army stood between them and the city and they were gathering into formations of blocks. She could see their banners fluttering in the wind and the horsemen riding around the army delivering messages and the like.

The army looked massive. It was a forest of spears that looked triple their own army. Greza looked around to the soldiers around her and she saw their pale faces and their wide eyes.

Horns began to blow issuing orders. Just like the training, they lined up into their formations. She knew exactly who was supposed to be on her left and right. Lieutenant Tezana stood behind them and drew her sword.

"Listen up, platoon! Don't mess this up. Fail me and I'll see your pay docked," the lieutenant said.

"So inspirational," Ox said somewhere behind her.

"I'd like to see that fat bitch get up in the front line," someone else said.

Greza was in front and she had a clear view of the army moving up to meet them. She could see the glint from their spears and their waving banners. There were thousands of them and they were marching right toward her to kill her.

How could they possibly kill so many of them? It was impossible.

Then she felt a hand on her shoulder.

"Steady, Grez," Burana said.

She looked back and nodded at her. Burana retreated back into formation and shouldered her gun.

Like an approaching storm the enemy army and their fluttering banners crept closer. As they got within shouting distance they stopped. The enemy was equipped with small round shields and long pikes. She knew that those pikes were for defense. Armies like that would attack with massed gunfire.

That was why she was there. She raised her shield and drew a pistol.

"Prove your worth," Greza said to herself.

She looked around for the Duke but didn't see him from where she stood.

Then the horns blew telling them that the battle had started. That was quick. She had expected the generals to negotiate. But apparently all the conditions had been set already and this was a serious battle. Whatever was going on was urgent.

"It's starting already?" Someone said.

"Man up, everyone."

"We can do this."

"We'll kill them all."

"Steady."

Then she watched as the enemy gunners began to move forward and prepared to fire.

"Targeteers! Ready shields!" Lieutenant Tezana shouted.

She kneeled down and she felt the gunners move behind her and leveled their guns.

Then the guns fired over her head. The concussion slammed her brain like a drum.

A second later she saw the enemy gunners fire. White puffs of smoke erupted along their line and a second later she heard the reports. Something struck her shield.

She had just been shot! Well, her shield. But it would have struck her. Someone behind her yelled out in pain.

The gunners that fired retreated and the second line moved up and aimed. Another concussive string of blasts gonged her head.

A horn sounded three times. The signal to advance.

She took a deep breath and shoulder to shoulder with her fellow targeteers she began marching forward as the third line of gunners moved up and fired on the move.

She readied her pistol. Their job was to take out the pike men and move in on the gunners. As they got within range she fired at the nearest pike man. The small buckler on their arms wasn't enough to defend against bullets and her man went down with a hole where his eye used to be.

They sheathed their first pistols and pulled and fired their second.

A pike man thrust his long spear at her head and she narrowly dodged. She batted it away with her empty pistol and moved in to where their long pikes couldn't get her. Now she was within range to do what she did best.

Gunshots ran out in front of her and she felt two separate impacts on her shield and a flash of pain along her shoulder. She looked down and saw a small cut where a bullet had grazed her.

More cries of pain came from behind her. A white fog of gun smoke was enveloping the battlefield and she could only see a few ranks in front of her. All around were gunshots and yelling.

She saw an exposed enemy gunner. This was her opening. If she could get inside the enemy formation she could cause serious havoc.

This was her chance.

Greza charged in with her shield in front. She barely felt an impact from a bullet before she crashed into the enemy gunner. She knocked the man down.

Now she was surrounded by enemy gunners. Some of them were backing up and one was frantically trying to reload. She tore off her shield and threw it hard at the loading man. The heavy iron shield knocked the gun out of his hand and she whirled on the nearest soldier. She grabbed his head and pulled it down hard to connect with her knee. She felt the bones of his face crunch and she let go.

She looked for another target.

One after one she grabbed an enemy and broke something on them. She'd smash them in the face with her armored gauntlet or break their necks in her arms.

An enemy soldier in armor and carrying a sword pushed his way through the ranks. By the way he moved she knew he knew how to fight. This was a veteran.

She looked around her. A gunner's helmet lay on the ground nearby. With her foot she picked it up and kicked it right at the armored soldier. He knocked the helmet out of the air with his sword and had time to swing at her as she rushed him.

She bashed the blade away with her armored gauntlet and reached for his shield. He managed to pull back but it left him slightly off balance. His belly was exposed.

Greza ducked down and wrapped her arms around the soldier's waist and pushed up. She picked the man up from the ground and heaved him up with all her might. Then she slammed him back down on the ground as hard as she could. She heard him grunt and the sword flew from his hand.

She opened his visor with her left hand and brought her right hand down in a bloody crunch.

Chapter Ten

GREZA SNATCHED UP HER SHIELD AS SHE saw a group of gunners running up to support the enemy unit she was fighting. This wasn't a place she wanted to be. She turned around to see her own unit rushing forward as well. The first line was raising their guns.

She ducked behind her shield as her unit opened fire. She heard the balls flying over her head with high pitched shrieks. A moment later the enemy returned fire.

As soon as they had fired she jumped up and rushed back to rejoin her ranks. She took her position again and raised her shield.

"You're crazy," one of her men said.

"I saw an opening," she said.

They advanced and their gunners kept firing.

"Almost out of shots!" Someone shouted behind her.

"Axes!" Lieutenant Tezana called out.

The gunners slung the flintlocks over their backs and raised their long, curved axes.

As one, they all advanced in a line, shield to shield. She fired the last of her pistols and put it back in its sheath.

The enemy pike men charged. A wall of spear points rushed right at her. She bashed several pikes away with her shield and saw one of the enemy gunners leveling their matchlock at her.

There was the white puff of smoke and she twisted her body to the side to avoid the shot. She felt the ball strike her breastplate and ricochet off into the air.

Then the two armies smashed into each other and instantly everything was chaos. Pikes were thrusting toward her. Axes were swinging around her. All over was the sound of metal on metal and the grunting and howls of men.

She was being pushed from behind and the front and from every other side. Her shield was pressed against her by an enemy pike man so that she couldn't move her arm at all.

Greza slipped her arm out and dropped the shield. Now that her armored hands were free she moved on the nearest enemy. She grabbed the man's pike and pushed it up into the air as she moved in. A metal fist to his face dropped him instantly.

Again she began tearing into the enemy. At that close distance the pike men couldn't defend themselves. They were great for keeping people away, but get too close and they were useless. No wonder Duke Verin chose to use long axes instead. Her men were using their axes in close quarters with no problem.

She grabbed a man's arm and brought her elbow down on it. She felt the bone break. Then she punched another man's throat and kicked another man's knee so that it bent the wrong way.

All of it became a violent blur and one action melted into the next. Though she couldn't tell exactly what she was doing, going on only instinct, she saw and heard everything. Never had her senses been more alive. She was enjoying it and she didn't care.

Then she stopped and looked around. The enemy was few and far between with many of them running away. Already she began to hear cheering coming from her side.

Greza raised her arms in the air and shouted out at the top of her lungs. Her armored fists were covered in blood up to her elbows.

Duke Verin! Do you see me? Look what I've done in your name! She thought to herself as she shouted.

Ox staggered up to her and leaned on his axe. He was covered in dirt and gore and a cut bled from his cheek. But he was smiling.

"I killed them," Greza said, feeling a toothy smile grow across her face.

"I saw. I couldn't help but see. You're a beast."

"They're running."

She turned back to make sure they kept running. They were running off to the sides. Troops from the besieged city were coming up from their rear and had been a hammer and anvil maneuver like the battle of Betetarnum in the War of Imperial Succession.

She had never felt such an energy pour through her as it did then. This had been the best day of her life.

Burana came up, limping and using her axe as a crutch.

Greza hurried over and put her arm around her to support her.

"You, alright?" Greza asked.

"A pointy stick scratched my leg. Nothing to worry about," Burana said.

Friendly cavalry rode up and one of the armored soldiers asked for a status report.

"Where's the sergeant?" Ox called out in his booming voice.

Turned out that the sergeant was dead. The lieutenant then told Ox that he was acting sergeant.

The officers then began reestablishing control and the army moved back and reorganized.

Her unit found themselves sitting on a grassy hill overlooking the battlefield that was covered in bodies and broken weapons. The corpses were in clumps where the fighting had been the fiercest and the medics were guiding their teams to pick up the wounded. The units that hadn't been at the front had clean up duty which was gathering equipment and putting bodies into piles for burial the next day. Her platoon sat around sharing dried pork and passing around canteens as they watched.

Now that the blood was slowing down she assessed the field and realized how many bodies covered it. The field was literally red and broken weapons and dead horses lay everywhere.

"You see it, don't you?" Ox asked.

"It was so wonderful, but now..."

"Now you see the real battle, Grez."

It had felt so amazing to win a victory for her Duke, but now she wondered if it had been right. Could so much death be good?

"Don't think about it too much," Ox said.

That was like telling her not to breathe.

He passed her a canteen and she took a deep drink.

She looked down at the dent in her breastplate where her heart was. That shot could have killed her. Several times she had been inches close to death. How pointless her life would have been to have ended there. She hadn't accomplished anything in her life and she wouldn't have been remembered by anyone.

How many of her fellow soldiers had died and would never be remembered?

"I can see it sinking in," Ox said.

"It's horrible."

"It is, but you can't let that rule you."

"Will I get used to it?"

"Unfortunately."

Then she saw the Duke and his bull and raven approach a group of riders from the city. Both groups had the banner of the Ekonian Army.

"Who's the Duke talking to?" She asked.

"Captain Richkurk," Ox said.

"Richkurk? He was the one that gave me the coin."

"That shows good judgment on his part."

The camp soldiers came up with their wagons and all their packs in neat order. A wagon came up and dropped off all their packs. The packs of the dead were split up among the unit and Greza got a shiny boot dagger. She used it to slice off a piece of pork and put it half way in her mouth as she chewed it.

She didn't know how long the battle had taken but the sun was already setting so it had been at least three hours.

The officers came by and ordered everyone to set up camp. The Duke and his men were still talking and she wondered what they were talking about. She could see them setting up a tent in the middle of the field as the Duke continued to talk.

"What are they talking about?" She asked.

"The Duke sent Richkurk ahead to organize everything for the campaign. I'd imagine they're having a strategy meeting and discussing everything."

"You know everything that's going on, don't you?"

"Not hardly."

They camped there outside the city for the next few days. There was no mandatory training and drills. It was a well deserved break while they rested from the marching and the battle.

"Don't you ever laugh, Greza?" Burana asked.

They were lying in their tent listening to the lute player from the next platoon over. This one seemed to prefer slow, melancholy songs to the usual drinking songs most army musicians played. She infinitely preferred this one.

"I laugh," Greza said.

"I've never seen you."

No, she didn't laugh. There was nothing to laugh about. Laughter was for people who had been allowed to be children. That was a luxury she hadn't had.

"You couldn't have been born so austere," Burana said.

"Perhaps I was."

She finished putting on her boots and then grabbed her pistol bandolier.

"Guard duty again? Are you scheduled every night?"

"The lieutenant has taken a liking to me," Greza said.

"Well, you did kill at least twenty men. As far as we know. That sort of thing doesn't go unnoticed."

"I don't need the medal."

"You're getting the medal whether you like it or not."

"And now the lieutenant's jealous? How petty."

She bid Burana good night and left their small, two-person tent and stood up straight. She looked around the camp, lit up by lanterns and camp fires of soldiers that didn't like to turn in early; which was most of the veterans.

The veterans usually gathered and shared stories of past campaigns. Some she had heard so often that she might as well have been there. Almost always the stories were humorous and almost always she doubted they had happened the way they were being told.

She donned her helmet without bothering to strap it down and began walking the perimeter. She knew the challenge code to say and she knew the camp well by now. They'd been there a week after the battle and were allowed within the city in small groups. Not surprisingly her name hadn't come up yet. Lieutenant Tezana had seen to that.

Greza walked a distance away from the camp and kept her eyes sharp. She had to stay alert at all times but even then she needed something to keep her mind occupied. So, she ran a philosophical puzzle through her head. If a boat called the *Sea Witch* was rebuilt piece by piece, and the old pieces taken to a different location and reassembled slowly over time, does the boat with all new pieces cease to be the same boat? Is the boat with all the old pieces the true boat and the new one false? Are they both the *Sea Witch*? If they are not both authentic Sea Witches, at what point does one boat stop being the *Sea Witch* and the other start?

She ran this puzzle all through her mind attaching it to different scenarios and objects.

Around midnight she heard a noise and stopped. Her ears quickly picked up the direction and she cautiously moved that way.

It was a group of fifteen riders heading away from the camp and toward the city. She stepped out into the road.

"Halt and identify yourself," she said.

The riders came to a stop in front of her. In the moonlight away from the fires and lanterns of camp she saw that it was a group of mostly civilians with a few Ekonian men in armor. Some of them were women in voluminous dresses and elaborate hairstyles. For a second she wished she could have dresses and hair like that and was aware of her own dirty uniform.

"What's this now?" One of the women said in a nasal voice.

One of the Ekonian men rode up. As he got closer she saw that it was Duke Verin himself. She stood straighter and tried not to look nervous.

"I'm the Duke, soldier. I can vouch for these people," he said.

"Of course, my Duke," she said and hastily got out of the way.

He didn't seem to recognize her from the library. Perhaps it was the helmet or perhaps she hadn't been important enough to remember.

"Is that an Ork girl?" One of the civilian women asked.

"I hear Ork females do the same work as the men. Can you believe that?"

"Orks are horrid creatures prone to ignorance and brutality."

"Simple creatures only understand survival and violence," a man said.

Her hand tightened on the butt of her pistol as she held her tongue. She was used to such insults from her masters, but not since she had become a free woman and had joined the ranks of the Ekonian Army.

"Leave the creature alone," another man said.

"Hold on, I want to ask her something."

One of the women rode closer to her and leaned toward her.

"Ork girl, some philosophers nowadays are saying that Orks are just as intelligent as any other race, that it's their upbringing that determines their behavioral violent lives. Tell me, would you agree with this statement?"

"Yes," Greza said.

The woman laughed.

"Such an eloquent statement infused with undeniable evidence!" The woman said to the laughter of the other civilians.

Greza looked to the Duke to see if he'd stop these insults. He sat silently by and watched with humorless eyes.

"Ork girl, can you support your bold statement?" The woman asked.

"Yes," Greza said.

"So direct!"

"You ask direct questions and I'll give you direct answers," Greza said. "If you want something more elaborate I suggest you ask a more open-ended question. As to the question of whether Orks are violent because of birth or upbringing I will say that it was not Ork society that taught me to be violent, but Imperial nobility; the ones that claim civilization that taught me to be a savage. As Denaria, the mystic philosopher of Old Alasatra wrote, 'Is it not the simple person that loves liberty and peace and the governments of the aristocracy that want confusion and war?'"

The woman looked at her with confusion all over her face. She glanced back to her fellow nobles for support but they were as confused as she was.

The woman then turned to the Duke.

"You let all your soldiers treat nobility with such insolence?"

"You asked her a question. She gave you an answer," Duke Verin said with little interest. "I fail to see the insolence."

The woman turned her attention back to Greza.

"Remember your place, Ork. You may pretend at learning and culture, but you're just a green-skinned brute like all your kind. You're a common soldier and will never accomplish anything of renown. You'll die unremembered and unimportant."

The nobles all laughed and rode off.

She wanted to punch the woman and all her friends in the face. They didn't care that she was educated. They only saw an Ork and no matter what she did, she'd never change their minds. They were set in their ignorance.

And to her own frustration, the woman's words stung.

She watched the group ride off toward the city and all she could do was stand there and smolder.

And the Duke had just sat there and let it all happen. He allowed them to insult one of his own soldiers. Had all the good feelings she had toward him been misplaced? If he was as truly noble as she had thought, then shouldn't he have come to her rescue?

Important men like Verin rescued damsels and ladies. Greza was no lady. She was and always would be "just an Ork."

She clenched her fist and punched the nearest tree. The bark shattered and flew in all directions and the frail, small tree fell to the ground.

"Easy, soldier," Duke Verin's voice said from behind her.

She instantly straightened up and stood at attention.

"At ease," he said with a small wave of his hand. "What's your name?"

"Greza."

"Ah, yes. I remember you from the library. You seem upset."

"No, my Duke."

"The tree would say otherwise."

"It's nothing, my Duke."

"Did you let that woman's words get through your armor?"

"No, my Duke. You shouldn't concern yourself with a simple grunt like me."

"I don't believe for a second that you're simple."

She didn't know what to say so just nodded. Was that a compliment? What did he know of her anyway? Perhaps she was simple.

"You must ignore, small-minded people, Greza. Good work, continue on."

He then rode off to catch up with the others.

She had been so lost in her thoughts that she hadn't noticed him approach. Now she felt like a barbaric imbecile.

The woman's words repeated themselves over and over again in her head all through the rest of her patrol.

When she was relieved she went back to her tent and crawled into bed next to Burana. She lay there listening to Burana sleep and thought about what the Duke must have seen. Did he believe that she wasn't a mindless brute? Did he think she was weak for letting the woman's insults get through?

Chapter Eleven

THERE WAS NO CEREMONY HELD FOR HER getting her first medal. Lieutenant Tezana came up to her one morning and threw the medal at her.

"There's your medal. I hope you feel big now with that unearned medal on your chest," she said and walked off.

And that was all the ceremony and praise she received. It wasn't the lack of ceremony that angered her; it was the lieutenant's mindless pettiness. How someone could be so shallow and angry was beyond her imagination.

The camp was full of rumors on where they were heading next. The only thing for certain was that the army was preparing to march. They'd be off to another battle soon.

She sat under a tree and ate her boiled eggs as she read her scriptures. Everyone that knew her was used to her scripture reading and she wasn't bothered except by strangers.

Then she saw Burana running up with an enormous smile on her freckled face.

"Grez, we got leave to go into the city tonight! You coming?"

She did want to see new places and finally this was her chance. Maybe even the lieutenant got tired of being vindictive once in a while.

"Yes," Greza said.

Together with Ox and a few other men from their platoon, they went into the city and showed their passes to the guards.

The city wasn't 'just a town but bigger' it had things she'd never seen before. The market place in the square by the main gate was filled with merchants, jugglers, acrobats and nobles. She also smelled the aroma of cooking food that she didn't recognize but wanted to become more familiar with. There was a fountain in the middle of the square with a statue of a man in ancient looking armor.

"Where to first?" Ox asked.

"Tavern!" One of the others said.

"Nah! Let's shop around first before the stores close," Burana said.

"Good idea," Ox said. "Split into groups. No one goes off by themselves and we'll meet at that tavern over there in an hour. Two at most."

Everyone agreed and began to split up. She went with Burana. The two of them chose a street at random and headed off.

"Looking for something particular?" Greza asked.

"No, just looking. You?"

"Just looking."

"I guess when we don't know what we want, we're always just looking. Next time we'll have a better idea of what we want."

"I just want what I have. Nothing more."

Burana laughed.

"I don't believe that. Maybe you fooled yourself into believing that, but it's not true."

"Then what do I want?"

"To prove yourself. I don't know who you're trying to prove yourself to, but something's pushing you."

"And what are you looking for?"

"A place to settle."

They walked by a shop full of mechanical toys and clocks. They stopped to look through the window at the machines before continuing on.

Burana seemed more interested in the clothes and such and dragged her into a store.

One thing did catch her eye though, a red scarf. It was beautiful. With her black uniform it would make her stand out. The weather was getting warmer but she wanted it. She paid the store man and walked out with the scarf around her neck. Burana had bought a blouse and vest that accentuated her feminine charms.

Greza wasn't interested in that sort of attention.

"Think Ox will like this?" Burana asked.

"I'd imagine so. You want him to like it?"

Burana didn't answer for a few seconds.

"Yes, I believe I do. Is that alright with you?"

"Me? I have no say in it."

"You certain that you don't seek his attention?"

"I don't."

Burana smiled and they continued on.

As the stores grew cheaper and more decrepit, they came to a small square with a broken down fountain. It didn't look like this area had many visitors. There were a few boarded up stores and a stall that didn't look as if it had been used in years.

Then something caught Greza's eye. It was a stone building sandwiched between larger wood buildings. It had a single tall door with a round stained glass window above it.

The stained glass window had the symbol of the Path of Light.

"Burana, hold on," Greza said.

"What? There's nothing here."

Greza pointed to the church and Burana nodded.

"I'll wait outside," Burana said.

Greza crossed the tiny square and stopped in front of the wooden door to the church. It looked old but it didn't look abandoned like many of the buildings nearby. The front steps were swept clean of leaves and the place was worn down but clean.

She tested the door and found that it opened. Greza stood there for a moment, frozen in excitement. She'd never actually been in a church before and didn't know what to expect.

Taking a deep breath she pushed the door open and walked in. She found herself in a round chapel with wooden pews in three rows of seven. Holy numbers. On the far side was the shrine and alter. A large book of scripture lay open on the altar. Incense was burning on either side of the book.

"Who's there?" She heard a man say in the almost unintelligible local accent.

"A worshiper," Greza said.

An old man in a priest's simple robe came out of a side door and he took a moment to look her over.

"You're not from around here," the man said.

"No, I'm with the Ekonian Army."

He frowned and turned away and walked toward the altar.

"What do you want?" He asked. "If you're here to mock, I assure you that I've heard everything there is to say."

"Not at all, I'm a follower of the Path."

He laughed.

"Of course, of course."

"I am. I've been reading the scriptures since I was a child but have never had an opportunity to attend an actual ceremony before."

"You're too young to be a believer."

"What does age have to do with it?"

He stood behind the altar and snuffed out the incense sticks.

"You must have been raised hearing stories of the Lost Victor. Why would you believe?"

"For the same reasons you do."

He shook his head.

"That doesn't mean much anymore."

She walked up the aisle and stood on the opposite side of the altar.

"I believe, sir. Please don't wave my conviction away."

He stopped and looked at her. Despite his age, his eyes were still clear and bright. He didn't appear as old as she had initially thought. It was his weariness and care-worn face that made him appear older.

"Why would you believe a religion that has had a false prophecy?" He asked.

"Don't you believe?"

"I asked you first."

"The prophecy hasn't been proven false. The Victor was lost, but that doesn't mean he won't be found again. Have the Divine Lights ever broken a promise?"

"The Child is dead. There's no coming back from that."

"Have the Lights ever broken a promise?"

"Not until this one, no."

"Then we must have faith that they will fulfill this one as well."

"Who are you?"

"Greza. I was a slave."

The man leaned over the altar and looked her right in the eyes. He held her gaze for several long moments.

"You are a true believer, I can see it. How curious," he said. "So, young Greza, what brings you here? Seeking truth?"

"I'd like to become an official member of the Path."

"That takes several weeks. I have to interview you and test your knowledge and ask family and friends and..."

Her hope sunk.

"I only have an hour, sir," she said.

He chuckled.

"Strange times we live in and this is a strange situation. I haven't had a petition for membership since...well, you know. Very well. We'll skip the other stuff. Kneel before the altar."

She quickly did so. Was he really going against tradition to make her a member? After all this time she was officially joining the Path of Light. Erinad would have liked to have been here and she hoped that he was watching.

"Hands together. Close your eyes. I'll say the words of the ceremony and when I tell you, you repeat after me."

She nodded.

"Greza of the Chimera Company, you have come to this sanctuary and this altar to petition membership among the Path of Light and to Worship the Divine Lights with all your heart and mind. This is no simple task to be taken lightly and will demand much of your life. Dying is easy, living justly is difficult. But you must endure and live a just life so that others may see the Path from your Light and choose to walk it themselves. Now repeat after me: I swear to follow the Path all the days of my life."

She repeated.

"I swear to treat others with equality, respect and charity."

She repeated.

"I swear to always keep faith in my heart, to pray always and never cease to trust the Divine Lights."

She repeated.

As he continued on with the ceremony he mixed up a bowl of herbs and paste. He then used the black paste to mark the curved "X" shape on her forehead. Then he sprinkled holy water on her hands and mouth.

"Rise, Greza of the Chimera Company and lay on the altar to offer yourself up to the Path."

He moved the book over to the stone shrine and she lay down on the table.

"Now I will pray and through me the Divine Lights will give you a blessing and with faith, a direction in life."

He placed his hands on her folded hands and closed his eyes.

"Divine Lights that rule the heavens and all above and below. Please hear your servant. Tonight we have a supplication for a new member. I know you all don't listen to me much and you're either deaf or you choose to ignore me, but please don't ignore this girl. She had come with earnest faith and honestly seeks your Path."

He made as if to continue but fell silent. Soon she began to wonder if this was part of the prayer and was about to ask if he was alright. But then he continued. But this time his voice was different. It was slower and quieter, almost like he was repeating what he was hearing.

"Greza, the Divine Path has led you here. All that has happened has led you here. You are placed to do a great work for the Path. Because of your unwavering faith you have been chosen for a great work; a work that may prove your destruction if you fail. This is a terrible burden but you are the only one of all the Path's servants to have the faith to be granted this purpose. Greza, you must seek out the Promised Victor. Find him. Show him the Path. Show him the Path or he will be doomed to wander in strange lands all his life and his work will be unfinished and lead to the destruction of this people. Your victory will not be pleasant and your chores will not be light. Just know that they are necessary and will earn you a great reward. Have courage, Greza. You are chosen."

Then the old priest broke off and stumbled backward, colliding with the stone shrine, causing the paper prayers to flutter to the floor.

"Impossible," he breathed.

She sat up, looking at her hands. They were shaking.

"What was that?" She asked.

"I don't know. It's impossible."

"Was that ... was that you?"

He shook his head.

"It wasn't. I've never...who are you?"

"I'm just a soldier."

She was nobody. She had just been a slave and nothing more. She meant nothing to anybody except one kind old man who was now dead. Who was she to be noticed by the Divine Lights?

"The Promised Victor is alive? Impossible," the priest said.

"That was them, wasn't it?" She asked.

"I don't know," he said. But by the look in his eyes she could tell that he knew.

The Divine Lights had spoken through him to her. She had read about such things and knew they had happened in the past to prophets and saints.

But she was neither prophet nor saint. She was just a slave and she had killed people with her hands. All her faults came rushing in one after another.

"They spoke to me. They know me," she said, the wonder of it all starting to sink in.

"I don't believe it," he said, shaking his head.

Then the old priest turned and rushed out of the room.

Chapter Twelve

GREZA WALKED OUT OF THE SMALL CHURCH in a daze. The Divine Lights had spoken directly to her. She had prayed to them in the hope that they were listening, but she had never imagined something of this magnitude.

On top of that, she was now an official member of the Path of Light.

"There you are!" Burana said. "I was about to gather a search party to find you. We got to hurry. Wait ... you alright, Grez?"

"I'm alright."

"You look a little dazed."

"We should get going."

They began walking back toward the tavern where they were to meet with the others. Greza stayed silent the whole time, contemplating what had just occurred. The Divine Lights had spoken to her through the priest.

The Promised Victor.

Erinad had been right. His last words to her were that he had protected her because she was destined for great things. She would never have imagined this though.

The Promised Victor. The Lost Victor. She had to find him. How? Why her? Perhaps she had faith, but nothing like the prophets and saints of old. Nothing like the heroes from the histories and stories.

"You sure you're alright? What happened in there?" Burana asked.

"I'm fine," Greza said.

Burana clearly didn't believe her but didn't say anything more.

They arrived at the tavern to find the others were already there. They cheered when they entered and called out their names. There were jokes and laughter but Greza barely heard any of it.

Then she heard her name.

"Huh?"

"Nice scarf, Grez," Ox said.

"Oh, thanks."

"You alright?" Ox asked.

"I don't feel too well. I think I'll head back to camp."

Without explaining or answering their questions she got up and left. She walked out the city gate and down the road to camp alone. The words of the prayer were etched into her mind and they repeated over and over again.

She had to find the Lost Victor.

What were the signs of the Victor?

The Victor was surrounded by other prophesized people. There was the Princess that the Victor would marry. There was the Defender that would save the Victor's life. There were the Bull and Raven, the Victor's companions and...

Bull and Raven.

Duke Verin had a Minotaur and a woman with raven hair as constant companions. She had seen the bull and raven the first time she laid eyes on them.

Duke Verin was the Lost Victor.

That couldn't be.

Where was the Duke from? Was he the original one or did the Path raise up another to keep the Promise?

She walked back into camp but didn't see any familiar faces. She found a camp fire still burning and sat down, not caring to which unit it belonged to.

The fire warmed her hands as she stared into it, thinking.

"If it isn't the scrawny Ork girl," a male voice said from behind her. She turned to see Captain Richkurk standing there with a beaming smile. "I was wondering if you ever made it," he said. "May I sit?"

"Of course, sir" she said.

He sat down next to her and prodded the fire.

"You made it. How do you like life in the Company so far?"

"I like it a great deal, sir."

"Glad to hear it." Then he paused to look at her. "You look like someone lost in thought. What's bothering you?"

Was it that obvious?

"Why did you give me the coin on the road?"

He laughed.

"I don't know. I guess I thought you deserved it. You showed spirit."

"Was that all?" She asked.

"Well ... I don't know. I guess I just had a hunch about you."

A hunch. The Divine Lights had pushed him.

"Without that coin I doubt I would have been accepted," she said.

"That would have been a waste."

The Divine Lights had spoken to Erinad and told him to protect her. The Divine Lights guided her path to Ekonia. The Lights put Richkurk in her path and prompted him to give her the coin. Everything had guided her to this place and time.

"Captain, may I ask a question?"

"You look like someone full of questions."

"What can you tell me of Duke Verin? Where did he come from? What of his childhood?"

"We don't like to discuss the Duke's past."

"Please."

He looked into her eyes and then nodded. His thick, bearded face that had seen countless battles had the look of kindness that most mercenaries lacked.

"I love the Duke like a son and I ask that you do not repeat what I'm about to tell you." She quickly nodded in agreement. "The Duke was born a slave. No one knows who his parents were. His masters belonged to the Order of Nyrulth and they were cruel, terrible people. He grew up and planned his escape. With the help of his fellow slaves, the Minotaur and the sorceress, he killed his masters and led a slave uprising. I was one of those slaves."

"So, it's true."

"Does this disappoint you?"

"I was a slave."

"Ah, then you understand better than most."

She kicked a log with her boot to get the unburnt part into the flames.

"No one knows where he came from?"

"Not even him." Then he put his hand on her shoulder. "I can tell there's something on your mind. What is it?"

"I suppose I'm contemplating my place in the universe."

"Aren't we all, but that wasn't much of an answer."

"It's the only answer I can give at this time."

"Greza, it's obvious that you're intelligent and educated. What position do you hold?"

"Targeteer."

"Targeteer? What a waste. What fool put you there?"

"They think me a dumb brute."

"Why?"

"I don't speak much and when I do I usually don't show myself."

"You're used to hiding."

She nodded.

"How would you like to transfer to the Scout and Ranger unit?"

"I would like that very much, but would they accept me?"

"I should say so, I'm their captain."

A scout? That would be someplace where she could show her worth. She'd be able to do something besides mind numbing guard duty.

"I'll put in the request tomorrow," he said.

"Thank you, sir."

He stood up and stretched.

"I'll speak with your officer tomorrow," he said. He turned and started walking but then stopped and turned back. "I got a good feeling about you, Greza."

He smiled and walked off, leaving her there with even more to think about.

The next morning Greza stood in line for breakfast which consisted of watery eggs and hard bread. Ox was telling a story of about last night at the tavern and Burana was squinting and trying to hold her head together from the pounding headache.

Drinking too much didn't look like a lot of fun.

"Greza!" Lieutenant Tezana yelled out.

"Here, lieutenant," Greza answered.

The lieutenant pushed her way through the crowd and stormed right up to Greza. She shoved one of her plump fingers into Greza's chest. The lieutenant hadn't earned her respect and Greza certainly didn't care about her opinion of things so it didn't really matter to her that she was angry.

"What is the meaning of this?" Tezana waved a piece of paper in front of her face.

"I don't know, what is it?"

"A transfer? To the scouts?"

Greza noticed the shocked expressions on Ox and Burana's faces.

"It's exactly what it appears to be; a transfer to the scouts," Greza said. "Richkurk talked to me last night and offered me a place."

"Richkurk? He talked to you?"

Tezana acted incredulous, like she wasn't worthy of being spoken to.

"You went over my head and stabbed me in the back. I want you out of my unit right now. I have no need of soldiers that don't understand loyalty," Tezana said and walked off, crumpling the paper as she did.

She enjoyed watching Tezana fume and smolder in her own petty hatred. She was a small-minded woman that had no thoughts beyond her own self. In her mind she set a goal to become higher rank than Tezana. Perhaps she was being a hypocrite and being petty herself, but she wanted to see Lieutenant Tezana taken down a few notches. She thought entirely too much of herself.

"You're being transferred?" Burana asked.

"I am."

"How?" Ox asked.

"Richkurk. We talked last night," Greza said.

"But what did he say?" Ox asked.

"He said my talents were wasted as a targeteer."

"I have to agree with him on that. I saw you during the battle. You're a monster," Ox said.

After breakfast she turned in her pistols and shield to the platoon's armorer and gathered her things. She promised to come back and talk to them when she could. She had no intention of making them into strangers.

Then she walked over to where the scouts had their camp. The camp there was far less organized. The tents weren't in neat rows. Laundry hung around on lines and soldiers stood around in various states of dress. Some had very little clothing on and bathed out in the open.

She averted her eyes as she hurried past. She had never seen a naked man up close and didn't want to start now.

Richkurk was sitting with a soldier over a strategaria game board. He was focused on the game and didn't look up at her approach.

"Captain Richkurk, Soldier Greza reporting for duty."

"Don't start with all that formal crap. That stuff will get you killed. In this unit we don't have ranks. A sergeant or even a soldier might lead the mission over the lieutenant. It all depends on merit. You know what to do better, then you're in charge."

She had never read about a military organized in such a manner. The only thing that came close was the ancient Death Legion and their absolute meritocracy.

"Is it a meritocracy like the Death Legion of old?" She asked.

He looked up from his board.

"You know about them, huh?"

"Yes, sir."

He looked back to the board and moved a piece forward.

"We only got one female in the unit so you're bunking with her. She'll be your partner so she's responsible for teaching you everything we do. I'll talk to you later."

She understood that as meaning "you're dismissed." So, she looked around for the only other female. A few inquiries later and she was standing in front of a Satyr woman. The woman had black hair that hung down over her pale face and looked as though it hadn't seen a comb in months. Her black eyes surrounded by dark rings looked up at her and she made a faint, humorless laugh. She was cleaning her armor and only wore a black sleeveless shirt and black pants. Her horns were long and only slightly curved. She looked young, only about twenty or so, but she had dozens of faint scars on her face showing that she'd experienced more suffering than someone twice her age.

"They sent me fresh meat," the Satyr girl said.

"I'm Greza," she said and held out your hand.

The Satyr shook her hand with a firm grip.

"Onata."

Onata's tent was right behind her but Greza didn't move toward it yet. This was Onata's tent and Greza would have to show her respect if she was to be accepted as an equal.

"We the only two women strong enough to be scouts?" Greza asked.

"Insane enough. I'm not going to lie to you, this job is dangerous. We'll be moving out ahead of the army, scouting out for ambushes and enemy movements. Sometimes we might have to infiltrate an enemy city or hold a bridge so it'll still be there when the main army arrives. Sometimes the only food we'll have is what we can kill or steal and the only shelter are the trees and your blanket. You sure you're stupid enough for this job?"

"I believe I am," Greza said.

"Go ahead throw your stuff in there. We got some training to do."

Onata spent the rest of the day teaching her how to start fires, skin animals, tie certain knots and which mushrooms to avoid. She spoke in short but clear sentences with no words wasted. She rarely smiled and most of the time she seemed distant, as if she was only partially there.

Despite her sickly appearance and obviously painful past, she never got angry or frustrated when Greza didn't learn something quick enough.

By supper Onata was talking about more than just training.

"Been in the Company for two years," Onata said as they stood in line for chow. "Front line infantry first year, scout the second. Now this is my third."

"Where were you before this?"

"A slave," Onata said as casually as possible.

She didn't show any shame or remorse. She said it like a simple fact, like she was stating that she was a Satyr.

Greza nodded. That explained the scars. Some masters took pride in their cruelty.

"I was a gladiator."

"I performed a different sort of show for those bastards. One of these days the Empire will have a nice little war and I'll be there. I'll make sure they pay me back in full."

"Is that why Richkurk put us together?"

"Nah, it's the gender thing. Its much less distraction to keep the genders separated, especially when out scouting alone for weeks at a time. Understand?"

She thought she understood. Bathing and using the bathroom while trying to find privacy was a distraction they didn't need.

If everything led her to be here by some fate of the Path, then was Onata part of the path or merely a part of the world? She could go crazy thinking about what was "destiny" and what was there just because it was there. She didn't want to think about it so she'd have to take everything as it came and go on as normal.

How was she supposed to find the Lost Victor?

She knew where the Victor was, but she had to be certain. And once she was certain, how could she prove it? The Victor had a finger severed and sent to the High Priest. Duke Verin had all fingers. Perhaps he was some kind of "Plan B" for the Victory.

This was too great a task for her alone. She wished that priest had been faithful enough to help her. He had run like a coward.

"Eat up, Greza. We have a long day ahead of us tomorrow," Onata said.

"Why?"

"Last I checked the enemy was still out there. Guess who gets to go find them?"

"That would be us."

"Damn right that's us."

Chapter Thirteen

IN THE MORNING SEVERAL PLATOONS OF SCOUTS moved out, dividing up into smaller and smaller groups until it came down to pairs. They had started off with a meeting around a map. Richkurk divided the areas that needed scouting into sectors and assigned units different sectors.

"We have to find the enemy and we have to find them quickly," Richkurk said. "They're invading our client's kingdom and if they find us first, they get the initiative. Once we find them, we do everything to disrupt their logistics. They outnumber us but that just means they have more mouths to feed. That makes them more vulnerable."

So they followed their assigned path and broke off into small and smaller units. It was just Onata and her then. Onata carried a large crossbow on her back, larger than any matchlock she'd seen. She had hatchets and knives all over her and she only wore the breastplate, no chain mail or helmet. Greza just did as she did.

Onata ran through the woods without making a sound and noticed things Greza would never have seen on her own. Onata pointed out deer tracks, edible mushrooms and berries and signs of other animals passing through. All while on the move.

"You know what Richkurk calls us?" Onata asked once they took a noon break. "He calls us the Thousand Cuts."

"Why?"

"No matter how large the animal, it will die of a thousand cuts. That's our job, to cut and cut until the beast bleeds out."

Onata sat down beside a stream and refilled her canteen.

"You know that speech they give about how important socks are?" Onata asked, and then held up one of her hoofed feet. "That lesson was lost on me."

"Onata, do you follow a religion?"

"Religion? The gods don't have time for me so I don't make time for them. Why? You religious?"

"I am."

"You ever get an answer why your gods made us into slaves?"

"No, but my gods promised to end slavery one day."

"What gods are those?"

"The Divine Lights."

"Aint they the ones that lost some holy child?"

"Lost temporarily."

"That's one way to look at it. If your gods ever stop making excuses and actually do something, then tell me about them."

They slept that night under a tree with only their blankets as comfort. They lit no fire and kept constant watch.

"When you escaped ... I'm assuming you ran, did you leave anyone? Family? Lover? Child?" Onata asked as they ate their small dinner.

"No one."

"No friends?"

"I left no friends. You?"

"I have a sister and brother somewhere, but we were separated when I was sold to a baron that took a fancy to me. Have no idea where they are."

Greza told her all about mother and Erinad and her escape. She liked telling people about Erinad's kindness. It felt like she was thanking him in a way.

"You were a toy as well?"

"Not in the same way. Erinad protected me from the worst of it."

"Sounds like your gods were watching out for you."

The Divine Lights were watching out for her. That was a comforting thought. She wondered how far that protection went. Would it stop an enemy bullet?

"Maybe they just like you better," Onata said before rolling over and going to sleep.

They traveled for three days on horseback without seeing any trace of the enemy. On the fourth day Greza was as filthy as she had ever been. The days were getting warmer and between the sweat and the dirt she doubted if she'd ever be clean again. She couldn't imagine how she smelled. Onata was positively a mess, but on her it seemed more natural and respectable, like she was made for it.

Then on the eighth day Onata held up her fist and stopped.

Greza didn't say anything. She knew enough to remain silent while she looked around. Onata pointed through some trees and Greza took a look. Through the trees she could see some rolling hills. At first she didn't see what Onata was looking at but then she saw a tiny speck of movement. It was on the crest of the hill. Then that speck became two, then three, then a dozen.

As they watched an entire army began cresting the hill and marching towards the west. Foot soldiers with long pikes and the same dark blue banners as before filled the view.

"We found them," Onata said.

They took out their paper rolls and charcoal pencils and began making notes of units, numbers, composition and weapons. They wrote down any other details they saw such as different banners or important looking people or equipment.

Greza tried to write what she saw as accurately as possible. This was her first time and didn't want to make a mistake.

The army looked big but she had learned that the size of the enemy force wasn't what counted. Verin would find a way to victory.

When they had a fair idea of the enemy force they turned and bolted away as fast as they could.

As the sun came down lower to touch the horizon they stopped and read to each other what they wrote. For the most part their estimates were very close. Then they wrote a scroll with a complete list of what they saw and also their own written observations.

"That was their main force, right?" Greza asked.

"It doesn't get more main than that."

This was great. They were the ones to spot the enemy main force. That meant she could be noticed by Verin. It wasn't the glory or prestige she wanted, but his attention.

The entire time back all she could think about was the fact that her new position moved her closer to the Duke so she could find out if he was the Lost Victor or if she was just an ignorant girl. Perhaps there would be some sign that she was correct about Verin. Maybe she'd see an angel or hear a voice. She silently prayed that she'd receive something to show her she was on the right path.

Two days later when they arrived back at camp they were ushered directly to the Duke's tent. Their horses had been to the point of collapsing and she didn't feel much better. Every muscle she had ached and even the space behind her eyes ached from lack of sleep.

A guard went in to Verin's tent to announce their return.

"Bring them in," she heard the Duke say from inside. It felt like a warm blanket.

The guard reappeared and opened the flap for them.

Inside the tent was a round table covered in maps and papers. Officers stood around the table and their quiet conversations ceased when they entered. Richkurk was among them and gave them a nod. The Duke was standing at the far side with his arms folded. The Minotaur stood behind him, his head almost touching the top of the tent. The raven sorceress was sitting on a cushioned chair painting her nails and eating grapes. She had to keep herself from staring at the obvious signs.

They both saluted and then Onata stepped forward and handed the scroll directly to the Duke.

"Thank you, scout," Verin said as he opened the canister.

Everyone was silent as he read the paper. Greza kept her eyes on the Duke. He was beautiful. His intelligence shone through his eyes. She didn't see any angels or saints, but if this man wasn't meant for great things then no one was.

"We have the position of their main force, gentlemen," Verin said. Then he turned to them. "You two, go rest up. I'll call for you later. I have a message to send."

They both saluted and left the tent.

"That should give us a few hours of rest before they call," Onata said.

Their tents were in wagons with the rest of the scout unit's possessions so they found a soft spot of grass and laid down for a nap.

"You did good," Onata said.

"I didn't slow you down too much?"

"Not at all."

And then Onata was out like a candle in a storm. Even while sleeping Onata seemed troubled. Her brow creased in the middle and she would frequently fidget and toss around.

Was this what Erinad had saved her from? She very well could have ended up like Onata.

When they were awakened it was mid afternoon. Richkurk stood over them with his hands resting on his sword belt.

"Get up, the Duke wants to see you," Richkurk said.

They scrambled to their feet and followed him back to the tent. Greza still only felt half awake and her body still ached all over. This time the officers were in clumps holding separate conversations and Duke Verin was by himself looking over the maps. The Minotaur and sorceress sat nearby eating cheese. She noticed the "unimpressed" look the Minotaur gave them as they entered. The sorceress hadn't even looked in their direction.

"Come look at this map," the Duke said to them.

They walked over and looked down at the table. The map showed the country they were in and all the towns, roads and bridges. Several red painted wooden markers showed the location of the enemy. Blue marked their position. There was a lot more red than blue.

"Thank you for coming," the Duke said. Not like they had a choice but it made Greza warm inside to hear it. "I need fresh eyes on this. My officers are in a disagreement about how to proceed. You scouts often have a different perspective. I'd like to hear your opinions."

"Our opinions?" Onata asked and then quickly added, "My Duke."

"Yes. How would you proceed with the campaign?"

Greza looked down at the map. The Company was still camped around the city and the enemy army was marching down the main highway as bold as could be. They were probably confident of their numbers.

She tried to think of a similar situation from history, but she needed more information.

"Do they have siege engines, my Duke?" She asked.

"Please dispense with the titles while in here. It wastes time," the Duke said. "Yes, they have siege engines."

She remembered a story from the Boshan Wars where the Terinad army marched right into the heart of the First Empire and surrounded the capital. They outnumbered the Empire by four to one. Everyone, including the Imperials, thought the war was over in a single stroke. But the Terinad's hadn't brought enough siege engines with them and the quick stroke turned into a two-year siege which hurt the Terinad's far more than the Imperials.

"Let them come to the capital," Greza said.

One of the officers looked up from his conversation and laughed.

"Let them walk in and take the city. Brilliant. We should have more Ork strategists," the bearded man said.

She suddenly realized that she had spoken too boldly. She was in a tent full of officers that knew far more about war than she ever would.

"I ... I was just thinking that we draw them in and close trap," Greza said, reverting back to her slave speech she was beginning to hate.

"And what trap would that be? You don't lure a bear to your position when you have nothing to kill the bear with. They outnumber us four to one, girl," another officer said.

"I thought scouts were supposed to be clever," another officer said.

They thought she was stupid. She wasn't stupid. She was smart and her father, Erinad had given her the best education he could.

"No, that's not what I'm saying," Greza said more forcefully than she would have liked.

All eyes turned to her.

"Tell us what you're thinking, scout," Duke Verin said with a smile she felt was directed at her alone.

She cleared her throat.

"We let the weight of their own army crush them," Greza said. "Just like the Terinad's from Juliaton's Histories of the Boshan Wars, we let them come in. Let them feel confident. Then we watch them starve as they find themselves besieged within enemy territory. On the way in, we ambush them, but only target their siege engines. Then when they arrive at the city, they'll have no choice but to lay a long siege without their machines. Then our army returns and surrounds them, cutting them off from resupply. In a battle of supplies, their numbers will work against them."

The Duke chuckled. Had she said something wrong? She should have just kept her mouth shut. People in power had no desire to hear what the lowers thought. She should have remembered that.

"Perhaps we should have more Ork strategists," Duke Verin said.

"But, My Duke..." the officer that doubted her cleverness started to say.

"Your idea of fighting them head on in a field battle was better?" The Duke asked. Then he turned to face her. "Greza, right? The reader. I see your reading has paid off."

Then the booming, low voice of the Minotaur sounded.

"You humans look at her and see an Ork. You don't see her cunning," the Minotaur said.

"Unless someone has a better plan, I say we start making preparations for Greza's plan," the Duke said.

"My Duke, I'm no strategist," Greza said. "Perhaps we should ... look at other plans."

"Already have and yours is the best. End of discussion."

****

SHE WAITED BEHIND THE FALLEN TREE IN SILENCE. Onata was a part of the landscape next to her. She gripped her giant crossbow but the only movement she made was the blinking of her eyes. Greza had her flintlock ready. Hers was loaded with shot. The enemy troops would be close together as they marched and she wanted to injure as many as she could. Killing was nice, but an injured soldier used up resources and manpower. An injured man was far more damaging to the enemy than a dead one.

Two loud clicks sounded: the signal that the enemy was in sight. The enemy, upon finding the main bridge of the highway destroyed, had split their army into three columns that would take smaller bridges and reform further down the road.

This column had the majority of siege engines.

The Kingdom of Larica had used a dispute over who the rightful heir was to the throne. The new king was a usurper and invaded under the pretense of establishing the rightful heir on the throne.

It was a shallow excuse and everyone knew it. Few cared.

After a few minutes she could hear the approaching soldiers of Larica's third column.

The two of them were a part of the distraction. They would launch a text book ambush on the front and a secondary force armed with grenades and small cannons would take out the siege engines being transported in carts.

Onata silently mouthed the words, "you ready?"

Greza nodded.

Twigs and branches were tied to Onata's horns and Greza had branches tied like a wreath over her helmet. They also had green and brown cloaks to hide them from sight.

All they had to do now was wait for the signal that Richkurk would give. He had insisted on leading this attack himself. If they destroyed the engines then their siege of the city would falter and leave them trapped like birds in a cage.

The sound of marching feet came up to their position and moved past. Then the first gunshots fired.

That was their rather crude signal.

Greza stood up and fired off a blast of shot at the thickest concentration of enemy soldiers. They wore breastplates and helmets but arm, leg and neck wounds were all she needed.

The blast of smoke kept her from seeing how effective her shot had been and she ducked back down to reload.

Onata fired off a bolt and ducked town as well.

Gunshots sounded and a bullet 'thunked' into the tree they were hiding behind.

"They know where we are now," Onata said.

"That was the purpose of this, right?"

Onata smiled and pulled out two pistols. She jumped back up and fired while Greza hurried to reload.

Once the ball was pounded into place she popped back up. The enemy were getting into formation and aiming their guns at her direction.

She ducked back down just as they fired. Thunderous reports sounded and bullets tore through the air above her. As soon as the balls passed over she jumped back up and fired into the mass of enemy infantry.

Again there was a burst of smoke that obscured her targets. This time she ducked down to get a look. In the half second glance she allowed herself she saw three soldiers wounded with dark blood staining their tan uniforms.

"Time to retreat," Onata said.

Greza fully agreed.

They picked up their things and ran further into the woods to the fall back position to continue firing. The secondary position was behind a fallen tree where they had dug a shallow trench. Onata and Greza grabbed the loaded long guns that had been placed there and they both took aim.

Then she heard the sound of several explosions followed by a great deal of shouting from the enemy. She didn't understand their language but she guessed they weren't happy words.

The explosions were the grenades going off on the siege engines. What wasn't blown up would hopefully catch on fire.

But their job wasn't finished. They had to hold their positions until the horn sounded. That would tell them that the siege engines were in fact destroyed.

Suddenly Greza's head was knocked back and she fell. She landed hard on the ground and for a second everything seemed so far away, like she was looking at the world through a long tube.

"You alright?" Onata asked as she bent down to get a closer look.

She was just a blur but a second later Onata's face came back into focus.

"I don't know."

She sat up and looked around. Her helmet lay beside her. There was a deep gash on the side from where a bullet had struck.

"One inch closer," Greza muttered and put it back on.

"Be careful." Onata said.

"I don't control where enemy bullets go."

There were more explosions followed by the blast of several horns.

"Signal!" Onata shouted.

They grabbed their guns and equipment and ran. Bullets zipped past them, hitting trees and leaves to their sides.

She ran too fast to think. She just ran.

They ran for a long time through the forest, dodging branches and logs. They didn't have time to look at a map so they had to rely on landmarks and the sun. If it wasn't for Onata she would have gotten lost a long time ago.

They reached the rally point where the others were. They did a quick headcount and ran again.

Once back at the forward scout camp they started a fire, began roasting a pig and sang. The scouts celebrated their victory. They had destroyed the siege engines and lived to tell about it.

Greza didn't join them. She knew what their celebration was going to be like. They would drink and tell foul stories. She sat off to the side and cleaned her guns and armor instead. She cleaned the gash in her helmet and thought how pointless it all would have been if she had died then. Why bother escaping? Why receive a mission from the Light if it just ended with a stray bullet?

Onata came up with a plate full of steaming meat.

"Don't you ever smile?" Onata asked.

"Sometimes," Greza said.

"I've never seen you."

Onata sat down next to her and Greza picked up a piece of pork between her middle finger and thumb.

"What food are you going to have once we get back into town?" Onata asked.

Greza shrugged.

"I don't know."

"What's your favorite?"

"I haven't had a lot of good food."

She'd never had good food except the few scraps she had stolen from the kitchen. She ate either slave food or Company food. She hadn't had a lot of variety in her diet.

"One of these days you're going to have to relax and celebrate. We're alive."

"We are alive."

But alive for what purpose? To find the Lost Victor? She had to start with Duke Verin, but she didn't even know where to start. It wasn't like she could go up and ask him.

Chapter Fourteen

THE ARMY MOVED EAST IN AN ATTEMPT TO corner the enemy and bring them to battle. After their defeat, the enemy retreated back to the eastern part of the country. Morale was high after their first victory but Onata wasn't overjoyed. She and the other veterans knew it was just the first battle and they had five more months of battles to go through.

None of them knew exactly what the over-all strategy was, but they had some educated guesses.

As the army marched Greza and the other scouts were sent ahead to search for signs of the enemy and to warn them of any potential ambushes. It was a job that had them out in groups of two, sleeping under trees and eating cold rations every day.

It was difficult but she had never felt freer. There were no walls or task masters and no daily schedule. If she wanted to walk over and see what was on top of the hill, she could. Sometimes she had called for a rest not because she needed it, but because she could.

Onata had point and was walking first when she suddenly stopped. Greza crouched down and scanned the area. They were in the forest covered, rolling hills. The terrain was rocky and the forest floor was a carpet of leaves that covered the soil with several layers.

"What do you see?" Greza asked.

"A stream."

"So?"

"Bath."

Onata spotted it so she bathed first. Greza kept watch while Onata stripped and waded into the calm stream. The stream was quick and shallow, but gathered into calm pools in some places.

They had been partners for the past three weeks and so far Greza had avoided bathing with her or anyone else. She usually bathed in the middle of the night when no one was awake.

Onata knew of course, but knowing and seeing were two different things.

As Onata washed herself Greza kept ideas running through her mind. She had to talk to Verin about the Lost Victor but everything she came up with sounded mad.

When Onata finished she still didn't know what to do.

"Your turn," Onata said as she strapped on her breastplate.

Greza nodded and walked to the edge of the water. She looked back to see Onata dutifully keeping watch and only occasionally glancing at her. Greza kept her back away from Onata as she removed her armor, equipment and clothes.

"Greza!" She heard Onata exclaim as she was bending down to remove the pants from around her ankles.

She looked up and saw Onata staring at her. She quickly straightened up.

"What's the matter?" Greza asked.

"Your back."

Onata began to hurry towards her. She must have seen the scars when she was bent over. There was no point in hiding it now.

She came over and stood beside Greza and leaned over to get a good view of her back.

"What happened?" Onata asked.

"It doesn't matter."

"What did those animals do to you?"

"Nothing that isn't done to other slaves."

Onata hesitantly touched her back and withdrew her hand.

"Don't tell anyone," Greza said.

"But, Grez..."

"Please don't."

Onata nodded.

Greza hurried and took her bath and dressed again. Once they were ready they continued on their patrol.

"Do you ever want revenge?" Onata asked.

She thought about it for a moment before answering.

"I used to, a long time ago."

"I do. I want to march back in there and burn my masters' house down. I want to see them lose everything."

"Hatred only hurts yourself."

"Maybe, but it keeps me going."

"There's enough hatred in the world. We don't need to add to it."

"Those scars weren't from fighting."

"I don't wish to speak of it. They already dislike me for being an Ork."

"No they don't."

"I hear how they speak of slaves. They use 'slave' as an insult and I'd be the brunt of more insults. The powerful Greza, the killer brute, was tied up and lashed repeatedly. That doesn't inspire confidence or respect."

She saw how Onata looked over to her with a look of pity. Greza turned away. She didn't want the entire army seeing her like that.

They marched until mid-afternoon and took a small break in a clump of trees on the top of a hill. Below was the end of the forest and the beginning of miles and miles of fields.

Greza dug out of her pack a hard biscuit and a dried piece of pork.

"No wonder you never complain," Onata said. "I hear these soft towners complaining of the work and the food. The farmers complain less. But the only people I've never heard complain were the former slaves. At first I ..."

"*Shhh!*" Greza said.

She thought she saw something.

"What is it?"

Greza pointed out past one of the distant farms. It looked like a cloud of dust in the distance.

"I don't see any ... oh, yes. I see it," Onata said.

"Enemy contact?"

"Maybe. We have to get a closer look and judge their Direction, Equipment, Size and Units."

"D.E.S.U. I remember."

They sat there and waited while the dust cloud grew bigger. Good, they were coming their way. They'd be able to stay on the hill and observe in safety.

It was a full hour before the enemy came close enough to gain any useful information. Their destination was the direction of the Chimera Company.

"Why have they turned around?" Onata asked.

"They're coming back to renew the fight," Greza said.

"Yes, but why now? Why not earlier? Something had to have changed to warrant their sudden reversal and desire for battle."

Greza knew that an army on the run doesn't turn and face its pursuers without good cause. It was their duty to find out what that cause was before reporting back.

She took out the spyglass from the leather case on her belt and rested it on a rock for a steady view.

Through the dust she was able to make out the dark blue flags of the Larica Kingdom. Their files of infantry were marching west flanked by their columns of heavy and light cavalry.

Then Greza saw something odd. She adjusted her spyglass and looked at the thing that drew her attention.

Behind the ranks of Larica infantry was a unit sporting a yellow flag. As the dust grew worse it became increasingly hard to see the specific units. But what she could tell was that there were many more of them now.

She saw a small unit of cavalry break away from the main force. One of them carried a yellow flag. The flag had an eagle's head on it.

"Roshan," Onata said.

"They met up with allied reinforcements."

"Now we know and now we head back."

The enemy army was now massive. She had no idea that the smaller kingdoms could amass armies that large. How was Verin supposed to stop an army of this size?

They put away their spyglasses and began running west. Onata kept looking at her compass and checking her map. Each time she did so they had to slow down, but now was not a time to get lost in unfamiliar territory.

As she ran the realization that she and Onata held the fate of the Ekonian Army in their hands sunk into her mind. Right now they were the two most important people in the entire army.

They stopped to rest only when it became too dark to run. They couldn't risk torches because the enemy had their own scouts. Sleep was only for a few hours and they were traveling again long before sunrise.

They ran for as long as they could and then they walked. As long as there was any kind of light, they didn't stop.

By sunset of the third day Greza was starting to feel the fatigue. Onata had circles under her eyes and looked pale. Greza's mind wasn't clear and she could feel her body fighting against every step. Her legs ached and her mind cried for rest.

"I see them," Onata said.

Greza looked where she was pointing and saw a few lights in the darkness. She didn't have the clarity to ask a useful question so she just followed Onata. As they crested a hill the entire camp spread out before them like a lake reflecting the stars. All the fires were in clusters showing the location of each unit.

Four soldiers approached with guns leveled at them.

"Sea Tiger," Onata said.

The guards accepted the password and let them through with an escort. All too soon she found herself standing in front of the Duke's red and black command tent. She was sweaty, covered in dirt and out of breath. She was so exhausted she wanted to collapse and her mind wasn't working properly. She could barely remember her own name.

And then the tent doors opened and she was ushered in.

Greza stumbled into the large, circular tent where men in heavy armor sat around a table. They seemed to be deep in an argument of some kind. They were gesturing wildly and pointing at different maps. The Minotaur stood a good head and shoulders taller than the others but he seemed to be the calmest of the ten. The Raven girl was standing next to him and arguing in a quiet voice that could barely be heard over the others. But the fiery look in her eyes demanded attention.

Duke Verin though, sat on the opposite side of the table seemingly lost in thought. His head rested on his hand while the other hand balanced a dagger on the arm of his chair.

No one noticed their entrance.

Greza looked to Onata to follow her lead, but Onata looked almost dead. Her mouth hung slightly open and her eyes stared off into nothing as if she didn't see the room or anything in it.

Greza hadn't been taught what to do in a situation like this. She didn't know who to address herself to or how to interrupt an argument between captains. The only one that wasn't occupied was Duke Verin and she didn't think it proper to go directly to him. If Richkurk was here she would approach him, but he wasn't.

But she had to do something. The news was too important to wait.

"Sirs, I bring important news," she said.

She had tried to be loud but her voice came out as a dry croak instead. She cleared her throat and looked around for something to drink. Her canteens had gone empty hours ago.

There were no basins or pitchers of water. The only liquid she saw were goblets of wine on the table where the captains were. No good. As thirsty as she was, she wouldn't break the tenants of her belief.

She stepped closer to them and cleared her throats.

"Sirs, I come with urgent news!"

This time she got looks from the captains and their conversation drifted into near silence. Now that she had all of these captains' attention she had to report. Her mind tried to focus and bring everything together.

"Sirs, I am Scout Greza. I have the enemy's location to report. We saw them..." She struggled to remember what the name of the place was. So she leaned forward and pointed on the map. "Here. They're heading west and ..."

She was about to explain but was interrupted by one of the captains.

"West? They were heading east!"

"Perhaps they desire to make a stand or have found a suitable ground to defend themselves."

She had to speak out.

"Sirs, they head west with reinforcements from Roshan," Greza said.

She was gripping the side of the table for support. Her eyes kept wandering to the goblets of wine.

When she looked up she noticed that they were all silent and staring at her.

"She must be mistaken. The Ork doesn't know the banners of the kingdoms," an Elf captain with long hair said.

"It was Roshan," Greza said.

"Impossible. They're Lerichstag's ally," a Human female captain said. Her hair was in several long braids that hung down her back like thick ropes.

"She's just an Ork."

"But what if her report is true?"

"Look at her! She doesn't know the difference between Roshan and Taranka."

"Excuse me," Greza said with her throat feeling like a dirt road. "I do know the difference. I know that Roshan began as a rebel province of the Second Empire and formed an equalitarian Republic that lasted nearly five hundred years before civil war tore it apart. I know that Taranka fought wars against the Minotaur clans and now have an elite core of Minotaur soldiers that pass the service down from father to son. I know that the philosopher Serato thought Taranka was a flourishing place for heretical, rebellious and insipid thoughts."

The captains stared at her. Some were scowling and could barely hold in their contempt.

Then they heard laughing. They turned to the sound and saw that Duke Verin was sitting on this throne, eyes closed and laughing a quiet but deep laugh.

"It appears that she does know the difference between Roshan and Taranka," Duke Verin said. "I'll take your word. You saw Roshan marching with Larica and they were heading our way."

It took her a moment to overcome her surprise. Her mind was muddled after all.

"Yes, my Duke."

"Any estimate as to their numbers?" The Duke asked.

"Perhaps double of what they were," Greza said.

"Double!" The woman captain said.

"It's true," Onata managed to get out.

"Double," Greza said.

Duke Verin stood up and walked to the table.

"Show me their last location and direction," he said.

Greza grabbed one of the red wooden markers on the map that represented army units and demonstrated for the Duke.

He folded his arms and stared at the map.

"My Duke," one of the captains ventured. "This is dangerous. We can't take on two armies."

"We don't have a choice. They made that decision for us."

"Doesn't mean we have to attack them," the elf captain said.

"If we don't attack them, they'll attack us," Verin said. "What we have to do is find a place where attacking them is advantageous to us."

"Lerichstag. Let them come there and we'll have the walls to protect us," another captain said.

"Then they'll lay siege and we'll be out of food before summer is through," Verin said.

"Attack them at their weakest," the giant Minotaur said.

They began discussing strategy and tactics and bringing out more detailed maps of smaller areas.

Greza retreated back to where Onata stood and wrapped her arm around the Satyr's waist to keep her standing. She turned them around to leave the tent when Duke Verin spoke up again.

"Loyal scouts. Please hold on. You've done us a great service by bringing this news to us." He then turned to the Minotaur. "Please take them to my tent and have them served a refreshing meal and plenty to drink."

The Minotaur nodded and strode toward them.

"Follow me," the giant said.

They stumbled their way out of the tent and followed the Minotaur to another large tent with guards that let them through without question. Inside were couches and beds with thick fur rugs, chests and racks of armor and weapons everywhere.

"Take a seat anywhere. Wait here and I'll be back with food. Help yourself to what you find here," the Minotaur said.

After he left she looked around and saw a pitcher of water and gave it to Onata to drink first. She gulped it down in deep swallows and then passed the remainder to Greza who finished it off.

She could feel the water go down and spread out through her body. It was a tangible rejuvenation.

Eventually the Minotaur returned with a platter of cut meat, fruit and cheese. He placed it down in front of them and sat down on a bed across from them.

"What're your names?" He asked in a voice that sounded more like a low rumble than a voice. It wasn't unpleasant and she didn't sense any hostility in it.

"I'm Greza and this is Onata."

"I'll remember those names," the Minotaur said.

"And yours?" Greza asked.

"It's been a while since I've had to introduce myself. My name is Tempest."

She speared a chunk of meat with her knife and bit off a small piece. She didn't want to eat too much too quickly.

"You're the new scout Richkurk told us about," Tempest said. "You trained many of our officers in hand-to-hand fighting."

Greza looked up from her meal and nodded.

"He said you were a quiet one. Yet tonight you spoke out more than others would have."

"I speak when necessary," Greza said.

"Which isn't often, I take it?"

"Not as often as many believe."

Tempest chuckled and then stood.

"Stay and enjoy the Duke's hospitality until you're refreshed. You did the Company a great service."

He bowed his massive head in a quick show of respect and left the tent.

Greza looked over and saw that Onata was already asleep on her couch.

Chapter Fifteen

GREZA STOOD BESIDE RICHKURK ON TOP OF the hill overlooking the battlefield. The two armies were facing each other and the number of red and yellow banners outnumbered the black and silver banners of the Company by a large margin.

Scouts generally didn't fight in the front lines during battles. They'd act as messengers, raiders, skirmishers and sometimes spies. Today she was a messenger. It was her job to run back and forth between Richkurk and the Duke.

"I see you fretting," Richkurk said.

"I'm not fretting, sir."

"You are. It's not as terrible as it appears. Look."

He pointed to where the Company was waiting. They were in a narrow space between a steep, rocky hill and thick woods. The enemy wouldn't be able to bring their entire army to bear and could only attack a little at a time.

"I see the strategy, sir. But they still have more men than we do."

"We're better trained and equipped. Quality is what's important in a battle like this. It's more a battle of wills, Greza. Our veterans are tough and won't run easily. Let's hope this enemy is comprised mostly of farm boys who miss their home."

"Yes, sir."

She heard the distant horns blowing in the enemy army and the long rectangles of infantry began to move forward.

"Look there!" He pointed to the far right flank of the enemy.

She squinted and saw cavalry moving through the woods. They were going to try to attack Duke Verin's flank in a surprise maneuver.

"Our men can't see them from where they are," Greza said.

"Not at all. Run to the Duke. Tell him."

She didn't waste time in responding or saluting. She took off running. She had gotten the position because she was the fastest of the scouts.

And now she used that talent to run as fast as she could to the Duke's position. She could see where he was due to the enormous flag that was black and gold.

She ran through the files of soldiers and past the cannons with their crews hurrying to load their artillery. Verin's body guard stopped her until she said the password and then let her through.

Greza ran up in front of the Duke's horse and kneeled.

"Sir," she said.

"Don't need to kneel in battle, scout. Report."

"Enemy cavalry is moving through the woods and making a wide circle to our right. They mean to catch us unaware."

He thought for a moment and then nodded.

"Thank you, scout."

A part of her wanted to stay and find out what he planned to do but her sense of duty overpowered her curiosity.

She returned the nod and hurried back up to where Richkurk and a few other scouts were stationed. They took turns delivering his messages to different units.

Richkurk had his spyglass out. He sent one runner off to the captain of the artillery to tell him where the highest concentration of enemy guns was.

The white puffs of gunfire began to erupt along the fronts of the armies. The delayed sound of their reports floated up to her. The guns made soft 'popping' sounds but when the cannons opened fire they sounded more like a bass drum and a snare drum being struck at once.

She watched the gunfire grow in intensity until it was a constant stream of smoke and noise.

She felt helpless to watch. She should be down there fighting. Ox and Burana were down there somewhere. All she could do was pray they survived. Her hand reached for her necklace of the symbol of the Divine Light, but it was safe under her breastplate.

"Greza, they're moving more men to our right flank. I think that's where their main push will be. Go tell the captain down there to bring up reinforcements to counter in case of a breach in the line."

Greza nodded and took off running.

She entered the ranks of the army and passed by hundreds of men and women in the rear waiting for their turn at the front. As a unit grew tired or took too many casualties they'd fall back and a fresh unit would take its place.

She saw the fear and nervousness on their faces and wondered if she wore the same expression.

She had to ask around for the captain's location. The closer she got to the front, the more chaotic everything became. Sergeants and officers were running around shouting orders to maintain the line. Wounded were crawling back toward the medical stations and water was being brought up for the units that were falling back to be replaced.

The captain was on his horse shouting at two lieutenants and gesturing towards the enemy with both hands.

"Sir, I have a message from Captain Richkurk," she said.

"Out with it," the captain shouted without looking at her. He kept his eyes forward.

"Captain Richkurk says the enemy's main push is going to be here. Be prepared to fill breaches in your lines."

His head shot toward her. She couldn't tell if it was fear or anger in his eyes.

"Tell Richkurk that we're already doing what we can to avoid being trampled over."

She nodded and was about to run back when a surge of yelling and gunfire erupted to her right near the woods. She looked and saw enemy infantry coming out of the woods and attacking their flanks. That couldn't be allowed to happen. If they rolled up the line from the side, the entire right flank would crumble and the enemy would pour through like a leak in a ship.

She checked the cestus on her fists and charged in. She had to blunt their attack to give reinforcements time to stop this.

Greza charged into the enemy front line where the gunners were using their arquebuses as great clubs. Some were using their long axes and a few pike men were running up to the fight.

It was a general melee, something she excelled at.

The first enemy she reached had a lance. She grabbed the end and broke it with her other hand. Then she rushed up to the enemy soldier and shoved the spear point in his face.

The enemy soldiers were wearing little armor and what armor they did have looked to be more decorative than useful. Some had gauntlets and greaves. Most had only round helmets and shields. Only their officers on horseback had breastplates.

She charged the next closest enemy and smashed him in the face with her gauntlet before he could raise his gun up to block her.

A man in yellow armor and wielding a saber rushed her. She narrowly dodged the downward slash and rewarded the soldier with an elbow to the face.

One by one she took enemies down. She'd crush their skulls with her fists, break their arms or smash their knees with well placed kicks.

Three men at once attacked her with swords, a spear and an axe. She grabbed the spear, dodged the axe and blocked the sword. It became a mess of dodging and getting in close so they couldn't fight back. They had been trained to keep people at a distance and she had to move in as close as possible to break them apart.

Then Greza looked around and found that she was alone. She was surrounded by enemy soldiers with no friendlies in sight.

She was tempted to curse but she didn't have time to curse or even think. She turned around and plunged into the enemies that stood between her and friendly lines. She grabbed men and tossed them into others and eventually found a small cluster of friendly axe men. They didn't have time to reload so they relied on their curved axes.

With every army having their own colors it made it easy to determine friend from foe. She backed up into the friendly circle of axe men and someone patted her on the back.

They fought on, completely surrounded by enemy.

This was bad. She wanted to break out and make a run for it, but she couldn't leave these men here.

"Who's in charge?" She called out.

"No one! Our sarge and lieutenant are dead," someone replied.

"We have to move back toward our men but we have to move as one!" She tried to yell over the din of battle and didn't know how well she was heard.

As her squad struggled to move back toward friendly lines she saw that there were too many enemy reinforcements coming their way. They had to be stopped or the squad would never make it.

"I need a volunteer to come with me and hold them off!" She shouted out.

"I'll come," a large man with a crescent axe said.

She jerked her head toward the enemy and he nodded. He came over and stood behind her.

"Everyone, make a run for it!" She shouted.

As the squad broke away and dashed back, she and the large man charged forward.

She grabbed the nearest enemy's pike, broke it and moved in on the man.

Before she could land a punch someone else was swinging at her with a curved sword. She barely managed to dodge and shoulder-rammed the swordsman. He fell back into another soldier and she quickly stomped on his knee, breaking it.

A spear gashed her shoulder and she ignored the searing pain. She moved to a man with an axe, grabbed the axe before it could swing at her and kneed him in the groin. He crumpled to the ground and she threw the axe at another soldier, hitting him in the face with the blunt end.

She didn't know where the large man was and didn't have time to worry about him. She was surrounded by enemy soldiers.

Greza grappled a man, broke his arm and elbowed him in the face. Another she grabbed by the head and threw him into his own men.

Suddenly something struck her in the back. It knocked the wind out of her despite the armor and she landed on her face in the dirt.

When she flipped over she saw several spear and sword points in her face.

An Elf officer with a uniform decorated with gold bird icons walked up and squatted down beside her.

"You fight good, Ork girl," he said with a barely intelligible accent. "But now you come with us."

Even if she hadn't been too out of breath to even speak, she wouldn't have a clue what to say.

She was a prisoner and there was nothing she could do about it. All she could do was hope that the squad made it back to friendly lines.

They led Greza and the large man to their rear lines. They were in a hurry and were pushing them hard through the ranks of their soldiers. Her hands were tied and they had taken her weapons from her. She still had her armor and Cestus though and that was all she needed.

As soon as they reached the enemy's camp that appeared to be packing in haste, they were thrown in a cart where three other captives were. They exchanged glances and no more. The tall man that had volunteered looked to be a veteran but she didn't know about the other two.

They had gone over what to do in the event of being captured. Their first duty was to escape. Their second duty was not to give away any important information. There were rules to war that governed how captives were treated but the instructor had said that not every country followed those rules. She wondered if this country did.

The uniforms of the soldiers told her that she had been captured by Roshan. They were a civilized country but she had seen how uncivilized civilization could be.

Horns began to blow in the Roshan army and the camp was being packed up in a hurry.

"Their getting out awfully fast," one of her fellow captives whispered.

"They're losing," the large man said.

"Small consolation," another said.

Greza watched their camp to see how it operated. If she did escape perhaps she could relay some weakness to their army.

Their jail cart began to move and a column of soldiers filed in behind and in front. For the time being she wasn't going anywhere.

She tried to get a glimpse of the battle but all she saw was a forest of pikes from the Roshan army that was obviously in full retreat.

As the road grew long she settled in and thought. She leaned up against the side of the wagon and put her feet out in front of her.

What a hero she had turned out to be. She had wanted to do her best so the Duke would notice her. Now if he noticed her it would be on a list of prisoner exchange. That would not impress him.

This was pathetic. She was on the back of a cart and was a prisoner. This was only the beginning of the campaign season and perhaps it would be her last.

"What's going to happen to us?" A Hobgoblin soldier asked. Hobgoblins were like skinny, hairy Orks without the strength. His yellow eyes darted around looking for any sign of hope.

"Normally there'll be a prisoner exchange," the large man said.

"When will that be?" The Hobgoblin asked.

The large man shrugged.

"Could be tomorrow, could be next year. None of us are officers so I don't think there'll be a rush to free us."

That wasn't sounding good. Instead of gaining the Duke's favor, she'd disappear into obscurity.

The Divine Lights chose the wrong person. She'd never find the Lost Victor in a prison.

But she had already found him. Deep inside she knew it was Duke Verin. Perhaps she just had to accept that.

Not that accepting it would do any good now.

The large man tapped her foot with his own.

"What's your name?" He asked.

"Greza."

"Tarak. You did good out there."

"Apparently not."

"I saw you. You fight like a mountain demon."

"I fought like a fool."

"Modesty?"

"No. I didn't do well because I'm now sitting in the back of a prisoner cart."

The Roshan army didn't stop until after nightfall. All around them soldiers began throwing up tents.

None of the Roshan soldiers looked happy. They had lost today's battle. At least she could take some solace in that. Her Duke had won a battle against a superior force. Everything he did proved that he was worthy to serve.

All her life she had served others and now that she was free she had found someone she wanted to serve more than anything else.

But being a prisoner wasn't helping him. It weakened his position.

Somewhere she had made a mistake. She tried to think back to what she should have done differently.

As the camp fell asleep around them it became obvious that they weren't getting fed or taken care of.

"Not even a stale crust of bread," one of the captives named Delun said.

"Its one meal. We'll live," she said.

"And what if it's tomorrow and the next day?" He asked.

"Then we go without. There isn't anything we can do about it so stop whining. It hurts my head," she said.

"See how calm you are when you're dying of hunger."

"I've starved before."

The next day they got a cup of water for breakfast and then they were back in the cart. They rode all day while the remains of the Roshan army and their allies marched. They weren't in a hurry which meant they weren't being pursued.

That night, what she guessed to be near midnight, they came to a fortress. It was an ancient fortress with one giant keep in the form of a circular, thick tower with a tall wall around it. The stones walls were worn and chipped from what must have been centuries of abuse. All of it was ugly and undecorated in a similar fashion to the Chimera fortress. Upon entering the gates she saw that there were several smaller stone buildings with wooden roofs stained dark from too many years.

The Roshan soldiers dragged them out of the cart and took them to the dungeon in the deepest part of the keep where they each were thrown in separate cells. Once the cell doors clanged shut they were left alone in the darkness. At least they had freed their hands and she rubbed her wrists to get feeling back into them.

She didn't know which one, but she heard one of the others crying.

Back on Roristan Manor she had often been thrown in the cellar for punishment. It was where they kept the ice and she'd be down there for days, shivering and starving. Privation was nothing new to her.

She tried to move her arms and found them painfully cramped. She lay down in the moldy straw and tried to sleep. There wasn't much else to do and her thoughts were far more disturbing than comforting. Back in Roristan she knew that punishment would end sooner rather than later. Here she didn't know if it'd end at all. Duke Verin wouldn't go out of his way to get back five low ranking soldiers.

No help would be coming. She had to escape or she'd be stuck down there forever. She had a mission and she had to do it. She had to prove herself to Duke Verin and stand by his side.

To do that she had to escape.

They had taken away the small boot knife she kept there but had left her cestus. They probably didn't recognize the battle gauntlets for what they were.

Unfortunately the cestus couldn't help her escape. With a knife she might have pried stones or bars loose.

So, she did the one thing she could do; she prayed.

Every morning the guards would come with their breakfast and slip the plate in through a slot. She didn't have opportunity to kill them or steal the keys. There were no windows and only a small grate in the floor which smelled of the sewer that was below them.

She tried and tried but she couldn't find a way out. She'd do sit ups and pushups to keep her body from weakening too much and she prayed to keep her spirit from weakening.

The Divine Lights gave her a mission and they'd provide a way for that mission to be accomplished. She just had to be patient.

They asked questions through the door with promises of better food or threats of no food. It seemed to her that they weren't putting great effort into questioning them. Perhaps they thought they had nothing to gain from low ranking soldiers. Perhaps they had better things to do. The questioning lasted three days or so; hard to tell due to no sunlight. After that she didn't hear from them again.

After the first month of being stuck in a hole her patience was starting to weaken. She tried to reassure the others that it would all turn out in the end; that they were being watched over.

After the second month her reassurances were starting to sound unconvincing, even to her.

Where was her Duke?

Why didn't he come for them?

He had left them there to rot because they weren't important.

By the end of the third month she wondered if her mind was slipping. She had already heard the others' life stories several times and knew them all completely. They now knew her story except the mission by the Divine Lights. That was something she couldn't share with them.

Not until she was sure her Duke was the Victor and not until he knew it himself.

Chapter Sixteen

THREE AND A HALF MONTHS OF ROTTING IN the prison. No word from anyone. She'd shout at the man who delivered her food; demanding to know what was happening. They never replied.

The only light she saw was the torch through the slot and under the door as a guard walked up and down the aisle. She probably looked awful from lack of sun.

"Hey, Grez, you awake?" Tarak asked.

"No."

"Good, didn't want to disturb you. But I got a question."

"Sure."

"How many Divine Lights are there?"

"Four, the Tetrarchy. Then there are seven Governors that act as mediators between the Tetrachy and Mortals."

"Do they have names?"

"Yes, but we don't know them."

"Why didn't they save the Victor?"

She often spoke to them of the Victor and her faith that he'd return to them. They had long gotten tired of the topic, or at least she had thought so.

"We've been over this hundreds of times."

"No, I mean, what was their purpose in letting him get taken?"

Letting him get taken? She had never thought of that. They had to have known he'd be kidnapped and accounted for it. If they had a grand plan in all of this, which she was sure they did, then she didn't understand it.

"Perhaps it was a test?" She said.

"I don't think they'd do things just to test. I think the test part is like a … side effect, not the main reason."

"I have to admit that I don't know."

"Assuming the Lost Victor is out there – and I'm not saying he is – then we need to look for the prophesized people that surround him, right? Let's see, there were the Bull, the Raven, the Guardian, and the Princess."

"Correct. The Guardian will protect the Victor's life. The Princess will marry the Victor and establish a new reign over all the lands."

"So, if we see these people surrounding a guy, that'll be him."

Delun spoke up from his cell.

"You want to know how I know it's all just a pile of crap? Because those old prophecies are so vague they can be applied to anything and only after the fact they say; oh yeah, see? It fits perfectly!"

"Sounds pretty specific to me," Tarak said.

"Take the Cow and Raven. Duke Verin has a Minotaur and a dark haired woman. This stupid prophecy could be thrown on them," Delun said.

It didn't sound absurd though. It sounded right to her. It wasn't her rational mind telling her but her heart.

"Yes it could," Greza said.

"See my meaning?" Delun said.

"Grez," Tarak said. "You knew that already."

"I don't know anything."

"But you've been thinking that, haven't you?"

Before she could answer the light from the torch appeared and they instantly fell silent. The guards didn't want them talking to each other.

The tin plate was slid through the slot and clattered on the floor, spilling some of the tasteless slop on the floor. Every evening they'd come by and demand the plate back. If they didn't give the plate back they wouldn't be fed.

She heard Yulof coughing. His cough was getting worse. The Humans weren't as resilient as the other races and the poor diet coupled with the poor conditions were starting to wear on them.

After her meal she knelt and prayed for release, rescue or escape like she did every day.

Then one day, about a week later, they heard several guards coming down the hallway toward their cells. This hadn't happened since their first week there. She stood up and quickly put on her cestus. Her armor lay in a heap in the corner of the cell.

The group of what sounded like four guards stopped at her door first. She heard keys rattling.

"Prisoner, you in there?" A rough male voice said in that strange Roshan accent.

"Yes."

"You're being moved. Don't resist or we will hurt you. Understood?"

"Understood."

She understood very well. She understood that this was her chance to escape. She hadn't had an opportunity like this in over three months. She didn't know if she was ready. She had tried to keep fit, but there was only so much she could do. If she tried and failed then she'd be beaten or worse and her friends would remain where they were.

Her heart began pounding and she limbered up her shoulders. She knew this feeling well. It was the feeling she got every time she was about to enter a match she wasn't sure she could win.

Four guards. If they were well trained soldiers she could easily be killed with a quick sword thrust to the gut. One small mistake and she was dead.

The lock turned and the door swung inward.

"Back against the wall and turn toward it," one of the guards said.

She took a deep breath. This was her one and only chance. She had no other choice.

As soon as the door was full opened and she saw the first guard walking in, she launched herself forward, to get out of the cell. She couldn't afford to get locked in.

The guard she crashed into wasn't incompetent because he was drawing his dagger instead of his sword. But he wasn't fast enough. She shoulder rammed him out into the hall, then pushed off of him and elbowed the next guard in his face.

The guard she rammed into the wall grabbed her from behind in an attempt to pin her arms. She let him push her face first toward the far wall. She kicked her legs up and pushed back with all her strength.

She slammed him into the wall and heard something snap and he let go. The third guard had gotten over his surprise and was swinging at her with his sword. She stepped into it, letting the sword swing uselessly past her and used her momentum to punch him in the face. She heard bones crack against her metal gauntlet.

The fourth guard grabbed her arm. She in turn, grabbed his hand and bent it back further than it had been made to go. He screamed out and fell to his knees where she kicked him in the face.

The last guard, the one that she had slammed against the wall had his dagger drawn and was in a fighting stance. She charged him and pretended to swing with her left. He began to raise his arm to block and she struck out with her right fist.

Metal collided with meat as she smashed in his helmet and he collapsed to the ground.

She was out of breath and only vaguely aware that the others were trying to say something.

"Greza? You alright? What's going on?"

"If you bastards hurt her I'll see your head on a pike!"

"I'm alright," she said.

"What happened?"

She bent down and took the keys from one of the guard's belts.

"I have the keys. We're leaving."

Greza opened the doors of the other cells and was surprised at how emaciated and sickly they all looked. She knew she must look the same.

"You took out all four?" Delun asked.

"Get their uniforms on," Greza said.

"How'd you kill all four?"

"One or two might be alive. Hurry!"

She watched them put on the guard's clothing and armor. It was all baggy on them but there was little they could to about that.

"You four will escort me as a prisoner," Greza said.

"But where are we going?" Yulof asked.

"On the way in I saw that we came in through a side entrance of the keep. It went straight down into this dungeon," Greza said.

"Are there any other ways out of the fort other than the main gate?" Tarak asked.

"I didn't see any. Let me go see if it's night or day outside," Greza said.

She went up the narrow stairs to the thick wooden door and peeked out. The sunlight felt like spears jabbing into her eyes. She closed the door again and waited for the pain to recede. Then she opened the door again but only a crack this time until her eyes adjusted.

It was a bright sunny day. Not good. They couldn't afford to wait for night because the guards were probably expected somewhere.

But then she saw that everyone was rushing about in a hurry. She opened the door a little wider to get a better view and saw that they were loading up wagons and forming into marching lines.

They were preparing to leave.

That's why the guards had come down. They were being moved. Perhaps that meant the Chimera Company was approaching. They could meet up with them with no problem.

She closed the door and reported back.

"They might not notice us in all the commotion," Tarak said.

"We need to go now before they're missed," Greza said.

"It's too dangerous," Delun said.

"No choice," Greza said.

She looked for more argument from Delun, but he kept his mouth closed.

They went up the stairs and Tarak peeked through the door. He winced from the blinding light and it took him a while before he could look.

"Can we get through the gate?" She asked.

"No, too many soldiers there, including officers."

"Wait ..." Tarak began to say. Everyone froze in silence. "They're moving carts out."

She understood. They could sneak onto a cart and ride out unnoticed.

"Alright. Follow me," Tarak said.

He opened the door wide and strode out into the painfully bright sun. None of them spoke Roshanish so if they were stopped they'd be found out instantly.

Within the fortress walls were carts, donkey's, horses and soldiers running around, scrambling to make their preparations for leaving. Commotion was all around them. People were shouting in a language she didn't understand and the light was still too bright. Their door was on ground level and the ground was all dark mud.

Tarak led them over to a line of carts and went between them and the fortress walls where they were less likely to be seen.

"Once we're out of the walls, what then?" Tarak asked.

"We look for a chance to run. Slip out if you can do it unseen. There's bound to be breaks for the people on foot. We might have to go separately. If we are separated, head west and try to find the Company."

They all nodded in agreement.

The carts were carrying all kinds of things. One carried all weapons and another was loaded with crates. Some had tarps over them. Those were the ones they wanted. As they looked she kept her eye on the doorway to the dungeon. So far, no one came near the thick side door.

She said a silent prayer to the Divine Lights to guide their path.

Greza helped them climb into the carts one by one. She insisted on being last because she had a better chance of silencing someone that spotted them. Tarak wasn't the most graceful person and she had to guide his foot in under the cloth.

Once they were all secured she found a cart that was carrying blankets and climbed in, burying herself beneath them.

She didn't look out but she listened. She listened for any shouting that might be an alert.

Every moment dragged on as the chances of discovery grew. If she was discovered she'd fight and hopefully make it to the gate. It was far from hopeful though.

Then the cart began to move.

She waited and prayed. No one could help her now but the Divine Lights.

She could tell by the echoing of the wooden wheels on the stone that they were approaching the gate.

They didn't stop and no one searched the cart or double checked it.

Once they were clear of the gate she dared a glance out. There was a cart behind her. It was a good hundred paces back but as soon as she left the cart she'd be spotted and put the others in danger. She had to wait for the right time or she and her friends would get caught.

Over the past four months or so she had gotten to know them. They weren't perfect men and some of them weren't even good men. Delun had a child with a woman he refused to accept. Under normal circumstances she wouldn't speak to the man. But now they were united in cause.

Inside she felt she had been abandoned by her Duke. He should have negotiated for their release or come to their rescue. But she had to remind herself that she didn't know what he knew. It was possible that he didn't know about their capture. Perhaps they had been pronounced dead. There was a nearly infinite list of causes that prevented their release.

She had to have faith and trust that the Divine Lights were guiding her.

For an hour or so the noisy cart plodded along the dirt road. Dust kicked up from the wagons filtered in under the blankets and covered her. They were in woods now and as soon as she lost sight of the wagon behind her she'd make a run for it.

She was on her way back to her Duke. She had embarrassed herself on her first campaign by getting captured. She would work doubly hard to make it up to him. She would show him that she was worthy of his attention.

She would show him that he was the Promised Victor.

Then she heard shouting. Riders on horses rushed passed her cart. A few minutes later the cart and the rest of the column stopped. Something was going on and she could guess what it was. Their escape had been discovered.

There was nothing more she could do for the others. They had to make it on their own and use their best judgment.

She had to run this moment or be caught.

Greza watched for the driver behind her cart to look away and she slipped out. No one yelled or said anything. The driver turned back and saw her. He said something she didn't understand so she just shrugged and shook her head, hoping her answer made sense.

Then she walked towards the woods as if everything were normal.

It sounded as if someone was calling out to her but she didn't respond. She just kept walking and acting as if she belonged there. It took everything she had not to run right then. Running would alert everyone to what she was. Best to keep them guessing.

She got to the wood line and then turned around. The driver was talking to some soldiers and pointing in her direction.

Now it was time to run.

Greza took off running as fast as she could. She dodged branches and jumped over logs. She needed distance. Distance was her friend. She didn't go straight either. She curved to the right.

It was too early to hide. They'd be searching the woods with everyone they had probably. No, she needed distance.

Once again she found herself running for her freedom. Her life depended on her ability to run. Normally she could outrun any Human, but she'd been starved and stationary for months. The trees would prevent horses but dogs were a possibility.

All other thoughts fled from her mind. All she could think about was running. Tarak and the others were forgotten. Just her breathing, where she placed her feet, and obstacles in the way were all she thought about.

Already she began to feel tired. Her legs were becoming less responsive. Her breathing was growing more difficult.

When a clearing presented itself she looked back to check on her pursuers.

She didn't see anyone. That didn't mean they weren't following. If they brought dogs then hiding wasn't an option. She had to keep going.

Greza kept running until she couldn't run any more.

Chapter Seventeen

GREZA TROD THROUGH A SHALLOW STREAM. The sun had gone down an hour ago and the temperature with it. Summer was already over. Soon it wouldn't be just the nights that were colder.

No one had found her. No barking dogs, no men on horses. She had gotten away and the further she went the safer she was.

Now she had time to pray for the others.

She found a mossy part of the shore and settled down for the night. She was cold, starving and exhausted but she had her freedom back like she knew she would. She was able to breathe fresh air again.

In the morning she looked down into a still part of the stream at her reflection. She barely recognized it. The pale gray/green thing with the wild tangle of hair wasn't the Greza she knew. Her hair had grown to the small of her back and hadn't been combed or washed the entire time. She looked like some half-dead, wild barbarian.

The thing in the reflection would only draw disgust from Duke Verin.

She took the time to wash herself head to foot and clean out her hair. Normally slaves weren't allowed elaborate hairstyles but for performances servants had done her hair in some fashionable way. All she knew how to do was put it in a pony tail.

Now that she looked slightly more civilized she found west and began walking. Along the way she managed to catch a fish with her hands and find berries. Even with that she was still painfully hungry most of the time.

On the second day she came to a road in the forest. It ran north and south. She paused to look each way and saw nothing. She chose north because Ekonia was north and if she couldn't find the army, at least she could return to the fortress.

On the fourth day she came to a town where she didn't understand the language. She stole a loaf of bread, prayed for forgiveness and continued on her way.

On the eighth day she came to Lerichstag. The capital city was full of more people than she had seen during the war and bright banners flew from the walls and towers. She passed through the main gate and found a merchant that spoke Imperial. That was a hard task because it seemed as if every merchant spoke a different language. At least in the Empire one could go anywhere and be perfectly understood.

"The war's won," the fat merchant said.

He was standing at his cart full of corn and beets. His young son sat in the cart with empty bags for customers.

"And the Chimera Company?"

"Went back north they did."

"When?"

"Bout two weeks ago."

"Thank you, sir."

She had no money and no food. How could she make it all the way north? She had barely made it to Lerichstag. She was weak from lack of food and if she continued on like this she'd get sick or collapse along the road, too weak to continue.

The city felt larger now that it was full of people again. It also felt more lonely. She was surrounded by thousands of brightly clothed people and she didn't know a single one of them.

The Temple of Light. They would give charity. At least they were supposed to. She doubted the priest would be happy to see her, but it was the only thing she could think of to do. It was that or starve to death in the street. She was light headed, numb and weak. If she didn't get a real meal soon she would die.

Dying from starvation. That was an inglorious end. She'd be just another body found in the street. No one in the army would ever know what happened to her.

She half stumbled to the Temple of Light and knocked on the door. After only a few knocks the door opened. It was the old priest. His brows rose high on his forehead and his mouth broke into a giant smile.

"There you are, I've been expecting you," he said.

He took her arm and led her in to the sanctuary. He sat her down on a pew.

"I've been having dreams about you," he said.

"I'm very hungry."

"You don't look well. Stay right here."

He hurried off through a side door. He returned a minute later with a bowl of bread and cheese.

"Eat," he said.

She took the bowl and began tearing off chunks of bread and stuffing them in her mouth.

"What happened? Why aren't you with your company?"

"Captured. Escaped," she said.

He sat down next to her.

"I must apologize for my reaction last time we met. It's often surprising how little faith I have."

She didn't say anything because she was too busy eating and right now, his lack of faith was not high on her list of priorities.

"What do you plan to do?" He asked.

"Get back to my army."

"You should be looking for the Lost Victor."

"I found him."

"Who? Where?"

She swallowed.

"Duke Verin of Ekonia," she said with pride.

"Him?

She nodded.

"Are you certain?"

"Yes."

"How?"

"He has a bull and raven with him; a Minotaur and a sorceress in black."

"Anything else?"

"A strong feeling."

He stood up and began pacing.

"I need your help," she said.

He was lost in thought and didn't hear her so she repeated.

"Help? Of course you'll have my help, but I have little to offer."

"Food. I need to get back to my company."

"What little I can spare is yours."

"Thank you."

"Rest here until tomorrow. You need it."

She spent the night in a small room that was probably meant for some lesser clergy. She must have passed out as soon as her head hit the pillow because she didn't even remember sleeping. She gradually woke up with daylight streaming in from a narrow window.

There was a cup of water and a bowl of fruit on the table beside her. She ate an apple and grabbed another to continue eating. She got up and wandered out into the sanctuary.

She felt better; not perfect, but better. She could walk without feeling like falling over, so that was an improvement.

The old priest was kneeling in front of the altar.

"You're finally awake. Half the day is gone," he said.

She walked over and sat down on the nearest pew.

"I need to go," she said.

He pointed over to the exit. A backpack sat beside the door.

"That's everything I could spare. Food, a rain cloak and a few things I thought you'd need. If I had more, I'd give more."

"Thank you, brother."

"You will find him, yes?"

"Yes."

"You will show the world what he is?"

"I will."

"You must for you play a part in this as well."

"Me?"

"Yes, you. You think you were randomly chosen? It's your task to find him and bring him out into the open. You're a part of this prophecy though I know not which part."

"Yes brother," she said, though she didn't know what to make of it. She was a part of the prophecy? She knew she was a servant, but what part could she possibly play? Perhaps she was the Protector. Maybe her part wasn't mentioned. Her part was probably small, but she would accomplish her mission even if it cost her life.

"Then go and waste no more time. I fear the threat to this world is approaching and he may not be ready."

He turned back toward the altar and closed his eyes.

There was nothing else that needed to be said.

She stood up and walked to where the backpack was. It was stuffed and the straps barely held it together.

"I won't forget your kindness," she said before closing the door behind her.

****

THE PRIEST HEARD THE DOOR CLOSE AND HE WAS LEFT alone in his crumbling temple. Everything he had was in that backpack. The few remaining coins he had saved were there as was all his food. He had nothing left. No donations were coming in. No alms and no food.

When he gave her that pack he knew he was surrendering his life. He had always wondered if he'd have the courage to give his all. His entire life he doubted. Now, at the end, he knew.

The thought filled him with peace as he knelt on the stone floor and prayed to the Divine Lights that he'd soon meet face to face.

The girl seemed a quiet, intelligent sort and he didn't doubt that she'd succeed in her mission. With the exception of his own case, the Divine Lights didn't choose fools for their errands.

How sad it was that they had to rely on him for a servant. The Lights deserved better.

He thought about Greza and her awe-inspiring faith. The Path needed more people like her and less like him so he spent the limited time he had in this world praying for her success and happiness.

****

GREZA TOOK THE MAIN TRADE ROUTE THAT WENT north. It was the same road the army had traveled south on. Just two weeks ago the army had traveled this way heading north.

She'd only stop for short breaks and only after dark. She had no tent to set up and she didn't need a fire yet. She slept under the stars. Without the trees to block the wind she found herself shivering at night. The wind would whip through the tall grass and sometimes kept her awake at night.

The problem was food. She was quickly running out. The priest had given her a good amount of money, she didn't recognize the coins so she could only guess, but there weren't any towns nearby to purchase anything. The few farms she saw didn't speak her language and those had become very scarce.

The land was flattening out into prairie and when it started to turn into moor she'd know she was getting close to home.

Home. That was a strange notion. Before, her only concept of home was her tiny room where she could be left alone for a few hours as she slept. That small room was her cave; her sanctuary against the world. Now she had the Chimera Fortress where she had her friends waiting for her. The Duke was waiting for her.

So far she hadn't seen any of her fellow escapees, but she didn't really expect to. The world was too big a place for a chance meeting like that. But a day didn't go by that she didn't think of them. She prayed they got to safety.

On the tenth day after escaping, the sky was gray and the flat land was growing more desolate by the hour. There was more moss now than grass and it made a relatively comfortable bed, especially compared to the bare stone floor of the prison cell. She was close to Ekonia if not already within its borders.

An hour after noon she saw a fork where another road crossed the highway and stretched off into unknown lands. There was a wooden sign with the directions of cities and countries.

There were also four men standing by the sign. They wore black and crimson robes with hoods. They stood there in a line, not moving.

Greza wondered if they were pilgrims or monks of some kind. But she kept herself ready for trouble if they were something else. Whatever they were she didn't get a good feeling from them.

Due to the low, flat land she saw them far off and they were sure to have seen her coming for miles.

When she finally arrived at the crossroads she only looked at them through the corner of her eyes. Other than the constant wind that moved their cloaks about them they made no movement. Their robes beneath their cloaks appeared to be richly decorated with gold buckles and strange symbols woven subtly into patterns.

As she was about to pass by one of them spoke up.

"We were guided by our God to be here to await the arrival of an Ork woman. And you have arrived," the man said.

She stopped and turned to face them. Their faces were concealed in shadow and they still hadn't moved, not even to face her.

"And which god would that be?" She asked.

"Nyrulth, the Dark Star, the Burning Mountain, the Annihilator."

She had heard of them. They were the illegal cult that had kidnapped the Victor.

Greza was about to turn and run when they all pulled out swords from beneath their cloaks. One of them pulled out a pistol which made her stop. She was fast but she couldn't dodge a bullet. Instantly she felt the familiar and sudden surge of alertness and strength in her body.

The man with the gun pulled his hood back to reveal a shaved head covered in red tattoos of the same symbols that were on his robes.

Cultists of Nyrulth and they were here to stop her. If her enemy moved against her that meant she was a threat.

"You have a very impolite way of asking for directions," she said.

As she spoke she unshouldered her backpack and held it with both hands by her side. She didn't want the pack slowing her down. The man had one shot. If she could avoid the bullet she had a chance of surviving.

"You know why we're here," the man said.

"I wasn't sure I was on the right path, but now I am. I should thank you for that."

"You won't get a chance to travel that path."

He aimed the pistol and she knew this was the moment to act because she wouldn't get another one.

Greza threw her pack right at the gunman and charged him. The pack hit his arm causing his shot to go wide and into the dirt somewhere behind her.

She reached him and punched him in the face with her armored fist. The metal met bone and his face collapsed under her blow.

The three other men were striking out at her with their swords and she narrowly dodged one in time to deflect a second one. She maneuvered to keep them in a line and not able to surround her.

That was the trick for fighting multiple opponents; make sure to only fight them one at a time.

She waited for one of them to strike again and when his swing went wide she moved in to his exposed side, grabbed his arm and with her free hand she struck his elbow so it snapped the wrong way. The bone collapsed as easily as a dry twig.

Then steel flashed from the corner of her eye and she tried to dodge but the sword bit deep into her bicep. She felt the blinding pain stab through her mind and felt the warm gush of blood.

She had to ignore it. Countless times she had seen pain distract a gladiator enough to give her an opening. She could not afford to give these men an opening.

Distraction led to death.

Greza turned on the man who had cut her and grabbed his sword arm. She smashed her knee into his groin and when he crumpled over she kneed him in the face sending him backwards with his teeth flying through the air.

Snatching his sword up she threw it at the remaining man. He dodged to the side and she was on top of him. She punched him with the strength of her arm and the momentum of her charge. His head jerked back with an audible 'crack' of his neck.

The man with the broken arm was struggling to get up. She paused long enough to look at her wound before dealing with him. Her arm was bleeding and already she could tell it wasn't good. It was deep and bleeding freely. If there was a doctor nearby there wouldn't be a problem, but there wasn't anything around, let alone a doctor.

She walked over to the crippled man and picked him up by his neck.

"Where did you come from?" She asked.

He looked up at her and smiled. Then he said some words in a language she didn't recognize.

"What are you..."

The man suddenly fell dead in her hands. Maybe it had been a spell or poison. She didn't know and she didn't care.

She dropped the corpse and staggered over to her pack. Her arm was bleeding and she had to get that under control. After digging through her pack she found the roll of bandages the old priest had left her and wrapped it tight around her wound.

It looked deep. She didn't know how much further she had, but she was sure the wound would give her serious trouble before she reached home.

When she tried to get her backpack on, her wounded arm felt weak. She struggled to get the pack over her shoulder.

Once the pack was on she searched the bodies of the men and found only a few coins but nothing that would tell her who they were or where they were from.

She had enough to think about to keep her mind off her throbbing arm.

She thought about this dark god sending assassins after her. That meant she was indeed an important part of this and that she was doing the right thing. It hadn't been their intention, but they had proved that Duke Verin was indeed the Lost Victor. If he wasn't they wouldn't have acted as boldly as they had.

She had to keep thinking of him. That would push her to keep going and get there before something terrible happened.

It grew night and she continued to walk. She didn't stop until she started to feel lightheaded and sick. She collapsed into the soft moss of the moor and took out the last of her dried bread and pork. She washed it down with water from her canteen and passed out for the night.

When she woke it was light and the sun was well up into the sky. She tried to get up but her whole body felt stiff and weak. Too many months of starving had left her ill equipped to deal with the tortures she was demanding of her body. Even her eyes felt weary.

She struggled to her feet, slung her pack over her good shoulder and continued on. It felt as if each step grew slower and slower. She more shuffled than walked.

At noon she stopped to rest and check her bandage.

When she unwrapped the bandage she saw that the wound looked red and angry. She was tempted to say a curse word but instead just put on a fresh bandage, for whatever good that would do. Once ready she hoisted herself up again and continued on.

An hour later she came to another crossroad. This was the same crossroad that had led her there the first time she came to Ekonia. Another day of traveling. She didn't know if she could make it one more day. Each step was a decision now.

She looked down each road until they reached the four horizons but saw no sign of a traveler of any kind. She was alone out on the desolate moor.

As soon as the sun dipped behind the land she fell down and slept.

She could no longer think clearly and instead of thinking through her situation and mission, all she could focus on was the same visual memory of Duke Verin. She remembered how he looked at her from atop his horse and told her she was better than those arrogant noblewomen.

That thought fixed itself in her mind until it was all she could think of.

That thought got her up in the morning and kept her shuffling forward. She couldn't quit or take a rest this time. In the back of her mind she knew that if she sat down again she wouldn't be getting back up.

So she stumbled on all day, thinking of Verin and trying to keep herself from that merciful rest her body craved so much.

Sometime during the day, she had no idea when, she saw the dark shape of the fortress right in front of her, taking up her entire vision. It had taken her by surprise and she wondered how long she hadn't been paying attention. The walls loomed tall and wide and she could see the guards on the walls.

She smiled and coughed out a dry laugh. Her stumbling quickened and she nearly crashed into the gate.

Greza tried to call out but nothing emerged. She pounded on the door with her metal gauntlets.

A slat opened up in the door.

"We don't give charity to beggars," the guard said.

"Private Greza, scouts. Chimera Company, Third Platoon," her unrecognizable voice said.

Then the gates swam in front of her and suddenly, for some reason, she was looking up at the sky.

Funny. The sky's turning dark. Is it night already?

Chapter Eighteen

GREZA AWOKE IN AN UNFAMILIAR BED IN AN unfamiliar room. It was a small but private room. The bed looked clean and there was a window.

She sat up. Her head hurt but it was nothing she couldn't handle. The window looked out over the courtyard where soldiers were training.

She was back home. She had made it.

Greza collapsed back down and stared up at the white painted ceiling. *Why was everything white in this room?*

Her arm didn't hurt and when she looked down she saw that there was no bandage and no sign of a wound. Had she hallucinated the whole thing?

"Hello?" She called out.

A few seconds later a Dark Elf woman poked her head in.

"Good, about time you woke up," the woman said.

"How long?"

"You've been out the entire week."

Greza nodded. She didn't know what to ask. What was to become of her? Was she disgraced or would she be allowed to rejoin her unit?

"Wait right there and I'll bring you something to eat."

The Dark Elf woman went back out into the hall and Greza heard her talking to someone else.

"Go tell him she's awake," she heard the woman say.

A few minutes later the woman returned with a bowl of something hot. Greza didn't care what it was and just started eating without tasting.

She didn't dare ask any questions about her fate. She feared the answers.

When she finished the bowl she was still hungry but the woman took it away and left.

She sat there, looking out the window and wondered about her fate for what felt like hours.

Greza thought about her time as a prisoner and it didn't feel real that it was over. It was like she was expected to go back into that dark, cold cell at any moment. That was the reality and this comfortable white room was the dream.

"They told me you were awake," she heard a familiar voice say from the door.

She turned to see Richkurk and Onata standing there. Onata rushed over and threw her arms around her.

"Don't ever do that to me again," Onata said.

"I promise."

Richkurk pulled up a chair beside the bed. Onata broke away and sat at the edge of the bed.

She couldn't stand looking at their smiling faces. How could they show such gladness when she had failed them? If she was in trouble then tell her. This protective façade wasn't helping her.

"What's going to happen to me?" Greza asked.

"What do you mean?" Richkurk asked.

"I allowed myself to be captured."

Richkurk looked to Onata who shrugged with a confused expression.

"I failed. I was captured. I put the Duke and the Company in a weaker position."

"What are you talking about?" Onata asked.

"Greza, we heard what happened. After the battle when we couldn't find you, we asked around and found out you had volunteered to hold off the enemy while others retreated. Then, three days ago Private Tarak returned and told us what had happened after, that you freed yourself and the prisoners. Greza, you're a hero. The Duke's been asking about you almost hourly and you're scheduled for promotion and at least two medals."

Richkurk's words flowed over her like a dream.

"I did nothing special to deserve any reward. I messed up."

Richkurk began laughing.

"Girl, you're either the most humble creature I've ever met or you're mud eating crazy."

"I think both," Onata said.

Still laughing Richkurk stood up and patted Greza on the shoulder.

"Glad to have you back, Greza. Get well and I'll see you soon."

Richkurk left and Onata climbed onto the bed to sit beside her. Her black uniform meshed with the black fur of her goat legs.

"We all thought you were dead," Onata said.

"Didn't they try to negotiate for prisoners?"

"They never told us they had prisoners."

"The Duke didn't even know?"

"No one knew."

Onata kissed her on the check and wrapped an arm around her.

"Can I still be your partner?" Greza asked.

"Maybe. Depends if you won't let your promotion give you a puffed up chest."

"We're the same rank now, right?"

"Yeah, but I have seniority."

She looked down to her arm.

"I was wounded on my arm," Greza said.

"The Duke had Alethia heal you."

"Alethia?"

"That sorceress he always keeps near."

"The Raven, yes."

"Well, you were a mess. I mean, they didn't think you were going to live. When the Duke found out you returned he ordered Alethia to heal you. Few get that privilege."

"Why? Can't she just heal anyone whenever she wishes?"

"No, every spell she casts costs her a memory. The more powerful the spell, the more powerful the memory. He only allows Alethia to use her magic in the most serious situations. For him to use it on a grunt is ... well, I've never seen it happen."

The Duke had her life spared. They thought her a hero for some reason, but why would he go through such great lengths to save her life? Her life wasn't worth the skin that held it together.

Her eyes were watering and when she tried to clear them she found tears running down her cheeks.

Onata just embraced her tighter and didn't let go.

After a long time Onata kissed her on the cheek again and broke off to stand up.

"I have to go, got a class to teach on camouflage. I'll be back later tonight." Then she leaned over and whispered in her ear. "Don't leave me like that again."

Then Onata left.

Hero?

That didn't make sense. Heroes were people in the stories that did great deeds. They were important people who changed the course of history. She was just a runaway slave who was good at one thing: killing.

But why would the Duke spend so much to save her?

She tried to get up. Her legs felt weak but strong enough to stand. She walked around her room for a bit and then went back to her bed to look out at the soldiers. This time it was with more joy because she knew she'd be rejoining them. She'd be able to serve her Duke again.

Onata came back that night and brought dinner with her. She sat on her bed and they ate their meal together. Onata told her all about the war she missed and Greza told her all about her experiences but left out anything to do with her divine mission.

There had only been a few skirmishes after her last battle. The enemy hadn't had enough strength to mount another full invasion again so the war remained in deadlock until Verin convinced other countries to ally with him. That meant Ox and Burana were most likely safe.

It was good to be back. She had friends here; people that cared about her. Erinad would be glad to know she was cared for. He hadn't died in vain.

When Greza woke up the next morning she felt the warm sun on her face and she stretched out. It felt good to be alive. That wasn't something she could say very often. She let out a little moan of pleasure as she finished stretching and opened her eyes.

Sitting on a chair at the foot of her bed was Duke Verin. He was sitting there as still as a block of stone, reading a book. He looked up from his book as she sat up, drawing her sheets around her shoulders.

"My Duke, I didn't know you were here."

He waved her off with a slight smile.

"We've heard a great deal about you, little reader."

"Why did you have me healed?"

"Was that a mistake?"

"But I'm just one soldier of no consequence."

He closed his book with his finger to mark the spot and looked at her with those examining eyes of his. She had to look away to keep the feeling that he could see her soul.

"Do you think so little of yourself?" He asked.

"I know what I am, My Duke."

"And what are you?"

"An ugly, escaped slave that's only good for killing."

His brows knitted in the middle and he cocked his head.

"And that is what you see?" He asked.

"It is what the world tells me."

He put his book down on her bed and steepled his hands on his chest as he thought.

Verin was the sort of man who thought about what he said. He didn't say vain, mundane things.

"That wound looked fairly recent. What happened?" He asked.

She thought about how to answer him and decided that the truth was the best. Perhaps this was the time to tell him.

"I encountered four men at the second crossroads. They were worshipers of Nyrulth and they were there waiting for me."

He raised an eyebrow and straightened up. He had been raised by worshippers of Nyrulth and must know about their cruelty.

"Nyrulth cultists were there waiting for you?"

"Yes, My Duke. They knew I have something important to do."

"How so?"

"Do you know about the Lost Victor?"

Her heart was beating faster than during a battle. Her mouth felt dry. This was the time. She was finally fulfilling her duty to the Divine Lights.

"I do."

"I've been told that the Lost Victor is alive and that I'm here to find him."

He leaned forward.

"Told by who?"

"The Divine Lights."

"If it was anyone else, I'd laugh. But I know you to be a serious-minded woman with more intelligence than a palace full of nobles."

"You believe me?"

"Not at all."

Everything froze around her. He didn't believe?

"But I know who it is," she said.

"Who?"

She looked at him directly in the eyes. He looked back for a few seconds and then smiled.

"Greza, I don't know what to do with you. I've never understood religious types. You're one of the smartest people I've met and I don't just mean your education. You have that fire behind your eyes that tells me that what you see isn't enough. You're always hungering to learn more. You're a wolf among the sheep, Greza. For that, I'll respect you're belief but you can't expect me to believe I'm some misplaced hero."

"You have a Bull and a Raven by your side."

"Is that the total of your evidence?"

"Then men tried to kill me because they thought I was right."

He held up his hands.

"I have all fingers."

"Yes, I haven't figured out that one yet."

"Tell me when you do. I'm curious to hear what you have to say."

"Thank you for not mocking me, My Duke."

"I would never mock you."

"Thank you all the same."

He stood up and walked to a window.

"Do you know how my company started?" He asked.

"I don't."

"A slave rebellion. Tempest, Alethia and I were slaves at a manor."

Then he suddenly turned towards her.

"Greza, I'm assigning you and Onata as my personal messengers."

"My Duke?"

"I've seen how you act under pressure and you're one of the best," he said in a formal tone. "I know you're intelligent and educated enough to parley with nobles and generals. I'll send Richkurk the order immediately, though I think he may be surprised by it."

"Are you sure?"

"Do you doubt my judgment or your ability?"

"My ability."

He gave a brief smile.

"Hurry and regain your strength."

He nodded and left her room, leaving his book on her bed.

She picked it up and looked at it. It was a history of a slave rebellion in the Empire. It was one she hadn't heard of so she opened it and began reading. She read it the rest of the day until Onata came in with dinner. She continued with her story of how they won the campaign.

Destroying the siege engines had been more of a crippling blow than they'd suspected. They had bought the engines and couldn't build new ones of the same quality. The battle that had seen Greza captured was a widely celebrated victory that boosted Duke Verin's reputation among the kingdoms.

After Onata left for the night she remained awake to think. She had almost too much to think about.

Verin hadn't believed her. She hadn't known what to expect, but she hadn't expected to be so thoroughly rejected. He had to be made to see. If the Lost Victor couldn't be made to see then no one else could be expected to see either.

Chapter Nineteen

"**W**ELL, EMISSARIES, I DON'T KNOW HOW much your duke has told you, but we're about to start a war," the Governor of Septium said.

The old governor was dressed in simple robes with a long thin beard that went to his chest. He dressed as simple as his palace and city. The place looked impoverished with beggars and boarded up shops everywhere.

The small office where they stood was cluttered with papers and looked more like an accounting office than a governor's. Books and empty ink bottles were scattered over the wide simple desk.

As Duke Verin's messengers, they had gone to the small Imperial province of Septium to deliver a message that was a complete secret. Duke Verin had told them that if there was a risk of it falling into the wrong hands they were to destroy the message.

Greza looked over to Onata to see if she had heard what she had. *Start a war? What was this governor talking about?*

"Explain," Greza said.

The Governor smirked.

"This war's been brewing for a long while. My province and thee others are about to rebel. We're about to find ourselves in a compost heap of problems and that's where you come in."

Rebel against the Empire? That's insane. No fighting force in the world could stand against the Imperial Legions.

Four out of twelve provinces. That wasn't good odds either.

"You don't seem very enthusiastic about the idea," the Governor said. He laughed and extended his hand. "Let me see the message."

Onata handed the leather case over to the Governor. He took it, opened it and began reading. Greza watched his face for signs of his reaction. The man was unreadable. He then handed the message over to one of his men.

"I see. This message wasn't what I expected. Your Duke is surprising."

When you don't understand, stay silent.

The Governor then took a pen and paper and began writing.

Onata was shifting her weight and looking around with wide eyes. She seemed as lost and confused as Greza felt.

After the Governor finished his message he rolled it up and put it in the case.

"Ladies, this message must reach your duke. I accept his proposal and conditions. He brings his army here in the spring and he will receive full payment then and there."

"Our Duke will get the message," Greza said.

"Be careful on the road. The Empire has many agents out there."

"He'll get it," Onata said.

"I'm sure that he will."

They left the castle and remained silent as they mounted their horses and made their way through the mud filled streets. She kept looking to Onata and wondered if she thought the same thing she did. This was bigger than anything they had heard of. A civil war within the Empire? There hadn't been a rebellion in the Empire for over six hundred years.

And that rebellion didn't end well for the rebels.

Neither of them said anything until they were well out of the city.

"What is the Duke thinking?" Onata asked.

"He knows what he's doing."

"Does he? Maybe this Governor is offering a fortune?"

"I don't think he'd risk his army for money."

"You have too much faith."

"You don't have enough."

Onata threw her hands up in the air.

"Greza, why do you think the Duke is perfect?"

"I never said that."

"You don't have to," Onata said.

"The Empire hasn't fought a real war in generations. It's not hopeless."

"It's crazy."

They rode on through the brown pastures heading back toward the border.

At night they stopped to make camp. It was Onata's turn to cook and Greza set up the tent.

"Are we allowed to read the message?" Greza asked as she took the saddles of their horses.

"Unless we're ordered not to."

Greza took the canister and removed the scroll. She unrolled it and began reading. Most of it was written in vague, symbolic terms and she only understood a little of it because she knew the basic idea behind it.

What she read told her that this was something that had been in the planning for a long time because there were references to many past messages. Then she saw something unusual.

"Onata, look at this. This message says that the Duke refused the Governor's first offer because it was too much."

"Too much? Now I know he's insane."

"There has to be more to this. I don't think they'd risk rebellion if they didn't believe they were prepared."

"Many armies that thought they were prepared met with destruction."

But they didn't have the Promised Victor with them.

The next day they continued on at a pace that was quick but wouldn't wear out their horses.

Eventually they arrived at the border station. But something was different. Last time they passed through the guards had been disinterested at best. Now the guards were standing at their post with spears in hand.

"Eyes open," Onata whispered.

They approached the station and one of the armored guards stepped up and raised his hand. He wore a shiny breastplate, arm and leg guards and a pointed helmet. His uniform was blue with white belts and harnesses. It was clearly meant more for show than for actual use.

"Halt and dismount," the guard said.

They did as instructed and the guards came up and began searching

"What's this?" The guard asked, pointing his sword at the message scroll.

"An official message from an Imperial official," Onata said.

By law, they weren't allowed to touch it.

"Open it up," the guard said.

"You know we're not allowed to let anyone see it," Onata said.

"Open it."

Greza stepped up in front of Onata and looked the guard up and down. She knew she could take all these men. She looked in the man's eyes and she knew that he could see it too. He stepped away.

Then a man emerged from the guard shack.

He was large, a good head and shoulders taller than Greza. He was also massive. Between his muscles and heavy armor he was almost as large as Tempest.

He didn't wear a helmet and had the shorn hair of a soldier with scars running up and down one side of his head. He smiled and walked up to them but the smile didn't reach his cold eyes.

"Guard, no need. I'm sure these messengers must be on their way."

"Of course, sir."

The guard saluted and hurried off to do anything else.

The giant man folded his arms and looked down on them.

"I'm sure you two aren't carrying anything of interest to the Empire."

"Not interesting enough for you, I assume," Onata said.

"But, there is a problem," the giant said. "We have word some Imperial officials are planning on doing some very stupid things. Of course you two wouldn't know anything about that."

"Of course not," Greza said.

"Mind if I take a look at the message?"

"Yes," Onata said.

"Now, do you actually think you're going to stop me?" The giant asked.

"Yes," Greza said.

She stepped up in front of him and looked him up and down. Strangely, he didn't carry a sword, only a knife.

This man would be difficult. His size and strength would make him dangerous but size and muscles didn't make a knee joint any tougher. A well placed blow to the right place will drop him as fast as it would drop anyone else.

"Onata, mount up. I'll take care of this man," Greza said.

Onata readily agreed and mounted her horse with the message.

"Just give me the message and you can continue on with your life."

"No."

He unfolded his arms. By the way he moved and positioned himself she could tell that this man knew how to fight. Simple tricks and distractions wouldn't work on him. If he got his hands on her his strength would be problematic.

Then the man got into a stance she recognized. It was her own style. This man knew how to fight like her.

He fought like her but was bigger and maybe stronger.

If she fought this man, she would lose.

"See something?" He asked.

"Where did you learn to fight?"

"The Old Imperial style of *Tarashreg*. You know it, huh?"

She took up her defensive stance and he nodded in recognition. She looked over to make sure Onata was ready to leave.

"Onata, go now."

The man laughed a low laugh.

"You know where *Tarashreg* came from?" He waited for an answer but when she didn't reply he continued on. "It came from a group of monks. Their religion is long dead but this one tradition of theirs has lasted. What does that say about their gods? Violence is eternal but gods are mortal? Do you think they'd be happy with their legacy? They should be. After all, they created the most efficient means to kill another living being that I've found. Wouldn't you go to church to learn how to kill better?"

"I think you don't quite understand religion."

"I beg to differ. I think I understand better than you. Really, what is religion? It's a means to motivate people. Motivate them to do what depends on the religion, but the purpose is all the same. Are you a religious person?"

She nodded.

"I see. What does your religion motivate you to do?"

"Become a better person."

"Exactly! Become a better person. My idea of a better person is one that has the power to do what he wishes. Right now I have the power to make you do as I wish. Give me the scroll and I won't make you beg for death."

She couldn't defeat this man. If he had half the skill she did, his size and strength would tear her apart. She wouldn't have time to get on her horse without him reaching her first. If she was to get out of this alive, then she had to escape.

Suddenly the man moved forward. He shot towards her and reached to grab her. She twisted to the side to get her arm out of reach while simultaneously moving backwards toward her horse.

Onata hadn't had left yet.

"Go!" Greza shouted.

Onata spurred her horse forward and took off at a gallop.

"Only me and you," he said. "Tell me where you learned *Tarashreg*."

"Why?"

"Only royal family or their trusted guards may learn Tarashreg."

"I was a slave. I learned what they taught me."

"And who taught you?"

She swept her arm near his face to distract him but he reacted by kicking out and striking her leg. She managed to move in time to avoid having her knee crushed while continuing backing up. He continued following.

"Don't want to talk? That's fine. I'll make you talk later," he said.

His footwork was perfect, never losing balance and always ready to strike. He left no openings.

She had to try though. She threw a quick punch to test him and he knocked it out of the way like she was an amateur.

Suddenly she found his hand around her neck, squeezing the life out of her. He was too quick. Grabbing her breastplate on the bottom with his free hand, he lifted her up.

"Give me the message."

He let go enough to allow her to breathe.

"Or you'll kill me?"

"No, I'll rape you."

Everything froze around her. She knew she could die but she never feared it. But now she was facing something worse than death. All her life she had feared this and now it was brute strength and not authority that would force her.

She had to remain pure. The Divine Lights demanded it. It wasn't just the simple rules of chastity, it was something else. She had seen the damage it had done to other women slaves and though she didn't understand much of it, she knew it would destroy her.

This man was going to ruin her in ways her mind pitilessly imagined over and over again in the fraction of a moment. And there was nothing she could do to stop him.

She tried to break free but every time she moved he would squeeze hard enough to make stars appear in her vision. He'd strangle her before she could do anything to hurt him. Never had she felt so weak and powerless.

Suddenly the man screamed out in pain and his grip loosened. She immediately knocked his hands off and kicked away from him.

Greza hit the ground and rolled to a crouching position. Then she saw what had saved her. A crossbow bolt was sticking into the ground from where it had passed through the giant's leg. A bloody hole marked its passage.

On the other side of the border station was Onata with her crossbow.

He gritted his teeth against the pain and fell to his knee.

Greza didn't wait one more second and ran to her horse. She jumped up and spurred the horse into a gallop. She sped past the guards and met up with

Onata. They didn't wait around and galloped as far from the Imperial border as they could before their horses needed rest.

When they finally slowed down Onata turned to her.

"Who was that man?" She asked.

"Don't know, but I can't take him," Greza said.

"Never thought I'd hear you say that."

Greza looked down to her hands and saw that they were still shaking.

"You alright?" Onata asked.

Greza shook her head.

Onata hadn't heard what he wanted to do to her and despite living under the threat of rape all her life, she had never come face to face with it. The reality was far worse than her imaginative fears.

Onata rested a hand on her shoulder.

"It'll be alright," Onata said.

Greza tried to manage a smile, but failed.

They rode hard the rest of the trip back to Ekonia.

The sight of the monolithic fortress looming over the cold moor made her happier than she had been in days. She was finally home where it was safe.

They were shown up to the Duke's office immediately. Upon entering the room she saw her Duke with all captains and advisors standing around a table. They were gesturing wildly and talking so loud that she had heard them from down the hall.

Apparently things weren't going well.

Tempest saw them first and nudged Verin. The Duke looked up and for a second she saw what looked like a smile on his face.

"What news do you bring?" Duke Verin asked.

Onata hurried over and handed him the message. The room fell silent as he laid the message on the table and they all gathered around.

After reading it one of the captains, a clean shaven man in full armor began to pace around the room.

"Even with us, the Red Dragons and the Varandi, we still won't be enough," the captain said.

"Our troops are better. We have veterans. When was the last time the Imperial legions actually fought?" Verin asked.

"This is still suicide," the captain said.

"That's why we're taking our payment and using it to hire mercenaries," Verin said.

"We're going to lose money on this. Even if we survive we'll be too impoverished to do anything else."

"But I'm not in this for the money. All of you and the soldiers will be paid like always. This is something different," Verin said.

"Yes, your dream of vengeance," the captain said.

"I'd watch your tone," Tempest said.

The captain didn't look at Tempest and only continued his pacing.

"If you think this war is suicide, then you're free to leave. I'll write letters of recommendation and there'll be no ill feelings," Verin said.

No one spoke up for a while. Eventually the captain spoke.

"Hell, Verin. You know this is suicide. I know its suicide, but I'm still with you."

"Gentlemen and ladies, this is the time. This is what I've been waiting for all my life."

Everyone nodded in understanding except for her. She had no idea why they were doing this.

"You two," the Duke said, pointing to her and Onata. "I'll send for you later. I'll want your full report."

"Of course, my Duke," Greza said.

They saluted and took their leave.

As soon as the door was closed behind them, Onata sighed and leaned against the wall.

"Now we have two days off. I'm going to go take a hot bath," Onata said.

That did sound nice, but what Greza really wanted was her own bed. She waved goodbye to Onata and walked down to her room. Once inside she stripped down and tossed all her gear at the foot of her bed and promptly fell asleep.

She woke up a few times but didn't mind because it reminded her how good the bed felt.

After a few hours of sleeping, she wasn't sure how long but the sun was down, she went to the bathroom and took a hot bath. She felt like a real person again and not some savage animal.

Just as she was getting comfortable on her bed with a book she heard a knock at the door. It was a guard telling her that the Duke would like to see her now.

"Should I go find Onata?" Greza asked.

"He just told me to find you."

She thanked him and closed the door. She threw on her boots and black uniform jacket and hurried up the stairs to the Duke's office. The guard opened the door for her without a word.

Greza had expected to see a room full of officers. Instead, the only person she saw was the Duke. He was sitting at the table with a glass of wine.

"Greza, come in," he said without looking up.

She walked in and the door closed behind her, almost startling her.

"Please, sit," he said, pointing to a chair next to him.

Am I in trouble?

She looked around but didn't see any guards.

She hadn't been alone with the Duke since that time in the library.

Greza walked over to the chair beside him and sat down, hands folded in her lap. She kept her back rigid and at attention.

"Greza, it's obvious that you're well educated. You're sharp, intelligent, clever and something everyone says about you; you're honorable. Those are all traits I'll need soon." Then he looked up from the maps and looked right at her. It was all she could do to not look away. "Greza, what did you see in the Empire. Do you think I'm crazy?"

"No, my Duke. I don't believe you'd go to war if you didn't think you could win."

"And what if I told you that the chances of victory were slim at best?"

"Then I'd say that you're following the path you were meant for."

"Of course, the Path of Light."

"You are the Victor."

"For the last time, I am not. The Victor was killed. I am still alive."

"And who were your parents?"

"Don't know."

"Where did you come from?"

"Don't know. But I do know that I have all my fingers."

"I can't explain that yet."

He laughed again.

"I didn't ask you here to discuss your delusions. In spite of your misguided belief in me, you're one of the smartest people in the Company."

"That can't be true."

"You believe I'm some lost prophesized hero, but you can't believe you're one of the smartest people I know? Please, tell me what you saw in the Empire. Tell me about the security and this Governor."

She recounted every detail she could remember and he listened. Occasionally he'd stop to ask a question or two, but mostly he let her do the talking.

As she talked she knew that she had to say something. He hadn't believed her last time she told him about being the Lost Victor, but she had to keep trying.

Chapter Twenty

GREZA TOLD HIM EVERYTHING ABOUT THE Empire as she remembered it. Her account of the man that attacked them at the border had him scratching the stubble on his chin. She left out what he had said though. It wasn't something she wanted to repeat.

"Someone that can take you down? He couldn't have gone unnoticed. Someone knows who he is."

"He's dangerous, he's smart and he's evil."

"Evil?"

"He ..."

"What did he do?"

She only answered because he asked.

"He said he was going to violate me, though not in that exact turn of phrase."

He nodded.

Then the door opened and Alethia came in. Her black cloak's hood was up and she caste a quick glance at Greza before facing Verin.

"We sent out messengers to the Krolak," Alethia said.

"Excellent."

"Still talking to the rookie?"

"Indeed and something interesting has come up."

Alethia rolled her eyes.

"What?" She asked.

"Greza here seems to think I'm the Lost Victor."

Alethia let out a burst of laughter before covering her mouth and regained control.

"Oh, does she? Why does she think that?"

"Several reasons, but it doesn't matter because I have all my fingers."

"Wait," Greza said. "Alethia healed me, correct? What if they used magic to heal your hand? That way no one would know."

"Then there's no way to know. Too bad," Verin said.

"This is idiotic. She's a rookie and a zealot," Alethia said as she turned to go. But then she stopped and turned around. "I can't believe this actually has me curious. I'll feel stupid enough tomorrow for it. Well, if someone's been healed or altered, there is a way to tell," Alethia said.

"How?" Greza asked.

"The magic twists and warps the fabric of reality. Where it's been changed there'll be permanent scars. If your hand has been healed, I'll know if I search for it."

"Excellent. Examine my hand and tell Greza once and for all that I'm not the Lost Victor."

Alethia shook her head.

"This is asinine," Alethia said, but took Verin's hand anyway.

She held it closer to her face and her eyes focused like she was reading a book. As the seconds ticked buy Alethia's face grew more contorted with concentration.

"Alethia?" Verin asked.

Alethia suddenly dropped his hand and stepped back.

"Have you ever injured your hand?" Alethia asked. She was breathing hard and had her eyes locked on Verin.

"You know I haven't."

"Verin, your pinky and ring finger have been restored by magic at some point."

"You're playing with me now," Verin said, waving Alethia off.

Alethia took his hand in both of hers.

"This is no joke, Ver; your hand has been healed. Your two smallest fingers were replaced a long time ago. The echoes are faint, but they are there."

The smile faded from Verin's hand and he snatched it back to get a closer look himself.

Greza remained silent. They were working it out on their own and didn't need help from her. Alethia would probably consider it interference.

But finally she had the proof she needed. He fit the prophecy's description exactly. Duke Verin was the Promised Victor. She knew it as much as she knew anything. She tried to contain her smile but felt it slipping.

"I never knew," Verin said.

"The Ork girl was right," Alethia said.

"You are the Promised Victor," Greza said.

"If I find out that this is some joke, Alethia ..."

"This is no joke," Alethia snapped. "You know I don't joke about my magic."

"Alethia, has anyone ever said you remind them of a raven?" Greza asked.

"No, but 'Alethia' means 'raven' in the ancient tongue."

"And Bull and a raven shall accompany him on each side," Greza said, quoting the scripture.

"This is ridiculous," Verin said.

He stood up and stormed out of the room before she or Alethia could stop him. They both stood there, silent in thought.

Finally Alethia turned to face her.

"You were right," Alethia said. Her voice was hushed almost to a whisper. "He's the Promised Victor, kidnapped as an infant."

Alethia looked down to the ground as the thought.

Greza waited for her to think things through.

"I've always known there was something different about him," Alethia said after a long time of silence. "He was always the smartest person in any gathering and he ..."

"He, what?"

"He glowed."

"Glowed?"

"Not literally, but I could feel it. Sometimes I imagined I could see it."

"You're the Raven of the prophecy."

"What does it say about the Raven?"

"That's she'll support and advise the Victor in the terrible war that is to come."

"Tell me about this war."

Alethia sat down and the two of them talked for the next several hours. Greza told her everything she knew about the prophecy and Alethia asked questions.

"So, what's your role in the prophecy?" Alethia asked.

"I don't have one."

"But you were chosen to find the Victor. There has to be something mentioned about you."

"How are you going to tell Tempest?" Greza asked.

"Me? You tell him."

"You're his friend. I'm just an Ork girl."

"He thinks I'm a dreamer. He never takes anything I say seriously."

"But he doesn't know me. I'm just a rookie scout."

Alethia waved her hands to dismiss the idea.

"No, everyone says you're one of the best scouts they've ever seen. They all respect you."

"And you?"

"Everyone liked you so I took the opposite view. I find mistakes are made when everyone agrees on the same thing."

"Oh."

Alethia then stood up and took Greza to Tempest's door.

"You're coming in as well, correct?" Greza asked.

"Right behind you."

She tried to relax and took a deep breath before knocking on the door.

Tempest answered the door and raised an eyebrow. He invited them in and sat down in a giant chair that was solid with no legs to break.

After telling Tempest everything they knew about Verin and the Lost Victor, Tempest sat back in his chair and thought. His face was completely calm. She looked over to Alethia for any kind of clue as to what Tempest was thinking. Alethia was likewise unreadable.

Finally Tempest spoke up.

"There are two possibilities," he said. "Either you're pulling a joke on me, in which case I'll react with anger and possibly violence. Or you are both delusional and need a holiday to get your heads turned around the proper way."

"It's true, Temp. He's the Lost Victor," Alethia said.

"Second option it is. At least I won't have to hurt any of you." The enormous Minotaur stood up and went over to his armor that was hanging from pegs on the wall. "I have more important things to do now. I must polish my armor, take a nap and get a snack."

Greza couldn't believe it. The Bull of the prophecy didn't believe it. After Verin she probably should have been expecting it, but she had imagined this going better than it was.

"Nothing we said sank in?" Alethia asked.

Tempest whirled around, snorted and barred his sharp teeth. His power and anger filled the room. Both she and Alethia recoiled back from the sudden fury of the great beast.

"Sank in? Yes, it's sunk in. Alethia, you chase dreams during the day. I know you have a need to collect all the memories you can, but this is ridiculous. I don't care if you waste your time but don't waste mine. Greza, you're one of the best scouts I've seen and a soldier like few others, but you're a fanatic that insists a dead religion is still true. It's not and no one cares about your Divine Lights anymore. The sooner you two see the truth the sooner you can get back to doing something useful."

They were then shown the door and had it slammed behind them.

"He took it better than I thought he would," Alethia said.

"At least you believe me."

"That's two of us. Now we need to convince others."

"Soldiers aren't known for being particularly religious or open minded."

Greza walked back to her room, disappointed that Tempest thought it foolishness, but excited that she had at least one other person who knew the truth.

When she got back to her room Onata was there playing a tuneless song on the flute.

"Where you been?" Onata asked.

"Talking to Duke Verin."

Onata's left brow raised.

"Talking, huh?"

"Onata, you're going to think I'm crazy."

"I already do."

"I told the Duke that he's the Lost Victor."

"You are crazy."

Greza explained everything that had happened about the priest, the prophecy and Alethia's discovery about Verin's hand.

"Very well," Onata said. "My dad used to do something with me when he didn't believe my stories. He would run through the scenario as if I was right. So, let's assume you're right about this. If the Duke is the Promised Victor, then who are these others that we can find?"

"The Bull and Raven I've already found. Then there's the Princess that will marry him and start a new dynasty. Then there's the Defender who will save his life on two occasions."

"How do we recognize these others?"

"I don't know. There is more scripture about the prophecies in books that I don't have. Those books are usually reserved for priests and such."

"Then it sounds like your next step is finding one of these books."

"You'll help me then?"

"Sure. Got nothing else to do. Just remember that I think all this is a chamber pot that hasn't been emptied in a week."

Greza would take any help she could get. She hadn't realized how tiring it had been to carry the secret alone. It felt good to have help. That night during her prayers she gave extra thanks to the Divine Lights.

Over the course of the winter she found herself training new recruits in hand-to-hand. The training masters told her story of how she was a hero to every new recruit and to her consternation they embellished it to the point where even she thought she was a hero.

She never yelled at the recruits like the training masters did. She spoke kindly to them and gave nothing but encouragement. Yet they were still frightened of her. Whenever someone did something wrong she'd ask them to step forward to spar. She gained the reputation of being able to transform into a demon. She just told them not to confuse meekness for weakness.

Greza checked the Duke's library several times but it did not contain the book she needed: *Prophecies of the Winter Prophet*. The book was considered by most to be too confusing, esoteric and boring for the lay people.

More messengers were sent out to other kingdoms and mercenary companies. Every day the war grew closer. Few people knew what it was about but some suspected that it would be the Empire.

"I've never seen this much preparation for a campaign before," she overheard one old veteran say.

This was only her second winter here but already she could see that the atmosphere of the fortress was different. Crates of provisions were being stacked already and the training was far more demanding.

Onata and she were sent out again to deliver a message to a mercenary company to the south that had their headquarters along the coast. The mercenary general in charge there laughed at first at the idea of a small kingdom invading the Empire but when he read Duke Verin's letter the smile vanished from his face.

"He's serious," General Decaron said.

He wore gold and blue silks and didn't look like a soldier to her, but Onata insisted that the Storm Spears were one of the best.

"He's very serious," Greza said.

"You know this is madness, right? No army can take on the Empire and expect to survive."

General Decaron picked up a jeweled chalice and took a deep drink. He held it like one of the dandy fops she had seen in her Master's court. This man had more in common with a woman than other men. His hair was long and braided and she saw traces of makeup.

"No one army," Onata said. "That's why we're getting many armies."

"No, no, no. I'm not going to risk my precious men on an idiotic adventure that's doomed to failure."

"It's not doomed to failure," Greza said.

"Oh? And how much does a grunt know about such things? You've fought in dozens of campaigns? Studied the art of war for decades?"

Onata gave a barely perceptible shake of the head to warn her about any mention of the prophecy.

"Lord Decaron, our Duke is not one to enter into such things lightly," Greza said. "He would never attack the Empire unless he saw a way to win. Also, think about what you have to gain if we win. Land within the Empire. Fortune like the kind that only Imperial nobles know of."

She was about to end it there but then she had a feeling to push further with this man. He dressed like a fop but she knew there had to be more to him than what was apparent. He was a famous and very successful mercenary. He didn't get that by being weak.

"Lord, also think of this as a chance to right so many wrongs. For generations the Empire has kept everyone in subjugation. The difference between slave and citizen is growing less and less every year. The Empire does as it wants; throwing anyone who dare questions it into dungeons where they're never heard from again. Whole families go missing and the rights that were once sacred to the People are all but gone. Tell me, Lord Decaron, what have you lost to the Empire and what would it be worth to get it back?"

Decaron's eyes went wide and his knuckles whitened around his goblet.

"You know nothing, girl," he whispered.

"I know that injustice can only reign so long. Justice will eventually prevail."

"What I lost cannot be regained."

"Then let it be avenged."

Decaron threw his goblet to the side and stormed out of the room. They waited the night in a guest room where Onata asked over and over again if she had lost her mind.

"Decaron will never sign now. I'm not sure what you said, but you pissed him off and that's seldom a good thing to do when trying to convince someone to join your side."

In the morning they were summoned to Decaron's office. He was dressed in thick robes and wore a thin crown on his head. He didn't look at them as the entered and only waved them to come nearer.

"Tell your Duke that I think he's insane," Decaron said.

Greza's stomach tightened as she thought about the report she'd have to give to Duke Verin. She had angered Decaron and practically ensured that he wouldn't agree.

But then Decaron continued.

"And tell him that he should make room for one more in the mad house."

He handed them a message scroll and waved them off with a calloused hand covered in rings.

★★★★

"He agreed?" Duke Verin asked.

"Indeed, my Duke," Greza said and handed over the message.

"I must admit that I'm surprised. I didn't think he would. I've been planning my campaign under the assumption that he wouldn't participate."

"Greza here spoke up and said a bunch of stuff that pissed Decaron off, but somehow he still agreed."

"What did you say to him?" Verin asked her.

"I asked him what he had lost to the Empire."

"And what did he say?"

"Nothing. He left the room."

Verin smiled and shook his head.

"Long before he was a self proclaimed 'lord,' Decaron had a wife. She was murdered by a young noble and the law wouldn't touch him. You are a strange one, Greza."

She didn't want to be strange. She knew her life was anything but normal, but strange made her feel like some kind of freak.

"Umm...thank you, my Duke."

"I could use more strange like you."

Chapter Twenty-One

FOR ALL HER TIME OUTSIDE, ONATA DIDN'T like the cold. She'd rather be inside any time. But she was good at what she did so she found herself outside far more often than she liked. What she wanted was a warm palace by the beach with servants bringing her sweet meats and cherries.

It was the winter's first field exercise and snow covered the frozen moors around the fortress. A vast white plain of nothing stretched out in every direction. A general couldn't ask for a better practice ground.

She could certainly ask for a better place to spend her day, though.

The Company was split into two equal sides and she stood off to the sides with her half of the scouts. Lieutenant Daran led her contingent and they were facing Richkurk's scouts.

"You're staring again," Onata said.

"No I'm not," Greza said and quickly looked away.

Onata just laughed. Greza's infatuation was too obvious.

"Oh, that's right. He's the Promised Victor. How could you not gawk at such magnificence?"

"It's true. He is."

"Magnificent?"

"The Victor."

Verin was still talking to his officers when the other army began to march. It was led by Tempest. Alethia sat this practice out. She preferred to stay in her quarters drinking wine and reading.

Onata and Greza moved closer to the Duke in anticipation of receiving messages. He had horns and flags for the basics and now they blew the one long note for "advance."

As one the Duke's forces began to march forward to meet Tempest's army, Onata watched as the blocks of infantry moved at a deliberate pace.

The cavalry advanced in stride with the footmen but stayed at the wings. A small reserve force remained in the rear to plug any holes in the line.

The armies grew closer and already padded arrows were filling the space between them. She tried to see how the enemy would react and see the battle the way Duke Verin did. The books said generals saw several moves ahead. It was a game of anticipation.

Greza was a fool, but a harmless fool. Aside from being a zealot, she was honest, kind and brave, three virtues lacking in the world.

Divine Lights: ridiculous. The idea that any powerful deity was watching them and helping things along was pig muck. No one was watching and if they were, they didn't care.

For seventeen years she had been a slave. Seventeen years of pain, degradation and abuse. No kind or caring god would stand by and watch that happen, not if he had the power to do something about it.

If there were Divine Lights, she wanted to punch them in the face.

Greza seemed to be studying the battle. She got that particular look she got when she was concentrating. Her lower jaw would stick out, showing off her enormous lower canine teeth. She'd probably stop doing it if she knew she was doing it.

The girl was as easy to read as a highway sign.

Still, Greza was kind of pretty. Orks were relatives of Elves and in Greza she really saw the connection. Her jaw was angled and narrow and she had beautiful black eyes. Her perfect posture and slender body didn't hurt either.

I'm prettier but Greza comes a distant second place.

Onata took off her helmet and straightened her hair. She had to take the helmet off over her horns. Only two holes cut into the helmet allowed her to actually wear it, but it made getting it off and on a pain.

She looked over to Duke Verin to see what it was that Greza saw in him. Yes, he was better than any other leader. He cared about his people and tried for justice. Perhaps that in itself was worthy of admiration.

Very well, the Duke was an amazing man, but she wouldn't admit that to Greza.

Then something caught her eye. Off behind the Duke and his entourage was a bowman. Nothing strange in that, there were hundreds of bowmen around. But this guy caught her eye because he was walking by himself. No one was by themselves except couriers.

She turned to get a better look at the man. He wasn't looking to the sides and had his eyes locked on Verin.

The arrow that was notched in his bow wasn't padded.

Suddenly the situation was obvious.

"Greza!" She shouted and spurred her horse forward.

She didn't have time to explain the situation. She had to stop him but the Duke was closer.

"Duke! Watch out!" She shouted.

Verin turned to see who was shouting at him. He still didn't see the danger.

Onata pulled the crossbow off of her back in one, well practiced move and threw a bolt on it.

The assassin was pulling his arrow back, preparing to take aim. She had to be faster or Verin would be dead.

She raised her crossbow and took aim. But he was standing and she was on a moving horse. She expelled all the air from her longs and tried to time her shot with the movement of the horse.

There was simply no way to make this shot in time.

He had his arrow back full pull and was getting ready to fire.

Onata fired and watched her bolt shoot forward as if time had slowed down. At times like this she was always amazed at how sharp her awareness became. She heard Greza riding behind her and saw the Duke's head turning to see the assassin.

She also watched her bolt fly through the air. It looked like a small dot with three fins.

The bolt slammed into the man's neck a half second before he fired. His arrow loosed and flew by Duke Verin's head, moving his hair by the wind of its passing. Her bolt had gone straight through the man's neck and blood gushed out both sides.

As soon as she reached him she jumped down, landing on her hooves and crouched down beside the dying man with her mercy knife in hand.

"Who are you?" She demanded, but quickly realized the futility.

Even if he had been inclined to talk, the bolt through his throat wouldn't let him.

Greza came running up beside her. She looked down at the man with a sneer of disgust. She then spit on the dying assassin.

"You recognize him?" Greza asked.

"No."

Then Duke Verin and his officers rode up. His officers were wide-eyed and looking around like panicked birds. Verin was calm as a windless pond.

She had to give him respect for that.

"That was a one in a million shot," Verin said.

"He was trying to kill you," Onata said.

"And you saved me."

"My lord," one of his officers said. "I think we should get you off the field. There may be more of them."

"You're right, but I'm not going anywhere. Onata, you have my thanks and I'll be more thankful later. Right now I want you and Greza to find out who this man was. Find out why and who his employer is."

"Yes, Duke!" Onata and Greza said in unison.

She turned to Greza who was looking at her with that "concentrating" look again.

"What?"

"You just saved the Duke's life."

"I don't have time to think about that."

She didn't do it for any fame or reward. She just reacted like anyone else would.

"Stop looking at me like I'm some hero," Onata said.

She wasn't a hero. In fact, she was a pretty horrible person at times. She drank too much, slept in other people's beds too much and only cared about herself.

"You don't understand," Greza said. "You saved Duke Verin's life. The life of the Promised Victor. You're the Protector."

"Don't get into that crap right now."

She dismissed it with a wave of her hand, but in the back of her mind she found that it wasn't nearly so easy to dismiss.

Out of everyone in the army, she was the only one to see the assassin. She pulled off that shot faster than the man and from horseback too. She shouldn't have been able to make that shot. She wasn't that good.

She looked over to the Duke and saw what Greza saw, a fearless man that wouldn't let anything stop him. He would win no matter what. Her mind filled with all the possibilities. All of Greza's evidence sorted out and fell into place.

He was the Victor.

****

GREZA DIDN'T SEE THE ASSASSIN UNTIL IT WAS TOO late. Now she stood over his blood-covered body wondering what would have happened if Onata, the Protector, hadn't been there.

"Who's trying to kill the Duke?" Onata asked.

Greza kneeled down next to the body and began going through it. They had people staring at them and the Duke, but she ignored them.

Rumors would be all over the barracks by dinner.

"My guess," Onata said, "is that it's someone who knows he's the Promised Victor."

"You're starting to believe, aren't you?"

"I didn't say that."

Greza didn't push the issue but inside she was smiling.

"Someone kidnapped him so maybe they want to deal with him now," Greza said.

From his "warrior plates" around his neck they found his name and unit. While the mock battle continued on they went to the man's barracks and began looking through his stuff. He had no journal, no letters and nothing beyond what the Company had issued him.

"This man left us with nothing," Onata said and kicked the man's foot-locker closed.

"You think they have more than one agent?" Greza asked.

"That's an unpleasant thought."

"We're not paid to think happy thoughts. We're paid to serve the Duke."

"Ah, yes, *Your* Duke."

"He's your Duke as well and if we can't protect him then we'll fail in our duty."

"Remember that man you fought at the border?"

"Of course."

She wasn't about to forget the only man to ever frighten her.

"You think this has something to do with him? What I mean is ... do you think this is the Empire? They have to know what the Duke's planning."

That was indeed an unpleasant thought. If the Empire wanted Verin dead, they had a lot of resources to throw at him.

"I think we need more information. If the Duke is in danger, we have to find out by who and we have to protect him."

"He has his officers."

"Who are too busy to watch his back all the time."

"Grez, do you want to watch the Duke's back or his backside?"

"What? How can you even suggest that?"

"Ha! It's true isn't it?"

What angered Greza the most was that Onata was partially right. She did enjoy looking at Verin. But it was more than that. He was the Victor and dark forces would oppose him. He needed to be protected so he could fulfil his destiny.

"If he dies, the darkness wins and we'll both be out of a job," Greza said. Onata elbowed her and winked.

"Say what you will, Grez, I can see the bloom of love."

"Shut up."

After the mock battle they interviewed all his squad mates one by one. By all accounts he was a quiet man who kept his own council and never made friends with anyone. He claimed to be from Ekonia but his accent had been wrong. It sounded more Imperial.

After dinner they reported what few findings they had to Duke Verin.

"It was a matter of time before they found out," Verin said.

"Then we don't have the element of surprise," Tempest said.

"I never counted on it. But their spies seeing a threat and the Emperor mobilizing his armies are two very different things. His spies deal with intelligence and politicians seem to avoid intelligence at all costs," Verin said.

"That's cute," Tempest said.

"I can use my magic to find out who this assassin was," Alethia said.

"No, don't waste it on this. He was one man," Verin said.

"For now. There'll be others," Tempest said.

"I agree, my Duke," Greza said. "We have to assume that whoever sent this man will send others."

She wasn't sure she believed that he was sent by the Empire. In her heart she felt the man had been sent by whatever dark forces had kidnapped the Victor. But evidence said "the Empire" so that was what she reported.

"Then what do you suggest? I lead a war with one eye on the enemy and one eye on my own back?"

"No, I suggest you have dedicated body guards with you at all times," Greza said.

"I concur," Onata said.

"Sounds like they're volunteering," Alethia said.

"Wait, that's not what I was implying," Onata said.

Verin laughed.

"Makes sense to me," Verin said. "Onata, Richkurk has told me on several occasions that you have the sharpest eyes in the army. And Greza, we already know that you can rip almost any man apart with your bare hands and your dedication is beyond question. I order you two to report to my quarters at seven in the morning. You're to follow me everywhere I go unless I say otherwise. That means you can't follow me into the bathroom."

"This is really no time for jokes, Ver," Tempest said.

"But ... but Commander Richkurk ..." Onata tried to say something.

"I'll tell Richkurk in the morning myself. Don't worry about him. I'm the leader of this army. That means I get to make decisions like this."

They were both stunned to silence as they walked back to their barracks. They undressed and climbed into their beds.

"That didn't turn out as expected," Onata finally said.

Greza could hear Onata chuckle in the darkness.

It was a surprise to say the least, but now that it happened it made perfect sense. Onata was the Protector so it made sense that she'd be close to the Duke. Every time she thought about it, it felt more right. Onata was a part of the prophecy.

It wasn't fair that Onata was named in the prophecy while she wasn't. After all, she had found the Victor, not Onata or anyone else. Since she certainly wasn't a Princess that left her out.

A follower of the Divine Path shouldn't seek out rewards or do the right thing because they expected compensation. Quite the opposite, in fact. Often good deeds were met only with scorn and hardship.

No matter how many times she told herself that, the pain didn't go away. As important as her work was, she herself wasn't important enough to be mentioned.

She began to wonder if she'd even be remembered. It was a selfish, vain desire but it was real and she had to deal with it. She was after all, just a mortal like anyone else. She wasn't a demi-god.

"Grez, you still awake?" Onata whispered.

"Yes."

"So, you really are a virgin?"

"How is that remotely important?"

"Just curious. You were a slave like I was and you're easy to look at. I don't see how you could have escaped what even ugly slaves can't."

"I told you, I had my protector."

"Yeah, but I always assumed that you and him..."

"He was like my father."

"So? 'Like' doesn't mean he was."

"I'm a virgin. Change the subject."

"Sorry, but I've been thinking. The Divine Lights love virgins, right?"

"It's considered holy, yes."

"Then it wasn't coincidence that you were protected. You've been set up to be Their servant for a long time. I can't think of any other slaves who were protected."

She hadn't thought of that. How long had she been preparing? Childhood? Birth? Did her mother have anything to do with it?

From what little she remembered of her Mother, she felt that she hadn't acted like the other Ork slaves. She was kind and intelligent. She taught her to hide her talents and hide her resentment. But she couldn't think of anything Mother said or did that related to the prophecy.

Chapter Twenty-Two

GREZA WATCHED LORD DECARON'S ARMY set up camp outside the walls of the Chimera fortress. Brightly colored banners and tents now covered the gray moor. Onata and she stood beside Duke Verin on the wall above the main gate.

"He doesn't try to hide, does he?" Onata said.

"I wonder where he could possibly be," Duke Verin asked with a smile.

The answer was more than obvious. In the middle of the camp was an enormous tent with more banners and colors than anything she had ever seen.

"At least he understands the privations of military life," Onata said.

"Let's go welcome our guest, the first of many," Verin said.

"How many, my Duke?"

"The moors around Chimera fortress will be covered with tents before spring."

They rode out to meet Lord Decaron. He had given himself the title of lord, but with one of the strongest armies outside the Empire no one refuted it.

Lord Decaron rode up to them riding a white horse that was covered in red silks. It's mane and tail were braided with ribbons flowing almost to the ground.

"Hail, Lord Decaron. I am truly honored that you accepted my mad proposal," Duke Verin said.

"Yes, yes. It's quite mad, but I shall get to that later." Decaron then pointed a jeweled finger to Greza without looking at her. "And speaking of mad things, the pretty Ork girl makes me madder than I have been in years."

"Would you like me to send her away?"

Send her away? Of course it made sense, but she didn't want to part from him. She had a duty to watch over him.

"No, you silly boy. Quite the opposite. She angers me by speaking truths no one else would be insane enough to utter. She is good to keep around."

"I thought so as well."

Decaron flipped some of his beaded braids back behind his shoulder and looked up at the Chimera fortress. One eyebrow rose along with a corner of his mouth.

"You still haven't gained any sense of beauty. Eyes always on what needs to be done at the moment and never on what gladdens the heart."

"You may decorate your quarters as you will."

"That goes without saying."

Then they led Decaron and his officers into the fortress where they dismounted and handed their rides to servants. As Decaron dismounted Greza noticed that his boots' heels were higher, almost in the fashion of noble women. He also wore a two-handed sword on his back. Unlike everything Decaron surrounded himself with, this sword was old, battered and undecorated. There were chinks in the blade and cuts along the hand guard. That blade had seen heavy fighting during its life. It was the kind of sword that was so large a soldier had to wield it more like a quarter staff than a sword. It took strength and skill and if Decaron wielded a blade like that, then he was no one to be trifled with. He dressed in silks but his sword was a well used tool for killing.

They led him into Verin's office where the war table was. A map of the Empire and surrounding countries covered it with red wooden markers showing the locations of every Imperial unit they knew of. Blue markers showed allied armies. There were more red than blue.

"Doesn't look promising," Decaron said.

"It's not as bad as it appears," Verin replied.

"And how do you figure that?"

"Each one of our blue chips is equal to two of theirs."

"That's optimistic."

"Realistic. Imperial troops are soft. Their officers haven't had real combat experience in decades. We're loaded with veterans and the best training. And it'll take twice as much to feed them."

"But that still wouldn't be enough. What's your game, Duke Verin?" Decaron asked.

Verin smiled and leaned over the map looking at it as if he saw something the others didn't.

"Rebellion. Insurrection."

"You think slave and peasant uprisings will be enough of a distraction?"

"No, I'm thinking that if we do it right, they'll be all we need."

Decaron laughed and waved his hand as if to dismiss the map.

"Be honest with me, Verin. What are our chances? I've been doing the math in my head over and over again and I keep coming up short."

"It's not about math."

"I beg to differ."

Greza saw the solution to Decaron's problem. He was looking at the Empire as a monolithic whole. It wasn't. Their armies wouldn't be gathered into one giant force. They would be spread out to protect the nobility's land and cities.

"My lords, if I may," Greza said. "The Imperial forces will be spread out all across the Empire. As a whole, yes, they over power us. But we will take them piece by piece because they will use much of their forces protecting the rich nobles. They won't send out all their armies because they are scared."

Verin smiled at her and turned back to Decaron.

"She understands."

"I understand as well, but I still wouldn't put money on our odds."

She watched as they got into the details of the planning. She was surprised to learn that the Duke already had agents within the Empire stirring up the peasants and slaves.

How long had he been planning this?

She looked for Roristan on the map and found the small province where her former masters lived. It was on the Eastern side of the Empire and was certainly in the path of the invasion.

She began to wonder what it would be like to return to her former masters as part of an invading army. Would they even recognize her? In all likelihood they would have fled before she ever arrived.

"So, why now, Verin?" Decaron asked.

"The emperor is on his deathbed. He'll pass on any day now. His heir is more concerned with debauchery than ruling the Empire."

"Doesn't that mean that his more able advisors and generals will rule?"

"He only takes the advice of his closest friends and all they care about is their vices."

Decaron nodded.

"A fault in leadership."

"Exactly."

"And he's as bad as you say? Let us hope he is. His stupidity is the only thing that can save us from yours."

As Duke Verin and Lord Decaron left the map to have some refreshments, she took the opportunity to peer over the map. A major highway led right past Roristan. The invasion would possibly travel along the highway. Returning to her former place of enslavement was avoidable.

She wasn't that slave anymore so why should she still be frightened? Deep inside her dreams she still feared being forced back into slavery where she had no free will and no choices. She would rather die than return to that life.

****

GREZA COULDN'T BELIEVE HOW MANY TENTS FILLED the moors around the fortress. She had thought Lord Decaron's army was an impressive sight. Three more mercenary armies had joined them. It was the largest army she had ever seen.

Their camp fires spread out in all directions and she stood atop the wall looking over the sight.

She couldn't sleep so she didn't want to waste her time lying in bed. The guards knew who she was and left her in peace.

Her hood was up to keep the wind off her face. The days were getting warmer and soon they'd be on the march, muddy roads or not.

"Couldn't sleep?" Verin's voice said from behind her.

She startled and spun around. He stood there with his giant fur coat looking out over the numberless camp fires. He had a slight smile on his mouth.

"My Duke? My I ask a question?"

"You don't need to ask permission. Just ask."

"Do you hate the empire?"

He rested his elbows on the battlements and his eyes seemed to lose focus.

"I hate what it does. Greza, I'm not out to destroy the Empire, I just want to force it to change."

"Ending slavery."

"And more. Equality."

"Equality?"

"I want a land where everyone is equal under the law and no one is superior to another."

"Is that possible?"

"It's happened before."

She hadn't read anything about a place like that.

"When?" She asked.

"Early in the First Empire."

The First Empire was nothing more than legends. She hadn't paid much attention to it because it wasn't true history.

"You believe those stories about a freedom loving Republic, then," she asked.

"I do."

"It sounds nice."

"It will be. But it can't be achieved without painful sacrifice."

She adjusted her coat's hood and straightened her gloves. Some cold air was getting through somewhere.

"Are we going to win?" She asked.

"I don't know, Greza."

He was always so confident about it and it was kind of shocking to hear him voice his doubt.

"What if we lose?"

"Then I'll lose everything and hopefully you can find better employment."

"I don't think this is something to joke about."

He sighed.

"Of course it isn't," he said. "I just don't know what else to do. Greza, if I was wrong, would you tell me?"

"I would."

"You're honest, Greza. I don't want you to guard me in silence. I picked you to guard more than my physical body."

"What more then, my Duke?"

"My soul."

She nodded in understanding. He needed someone to keep him honest and on the right path and to tell him when he was being foolish.

"You trust a religious fanatic to tell you when you're wrong?"

"Sure, you're a little crazy, but aren't we all?"

He said it with that half smile that was particular to him when he was joking.

She couldn't help but smile back.

"I suppose we are, my Duke."

"Then I can count on you for brutal honesty?"

"Always. Though you might come to regret this."

"Most likely, but if I fail then I won't live long enough to suffer from it."

"Please don't speak like that, my Duke."

"Tempest accuses me of being fatalistic."

"Then don't be."

He fell into silence and she could tell that he was thinking. She didn't want to disturb his thoughts so she fell silent as well.

"Does this Victor prophecy mention anything about a war against the Empire?"

"No, just that you'll save the land from a terrible threat."

"Does that mean I'll win this war?"

"If anyone can, it's you."

He looked out over the armies one more time and then turned around.

"We march in a week, Greza. After years of planning it seems like such an impossibly short amount of time. One week and then I head out to meet my destiny. If it was just me, I wouldn't be worried, but I'm dragging thousands of people with me."

"They all march for their own reasons. It's their choice, my Duke."

He nodded and then began walking away.

"Walk with me, Greza. If you can't sleep, you might as well keep me company."

She hurried to catch up.

"My Duke, may I ask another question?"

"You don't have to ask to ask, just ask."

"Why do you believe in me?"

"Why not?"

"That's not an answer."

He sighed and adjusted his robe before answering.

"Do you believe in yourself?"

She fell silent in order to think about his answer.

Verin led her to his study where the war maps were laid out. Charts with numbers marking their supplies, weapons and men were hanging on the walls in a seemingly chaotic manner.

He sat down in the chair in front of the map table and stared at it.

"I've been studying these maps for years. I have them burned into my memory yet I can't help but look at them. It's like I expect to see some flash of insight that will direct me to a miraculous victory."

"No miracles, my Duke, just careful application of the basic tactics and strategies you already know."

"Basic tactics and strategies," he repeated. "Nothing too crazy. Focus on the essentials."

He spoke in a distant voice as if he was talking to someone while in a trance.

"You can win this war, my Duke. I have faith in you."

He smiled and picked up a bottle of wine.

"That's at least one of us."

He passed her a plate of cheese and she sliced off a chunk.

"One thing I like about being free, the food is much better," Greza said.

"You like that? It's particular to Ekonia."

"As a gladiator I got more meat than the worker slaves, but none of it was what you could call good."

"Now it's my turn: do you hate the Empire? We're going there in a few weeks. You might see places you know."

"I don't hate them. I just want to see it all end. Hatred only serves to cause more suffering."

"Is that from your Path of Light?"

"It is, but I also believe it."

"Do you ever doubt?"

She immediately thought of the Princess and how there was no part in the prophecy for her. She was the last true believer it would seem, yet she wasn't to be remembered or rewarded. The only thing she'd earn was to see the man she loved fall into the arms of a more worthy woman.

"I do," she said.

Chapter Twenty-Three

IF SHE THOUGHT THE SIGHT OF THE EKONIAN Army marching out had been an impressive sight then she didn't know what impressive was. She was watching her army and four mercenary companies setting out on a long march to the heart of the Empire.

The columns of troops stretched out forever and she didn't see the beginning or end of it.

"It's hard to imagine defeat looking at this," Onata said.

"I'm sure they think the same of the Imperial armies," Greza said.

"Hey, we have the Victor on our side, right? What does the Victor do but win victories. Don't worry."

"Of course I'm worried."

She patted Greza on the shoulder.

"We'll win."

"But at what cost?"

She looked over to where Verin was talking to the other mercenary generals. They all had their captains surrounding them. Bodyguards weren't needed at the moment.

The generals rode together in the middle of the army so they could continue to plan and discuss. Onata and she kept a respectful distance away.

As they rode out through the main gate of the fortress she turned back to see the lone guard atop the battlements. Only a handful of soldiers were remaining and they were mostly the old and crippled retirees that helped train new recruits.

This imposing fortress had become her home. She had made friends there and it was where she could be an equal. She was respected and sometimes even liked. As a slave the Master's manor was never a home; a refuge from the world. But this ugly fortress was and she silently prayed that she'd be able to see it again one day.

Ever since the generals arrived Verin hadn't had time to say two words to her. She understood of course, but it still hurt. Once they find the Princess it would only be worse. Then he wouldn't even remember she existed.

Onata talked on and on about possibilities of the campaign while Greza listened. She didn't feel much like talking.

The army marched at what she thought was too slow a pace, but she had to remember that humans weren't as durable as she would like to think.

At night they set up camp and Onata and she took turns at watch during the night along with other hand-picked guards.

When it was her turn it was sometime around two in the morning. The wind from the moor was still bitingly cold and she sat down near the fire. The Duke's tent was just off to the side. He had feasted with the other generals but she had not been allowed inside.

Now everything was silent except the wind. She looked up to the moon with a single wispy cloud in front of it. The moon was enormous and cold. Its dead light cast everything in gray/blue outlines. At night everything was just shapes. She saw the shapes of tents. Shapes of stacked weapons and shapes of horses.

None of her thoughts had been cheerful as of late so it was better to just ignore them until they turned to more pleasant topics.

Once relieved she went back to her tent and lay down next to Onata. Onata was the kind that when she slept she could pass for dead. She didn't move, didn't snore and didn't roll around. Greza wasn't sure if she snored or not, but she definitely rolled around. Every morning she woke up to find herself tangled in her own blankets.

She awoke to the blaring horns that marked the general wake up. It was the start of a new day and she hurried to get dressed. She strapped on her breastplate while Onata was still struggling with her shirt.

If she got there before the allied generals arrived then she might have a chance to speak with Duke Verin.

Once ready she went out into the gray sunlight of a clear, late winter day. She didn't see any generals so she ran over to the Duke's tent and took up her position beside the entrance.

The guard that was the last of the night watch was sitting by the fire, staring into the embers. When he looked over and saw her he stared at her for a few moments and then scratched his face. She recognized that look of only being half awake.

"The Duke wants to see you as soon as you arrive," he said.

"Right now?"

"Yeah, he told me about a half hour ago."

"Of course."

She straightened up, cleared her throat and rang the small bell beside the entrance.

"Who is it?" Verin called out from inside the tent.

"Scout Sergeant Greza. You wished to see me?"

"Come in."

She entered through the flap and found Verin fully dressed in his armor standing over a table of maps. He wore a solid metal breastplate with chain mail on the sleeves over his black winter coat. His thick leather belt held two pistols and a long curved sword. His conical helmet with chain mail hanging off the sides and back sat on the table covering a few maps.

He didn't look up.

"Greza, come take a look."

She walked over and looked down at the map.

"Here we have what we know to be the Second Imperial Legion. They're marching towards the city of Ishover and we can't take them in a stand up fight. Ishover sits at a four way crossroads for major supply routes. Strategically it's vital. Over here we have the city of Doranav where a slave and peasant uprising is taking place. If we hurry we can aid this uprising and capture the city without much of a fight, but the city isn't strategically useful."

"What do your allies say?" She asked.

"To take the more important Ishover."

"And what do you say?"

"I say...I say that I don't know."

"But you do, don't you."

"My heart says to help the rebellion in Doranav. We can add their strength to ours and encourage more revolts across the Empire."

"Then why ask me?"

"I like different points of view."

She could tell he was hiding something. She could always tell when he was uncomfortable.

"Is that all?"

She made sure to lock her eyes with his. He looked away first.

"I trust your opinion," he said.

"I'm just a soldier."

"You're not just a soldier. Now tell me what you think."

"In the short term, yes, the crossroads would be better. But if we can help the rebellion and other rebels see this, they'll be more inclined to help us and it'll be better in the long run as we march through the Empire."

"Can we survive the short term until we take the crossroads?"

"Depends on how fast we can march. Most of your army is human."

"And we're weak and slow."

"They have limitations."

"So, if we can march to Doranav and then to Ishover fast enough, we can secure it in time."

"That's my opinion."

"Then that's what I'll tell the others."

"Don't base your judgments on my assessment."

He only smiled.

Then the other generals came in. They were talking loudly and making jokes she had heard from them before. Lord Decaron was leading the way and when he saw her he threw his arms open.

"If it isn't my favorite Ork girl! Please, sit with us and share in our council," Decaron said.

"I already asked her what she thought," Verin said.

"Oh, what a shame. I missed it."

"What does it matter what she thinks?" One of the other mercenary generals asked.

"Because she's probably the smartest person in this room," Verin said.

Greza had to keep herself from smiling. She was glad she didn't blush because she'd also be blushing now. Verin was defending her and everything else faded away into the background.

****

THREE DAYS LATER GREZA SAT ON A LOG NEXT TO Tempest as engineers threw up a pontoon bridge. The Imperials had destroyed the wooden bridge to slow them down. It was a minor inconvenience at most.

Tempest was carving something from a thick branch he picked up from the ground. He was relaxed. They were all too relaxed.

"We haven't seen a single Imperial soldier. Why aren't they harassing us: attacking our baggage train?" She asked.

"Because they have no experience at war. They're probably still trying to agree on a plan."

They couldn't be that stupid.

Tempest chuckled and continued carving. His fingers were agile and he

179

carved like he could do it blindfolded. How was he so dexterous with fingers so large?

"Do you think we're going to win?" She asked.

"It's possible."

"Technically, almost anything's possible. It takes a great deal to list something as impossible."

"Then it's probable."

"Is it probable that the Duke's the Promised Victor?"

"Possible, but not likely."

She continued to watch the bridge being completed as Verin conversed with his generals. Other pontoon bridges were being made further up stream. Their combined armies were too large for one bridge. They couldn't spend all day filing across one narrow bridge.

Onata came running up with two bowls of something steaming.

"Got lunch!"

She handed them each a bowl and Greza sniffed it. It smelled good, but not like anything she had ever had. She sniffed it a few more times and looked up to Onata.

"It's some southern food. I don't know what it is. Just eat it," Onata said.

She took a bite and it tasted as good as it smelled, but it made her mouth tingle almost like it was hot.

"Caranum spice. Love it," Tempest said.

Greza then saw movement off to the side of the camp. Two scouts on horseback came riding up to Duke Verin.

"Looks like they found something," Tempest said.

She watched the scouts dismount and begin talking with wild gestures.

"Definitely found something," Onata said.

Something always had to happen just as she was about to eat or go to sleep. She shoveled a few spoonfuls into her mouth, quickly regretted it because of the spice, and hurried over to where Verin stood with the scouts. She looked for a water skin the whole way. Whatever that spice was, it was delicious, but painful.

Verin watched them approach with a cold look in his eyes that she had seen on only a few occasions when he was truly angry.

"You alright, Grez?" He asked, but he continued on before she could answer. "They found a manor a few miles from here. Ride with me."

Before they could find out more he was already heading for his horse. They had no choice but to mount up as well. Tempest and two dozen cavalry went with them. Tempest rode in a wagon with crossbow men in the back.

When they reached the manor she saw that several scouts were already there. It was a sprawling stone building with several wings that looked like additions and a few round towers. A low stone wall surrounded the place and there were many wooden outlying buildings. Some guards were guarding what were obviously the owners of the estate. They were finely dressed elves and they were kneeling on the ground with their hands on their heads. Other scouts were keeping guard while people dressed as slaves were carrying furniture, paintings and other valuables out of the mansion. Some slaves were breaking windows and smashing vases on the front lawn.

"What is this?" Greza asked, but no one answered.

Verin dismounted and walked over to the five noble prisoners. He had his hands on his sword belt and looked down at them. There was a middle age woman, two teenage boys, probably her sons, and a girl that looked about ten or eleven. They all had the same silvery hair and silver eyes.

"Why are you doing this?" The mother asked.

"Please don't hurt us," the girl whimpered.

Verin didn't say anything for a few moments. He stared down at them until they looked away.

"Your property is forfeit. It all belongs to what used to be your slaves," Verin said.

"And us?" The woman asked, fixing her gaze at Verin.

"You also will belong to your former slaves. I don't imagine they'll treat you with more kindness than you treated them."

The girl began crying.

Greza had thought about this moment for a long time. She had wondered what she would do if she were suddenly the master over her former owners. Vengeance was usually the first thing she thought of. She thought of the slaves that killed each other for amusement and the ones that found themselves mysteriously pregnant with babies that had remarkable similarities to their masters.

They deserved to be punished, absolutely, but handing them over to a mob wasn't justice: it was vengeance and nothing more.

She looked down at the two boys and the young girl. They were wide eyed and shaking. They couldn't keep their eyes off their home being destroyed by their former slaves. Their world was being torn apart in front of them and they probably didn't understand it at all.

Did they deserve this? What would happen to them once turned over to their slaves? What would happen to the girl? Greza could imagine it too well.

Perhaps they did deserve this, but something didn't feel right about it.

"Verin," she said.

He didn't hear her or chose to ignore her.

"Verin!"

He looked over and she saw the cold look in his eyes.

"Verin, can I talk to you in private?"

He nodded and they walked a little ways off and stood under a bushy tree covered in blossoms.

"Isn't this wonderful?" He asked.

"This isn't right."

"How so?"

She waved her hand to indicate all the chaos.

"This isn't right. This is vengeance, not justice."

"So?"

"They'll tear these people apart and if they live, they'll be left with nothing."

"Sounds fair. But can you honestly tell me that you don't want to punish your former masters?"

"I do, very much so, but not like this."

He folded his arms and looked out at the manor with the looting slaves and the noble captives.

"They all deserve to be punished, Grez. They deserve worse than this."

"Do you really want to be known as the man that sacked the Empire and killed its civilians? I thought we were above them. Right now you're no different from the people that kept me as property."

He shot an angry look to her. She didn't turn away. Let him be angry, but she was going to tell the truth no matter what.

Then he let out a long sigh and shook his head. When he looked back to her he had a smile.

"That's why I keep you close to me," he said and then turned and walked back to where the captives were.

Verin stopped the looting, made the slaves leave with as much as they could carry and let the nobles go. There would be no prisoners, no house burnings and no looting. Their army would take supplies and such, but nothing else.

As they rode back to camp she leaned over and whispered to him.

"Thank you."

"I need a good kick in the face once in a while. Who better to give it than you?"

"Tempest, maybe."

"He might be the one person that could take you down, Grez."

She looked back at the hairy, horned giant. The Minotaur was all muscle and was surrounded by an air of raw power, like an approaching black storm.

"You're probably right about that."

Looking at Tempest only made her think of that man from the border station. She hoped she never had to see that man again because she doubted very much that she could ever beat him.

Chapter Twenty-Four

THE IMPERIAL ARMY SPREAD OUT IN FRONT OF the city was impressive. She counted the units, taking their size into consideration and saw that they were outnumbered three to two.

The Imperials had moved an army to block their way into Doranav. Verin thought it was great news because it showed how frightened they were of the slave revolt. It also weakened the army at the crossroads.

"Never stop an enemy when he's doing something stupid," Verin said.

The Imperial army looked very pretty all lined up with matching armor and flags. Their combined mercenary army in comparison looked like a rabble.

But she wasn't concerned. From what Verin said, the Imperials spent more time polishing their armor and marching in parades than learning how to fight.

They were about to find out.

She was mounted next to Onata and they were both behind Verin. It felt strange not to be on the front line. The only way they'd see combat today was if their side lost and the Imperials managed to penetrate their center.

Tempest was off commanding the left flank of infantry.

Alethia, dressed in a long black robe walked up from the direction of the camp and tapped Verin on the knee.

"I don't think we'll need you today," Verin said.

Alethia nodded and walked back to her tent.

"That's reassuring," Onata said.

If they didn't need the sorceress then Verin felt confident of victory. She hadn't seen him wrong about a military matter yet.

"Men," Verin said. "Advance."

The officers immediately began shouting orders. Signal flags were waved and then horns began blowing.

The combined mercenary army undulated forward. The blocks of front line infantry were in the front with archers in the rear and cavalry on the wings. Reserves of pike men were behind everyone to plug up holes and to counter charge if needed.

Verin and his fellow generals had discussed the strategy until dawn. Their plan was as good as it was going to get. From what Greza understood of it, it was very basic. No fancy maneuvers, no tricks. Just simple movement and aggression.

Victory would come down to the generals exploiting weaknesses and openings in the enemy lines and the quality of their troops.

"I bet the Imperials are feeling right confident about now because they outnumber us," Onata said.

"You really think they're that bad?"

"Hope they are."

A part of her wanted to be up front with her old squad mates in the thick of it. She couldn't deny that she loved the surge of power she felt during battle. Never did she feel so alive than in a fight. It was a terrible thing to feel, but she felt it.

The sun was just over the distant mountains and the sky was still shaking off the dawn's purple. Dew covered the grass and it was a beautiful morning. Shame it was about to turn ugly.

Even if they won she knew this was going to be a horrible day. So many people dying. Mothers, daughters, sons and sisters were going to mourn by this night. Each one would be a personal tragedy.

She watched as the two armies collided like distant clouds, so slow but so awe inspiring. Flocks of arrows filled the sky going in both directions and soon white clouds of gunfire obscured much of the battle. She could see cavalry units riding around and pike men charging forward.

Somehow Verin was able to make sense of it all. He would point, issue orders and discuss with the other generals. All she saw was a chaotic mess.

She rode up closer.

"How goes the battle?" She asked.

Verin turned to her and smiled.

"We're pushing them back already. Two of their left flank units have already crumbled and ran back into the city."

It had only been a half hour. That did not speak well for the Imperial troops.

Decaron was holding a thin glass of wine and a servant stood by with a plate of salted meats and cheeses.

"Care for a snack?" Decaron asked her.

She picked up a slice of meat and tossed it in her mouth without tasting it. Her attention was on the battle and trying to see what Verin saw.

"What's your assessment?" She asked.

"My assessment is that this display of soldiering by the Imperial army is pathetic. But this is just one of their armies. They have eleven more."

He then smiled and went back to his wine.

Greza then began to feel uneasy.

"Something's wrong," she said.

Verin gave her a raised eyebrow but didn't comment.

Then a purple swirling mist appeared in the open space in front of them. The horses recoiled away and nearby soldiers readied their spears or pulled out their swords.

"Magic!" Someone shouted out.

As she watched, the smoke coalesced into a looming shape. A moment later the smoke was gone and in its place stood a troll. It was covered in armor and carried what looked like giant cleavers in each hand. It loosely resembled a twisted man covered in thick, green hide. It was tall and lanky and its jaws were massively over-sized and filled with sharp teeth.

Decaron pulled his two-handed sword from his back while the nearby spearmen charged the confused monster.

The thing was massive. It made Tempest look small. The gray armor was strapped on and not fitted like true plate. Its sides, armpits and face were exposed. That was little comfort because once it started to move, it moved fast.

With one swing of its long arm it knocked several of the spearmen into the air. The swordsmen spread out to get behind it while it tore into the spear platoon. It picked up one man and tore his head off and tossed the body at the other spearmen.

It all was happening so fast. It seemed like everyone else was moving under water. There was nothing that could stop this troll from getting to Verin. The spearmen would stall it at best and the swordsmen had less of a chance. Onata was trying to load a bolt into her crossbow but her openings were small on a moving target.

It was up to her.

She had to go for the face. If she had a blade she'd go for the armpit, but with her cestus, smashing the face would be best. Two problems though. First: she didn't know how tough a troll's skull was. She might not be strong enough to break its skull. Second, the rampaging monster was three times her height. How would she even get to its face to land a blow?

Verin and the other generals were turning their mounts away. Why was everyone so slow? One of the officers fell off his horse as it startled because of the nearby murderous beast and it was like she watched him falling at half speed. The horse was right between her and the armored monster.

That was her way to the troll.

Without stopping to second guess herself, she charged forward, vaulted up onto the officer's horse and jumped off with all the strength she had.

Greza sailed through the air over the surviving spearmen and right towards the enormous troll.

Its small red eyes saw her coming and its long arms began to move toward her. It opened its mouth to let out a roar and revealed fat, sharp teeth like a dog's. She couldn't control her direction and was like an arrow that had been fired.

Its clawed hand reached for her but missed and she flew past it and right at his face. Greza had her punch wound up and now brought it forward with everything she had. If she didn't break its skull then it would grab her and tear her to pieces.

Her metal fist smashed into the creature's nose. Immediately she heard bone cracking and felt her fist sink into its face. The blow shook her arm and a stabbing pain raced up her hand and to her shoulder.

The beast tumbled backwards with her on top.

Once the giant hit the ground she rolled off and ran away to gain some distance in case it got back up.

The beast was holding its face with one hand and thrashing around with the other. Its legs kicked out in every direction.

Then something flew past her head with a faint whistle sound and struck the troll in the neck just above its armor. It bellowed in rage while spitting up blood.

The soldiers moved in and began hacking away at it. Within moments the troll was just a bloody mess.

Onata rode up next to her. Greza looked up and saw that Onata's eyes were wide and she was breathing hard.

"I've never seen a troll up close," Onata said.

Greza then looked over to Verin and the other generals. Verin's eyes were still on the dead troll.

Then he looked towards her.

"I don't believe it," Verin said.

"Did your bodyguard just take down a troll in one punch?" Decaron asked.

Greza looked down at her gauntlet and saw it was covered in blood. Her arm felt numb.

Slowly she took off the cestus and felt her swollen hand. More sharp pain.

"I think it's broken," Greza said.

"A broken hand? Troll bone is tougher than iron. You should be dead," Decaron said.

"Greza ..." Verin said.

"I'll get her to the medic," Onata said.

Verin swallowed and then nodded his approval.

"Grez, that was amazing. That should have been impossible," Onata said as she walked along side her.

"I saw an opening."

"What made you think you could take on a troll? Never do that again."

"Don't want me to fight a troll then don't threaten Verin with one."

Onata shook her head.

"Promise me you won't do something that stupid again."

"I can't promise that."

Onata sighed.

"Sometimes I wonder if you're as crazy as they say you are."

"Who says I'm crazy?"

The rest of the battle was a mop up. The Imperial army broke and most ran off. Some ran to the city.

The combined army marched into the city of Doranav through the open gates. The remains of the Imperial army had tried to hide behind the city walls but the citizens threw the gates open.

If this wasn't a righteous cause guided by the Divine Lights then nothing was. The Divine Path was more necessary now than ever.

Verin was riding his black warhorse through the gates and looked every part the hero.

Right then she knew that there was no greater man in the world. She would do anything for him.

She watched his entrance from inside the gate while she kept an eye on the crowd. Onata was on the other side of the gate watching for trouble.

She grabbed the pommel of her saddle with her broken hand and immediately regretted it. The medic had bandaged it up and gave her some horrible drink that killed the pain, but it still throbbed. The medic said it wasn't bad, but it certainly felt bad. Medics always seemed to have an underestimation of pain.

Just in case there was trouble she had a brace of pistols slung across her chest. She wouldn't be much use in a fist fight so she had to rely on more range.

"How's the hand?" Tempest asked.

She hadn't seen the giant Minotaur approach and mentally scolded herself for being distracted.

"Hurts."

"I'd imagine. Heard what you did. Impressive."

"They tell me it was foolish."

"It's never foolish to fight to protect someone."

She didn't know if her hand would agree.

"How did our forces do?" She asked.

"We did very well. It was the first real test of our unit cohesion, but everyone did their part."

"Casualties?"

"Low."

"Lower than expected?"

"Slightly. You know, you really should be looking out at the crowd and not at Verin."

"I ... what? I'm not."

She tore her eyes away from Verin and went back to scanning the crowd for weapons or sudden movements.

Tempest chuckled and she would have hit him but he was on the side of her broken hand.

"He's not a god you know," he said.

"I know."

"Do you?"

She looked over at him to see how serious he was. Apparently 'very.' She turned back to the crowd.

She wasn't deifying him. She respected him a great deal and would die for him. She wanted to be with him always. That was all.

"There she is," Alethia's voice came from behind her. She turned to see the black robed sorceress push her way through the crowd. Her hood was down and her long black hair cascaded over her shoulders. Her skin seemed even paler in the bright sun of early afternoon.

"Let me see your hand," Alethia said.

Greza held out her bandaged hand. Alethia took it and turned it around, making Greza wince.

"Seems bad," Alethia said.

"Decaron says that's what happens when you punch trolls," Greza said.

"That's what happens when you play the fool, but I'm glad you're our fool. You saved Verin's life today."

"I wouldn't say that. There were plenty of soldiers around."

"But none that could have stopped a rampaging troll. Maybe if we had some gunners there. No, stop being modest. Modesty angers me. You saved his life," Alethia said.

"And the sorcerer that sent the troll?"

"Fled," Tempest said.

Alethia then took Greza's hand in both of hers and she was about to pull it away from the sharp pain but suddenly there wasn't any pain at all.

Greza wiggled her fingers and everything felt perfectly normal.

"Alethia, you shouldn't have! I'm not worth it."

"You are important. More so than you realize," Alethia said as she walked off.

She was just a bodyguard. She wasn't worth Alethia's memories for a simple broken bone. It would have healed.

Alethia shouldn't be so wasteful about her memories.

Greza followed Verin's procession to the castle in the middle of the city. With a determined force the Imperials could have held the city for weeks, maybe months. As they passed from the city and into the castle's courtyard she was glad it hadn't come to that. The walls looked very high.

The mayor of the city and all his nobles were out in the courtyard to greet their conqueror and were dressed in their finest. They wore purple and gold robes with cylindrical hats with the enormous image of the Imperial Sunburst.

She walked just behind Verin and to the side so she'd have a view of any danger. She tried not to be distracted by the enormous honor it was to be standing with him at this moment of triumph.

She couldn't stand looking at the officials. They came to grovel and beg for mercy. They assumed Verin was as cruel and petty as they were.

Verin and the other mercenary generals dismounted and approached the group of city leaders. The one in front, with the fanciest robes was a Satyr with gold rings decorating his horns and a silver bell hanging from his pointed beard.

The satyr made a deep bow.

"We welcome you, Lord Verin to Doranav City."

Verin didn't return the bow.

"You're the mayor?" Verin asked.

"Um...no, I'm his third advisor. My name is Daralan Serotatian Beranii. The mayor and many of his staff left an hour ago. I am the highest ranking official left."

The mayor had fled. Typical. These nobles seldom had the courage to stand up against an actual threat. They were cowards.

"Well, Beranii, Doranav is now under Combined Army occupation and there will be a few new rules. As of this instant, all slaves are set free with no compensation to their former masters."

"I assumed as much," Beranii said.

Beranii looked as if he had more formalities he wanted to go through but Verin hated such pomp and ceremony. He had too much to do to worry about niceties. He led the group inside and Greza followed.

The Grand Hall of the governmental palace was dark and quiet as the doors shut behind them. The crowds were shut away from the discussion which meant they were free to say what they meant.

Verin had his bodyguards and officers with him and outnumbered the remaining city officials three to one. At least they had the sense to look nervous.

"You are to surrender half your property to the people you've enslaved their entire lives," Verin said.

"Half!" Beranii said.

"Yes, half. You took everything away from them so its more than fair you give them something back."

"That's too much. You'll ruin us," a fat human official said.

"I'm not done," Verin said.

He turned to them and looked them each in the eye.

"Your oldest son or daughter will join our army or pay a fine of five thousand Soldati."

The officials burst into protests but Verin ignored them as he walked down the Hall toward the throne at the end.

It was a harsh judgment, especially for officials that were willing to work with them. Aside from the counter-productive fear it'll put into nobles heads, it felt less like justice and more like revenge.

She watched Verin and didn't see any concern in his eyes.

Chapter Twenty-Five

SHE WAS ASSIGNED A LARGE BEDROOM SUITE in the palace to herself. She didn't know who used to live there but it had been a woman with expensive tastes. Dresses lay strewn about the room from where the occupant had packed what they could in a hurry. Embroidered curtains with subtle floral patterns blew from the open window almost touching the enormous four post bed that was covered in satin pillows. How many pillows did one person need?

Greza picked up a crimson dress and felt the unearthly softness of the silk. It was wonderful. She'd never dressed in anything like it before and had only seen ladies wear them during her gladiatorial performances during parties. Even though she could barely look at them or risk showing her hatred for them, they always looked regal and beautiful.

She was neither regal nor beautiful.

Greza let the dress fall to the floor. She walked over to the open, door-sized window and looked out over the city that was growing dark as the sun sunk below the distant mountains. Most of the army was camped outside the walls with only a few units let inside to keep the peace.

She could see the campfires of the army spread around the city like a premature night sky full of stars. There were so many of them that it was hard for her to understand the entirety of it all.

The sound of light hoof falls entered the room.

"Ready for the party?" Onata asked.

She turned around to see Onata wearing a black knee-length skirt, a black vest and her pistol belt. Her hair was done in a simple pony tail but it was neat and clean.

Her dark eyes looked Greza up and down. Greza hadn't prepared. She had no desire to spend all night around a bunch of drunken people. Also, she had nothing to wear and she didn't want to show up looking like a mud-covered brawler.

"Not going?"

"It's mandatory?"

"Afraid it is."

"You can come up with an excuse. Tell Verin I'm getting my hand looked at by the doctor."

"He knows Alethia healed it. Why don't you want to come?"

Greza sat down on the bed and kicked a fluffy dress away from her.

"These kinds of parties are a waste of time."

"You've never been to a party like this so how would you know?"

Onata picked up one of the dresses and turned it over in her hands. She then looked back to Greza.

"This might fit you."

Greza looked at the dark dress. It was very pretty.

"Really?"

"It might. If not, I can make it fit."

She thought about walking up to Verin wearing something so gorgeous. She imagined the smile on his face.

"You're smiling about something," Onata said. "That means you're coming. Now try this on."

Greza, not as reluctantly as she pretended, put the dress on. Then she washed herself as Onata made some hasty improvements. When Onata told her the chest had to be taken in Greza almost punched her for laughing. It wasn't funny. She was an Ork runt and couldn't help it.

Onata told her not to pout and tossed the finished dress at her.

She tried it on and found that it fit well enough if not too tight. She didn't know enough about fashion to know what everyone considered to look good. She then put her hair up in a simple bun and Onata put in a decorated pin with pearls on it to add some style to it.

"This alright?" Greza asked.

It felt more odd than alright.

"You look great. Now let's go."

She followed Onata out into the halls where she could already hear the music and laughter coming from the party. Verin had sworn that it wouldn't be a feast. Being in a war had a way of limiting food. Still, a victory party didn't seem exactly the right tone to set. They should be working on the people of this city to see that their needs were being met.

Then they came to the open doors to the Grand Hall and she stopped.

On the far side of the Hall was Verin. She looked down at herself to make sure everything was in place and that she didn't look too ridiculous. At least it didn't have a low back or short sleeves to show her scars off to judging eyes.

Onata was peeking around the doorway inside. Good. That meant Onata wasn't paying attention to her because she would have told her to stop acting so nervous.

Why, by the Divine Lights was she nervous? Verin cared about her skills as a soldier, not a woman. No one cared about her as a woman. She was a weapon and nothing more.

She took a deep breath and tried to put on a calm face as she walked into the room.

Long wooden tables had been brought in and soldiers were drinking and laughing while musicians played in the background. Maybe it wasn't a feast but there looked to be more food here than was necessary.

She looked around but didn't see Verin through the crowd and somehow she had lost sight of Onata.

"Who is this stunningly beautiful woman before me? Have we met?"

She turned to see Lord Decaron approaching her with a goblet in each hand.

"Flattery works better when it's believable," Greza said.

"You're gorgeous, woman. You're going to have to come to terms with that."

It would take more than one drunken fop to convince her of a lifetime of insults. It seemed that alcohol had a way of making everyone appear attractive.

He offered her one of the goblets.

"Don't drink."

"More for me then."

He then drank the offered goblet in one swallow.

"Have you seen Lord Verin?"

"Over there, surrounded by the remnants of the local nobility begging for leniency."

That didn't improve her already souring mood.

She excused herself and he gave her a polite bow. As Decaron had said, there was a swarm of local nobility surrounding Verin. Tempest and a few other officers were there along with some scribes that were scribbling faster than she ever could hope to do.

He was busy. Of course he was. He had a war to run and a country to put back together. There was no way he would have time for an Ork body guard. She was fortunate that she was even allowed near him.

Then he looked up and saw her. He stopped talking and sat up straighter. He was probably wondering why she was dressed this way. He'd ask why she wasn't in uniform and that she didn't have time to play dress up.

He stood up and his crowd of petitioners fell silent as they saw they were being ignored. She gave him a polite but awkward curtsey. She had seen it done but had never tried it before.

He stood in front of her for several moments before speaking.

"You saved my life today."

He didn't comment on her dress. Perhaps it wasn't remarkable one way or another.

"I only did what anyone else would have done."

He laughed.

"Take out a war troll with their bare hands?"

"It was my duty."

"I owe you. Tell me what you wish and you can have it."

"I ... I don't need anything," she said.

There was nothing she needed beyond what she had. She got to serve at his side and see him fulfill his destiny. She was a witness to the Divine Lights' plan. What more could she possibly want?

"I don't leave debts unpaid. Consider it for a while. One way or another you will be rewarded. It's a matter of honor."

"Yes, my Lord."

He brought her back to the throne and had her stand right beside him.

"Greza, these people think I am treating them unfairly by taking away from them to give to their former slaves. What do you think?"

Suddenly all eyes were fixated on her.

"I'm not anyone to comment on such things," Greza quickly said.

"Come now, Grez, you're the most moral, intelligent person I know. If anyone has an opinion on this, it's you."

She couldn't refuse. She did have an opinion and the Divine Lights frowned upon people that kept silent when they could remind people of what was right.

"My Lord, I do think you are being too harsh. Yes, what they did was wrong. I know how their kind treats slaves. But if we want their support and the support of nobles and merchants from other cities, then we need to show leniency. They're lost and confused and need guidance, not punishment now."

"So, I should pat them on the back and send them away with a piece of cake?"

Verin was smiling but she could tell he wasn't being humorous.

"No, they need to know that what they did was wrong. Perhaps they could pay a tax to help the former slaves and hire them on as paid workers."

"I didn't think you'd be so forgiving towards the people that treated you like a beast."

She looked away from Verin and towards the cowering nobles. They looked frightened and pathetic. They did deserve to be punished and she wanted to punch all their teeth out and decorate her saddlebags with them. She wanted to break their fingers and see the pain in their eyes as she snapped the bones one by one.

But that wouldn't help anyone. Justice wasn't about punishing wrongs, but about what was best for society. Right now, society needed these nobles to willingly help their cause against the Empire.

"My forgiveness is irrelevant. Their support is very relevant," she said.

His eyes bored into her as he sat rigid in his chair. Then his look softened and he shook his head.

"I don't know where ..." he started to say but then smiled. "You make a lot of sense, Greza. Perhaps you're right." He looked back at the nobles. "I'll have your answer in the morning."

He dismissed them with a wave of his hand.

She stood by his side in silence as the officers argued about what to do.

"You're always going to tell me what you think, aren't you?" Verin said just to her.

"Always, even if you don't want to hear it."

He nodded.

More people from the city came with petitions for emergencies the war had brought. Verin listened to them all while she stood there as a silent guardian. She could have been eating and telling stories with the other soldiers, but her place was here.

As the night progressed more food and drink was brought in. She frowned but it wasn't her place to dictate what was appropriate. Verin was laughing and sharing stories with the mercenary generals. It wouldn't do to have a mere bodyguard correct her lord in front of the allied officers.

Occasionally she'd catch a glimpse of Onata in the party, usually surrounded by men like a mother duck with her hatchlings.

Then she saw a familiar head of flaming red hair approach.

"You've done well for yourself," Burana said.

Burana held out a tankard of foul smelling ale.

"You know I don't."

Burana smirked.

"Thought I'd try. It's been a while. I thought maybe other things had changed as well."

"Not my faith."

"Of course not, but can that last forever?"

"How are you doing?"

She tried to give an honest smile. She was happy to see her, but Burana had an edge in her voice that was confusing.

"Not as good as bodyguard to Lord Verin. I hope you won't sneer at us lowly rank and file soldiers."

"Of course not."

"Do you think your gods gifted you this lofty position?"

"Are you drunk?"

She looked down at the other goblet in her hand.

"I hope so. I've been drinking enough."

"I'll find you tomorrow and we'll talk then."

"I want to talk now."

"No, I can't be distracted right now."

"Too good to talk to me, huh? Too good to talk to the unbeliever?"

Greza didn't know what to do. Burana was only getting worse and if she got more belligerent it could embarrass her in front of Verin or worse: embarrass Verin in front of his allies.

Then Tempest stepped in.

"Soldier, unless you have important business with Lord Verin, I suggest you leave."

Tempest's voice was low like distant thunder and didn't carry beyond their ears.

Burana looked up at the horned giant and backed away without another word.

"Thanks," Greza said.

Tempest gave her a nod and went back to his place behind Verin's throne.

Verin said he wasn't going to drink tonight so he could keep a clear head, but he held a giant goblet in his hand that had been full an hour ago.

As the hours ticked by the room became more vacant as the soldiers went off to sleep, "patrol" the city for more entertainment or retire to their rooms for love making.

She knew from history that every army had problems with morality. It came with the stress of never knowing if it would be one's last day or not. Still, she hated how the Divine Lights' mission was being carried out by people doing such immoral things.

"Well, gentlemen, I'm calling it a night," Verin said to his generals. "See you in the morning and we'll get back to conquering an empire."

He stood up and waved for her to follow him. She was going to regardless. He had been drinking and she didn't know his level of inebriation. His coordination could have been thrown off, leaving him vulnerable to attack.

They walked down the hall that lead along the outside of the wall. An arched colonnade gave them an open view of the city below them. The wind still had a touch of chill to it but Verin didn't even have a cloak on.

She wondered if he came from a cold place or if he just didn't mind it. She minded. The wind was coming right up her dress. It was very pretty but it wasn't at all practical.

"What do you see down there?" He asked.

She walked to the ledge and rested her elbows along the wall. The stone was cold and seeped through her sleeves almost instantly. Greza saw that most of the lights had gone out and only a few stars remained in the man-made sky.

"A sleeping city."

He looked at her and shook his head with a smile.

"I didn't mean so literal."

She looked again.

"I see an uncertain future."

"I thought certainty was the one luxury religion gave a person."

"Only in a few areas."

He turned away from the view and leaned back against the short wall.

"I keep wondering what chain of events brought you to me."

He spoke without looking at her. It was as if he was talking to himself. She examined his face for signs of being drunk. He didn't look it but he didn't look himself either. It was like a perfect song with one of the instruments out of tune.

"That's one of the certainties I have," she said.

"You have some crazy ideas about the gods, but you are one of the most exceptional women I've ever met."

She warmed and cleared her throat at the complement. He must be drunk. No one complimented her like that. She was a good fighter, sure, but she was hardly exceptional.

"I think my Duke is exaggerating."

"No," he said, the smile disappearing from his face. "If anything, I'm not doing you justice."

She didn't know what to say. She folded her hands and stared at the city with all her attention. This sudden praise was as undeserved as it was unexpected.

"You look beautiful tonight. You look beautiful every night, but especially more so tonight. You're strong, pretty, innocent and probably the most intelligent person in the army."

"I ... I hardly think that's the ... the case, my lord."

Beautiful? She wasn't beautiful. Everyone agreed that Orks were ugly and she was an Ork. She knew she wasn't pretty which meant only one thing: Verin was drunk.

He fell silent and she didn't dare look at him in case he was looking at her.

Did he really think she was pretty? She didn't see how unless he had problems with his vision that she was unaware of. But if he did... What if he really did think she was pretty?

She felt her cheeks grow warm and a strange tingling sensation ran up and down her back.

He moved closer to her and rested a hand on her shoulder. If felt like the heat of a fire through her dress.

"Greza, come to my room tonight."

She gasped and held her breath as her hands shot up to cover her mouth.

There was no denying what he was suggesting. She had been around masters and soldiers long enough to know what he meant.

Two powerful ideas instantly began battering around inside her head. One side was horrified at the idea. Everything her religion taught her told her that sex outside of marriage was a sin. It caused pregnancies which led to children without fathers and proper role models, it lead to disease and led to bastards living in poverty. All her life she had run from it with a desire to be pure for the one man she would marry.

The other part of her mind screamed at her to say 'yes' and let him take her to his bed where she could be with him. She'd have his lips on hers and his hands on her body. Despite her best efforts, she had imagined such a thing more times than she was proud of. Every inch of her body burst with its desire to have him on top of her. She really had no idea what it was like but she had a strong imagination.

She wasn't ignorant about the technical aspects. She had seen it done at parties in front of her. She had heard the moans of pain/pleasure and seen the looks of absolute ecstasy on their faces. There were few things she wanted more than to experience that with Verin.

But Verin was above her. He wasn't hers to have. He belonged to the Princess that was to appear. That meant she was meant for someone else and she had a duty to whoever that person was.

Verin's mission in the prophecy was too important to ruin because of her selfish wants.

"I can't."

His brows lowered.

"Can't?"

"It's not right."

"Is this a religious thing?"

"Partially."

He stepped away and looked her up and down.

"Do you want to?"

"Well ... that's a complicated answer. There are several simultaneously ..."

"Do you want to, yes or no?"

"Yes," she said before she could stop herself.

She was about to take it back but then she realized that it was true. She did want to. She wanted it very badly.

"Then let's go."

Right then all she had to do was remain silent and she'd get her secret desire. She'd be with Verin like no one else was. She'd feel what it was like to have him press down on top of her and feel his breath on her skin.

All she had to do was stay silent and take his hand.

But the cost was too high. She'd be robbing her future husband and she'd be going against the commandments of her gods. She knew what was right. She just had to have the courage to do it.

She swallowed before answering.

"But I can't."

He sighed.

"I'm getting tired of your religious piety. If you want to, then don't let some fake spirits in the sky tell you otherwise."

"They're not fake. They're real and I follow them. If I betrayed them then I could betray anyone and then how could you ever trust me?"

"I don't care," he snapped.

His flash of anger made her step back.

"Come on, let's go," he said and held out his hand.

If he continued this she knew she'd give in eventually. Already she felt more like following him to his bed. But then, he was drunk and he'd regret that he'd sunk so low once he sobered up. She couldn't let him soil himself with her lowness.

"No," she said.

Then she turned around and ran.

She ran back inside and through the halls to her borrowed quarters. There she slammed the door and locked it.

Her breaths came in great heaves, but not from the short run. Her heart was pounding like a woodpecker's tapping and her eyes were burning. When she rubbed them her hands came away wet.

This had all gone horribly wrong. Now he would hate her and send her away. He hated her religion and now he hated her.

Greza sat down on her bed and collapsed backwards into the mountain of pillows.

How was she supposed to face him in the morning? All she wanted to do was run and hide. He had offered her his bed and she'd rejected him as if she were somehow better than him.

Was she being punished for her sinful thoughts? Was this a test of fate or was this just one of the unfortunate aspects of normal life? Whatever it was, it was unfair and it hurt.

Chapter Twenty-Six

GREZA DRESSED IN HER UNIFORM AND straightened herself out in the mirror. If she was going to be exiled from Verin's presence, she might as well look her best.

Once her uniform was perfect she took some oil and a rag and polished her breastplate before strapping it on.

Lastly, she did her long hair in a simple tail. She wanted to look professional, not pretty. She wasn't pretty but Verin had been drunk enough to think she was. She had heard of this phenomenon before but had thought herself immune to it.

Now she was alcohol's victim. Verin would never have said those things and forced her to insult him if he had all his faculties.

What right did she have to refuse him? How arrogant she must seem. He probably thought she imagined herself to be better than him.

Verin, beneath her? Ridiculous.

Just remembering him calling her "beautiful" made her feel warm inside, but it wasn't true because it was the spirits talking and not him. That put a disharmonious note in last night's song.

Drunk or not she felt honored at his attentions. It was more than honor. It was hope. Perhaps one day he could see her as beautiful. She would never assume that he'd have feelings for her, but just him thinking kindly about her was enough.

All that might be over though. She could march into that hall and meet his furious gaze. She didn't know if she could take it.

After kneeling down and saying a quick prayer, she brushed her knees off and walked to the Great Hall where Verin held court.

Her boots were nearly silent on the thick rugs that led to the Hall. All she could hear was her own breathing that sounded heavier than she would have liked.

When she came to the open door where two guards stood, she wiped the sweat on her palms off on her pants and walked in. The generals were gathered around the table eating bread and sausages while arguing over maps. Verin was, like always, in the middle. He glanced up briefly at her entrance but went back to his maps. He didn't greet her but he didn't show scorn either.

Was this good or bad?

She walked to her usual place behind and to the side of Verin. Onata was nowhere to be seen and neither was Alethia. Alethia kept her own hours and if anyone saw her before noon that was counted as an early day.

It wasn't till a half hour later that Onata arrived. Her uniform was rumbled and her hair was messier than she had ever seen it. Her eyes were half closed and she looked almost as if she were in pain.

"Are you alright?" Greza whispered once Onata had taken her place.

Onata made an unintelligible groan in response and Greza decided to drop it until Onata regained the power of speech.

There was no one allowed in this room except officers so Greza allowed herself to listen in. They were discussing troop movements, logistics, where to go next and where the enemy might be.

Some wanted to split the army and take several weak cities but Verin insisted that they stay together. His argument was that if they continued as one massive army, the Empire would have to gather several of their provincial armies just to slow them down.

"It's almost as if you want them to," one of the generals said.

"And why not?" Verin said. "If we can smash them in one day, wouldn't that be better for us and the people? The longer and more spread out this war gets, the worse the common people will suffer."

"This is a war; of course they're going to suffer."

"I'm going to minimize that."

"He's right," Decaron said. "If we can draw them out we can end this right then and there."

"The longer we wait increases the chance that they'll learn and start cutting off our supply lines and setting ambushes for us."

"We've already planned for that," an Elf general said.

"And I've already sent an agent to bribe some Imperial commanders to start pushing for a confrontation," Verin said.

"What?"

"Are you mad?"

"Oh! This should be fun," Decaron said, clapping his hands.

They argued more but Verin got them to go along with his plan, at least for now. He listened and reasoned but he didn't change his opinion. Once the generals were dismissed Verin began rolling up the maps.

"I thought they'd be angrier about that," Tempest said as he walked up and patted Verin on the back.

"It wasn't fiery anger, more a boiling resentment. I can't push them too far, Tempest. They're already sacrificing enough."

"And they also know what they stand to gain. Being a governor of a province isn't a bad reward for a war."

"If they get it. That's the problem with gambling."

"You can't start having doubts now. Too late for that."

"Of course not. I never doubt anything ... ever."

Tempest chuckled and shook his head before leaving.

Verin gathered the maps under his arm and began walking toward the door. Onata and she began to follow.

"Just Greza, please. Onata, you can meet me back here during lunch."

Greza almost stumbled. All morning she had dreaded this. He wanted to talk to her alone. All the reprimands he would throw at her flooded her mind. She pictured his angry face or worse, a dismissive expression.

Onata didn't know what occurred last night and she waved with a headache fueled grimace before wondering off.

She followed Verin in silence as they left the Hall and walked back toward his room. She tried to walk as silently as she could to not disturb him or draw his notice. It was foolish and she knew it, but she didn't know what else to do. All she wanted was to run away.

Then he stopped walking and she swallowed.

"About last night ..." he started to say.

This was it.

"I wanted to apologize for how I behaved," he said.

What?

"I acted rudely to you. You deserve better treatment than that."

"My lord ..."

"You must think I'm a beast, but I swear that I am not. I'm sorry if I hurt you."

"But, my lord, I should apologize."

"You? For what? What imagined insult did you think of?"

"My lord, I'm a nobody. I didn't want you to think that ..."

"Greza, shut up."

Her mouth snapped closed.

"How can you think so little of yourself that you'd apologize to me?"

"Because I didn't want you to think that I was better than you."

It sounded weak as it left her mouth and she knew she must seem ridiculous.

"But you are."

She struggled for words but nothing came to her lips.

He turned back around and continued walking.

She tried to understand what he had said. What did he mean when he said she was better than him? He had to know that that was ludicrous. Was he trying to tell her something that she just didn't understand?

They came to his door and she didn't know what to do.

"Greza, please forget last night happened."

"Of course."

Of course there was no way he would find her attractive. She knew that.

She smiled and saluted as he closed the door behind him.

Greza went back to the Great Hall and sat down on one of the benches lining the wall. Only an occasional servant or messenger would pass by. Outside she knew the armies were readying to move out. At dawn they would march towards another battle.

She was a witness of the most important event in history for hundreds of years and she was honored to just be a part of it.

****

THE NEXT DAY WORD REACHED VERIN THAT THE CITY of Fairfield in the province of Spetium had raised in armed revolt along with two other provinces. The mercenary generals were surprised and cheered but Verin didn't seem at all surprised.

Greza remembered Fairfield as anything but fair. It was a dingy, poor place with no cheer. She knew the Empire taxed them heavily and put their hands in the people's pockets every chance they got, but there had to be more reason to rebel and she wanted to know what it was. She knew the message she had delivered to Spetium's Governor had lead to this.

Three provinces in rebellion were disastrous for the Empire and there was no way they could deal with that and Verin's invasion at the same time. Even if the provinces didn't send aid, their lack of support for the Empire was enough.

The next day the army moved out and kept only a token force behind.

The dust clogged the air and Greza had to wrap her face in order to breathe. Thousands of soldiers marched by and the carts kicked up more dust which made the air almost unbearable.

"If it would rain we could breathe," Onata said.

"But then we'd be up to our knees in mud," Tempest said.

"Just enjoy it for what it is," Greza said.

They both looked to her.

"Enjoy?" Tempest asked.

"We're part of this great mission," Greza said.

"Not this holy mission dung," Tempest spat it out like a bitter taste.

"Why not? It might be true," Onata said.

Tempest laughed and walked off to check on the baggage train.

Onata shook her head, making the tiny bells on her horns jingle. She liked to indulge in such vanities when silence wasn't necessary.

"No matter what you do, some people won't believe."

"Lord Verin will prove the prophecy. They won't have a choice but to believe."

"Of course. And this coming battle?"

"We'll win."

"Just like that?"

Onata was teasing her and she wasn't going to fall for the bait.

The Combined Army was approaching a city that sat on a three-way crossroads of the major highways. Everyone expected the Empire to send an army to stop them. The city was too important to let fall. What she heard from the soldiers told her they wanted the fight.

Then distant horns blared at the front of the army. Three long notes, the signal for enemy contact.

"I guess we're going to find out how good your holy boy is," Onata said.

"Please speak with respect."

Scouts were rushing up and giving reports and officers began barking orders all around her. It was an army preparing for a fight and the smiling faces on the running soldiers showed that they were ready for it.

She silently prayed that their confidence was justified. She wasn't foolish enough to believe that just because they were on a sacred mission that they couldn't fail. There would always be setbacks and disappointments.

The enemy army force was marching to catch them before they got to the city. Many officers wanted to rush and reach the city first to get inside the walls. Verin wanted to meet them head on.

Verin won the argument like he usually did and they moved their armies into position. The two armies came within sight of each other before either could reach the city, just as Verin wanted. It took hours for the ponderous armies to line up and face each other. By then the sun was setting.

She noticed the narrowed eyes and closed mouth on Verin. He sat on his horse watching his army and remained silent.

Something was wrong with him. She could see it but too much was happening to ask him. It wasn't her place either.

As she watched the scouts rushing around she recognized a few of them. She wanted to be with them, riding at the head of the army, finding enemy positions. It was so much freer out there, but here she could be near Verin. Whatever purpose the gods had for her, she was where she needed to be.

"Tomorrow," Decaron said.

"They outnumber us two to one," the fat general said.

Normally there would be jokes about the upcoming battle, but Verin's mood was dampening everyone's joy.

Something was wrong and he wasn't speaking to anyone.

The camp fires began appearing and music began playing. As she walked by the soldiers plucking on their lutes, she wanted to join them. She wanted to learn the songs they sang and learn to play those instruments.

That was a brotherhood she would never share.

It was just one more sacrifice to make for the Divine Path. It wouldn't be the last.

The sound of tinkling bells approached from behind.

"I think Verin's nervous," Greza said.

"He should be."

"How many enemy?"

"More than twice our number."

She looked over to where Verin sat by a fire with his generals. He and Decaron were talking quietly to each other.

"I wish I could do something for him."

"Just let him know you're there."

"How would that ..."

"Go over and stand by him. He needs you."

Onata pushed her towards the circle of generals. She managed a scowl at Onata before walking over and standing behind Verin. He glanced at her but didn't say anything to her.

Still, she saw a faint smile on his face.

Eventually the generals turned in for the night and Verin retreated to his tent. She waited until she saw the night guards doing their rounds before she went to her own tent. Onata was asleep inside, still wearing her uniform and boots. Everyone slept with their gear tonight.

Greza stretched her sleeping roll out and lay down. All she took off were her gauntlets. Her boots stayed on in case of sudden trouble.

THE MORNING CAME WITH LOUD TRUMPETS AND drums. Her eyes snapped open and she sat up.

Onata was stirring and grumbling something under her breath.

Greza helped Onata get into her armor and then Onata helped her. Then they strapped on their bandoliers of powder canisters and pistol belts with a speed that comes only from doing a thing so many times that the mind wasn't needed; the muscles knew what to do. Once they were kitted up they rushed outside to Verin's tent.

The sun was a purple smear in the distance. She couldn't count how many sunrises she had seen since joining the Ekonian Army. They always had to be up too early. This just happened to be one of the rare days that getting up before the sun was justified.

A few minutes later Verin came out of his tent in full armor. It was going to be a warm day so he didn't wear his long coat, only his cotton shirt under his armor and padding. He held his helmet down at his side and looked around with a smile in his eyes.

Whatever dark thoughts he had during the night were gone.

"Good morning, my lord."

"It's going to be a great morning, Greza. Stay close. I don't want a troll coming to shake hands with me again."

"If there's a troll, I'll kindly ask him to leave."

An enormous grin crossed Verin's face and he strapped on his helmet.

"Fellow generals! On me! We have a long day ahead of us!" Verin shouted out.

An orderly brought her horse to her and she mounted up. Onata wasn't there so she held the reigns of her horse until she returned. Onata came back with two apples and tossed one to her.

"Can't fight on an empty stomach," Onata said.

She looked out at the camp fires that covered the plain a few miles away. This was probably the only food she'd have for a while.

Greza took a bite and watched the armies form up into blocks and lines. Targeteers got into rows with the gunners behind them.

This was going to be a horrible day. It was like watching an accident in the slowness of a dream. She could see everything that was about to happen and was powerless to stop it.

But Greza didn't want to stop it because this had to happen.

The two armies faced each other across an empty space filled with potential death that everyone could feel. Greza knew this feeling. Already she thought she could smell the blood.

Greza pulled her carbine out of its sheath and laid it across her lap. Something didn't feel right. The itching that had been building up since last night was now like a burning coal in her stomach.

"Watch Verin with both eyes," Greza said.

"Always do," Onata said.

"More than usual."

Onata cocked her head.

"Something wrong?"

She wasn't sure how to answer that without sounding crazier than people already thought she was.

"I don't know."

Then a black horse with a black rider trotted up next to her. What was Alethia doing there?

"You should probably stay in the rear, Alethia," Onata said with a raised eyebrow.

Alethia shook her head and Onata shrugged.

Greza leaned over and whispered to Alethia.

"Why are you here?"

"I have a bad feeling."

Greza closed her mouth and tried to block all faithless thoughts from her mind. Yes, there was danger but she had to put her trust in the Divine Lights. If Alethia felt it as well then the danger was serous. She hoped knowing of the danger was enough to guard against it.

"I won't let the Promised Victor come to harm," Alethia whispered.

"We'll both watch over him."

Alethia narrowed her dark eyes and gave one nod.

Horns and drums blasted out the signal to march. As one, the brigades moved forward with the thunderous trampling of thousands of feet and the deafening clanking of armor and weapons. The back ranks had to wait for the front to move, like the bellows of a blacksmith.

Two miles away the Imperial army lurched forward. They had many more impressive looking banners than the combined army and their cavalry had silly looking plumes of bright feathers.

"The Imperial Chargers," Onata said. "The best they have. They call them the Sword's Edge."

"How experienced are they?"

"Their last battle was ninety years ago."

Verin had set their command on what passed for a hill on these plains. It was a slight rise that gave them just enough height to see what was happening. She looked to the left and right and saw that the ranks on the wings were twice as deep as the center.

Greza pointed a metal cestus at the right flank.

"Why the double depth?"

Onata raised her hands and shrugged.

The Imperial Army didn't have the well practiced precision of the Combined Army's veteran mercenaries and soldiers. Their advance was loose and sloppy with some units going ahead of others, thus creating gaps in their defense.

Their garish cavalry were charging in from the flanks, much too soon from what she could tell, but then she wasn't an expert general. The Combined cavalry hadn't moved from their position as they kept pace with the infantry.

She hadn't read any of these tactics in a book and never heard them in a lecture. Verin was trying something unheard of. Perhaps that was why he was worried.

She wished he had told her. Did he not trust her or was she still not back in his good graces despite what he said?

The Imperial army was rushing right for their center. They probably felt confident about their numbers and wanted to smash the Combined Army right there and then. If she knew she could win, that's what she'd do.

But to assume they'd win sounded like supreme arrogance.

The first volleys of gunfire opened up like distant popping and gray clouds of powder smoke emerged from the front lines. The battle had started.

The tempo of the gunfire increased until individual shots blurred into one massive sound like a roaring river. Blocks of Imperial infantry moved closer in preparation for a pike charge to break their center.

Verin raised his hand and scouts ran off to relay orders. A few minutes later the cavalry moved out. They raced out to the sides and met the enemy cavalry. She saw less puffs of smoke from gunfire from the Imperials. They used older style chargers with sabers and the Combined forces used far more guns.

Greza watched the cavalry battle unfold and almost ignored completely the rest of it. The Combined cavalry were outnumbered but their massed gunfire soon had the Imperial horses on the run.

A cheer rose up from the allied generals and officers. She thought it was a little premature for all of that.

The two armies continued sharing gunfire as the Imperials crept closer. If they charged too far away, they'd be slaughtered by gunfire. Charge too soon and they wouldn't get enough momentum.

Instinctively she knew the golden moment they should charge, so she was taken back when they broke into a pike charge too soon.

Fools.

Onata laughed.

Even with pike men dropping in disgusting numbers, they crashed into their front ranks with a rise in noise she heard from the rear.

Artillery was focusing their bombardment on the wings of the Imperial army, keeping them from charging. Still the heavy combined flanks didn't move in to support the center. What was Verin thinking?

The Imperials were losing far more men than the combined army, but if they broke through the center it wouldn't matter, the battle would be over. She continued to watch from her saddle as the Imperials slowly pushed their center back. If it stretched any more it would break.

"Greza!" Verin shouted.

Her head snapped over to look at him.

"I need you, Onata and Tempest to take our reserves and support the center."

She didn't want to leave him in a battle, especially with this bad feeling, but an order was an order.

"Yes, my lord!" She shouted and then spurred her horse over to where the reserves were. Tempest was right behind her, already barking out orders. Onata was rounding up some halberdiers and once they had a sizable force together, they charged for the front.

She had to trust Verin's safety to Alethia for now.

She left her horse in the hands of a young boy and she charged forward on foot with the infantry. Onata stayed mounted and Tempest was next to her. Even from her limited view and knowledge, she could tell that the center was bowing inward under the pressure of the enemy assault.

An enemy pike man bust through the ranks and he was followed by several others.

"There!" Tempest bellowed.

The Minotaur charged forward and crashed into the Imperial soldiers. Onata fired her crossbow and instantly pulled out and fired a pistol.

The hole in their ranks was made and they had to plug it or the entire battle was lost. What was Verin thinking with this formation? It was obviously too thin in the center.

The auxiliary infantry ran forward and engaged the escaping infantry.

Greza stood back and watched. The sickening feeling was only growing stronger. Something was wrong.

Then her head hurt as if a bullet had struck it. Clutching her temple, she turned in the direction.

A giant man wearing heavy battle armor shoved his way through the mass melee and walked directly towards her. She knew him. She recognized the shaved head and scar. He was looking at her and cracked his knuckles.

It was the man from the border station, the man she couldn't beat.

He took up the same fighting stance she was about to take up.

She looked for Tempest and saw him surrounded by enemy soldiers and Onata was too far away to notice her.

She was alone.

Chapter Twenty-Seven

GREZA FACED THE GIANT HUMAN AND WENT into her defensive stance. She looked him over for weaknesses to exploit. He wore heavy armor that would stop her punches. He was large and strong so she couldn't grapple with him.

Only two things she could do. She could try to go for his head, but it was out of her reach most of the time. Or, she could go for his joints. No matter how big and tall he was, a well placed strike would still break them.

Those were her only options.

The giant charged forward at a calculated pace she recognized from her own training. He maintained control of his movement, able to act and react with little hindrance.

She took up a defensive stance with her arms up and to the sides so as not to block her vision. It was called the "Bull" stance.

The man reached her and jabbed at her. It was a probing attack to test her defense. She knocked it to the side to open him for an attack of her own but his other hand was already reaching for her. If he managed to grab her, the fight would be over. He could pick her up and do whatever he wanted.

She stepped back out of reach just in time to dodge another fist. He was fast and kept her ducking and weaving to avoid being hit. His reach on her was so great that she couldn't get in close enough to land a shot.

There was no way she could win this fight without getting very lucky. All she could do was wait for an opening that might not happen.

He punched with his left arm and left his side open for just a fraction of a second. She took it. She pushed his arm further in the direction it was already moving to throw him off balance. As his side was open she snapped a kick to his knee.

Before her foot connected his left arm surged back like a landslide, pushing her away and she struggled to stay on her feet. He was strong. She was strong as well, but this was about weight. He could push her around all day because he had the leverage and she didn't.

She backed away from him as he approached at his measured pace. His arms were up and ready to attack.

Greza knew she couldn't beat him. He was just as strong as her but had more reach and weight. If she ran she'd leave the path open to Verin and that wasn't going to happen.

Her trainers would tell her that when she was in trouble to open her eyes and look around her. Right now she was definitely in trouble.

Greza continued to step away from him while keeping her guard up and looked to her sides and glanced very quickly behind her.

Nothing to her sides, but behind her was a squad of gunners running up to the front lines. Only there were allies on the other side of this man. If they missed, they'd hit friendlies. She had to get him closer, but she didn't know if she had time for that.

The man charged her, ignoring caution. He was confident and had every right to be so.

She continued to retreat while fending off his attacks. What she didn't dodge she deflected out of the way.

"Gunners!" She shouted back while keeping her peripheral vision on her enemy. "Gunners! Shoot this man!"

She spared a quick glance and saw that two of them were pointing her direction.

That glance cost her. An armored fist struck her breastplate and she was lifted into the air and landed on her back. Her helmet flew off and for a second she couldn't breathe. Blackness threatened to encircle her but she remembered her training and rolled out of the way just as his foot came down right where her head had been.

She felt the thump the ground took from his massive weight. As strong as her bones were, he would have crushed her skull.

An enormous hand clamped down and grabbed her by the hair.

"You were entertaining, Ork."

She tried to pry his hand off but this man was unusually strong, stronger than what was natural.

Then there was a loud crack and the metallic 'ping' of metal striking metal.

The man let go of her hair and stepped back.

Greza rolled away and leapt to her feet.

There was a small hole in his breastplate. Then another gun fired and another hole appeared in his bicep armor.

The man looked up at the gunners and bared his teeth. Another gun fired and she heard the ball streak through the air just passed the man's unarmored head.

He brought his forearms up to cover his head as he turned and ran. Gunfire followed him as he disappeared into the chaotic battle.

She took a moment to catch her breath.

One of the gunners ran up to her. He had a simple breastplate and helmet with wide circles for eyes.

"You alright, mam?"

She nodded.

"I am now."

She couldn't rest. The giant was gone but the enemy was still pushing their middle back.

After resting for a minute, she dove back into the battle. She grabbed an enemy soldier's halberd and bashed the haft into his face. Another enemy she punched his helmet in. Blood spilled down onto his shiny but thin armor.

She could tell they were winning. Even from the most chaotic mess of things, she could see the enemy was falling back.

Suddenly there was a loud 'thump' sound that she felt as a warm wind on her face. She looked over and saw a giant fireball rising up from the middle of their army. Bodies flew into the air as another explosion blasted a hole in their army.

"Magic!" Someone shouted. Then dozens more began shouting something about a wizard. Many began running away but she ran towards the trouble.

A blast of lightning shot into the air followed by another one that she saw tear through their ranks. Arcs of purple lightning weaved its way through several squads at once, locking its victims in place as they cooked in their armor.

A unit of gunners opened fire but their bullets hit an invisible wall before they reached their target.

The enemy sorcerer was a clean shaven human. He was old but was standing upright with the health of a young man. He walked at a leisurely pace as his stretched-out hands shot lightning and fire.

Then a streak of what Greza could only describe as 'black light' came from behind her and hit the enemy wizard. An explosion of white light erupted a few feet in front of the wizard. The dark ray left the afterglow of bright light on her eyes as she tried to blink it away.

Greza looked over and saw Alethia strolling through the retreating troops. Her black hair was blowing behind her from the wind of the explosion.

The Imperial wizard looked around and backed up a few steps.

"Run and I'll let you live," she said.

"What are you willing to sacrifice to beat me?" He called back in a clear voice.

"Everything," she said.

They looked at each other for a long moment, judging who would give up their most cherished memories to defeat the other.

Apparently the wizard saw something in Alethia's eyes because he nodded and turned away.

She had never seen magic unleashed on the battlefield before and now she wished she never had to see it again. If Alethia hadn't been there, they couldn't have stopped the wizard.

She had read of battles where dozens of wizards had unleashed everything they had. Those battles must have been nightmares.

Greza looked over to Alethia and gave her a nod.

Would Alethia really have given up all her memories or had it been a bluff?

Then more horns blew giving orders that she didn't recognize. She looked around and saw the far flanks stretching out even further. With the pressure off of the center she ran back up the hill to where Verin was.

He pointed at the battle.

"It's actually working," Verin said.

She watched as the flanks spread out and moved forward. The extended wings then charged in, surrounding the enemy in a complete circle. It happened so fast that the enemy general probably hadn't had time to come up with a counter move.

Within minutes the enemy army was completely surrounded. They were being attacked on all sides while artillery and arrows poured into their center. The battle was over. Either the Imperials would surrender or they would be slaughtered.

"I see white flags," Verin said.

She was too tired to form a coherent sentence so she just nodded.

"Glad you're here," he said.

He broke away from his officers and walked over to her.

"You're unhurt?" He asked.

She nodded.

"Thank the Divine Lights."

He paused, and then patted her on the shoulder before returning to his men.

Onata came up and sat down beside her. She was covered in black gunpowder marks and dirt. Her hair was a mess and she was holding her dented helmet in her lap.

"Hard day?" Greza asked.

Onata nodded.

✳✳✳✳

GREZA HATED THESE CELEBRATION PARTIES. SHE UN-derstood them and in truth, wanted to celebrate herself, but not like this. It was all the loud laughing and constant talking. It hurt her ears.

She appreciated the music but thought the feasting was a waste. No one else seemed to share her opinion so she kept her mouth shut.

Verin was at the head of the table and she was sitting on a chair behind him and away from the table. Onata was walking around the crowd, talking, eating and laughing with the others. She didn't drink at least. Like her, she was still on duty.

An endless parade of local dignitaries, businessmen and nobles came to see Verin, the new conqueror of the city. The rumor going around was that it had been the Empire's largest army. They had several more but that was the capital's elite divisions. If that was true then victory was possible.

Verin was talking to a Minotaur in simple robes. He didn't look like a noble. Probably a religious figure of some kind. Aside from her own, she had no interest in religious discussion.

"Greza, come here. I think you'll be interested in this," Verin called out. Greza approached his impromptu throne. He indicated the robbed Minotaur. "This is Dattano; he's a monk of the Church of the Exalted Hero. He says there's an ancient monastery of the Divine Path not far from the city."

Greza paused and looked to the Minotaur. He nodded a greeting to her.

"What's in the Monastery? Is anyone still there?" She asked.

"As of last year there was still one monk there. I know there is a relic and a library at least. I've only been there once."

She looked to Verin who smiled and nodded.

"Grez? You want to go there?"

"But, my Duke, you have many enemies here."

"I do, but I also have lots of friends. Tempest will take your place while you're gone."

"Really?"

This was more than she could hope for: one of the ancient Grand Monasteries of the Divine Path. If the monk was still there he could teach her far more than she'd ever learn by herself.

The rest of the night passed with her eyes on the crowd but her head filled with books of heavenly knowledge. And the opportunity to talk to a monk who had devoted his life to learning of the spiritual was even greater.

She barely slept that night and got up before dawn to head out on her own. It would be safer to travel with someone, but this was for her alone.

Greza rode out of the city gates with a wave to the guards and followed the directions Dattano had given her. She travelled down a narrow dirt road that wound through low hills covered in short but wide trees with some kind of purple fruit on them.

As the sun rose above the distant mountains it revealed a cloudless sky and singing birds. It was a beautiful day and she closed her eyes and let herself feel the sun on her face. The gods were generous at times.

Five miles out of the city she saw the monastery up on the hill, just like Dattano had told her. It had tall and simple gray stone buildings rising up from behind a wall that looked more like a fortress than a holy place. The buildings had tall spires rising up from the middle of the roofs. She had never seen architecture quite like it before.

As she came closer she saw the thick wooden gates were closed. Weeds and vines covered the walls almost completely obscuring the carvings of men and women in elaborate robes that were spread out evenly near the top of the wall.

How ancient was this place? Was it from before the First Empire and the time of the Falling? If so, how had it survived the massive destruction that tore across the continent?

It was another question she'd have to ask the monk.

She rode up to the door and knocked with her steel cestus. She waited a minute and knocked again, louder this time. If no one answered, she was going in.

On the tenth knock she heard the sound of the locking mechanism turning with a terrible grinding sound. It was rusted and hadn't been used or oiled often.

When the door opened an old man, hunched over with age, walked out. He had a long white beard that went to his waist and his eyes didn't see her. They were as grey and lifeless as the stone of the walls.

"Hello?" He called out.

"Hello, I'm Greza, a follower of the Path."

He faced her and he raised an eyebrow.

"Tell me, follower, what do you expect to find here?"

"Knowledge."

"Any other library would do then. I hear the palace in the city has an extensive library."

"I want to learn more about the Divine Lights."

"There are books about that too."

This man didn't seem to want visitors. That or he wanted something else. The Path was about walking through life being true and honest with ones self and with others. The monk had no time for vagueness and half truths.

"I come seeking knowledge about the Promised Victor and his mission."

The monk smiled.

"Finally, progress. Why do you want to learn about him? Isn't he dead?"

"I believe I've found him."

"Believe?"

"Know."

He nodded his head and ran his hand through his beard.

"So, you found the Victor. What more could you need to know? Let him do his job."

"I need to know the nature of the great threat and also his companions."

"Don't the Teachings tell us who the companions are?"

That they did. She knew who they were. All they lacked was the Princess. But she hadn't come here to learn about them. If she had to be honest with herself, she came to find out if she had any part in this.

"I sense hesitation, child," the old monk said.

"I fear that my answer may be selfish."

"Perhaps, but will it be honest and true?"

"Afraid so. I've found the Victor and most of his companions. Many things in the Victor's life are told in the scriptures, but ..."

"Tell me, child."

"But I came to find out if I had a place in this or if I'm just a bystander with no role."

He smiled showing a mouth with only half its teeth. He then led her inside the courtyard where she tied her horse and followed him inside. There were no candles or lanterns inside the dark monastery. Only a few slits let in streams of light.

He took her through the chapel that was filled with cobwebs and the statue of the Personification of Light which was a woman with raised arms. A giant cobweb stretched from her left hand to the nearby pillar.

Greza wondered what the Lights thought of the statue and its condition.

He took her through a side passage that was almost completely dark but he didn't even pause. He was used to the darkness.

Finally he led her to an octagonal room with windows around the base of the domed ceiling that were made from thin slices of bone. It was pretty but didn't let in a lot of light for reading.

"So, you wish to find out if you're mentioned in the more obscure scriptures."

"I want to know if I belong here or not. Am I a part of this or is my small mission accomplished?"

"Do you think it's done?"

She thought about it. Verin himself still didn't believe.

"No."

"Then it's not done yet."

He walked to a shelf and ran his fingers down the spines, counting the books as he went. Then he pulled out a book that was so ancient the cover was crumbling and the pages were brown.

"I believe you may find this enlightening." He turned around and extended the book. "I'll be in the chapel praying. Come find me when you've found what you seek."

He then left through the passage they'd entered in from. Now she needed a place to read. She went to the far door and had to shoulder it open. It led to a well maintained garden full of vegetables of all kinds. The old blind man was remarkably self sufficient.

She found a stone bench and sat down.

The book had no title on the cover. She opened it and the dried leather cover creaked. The pages were thin and brittle and she treated each one as delicately as she could. She took off her gauntlets and got comfortable.

The inside said the book was copied form the original and was the writings of "The Mad Prophet, Ezzanshial" in the time of the falling, before the first written prophet of this new Age.

She had never heard of this book. There were many lost books of scriptures, some only hinted at, others mentioned by name but lost forever. This one had had no mention from anything she had ever read.

Greza began skimming through the pages looking for anything relevant to the prophecy. He appeared to have several prophecies, many which had already come true. Either this book was a fake or this man had truly seen the future.

An hour later she reached a chapter where he first mentioned the Promised Warrior King. She slowed down and began reading with more attention.

Here this Mad Prophet Ezzanshial told of the Warrior being taken as a baby and hidden away for years. Why hadn't anyone else written about that? It didn't make sense. That seemed to be a rather important detail. She continued reading.

78. And in the time of the Confusion where men grow idle and proud, where mothers forget daughters and sons forget family, war will rage across the continent. The Promised Warrior will return to his people that he too had forgotten and conquer the kingdom in the name of peace.

79. But he shall not be alone. Ever with him are his Companions, his lieutenants set for him from the foundation of the world. Long has Zarrandal spoken of the Bull, the mighty warrior that shall be the Warrior's strength. Iriasas has told you of the Raven, the sorceress that bends the world to her sardonic will.

80. There will also be the Guardian, the dark woman that shall protect his life against all threats not of the Path's making. The Promised Warrior, upon the eve of victory shall find the Consort. This royal princess shall marry him and together they shall start a dynasty that may last two Ages if the Divine Lights will it.

A royal Princess. That narrowed it down to very few people.

81. And the Dark Prophet Aurian dreamed of the Assassin. The Assassin will strike the Promised Warrior down after the Enemy has been cast down.

She almost dropped the book. Assassin? There was a part of the prophecy that was going to kill Verin? She would never let that happen. Even if it meant breaking the Divine Light's plan, she would stop this Assassin no matter the cost.

Greza took a deep breath and continued reading. She had to know, no matter how painful the truth was.

82. But the Assassin is only a part of the Divine Light's path. For he is sent to fulfill the prophecy as instructed. The Promised Warrior will save the Empire from annihilation as he was willed to do. However, he was not created for the throne. He will grow more cruel with time until he becomes the Scourge.

83. The Scourge will lead the Empire down a path devoid of light from which it will not emerge for a thousand years.

84. For that, the Assassin will slay him and maintain the Path of Light.

This time she purposefully threw the book down.

That was wrong. She wasn't going to listen to some lunatic. He had to be wrong. Otherwise the other prophets would have mentioned him.

None of this made sense. Who was this assassin? There was no possible way Verin would turn into this Scourge. It was all wrong. Whatever it took, she was going to protect Verin from this Assassin. She didn't care about anything else.

She stormed into the chapel and found the Monk kneeling in prayer.

"That book is full of lies," she said and pointed back toward the library.

"It is? Aside from the part you clearly did not appreciate, what was a lie?"

She thought about it. Technically, nothing. Everything the lunatic had said had come true, but that didn't mean this Scourge business was true.

"Well, nothing, but this business with the Assassin ... I can't believe the Promised Victor turns evil. That's impossible."

"You're angry. You didn't find what you came for and instead found something that displeases you. I am sorry, I really am, but that is the will of the Divine Lights. Do you have faith?"

"Of course I do."

"Isn't faith about believing, even when you don't wish to?"

"I suppose."

"So, you are not a part of the Victor's prophesied companions. Is it fame you seek or justification? Your faith should be justification enough."

"He can't turn evil."

"That's why the Assassin is there, to prevent that from happening."

"What do you know of this Assassin?"

"Hardly anything. There is a book out there that speaks of him. All we know is that he will come after the Victor sires a child and defeats the Enemy."

Greza sat down on a creaking bench and rubbed her temples.

"Not what you expected, huh?" The monk said.

He stood up with some effort and came over to sit beside her. He patted her knee.

"This can't be right," she said.

"It is. That is not the only book that speaks of this."

"How do you know so much about what I'm seeking?"

"Simple. I was told you'd come here one day and seek to find your place, that you would not find it and that you will have a terrible choice to make."

"Told? By who?"

He pointed upward and smiled his haggard smile.

Chapter Twenty-Eight

GREZA RODE BACK TO THE OCCUPIED CITY and went straight to her room. All she could think about was Verin dying from some Assassin's blade. If this Assassin appeared, she'd kill him.

So many of the Victor's Companions had appeared, all that was left was the Princess and the Assassin. But what if the Assassin was already here? It wouldn't be until after the Victory that he'd make himself known. It could be anyone and if she ever found him, she would kill him before he could destroy Verin.

Onata knocked and let herself in without waiting for an answer.

"They said you were back. We're having a meeting in the throne room," Onata said as she walked in and looked around. "You're much neater than I am."

She wanted to tell Onata to go away because she couldn't think of anything good to say and wasn't in the mood for any of her jokes.

Onata paused and cocked her head to the side. The bells on her horns jingled.

"You alright?"

"I'm well enough."

"You don't look well enough."

If she didn't do something Onata would keep pestering her. So she slid her feet onto the floor and stood up.

"We have a meeting to go to," Greza said.

"Wait, did something happen?"

"It's nothing."

Greza led the way to the meeting where all the mercenary generals and captains were. There were about thirty of them with their most trusted assistants. As usual, Verin was in the center pointing at a bunch of maps with colored wooden pieces.

She took her place behind him and he gave her a quick nod and a warm smile.

For once that smile didn't comfort her. Now when she saw his face she saw his death by an assassin.

Even worse was the thing she was trying not to think about: the Scourge. Verin turning into a tyrant was impossible. He was the Promised Victor. He was the blessed child that would grow up to save the world.

"Three armies?" Decaron asked in his overly dramatic manner, but it did get her attention.

"That's right," Verin said. "The Empire's sending three armies our way. We're good but we can't take on three at once."

"Then we can't allow them to meet up," Decaron said.

"Clearly," another general said.

"My Satyr scouts can destroy bridges, block passes and cut down trees," the blonde woman general said. She was a large woman with her hair in several thick braids. She usually stayed silent during the meetings and seemed content to go along with what the others said. Maybe she was just quiet.

"We'll need to send every scout we have to delay two armies," Verin said. "We can take them if we face them one at a time. It might be one battle after another, but we can do it."

He was sounding far more confident about this than she did. She wasn't feeling confident about much at all at the moment.

They continued on to discuss the best place to face the enemy armies. The vast plains of the eastern provinces didn't give them a lot of variety in their choices.

Greza tried to pay attention. This was important and she had to understand it. However, her mind kept wandering to that book written by a forgotten mad prophet. He had been right about everything. Was it possible that he was wrong about Verin?

✶✶✶✶

IT TOOK TWO WEEKS FOR THE FIRST IMPERIAL ARMY TO arrive. They were supposed to have linked up with two other armies but due to the scout war that slowed them down, they missed their deadline and Verin's armies attacked and routed the first army with little trouble. The Combined Army charged into the defending Imperial lines and they broke after two assaults. Their cavalry was chased off in the very beginning, leaving their flanks wide open.

Their spies reported that it was an enormous embarrassment in the Capital and that the people were questioning their soldiers' and generals' ability to defend them. Their civic morale was at an all time low.

Also, three provinces were now in open rebellion. Their small rebellions weren't a threat individually, but uncooperative provinces denied resources to the Imperials while at the same time adding strength to the Combined Army.

Their army was camped on the plains waiting for their scouts to report the position of the nearest enemy army.

The mercenary officers and generals were gathered around their fires. Verin was standing off to the side, lost in thought in the deep grass. She knew that expression well. He seemed to wear it more often these days.

She shook thoughts of him becoming a tyrant out of her head and approached him.

"What worries you, my Duke?"

"Rumors and hearsay."

She took a few more steps closer so she could be right in front of him. He looked up from the ground and gave a half smile.

"It's my job to worry, not yours," he said.

"It's my job to worry about you."

"I don't understand why you believe in me. Yes, I know about your silly prophecy, but can't you see that I'm nothing special?"

"No, I can't see that."

He was anything but ordinary. He was unlike any man she had ever known. He was the only man she cared about. If she could spend the rest of her life at his side, she could die filled with joy.

She loved him.

She had never been in love before, not even close to being so, but she knew that this was love.

She loved Duke Verin and knew perfectly well how ridiculous that was. He would never look at her with any degree of equality. She was just a soldier in his army.

Then she heard orders being shouted out in the camp and a few moments latter a soldier from one of the allied mercenary armies ran up to Verin and saluted.

"Duke, an ... ambassador from the Empire is here and wishes to speak with you."

"How many with him?"

"He has a whole entourage. Maybe thirty."

"Not some local official then. Good. That means they're taking us seriously."

"Bring them up?"

"Only bring him and two others."

"Yes, Duke."

The messenger then ran off.

All over soldiers were coming from their fires to get a look. There wasn't much else to do at night and this promised to at least be a diversion.

She hurried and found Onata near the kitchens and dragged her to where the meeting was going to be. They took their places behind Tempest and Alethia who were standing on either side of Verin sitting on a folding chair. There was another chair placed on the other side of the fire. A circle of officers and soldiers surrounded them a good fifty feet away.

She tried not to get distracted by wondering what an official from the Empire wanted. She was distracted enough as it was.

The crowd was parting to make way and soon the three men in bright blue and white robes covered in gold 'Seals of Office' appeared. The seals were round with the image of that lion the Empire liked so much. They also held tall staffs with the Seal of the Empire on top. It seemed so pompous and hollow.

The lead one was the youngest. He was clean shaven and probably considered handsome, but he was nothing in comparison to Verin. His hair was in a neat tail and he had bright blue eyes that were almost startling in clarity. The other two had long white and gray beards.

"Welcome to my camp. Have a seat if you would," Verin said.

The young official nodded and took his seat. The two old men took positions behind him, mirroring Onata and her.

"This is an unexpected honor. What may I do for you gentlemen?" Verin asked.

"Duke Verin, I am Barilus Togasha. May we dispense with the pleasantries?" The young official asked.

"I'd be glad to, but I must say that that's not very ambassadorial of you. Shouldn't you be smiling and acting nice?"

"Not to honorless barbarians."

Verin leaned back with a large grin on his face.

"At least we're being honest," Verin said.

"I've come to demand the cessation of your raids on our western borders. Your savagery and wanton murder will not go unpunished."

Verin sat up and cast a confused glance at Greza and then at Tempest. Tempest gave him a barely distinguishable shrug.

"I don't follow," Verin said.

"And here I thought we were being honest," Barilus said.

"What western raids? As you can see, we're still stuck here in the east. I have no forces in the west."

"The western border provinces are some of our weakest but most loyal. They'd be easy pickings for a small diversionary force."

"I think I like that idea. Tempest, make a note to send a diversionary force off to someplace useless."

Verin waved his hand as if to dismiss the issue but Barilus leaned forward.

"You listen to me, peasant Duke. Five towns have been slaughtered leaving no survivors to tell the story. The news that sent me here out of my warm palace was that Dynastak, the largest border city, was burnt to the ground with everyone in it."

"You can't expect me to believe that an entire city was destroyed with no witnesses. If you're going to feed me swill, at least make it look like real food."

"There were witnesses. A group of hunters saw the whole thing from a distance."

"I'm still waiting for the part that's supposed to be interesting to me."

"They said they saw an army of horsemen, so many that the dust cloud filled the horizon."

Verin let out a long breath and then theatrically looked around.

"I know we've been destroying your armies like we were fighting little girls, but there's not that many of us. We're mostly from poor countries that don't use a lot of horses. War horses are for rich folk. We're heavy infantry because that's what we're forced to be. If I could field an army of numberless horsemen, I would. But I can't so I don't."

"I have your word, your sacred word that these raids are not your doing?"

"If it was, I'd tell you to your face and gloat over it."

"Your word?"

"You have my word that it isn't me or anyone I'm connected with."

Greza cracked her knuckles as she thought. A numberless host of destructive enemy from nowhere. No one had explored what was past the vast Wasteland. Expeditions had gone in without coming back.

She leaned over and whispered into Onata's ear.

"The Great Enemy."

Onata had been reading the sacred book and her brow furrowed.

"From the prophecy?"

"Who else could it be?"

Barilus cleared his throat and spoke up.

"It seems your two companions have something interesting to say."

Verin turned around and raised an eyebrow.

"We were just ... it's not important," Greza said.

"No, please, let us hear." Barilus said.

Verin shrugged and waved his hand for her to speak.

"It's just from the prophecy, my Duke."

Verin rolled his eyes.

"Prophecy?" Barilus asked.

"It's a silly idea they got from their dead religion."

"I would like to hear them, if you would humor me," Barilus said.

"Well, Grez, you opened your mouth. Time to step up and speak."

Barilus' face was an unreadable wooden mask. They both sat there, watching her and waiting. Such attention was always as comfortable as being trapped out in a hail storm.

"Ambassador, I and my companion here are followers of the Path of Light," Greza said. Barilus's mask slipped and for a moment he seemed genuinely surprised. "According to the prophecy of the Promised Victor, there will rise a threat that would destroy the Empire if not stopped by the Victor."

"See?" Verin said. "It's silly. Let's move on."

Barilus held up his hand.

"You are followers of the Path of Light?"

"Yes, sir."

"And you believe the prophecy. Wasn't it already proven to be false?"

"Greza, that's enough. Let's move on to something important," Verin said.

Barilus shot a glance to Verin.

"You're invading my homeland and I'm not trying to kill you at the moment. The least you could do is permit me to hear this woman's story."

Verin threw his hands in the air.

"Please go on," Barilus said.

"Well, we believe the Victor did not die. He was kidnapped and raised as a slave. He does not know who he is but I do. He is alive and fulfilling his divine mission. I also believe that these raids are the first wave of the Great Enemy that will come and threaten the existence of the Empire. Only the Victor can save us."

Her voice had been clearer than she could have hoped for and she didn't feel like a total idiot.

"See? Ridiculous, isn't it?" Verin said.

Barilus smiled.

"I find it fascinating. I suppose the next question is obvious. Who do you believe to be the Lost Victor?"

She looked around at the hundreds of people standing around the fire. Soldiers and officers from every army were all listening to her at that moment. This was meant to be. She only had to have the courage to speak the truth.

"Duke Verin is the Lost Victor. At his side here are the Raven and the Bull. He has united the most powerful army on the continent in time to meet the threat that could destroy us all. The prophecy is true and here he is."

She waved a hand at Verin and held her gaze on Barilus to judge his reaction.

The crowd was silent and she wasn't brave enough to look up and see why.

Barilus sat there with his hand on his chin, moving his gaze between her and Verin and back again.

Hushed whispers began spreading through the crowd and soon the roar of debate was sweeping through the army.

"And you don't believe this?" Barilus asked Verin.

"Not a word."

Barilus looked to Greza.

"And what is your name?"

"Greza."

"Just Greza?"

"Just Greza."

"I will remember you. This has been far more fascinating than I had imagined." He stood up and brushed his robes off. "I believe that these attacks are not your doing, Duke. We will send further word within the next day or two. Our armies will not attack you in that time. May I ask for temporary truce until we receive more word?"

"You have one week," Verin said.

Barilus thanked them and left with his men.

Greza watched them go and heard the crowd erupt in whispers.

Verin turned to Greza.

"That was odd, Grez. I don't know if I should be furious or if I should be laughing. I think you just convinced half our men that I'm some prophesied hero."

"The evidence fits."

"It's too early to tell if I could use this to my advantage or not. I really hope this doesn't backfire in my face."

Chapter Twenty-Nine

FOR THE NEXT WEEK, THE COMBINED ARMY camped within sight of two Imperial armies. Neither side moved while they waited on the temporary truce. By the eighth day Verin's own spies were sending word of an army from the west poring into the Empire's territory. Each day's message made the image clearer and clearer.

Barilus returned two weeks later with a larger delegation of men and women in more elaborate robes than his. Some wore decorative armor with swords on their hips that had never been used in anger.

"Looks like they brought us some counts and barons, maybe a few generals," Verin said. He didn't sound impressed.

"They come to beg surrender, I imagine," Greza said.

Verin chuckled.

"If only, Grez. If only." Then the smile vanished from his face. "No, I imagine they'll try to get a truce with me while they deal with this new enemy. They'll send their armies west, fight off this threat and then return to me with an army that actually knows how to fight."

This time the meeting place was a cleared out circle with cushioned benches. The soldiers were to remain out of hearing range.

Verin stood in front of his simple chair. Tempest and Alethia were on either side and Onata and she were behind them. Decaron and the other mercenary generals were also there, whispering to each other about what this meant for their profit and chances of victory.

The Imperial delegation made their way through the camp. Their progress was easy to track because they carried tall banners and the Imperial symbol of the Golden Lion.

It was all so hypocritical. They spent so much time and effort to make themselves seem so important. Yet all they did was sit around trying to think of new ways to entertain themselves. They made their peasants and slaves do all the work while they sat on couches fanning themselves. How long could society withstand supporting such useless people?

She tried not to show her disdain as the delegation entered the circle. Barilus was at the head but he was no longer the leader. A man with a bigger staff and taller cylindrical hat was the one everyone circled around.

"Duke Trimalius, the Emperor's brother," Decaron whispered to Verin.

"Moron?"

"Quite intelligent, actually. More so than his brother."

The procession came to a halt and Barilus stepped forward. This time he did all the formalities Greza remembered from the nobles and then some. He introduced everyone in the procession and went on to explain that they were sent by the Emperor himself.

That got her attention. Only the most important issues received the condensation of the Emperor. The large delegation and the Emperor's authority told that this wasn't an ordinary meeting.

She saw that the others felt it as well. Something was different.

"I'm Duke Verin and these are my people." He waved his hand around to indicate everyone on his side. "Please have a seat and let's talk."

The delegation took their seats in a half circle with Duke Trimalius at the center. The Duke cleared his throat.

"Duke Verin of the Combined Army, I have been authorized by the Emperor himself to treat with you," Trimalius said. "I bring a matter of urgency to you that we must discuss."

"I'm listening," Verin said.

"We request that you cease all hostile action against the Empire."

"Why should I do that?"

Greza noticed the lack of disrespectful tone from the emissary. Usually the Empire loved to talk down to everyone, but they were treating him as an equal. Things must be more desperate in the Empire than they realized.

"As you have heard, there is a vast army from the west. They crossed the wastelands and arrived at our borders and are currently causing untold devastation in our western provinces."

"Why should I care? Isn't that good news for me?"

She knew Verin. He was playing a game with them, pretending he wasn't worried about this new army. The fact that the cease-fire had ended a week ago and he hadn't attacked showed otherwise.

Duke Trimalius cleared his throat and for the first time looked uncomfortable.

"I'm sure, Duke Verin, that you've heard details of this army. As of yet, all reports have been vague and from a distance. We received our news from a carrier two hours ago. This army from the west is a race we've never encountered before. They are not an army of riders as we previously thought. They are a race of half man, half horse. They wear heavy armor, are well practiced with the bow and will slaughter everyone they see."

Verin shot quick glances to his companions and Greza shot one to Onata whose narrowed gaze told her that Onata was worried. Onata didn't get worried easily.

The Duke continued.

"That is not all. They use another previously unknown race as scouts: a race of half woman-half bird. They ride as one vast horde, far more numerous than all our armies combined. They charge in fast and hit with the power of a lightning bolt. Our Western Territories Army has been annihilated in our first encounter two days ago."

A burst of murmuring came from the mercenary generals. Even Decaron seemed unsettled.

"You are being uncharacteristically forthcoming with me," Verin said.

"Indeed. It is because we have no other choice. I don't need to insult your intelligence but you see that the Empire is on the threshold of destruction. Your army from the east and this unheard of enemy from the west. As our recent battles have embarrassingly proven, we are not in a position to defend from one, let alone two."

"Why not make a truce with them?"

"There is no dealing with them. They kill every messenger we send."

"So then, why tell me?"

Duke Trimalius looked to his fellow officials and they gave him their nodding permission. Then the Duke stood up and banged his staff on the ground five times. It was the ceremonial signal that what came next would be an official proclamation from the Emperor.

"The Empire is in dire need now more than ever in its entire five thousand year history. We need someone who can lead our armies to victory against this unknown enemy. The Empire is prepared to grant you land and titles in exchange for leading your and our armies against these western foes."

The mercenaries again burst into conversation but Verin held up his hand.

"I have no use for land or titles."

Then Barilus stepped forward.

"Duke Verin, you claim to fight for the people, the same people that are being slaughtered by the thousands. They're my countrymen. If you truly came to help them, then save them."

Duke Trimalius patiently waved for Barilus to sit back down.

"Very well. The Emperor did not believe you would be swayed so easily. We know why you have come. You may not believe it, but we do understand."

"You're right. I don't believe it. I know this army is slaughtering people and I will cease further hostilities against the Empire until you can deal with this enemy yourselves. Once that is over, then we will continue our war here."

"No!" Barilus shouted. "You still don't see, Verin. This isn't an army like yours. They cover the horizon. They shake the earth beneath their hooves. Our scouts have estimated that their forces number at least two million."

"Two million?" Verin blurted out. "Impossible."

"Not impossible. True. If you stand aside now and let them destroy the Empire, there will be nothing left for you to claim and then this savage horde will descend on you and destroy everything you hold dear. If we don't work together now to stop them, we are all dead."

Trimalius stepped forward.

"As reward for your service to the Empire and leading our armies against this enemy, the Emperor will crown you heir to the Empire and give you his daughter's hand in marriage."

Greza sighed.

This is how Verin finds the Princess, then. She was watching the prophecy unfold before her eyes. She didn't feel nearly as surprised as most everyone appeared to be. The details were certainly horrifying and the number of enemies seemed impossible to overcome, yet she knew this was all meant to be. There was a way to defeat them and Verin would find the way.

Still, being proclaimed heir was surprising. That would explain how Verin could start a dynasty. She would never have thought the Empire willing to give a mercenary such honors.

"Think about it, Verin," Barilus said. "Once you are Emperor, you can make whatever laws you deem just. You can free the slaves and make the world how you wish; all you need to do is defeat this enemy."

Verin scratched his head and looked over to her. Greza nodded for him to accept it. His shoulders sank.

"Tell me what else you know of this enemy," he said.

"They seem to be organized into twenty separate hordes. At times these hordes will split up to forage for food and scout. They strip the land of anything edible. In battle they are unstoppable."

Verin stood up and began pacing around.

"What think you, gentlemen?" Verin whispered to his generals.

"You think it's as terrible as they say it is?" Tempest asked.

"They are telling the truth," Alethia said.

"You don't need magic to see how desperate they are," Decaron said. "I've never seen Imperial officials act so ...frightened. They're not telling us all, but I think the part they aren't telling is the gory details."

"Two million horsemen?" one of the generals said. "How are we supposed to face two million fully armored horsemen?"

"We have our Combined Army, the rebel provinces, and the five remaining Imperial armies," Verin said.

"Which aren't worth a damn," Decaron said.

"Not yet, but we can make them," Verin said.

"You have a plan already," Greza said. She could see it plainly on his face. He smiled.

"I think so, Grez."

Verin then turned around to face the Imperial delegation.

"Tell your Emperor that I accept his conditions. I will lead your armies to victory against this savage enemy. I will need to consult with your generals immediately. We need a war council."

Within the hour they had Verin's generals and five Imperial generals gathered around a table arguing over maps. Word was being sent back to the Imperial Capital by carrier hawk.

It was strange to watch these men, who just hours ago were enemies, talk and discuss matters of war like they were familiar colleagues. Verin had a disarming way about him that seemed to put the Imperials at ease and they had a common language: war.

"I've been doing some math in my head," Onata said.

"I hate math."

"So do I, especially after this. Our Combined Army with the Imperial armies comes out to about two hundred thousand. At most."

"Ten to one."

"And we've seen the quality of the Imperial forces."

Greza cracked her knuckles and tried not to let worry cloud her face.

"This won't be an easy fight."

It's not just the war. It's what comes after the Victory that worries me.

The meeting was mostly about immediate concerns with integrating the armies and of course, logistics. Verin didn't seem to care that the men standing beside him were Imperial. He only cared about victory now.

After the strategy meeting that had lasted four hours, Greza followed Onata, Tempest, Alethia and Verin into his personal tent. She closed the flaps behind her. Verin went to his table that was covered in maps, reports and a large two-handed sword. He picked up a jug of wine and poured himself a glass.

"What did I just agree to?" He asked after taking a drink.

"I'm not sure," Tempest said.

"I believe you just agreed to become the heir to an empire you despise," Alethia said.

"Desperation," Greza said.

"It's the Enemy from the prophecy, Verin. Accept it," Alethia said.

"Not you too. I get enough of that from Greza."

"Maybe they're right about this," Tempest said.

Verin lowered his glass and cocked his head at Tempest.

"They got you believing?"

Tempest shook his head.

"I don't know about all that Victor garbage, but they might have been right about the Enemy. The timing is correct and if we don't stop it, sounds like they'll destroy the Empire and us along with it."

"A new race," Alethia said. "I wonder who they are."

"Doesn't matter. We have to destroy them," Verin said.

The coldness in Verin's voice seeped into her chest.

"And that leads me to the next matter," Tempest said. "You've just agreed to fight for the Empire against an army of two million armored horse-men. Not one million, but two. What are we supposed to do?"

"I think fleeing might be called for," Alethia said.

"Greza? What do you think?"

Greza had to clear her throat before answering. She still wasn't used to being asked her opinion.

"I think we can win. It won't be easy, but I know we can."

"Because your religion says so?"

"No, because they've already shown their weakness," Greza said.

"Unless being numerous and ultra powerful is a weakness, I haven't seen it," Onata said.

Greza looked to the others but they seemed as baffled as Onata.

"They're stripping anything edible from the countryside. Think of it.

Two million horse-men. How much food do they need on a daily basis? They crossed the vast wasteland to get here, so they either have one extremely long supply train or they have a limited and shrinking supply with them."

"We starve them," Verin said with a growing smile.

"Yes, I thought this was what you meant when you said you had a plan," Greza said.

"No, I was thinking something else. This is better."

"Starve them, eh?" Tempest said.

"At what sacrifice?" Alethia asked.

"It won't be pleasant," Greza said.

"Verin?" Tempest asked.

"We'll have to evacuate every farm and town in their path: basically all of the western provinces."

"That's impossible," Tempest said.

"Impossible or not, we have to do it and put everything we leave behind to the torch."

"You're talking about destroying half the Empire."

"To save the whole, yes. Once the Enemy is gone we can rebuild."

"It won't be that easy," Alethia said.

"No, it won't be," Verin said. "They'll come to battle sooner or later and we'll have to face them."

"And you have a plan for this, correct?" Tempest asked.

"I believe so."

They spent most of the night discussing strategy and tactics, mostly about how to deal with overwhelming cavalry formations. When Tempest and Alethia went off to bed she was about to leave with Onata.

"Greza, could you stay a while?" Verin asked.

Immediately she began to plan out her apologies for having refused his advances. Was this the conversation she had been dreading? Had she lost his confidence?

She nodded to Onata to go on without her and she turned around to face him.

"Of course, my Duke."

He held out a glass of wine for her and she shook her head.

"I figured now would be a good time to start drinking," he said.

"Now would be the worst time."

"Probably true. Come, sit."

He took a long drink.

He sat down in his cushioned chair and leaned back. She took the simpler chair by his side.

"Grez, you really believe that all this is your prophecy coming to life."

"It's plain to see."

"And I'm destined to save the Empire and start a dynasty, right?"

"That is correct."

"What if I don't want to?"

"Don't want to what?"

"I don't want to be an emperor. I don't want some forced marriage to same vapid royal slut. I already have most of what I want. If I can free the slaves then I'll be more than satisfied."

"Then this is your chance."

"But I don't like the price."

"We don't always like the role required of us. You don't think I have other desires?"

"You? I thought you wanted this?"

Greza shook her head and held up her battered gauntlets that had killed too many people to count.

"Then what would you want?" He asked.

"I just want to be left alone where I can read and maybe find new talents. Maybe start a family like the one I never had."

I also want him. More than anything else I want to be with him and for him to notice me for what I am on the inside.

He put his glass on the table and leaned forward.

"I thought you loved all this."

"I could never love this."

"I had no idea."

"And you, my Duke? What is it you want?"

"Safety for my people. I'd do anything to make sure everyone has enough to eat and a roof over their heads. I'd make everyone equal. No one would hold the lash over another again. They'll regret making me heir. If I become emperor I'll tear down their high palaces and use the rubble to make houses for the poor. I'd kick them all out into the streets and let them beg."

Greza watched his face as he spoke. He wasn't joking or exaggerating. He was saying exactly what was on his mind.

"Wouldn't that only cause more suffering?"

"They deserve to suffer, Grez. All their lives, for countless generations they grew fat off the labor of our brothers. They have to be punished."

She had to stop this before he grew into the prophesized tyrant.

"Many don't know any better. They were born into this life and told from birth that this is how things are. Things need to change, but not with violence."

"They have eyes, Grez. Don't try to defend them. You of all people know what cruelties they're capable of."

"I do, but that's because they haven't been taught. Teach them, don't destroy them."

"Justice. I'll teach them about justice. Maybe after they learn their lessons I'll show some mercy." He chuckled and shook his head. "Maybe."

"Revenge is beneath you. This is your chance to create the peaceful society the world needs."

"I'd love to believe you, Grez, but I don't see people accepting a bunch of good will. I'll have to be harsh to change anything."

She left his tent more saddened than confused. This wasn't the Verin she loved. This was something else. Had he been hiding this bitterness beneath his smiles or was he just voicing dark thoughts that he'd regret in the morning?

She didn't know the answer and the possibilities kept her awake most of the night.

In the morning Verin met with the Imperial generals and they all began to make plans. They showed Verin the movements of the Enemy horde. They were slow and methodical with occasional bursts of shocking speed and savagery.

Their only chance to prepare the evacuations and burnings was to slow the Enemy down.

"You really think we'll win?" Onata whispered.

"I do. But I think the cost will be very painful."

"How bad?"

"Very bad."

Chapter Thirty

THE CAMP WAS NOW FILLED WITH IMPERIAL soldiers. Their shiny armor and fancy banners were everywhere. Mixed in with them were mercenary veterans teaching them how to actually fight. It was Verin's idea to spread his men out to teach the unwarlike Imperials. They were great for beating up beggars and slaves, but not much else.

This mixture of grizzled veterans and shiny parade armor was three days from the Imperial Capital. There, the Emperor would meet Verin personally and Verin would meet his bride-to-be, the Princess.

Greza hoped she would be stupid and annoying. She didn't want to meet the Princess even if she was a part of the Prophecy.

The scouts and Imperial rangers were already out, burning evacuated farms, blocking roads and picking off small groups. They were good at what they did and every bit helped. It was their only chance. Starvation was their greatest weapon. Their armies could never defeat these hordes in a battle, but they could delay them until they starved. It was a simple mathematical formula, as Onata said, "Bodies plus time plus amount of food destroyed equals victory.

Every unit in the army here was in a massive push to train. It wasn't just making Imperial soldiers into actual soldiers, but also about countering massive amounts of heavy cavalry. Cavalry was usually a very small percentage of the army and heavy cavalry even more so. Riders were mostly scouts or flankers.

What would a wall of fully armored horsemen riding right at her look like?

She shook her head to avoid imagining it and went looking for Onata. Verin had a meeting in an hour and wanted his bodyguards with him. They were sending out another brigade to hold off a horde incursion while another city was evacuated.

That's what everyone around camp was calling them, the Horde.

Then she saw Barilus walking towards her. She looked away and tried to find something else to do. She didn't want to kill them for revenge, but she didn't want to be their best friends either. This man was an important part in a system that destroyed her mother and thousands of others.

"Greza, I've been meaning to speak with you," he said.

She looked up as if she hadn't noticed him.

"I'm awfully busy," she said.

"I won't take long."

She sighed as she realized she wasn't a good enough liar to get out of this.

"Very well," she said and folded her arms.

"I'm very interested in how you came to believe that Lord Verin is the Promised Victor."

Everyone had been asking her about that. Ever since she'd announced it in front of the entire army, people had been approaching her and asking if it was true.

"Is that a polite way of asking if I'm crazy?"

He shook his head.

"Not at all. If you would, please tell me."

Might as well get it over with.

She went through a basic but complete account of why she knew he was the Promised Victor. She left out what she discovered in the monastery library about the Scourge and the Assassin.

"It's a rare day to find a true believer, let alone a young one. Most of the old ones only hold to it out of habit."

"Yes, I've discovered that for myself."

He smiled and leaned against a tree. The camp was on the edge of a forest with most of the army spread out in what used to be farmland.

"You don't like me," he said.

"I don't know you."

"No, but I'm a part of the Empire that enslaved you."

How did he know she was a slave? Was there something obvious about her?

"It doesn't matter what I think about you."

"It does. Do you want revenge, Greza? Do you want to see me and my fellow nobles torn down and trampled in the mud?"

"No," she could say honestly.

"You should."

"The Divine Lights teach us that revenge only causes more pain and suffering and the cycle continues."

"They also teach us that justice cannot be ignored."

"Well, maybe once Verin's on the throne we can have justice."

"Doesn't it burn you to see us in all our finery, asking for help? We clearly don't deserve it. Instead we're asking the people we oppressed for help."

"I see people that need help. Yes, a small elite group of them is responsible for horrible things, but we need to save the people first."

"And there you have a good mixture of mercy and justice. The Divine Lights would be pleased."

She laughed.

"And what would you know of them?" She asked.

He reached down into his robe and took out a small necklace. It was a gold circle with a starburst in the center. It looked just like the one Erinad use to wear.

"You?" She asked.

He nodded.

She didn't want to believe it, but the man who had taught her the Path had been an Imperial noble as well. She had to remember the Path and know that she couldn't judge people by outward appearances.

"My father was the High Priest. When the Victor was lost, he retired to his villa and stayed there."

"But why you?"

"A noble can't be a good person and try to make the world a better place?"

"In theory, yes."

He sighed and put his necklace back inside.

"It didn't used to be like this, Greza. The Empire used to stand for something. It was founded by rebels fighting for freedom and now look at it. It's far worse than the tyrant we rebelled against."

"Are there any others?"

"A few. We keep quiet mostly."

"Do you have a plan?"

"Just trying to change things from the inside. I was getting discouraged when suddenly I hear this young woman say she'd found the Victor."

"Do you believe he is?"

"I do."

"And you know the prophecy?"

"I do. When you said he was the Victor, everything tumbled into place in my mind. Before, I didn't understand why the Emperor would offer his daughter. Now I know. It was meant to be."

Greza didn't find the thought of the prophecy being unavoidable at all comforting any more.

"We're on the Path. Verin will meet the Princess and they will marry. He will then defeat the Horde and raise a family, the beginning of a dynasty," he said.

"Have you heard anything else?"

"Of the prophecy?"

"Yes, about what happens after the Victory?"

"There's a new Imperial dynasty that will last at least a thousand years if the Divine Lights will it."

"Nothing else?"

"No, why? Have you heard something?"

"No, nothing."

He squinted at her.

"What aren't you telling me?"

"Nothing. I have to go."

He stepped in front of her, almost too close. This was a man used to giving orders and his confidence surrounded him like a haze of smoke from a fire.

"Greza?"

There was no escaping him. Even if she fled now, he'd find her later and maybe draw it out of her where others could hear. She was trapped.

"There's one more person from the prophecy. Mad Prophet Ezzanshial said that there will also be the Assassin and that he will kill the Victor after he conceives a child."

He remained silent for a few moments as he thought.

"Is there any information on who this Assassin might be?"

"None."

"I'll see what I can find. In the meantime, guard Verin with your life."

"Of course."

He gave her a respectful bow and left.

She was glad and bothered at the same time. She had finally found another believer, but he was a noble. The Divine Path dictated that everyone was equal to the gods. She wasn't sure she could live up to that standard.

Her eyes saw a man who had grown up in luxury while stepping on the backs of the poor. How could he be a righteous person? It was impossible.

Her emotions told her the man was a dog, but her mind where her beliefs held residence, told her that she knew the man was a brother in the faith and that right now, she had to take whatever help she could find.

★★★★

THE MERCENARY AND IMPERIAL ARMIES MARCHED TO within sight of the Capital. The ancient city of Torna was a sprawling ocean of buildings that had long since overrun the protective walls.

The River Apia came down from the mountains to the east and twisted through the plains and through the city where it split. From Torna, the Apia went to the two Empire lakes that were to the north and south of the city. The only way to approach the city with a full army was from the west: which happened to be the way the Horde was coming from.

Even from several miles away Greza could see the hazy outlines of impossibly tall towers with glittering roofs. She saw the fat shape of enormous domes and the dark gray line of the defensive wall rising above the vast city.

But the most impressive thing about the city was its immense size. They were still a long way off and already she could make out shapes of individual buildings. The walls of the city had to be higher than the walls of other castles.

"Impressive, isn't it?" Onata asked.

"But will it look as nice up close?"

"Maybe more, maybe less."

"You've been here before?"

"When I was young. Before I was sold."

Onata tapped her hoof to her horse's flank and rode forward. Greza stayed and looked at the giant, hazy city.

In that city was the Princess. That was who Verin would marry and there was nothing she could do about it. But what was she supposed to expect? That he would fall in love with an Ork soldier?

Even before she knew she was dreaming it she knew the dream was ridiculous. She shouldn't waste time longing for things she could never have.

An impossible desire if left to fester like a wound, will twist and malform the one who lets it worm into their mind. – Book of Cannitas, Scroll 8, Verse 14.

She had to let him go and stop thinking about him. He was so far out of reach that it was foolish to even entertain the thought.

Then he rode up beside her and all thoughts of giving him up vanished. She watched him from the corner of her eye. Every move he made was deliberate and powerful. When he looked around he was seeing everything. He watched the way the mule drivers managed their heavy cargoes. He saw how his troops marched in formation and the state of their equipment. Nothing escaped his notice.

"It's a beautiful city, isn't it?" He said.

"Have you seen it before?"

"No, but it's as good a place for a last stand as any."

"They're not unbeatable."

"They are now, but they won't be."

"And how is that going?"

He shrugged.

"As good as can be expected. It's like trying to drain a lake with pin holes. But that's not what worries me at the moment."

"What else, my Duke? Is there more news from the front?"

He pointed a gloved hand at the city.

"I'm about to walk into the capital of the Empire and meet the Emperor face to face."

"Oh, yes. Of course."

He would also meet his fiancé there. She had no doubt that the Princess would be gorgeous. She would have flowing hair and gowns made of the most expensive silk. Her skin would be smooth and not have a single scar.

Greza in comparison wore army wool and leather. Her unwashed hair was tied in a simple, unglamorous bun and countless scars marred her skin.

Verin had tried to get her in his bed because she had been the only female around. Now that there were actual beautiful women around, he wouldn't cast his eyes in her direction again.

Entering the city meant an end to her dream.

The army camped well outside the city while Verin, his entourage and Imperial officers and diplomats continued on. They had stopped long enough for everyone to freshen up. Verin had some of his men polish Greza and Onata's armor for them. When the two of them stepped out of their tent, they looked better than they had for months. Even their boot buckles were polished to a shine.

"We look good," Onata said.

"Yes, but you look better."

"Shame we won't be very popular in there. We were attacking their Empire a short while ago."

"Which means we have to be extra cautious in there. This still might be a trap."

"Or some noble with a grudge."

They didn't have to say more. They knew their job.

The procession, escorted by mercenaries and Imperial soldiers, made their way through the sprawling "Out Town" and through the massive defensive gates of the "Old City's" walls. The city walls were as tall as the Chimera's fortress's towers and the palace's walls were going to be even taller.

Once inside the city, the buildings changed from wood to stone and grew taller and taller as they rode closer to the palace. There were cathedrals that once belonged to the Divine Light that were now owned by other, smaller churches. There were bright colors everywhere. Houses had gold and brass pipes and figurines of Imperial heroes on their roofs. There were mansions, public theaters, coliseums, government buildings and finally they came to the walls of the Imperial Palace. The walls towered over all but the tallest cathedral domes and she had to crane her neck to see the top.

The streets were lined with people. There was no cheering or booing. They watched the procession in silence and Greza could see the fear on their faces. They knew what was coming. Some looked at Verin and could barely contain their disgust. Others looked at him as their hope for salvation.

The historian in her wanted to know all about the walls. She wanted to know how and by whom they were built. Dozens of questions rose up as they made their way through the gate. She kept her mouth shut though. Now was not the time for her idle curiosity.

Her attention snapped back to Verin and looking around for any movements that might be a clue to an attack. She scanned the crowd of people. Onata was doing the same. Both of them had their hands on the grips of their carbines.

Once inside the palace walls, the gates closed behind them. Within the walls was a vast compound covered in gardens, fountains, buildings that were decorated with marble columns. It seemed that each building was done in a different architectural style: the only commonality between them was the obscene wealth they took to build. A building to her right had three stories and each one had colonnades supporting the wrap around balconies. It was one of the smaller, less impressive buildings.

In front of them was the tallest building she had ever seen. It was like a man-made mountain of towers that grew taller and narrower as it reached up to the sky. The central mass of the building was a somewhat brutal looking fortress, but it seemed that towers were added on later and more after that until it was a forest of towers. The practical beginning had been covered by useless vanity. The doors at the base of the man-made mountain were at least five stories tall and made of brass with wide marble steps leading up to them. Scenes from the Empire's history in frieze covered the doors. Again, she wished she had time to stop and study.

Suddenly horns and drums played in a painfully loud song that she'd never heard before. She could tell the song was supposed to be powerful and majestic, but instead it just sounded pretentious and overbearing. Everyone that was mounted, dismounted and servants came and took their horses.

The great, vaulted doors of the palace opened. A procession of women holding colorful streamers danced out, followed by men in gilded armor and giant two-handed swords. Next were nobles in ridiculously extravagant robes and it looked like a rainbow coming down the steps. Finally, after a silly display of pageantry, the Emperor appeared. She almost laughed. After all that display of power, what walked out was an old man in robes that looked too large for him and a crown that added a good two feet to his height to compensate for his natural lack thereof.

Her smile vanished when she saw who stood beside him. Greza immediately know who it was. It was the Princess and she was the most beautiful woman she had ever seen. She had long, glowing blond hair that almost reached the ground with locks of hair tied in intricate loops decorated with pearls. Her silk dress was black decorated with massive silver jewelry that glinted in the sun. Her pale blue eyes looked out disinterestedly at the scene before her.

That was the woman Verin was to marry instead of her.

"The Princess, I assume?" Alethia said from behind her.

Greza hadn't noticed her approach.

"It is," Greza said.

"Definitely," Onata said.

The idea that she could have ever competed against the Princess seemed more and more absurd by the second.

"That the Princess?" Tempest said as he walked up to them.

"Clearly," Alethia said.

"Yeah, I can..." but Tempest trailed off and never finished the thought. He was too busy gawking at the gorgeous creature that stood at the top of the stairs.

Greza tore her eyes away and looked to Verin. He was staring as well. How could he not. Verin would be glad now that she had refused him. No one could think of her with any amount of joy when they had the Princess in front of them. It would be like offering a full eight-course meal with spiced duck, roasted pork and aged wine after a meager bowl of gruel. Once a person was starving, sure the gruel looked nice. Show him the full feast and he wouldn't touch the gruel if he was offered coin.

She hated being gruel.

She wasn't in the prophecy and had no part in Verin's story and now she had to deal with being gruel. The afterlife promised her a reward for being faithful, but for just once she'd like something nice in her mortal life.

The Emperor greeted them and the ceremony began. Verin dismounted and handed over his sword before approaching the aged ruler. He came to within a few paces and knelt down on both knees.

The Emperor then began some long speech that she couldn't even hear. She was about to try to move closer when something caught her eye. Onata's head jerked in the same direction so she hadn't imagined it.

The crowd was mostly still but they saw one man moving close to the stairs where Verin and the Emperor were. He was moving too slowly but in the wrong way. His eyes were fixated on Verin and he had a long jacket that he kept closed with one hand.

They didn't have to say anything. Both of them poured through the crowd on an interception course. They had to cut the man off.

The man with the coat and long pale hair went behind a pillar and didn't emerge. Greza pointed at Onata and then at the right side of the pillar. Onata nodded and hurried off to the right to cut the man off.

Greza pushed her way through the assembled people and into the colonnade. But the man wasn't there. Onata appeared and looked around, then threw her hands up.

They began scanning the crowd again. Onata jumped up on to the base of a statue of some half naked hero and Greza continued to push through the crowd, looking for the man with long hair. She kept her hand on the short carbine on her thigh.

Then she saw him. The man was near the front of the crowd, pushing his way through. Onata was up near the stairs and saw the man at the same time.

"Get down!" Greza yelled.

Heads turned toward her instead of ducking down. She pulled her carbine out and charged forward.

The man heard her and without turning away from Verin, pulled out two pistols and took aim.

Onata ran for Verin. The guards in gold tried to stop her but she slipped past them like she was made of mist.

Onata reached Verin and managed to fire just as the man fired at the same time. There were puffs of grey smoke and Greza saw the man's head open in a burst of red. But Onata was hit. A bullet struck her in the neck and she tumbled to the ground.

Verin bolted around and crouched beside Onata. The guards in golden armor rushed forward and stood in front of the Emperor who was instantly rushed away. The Princess paused and looked at the bleeding Onata before also being rushed off by guards.

Greza came to the dead assassin and searched him over. He wore fine clothing and the guns he was using would pay for a family of eight to eat for a decade.

Then her eyes shot up to Verin who met her gaze. Onata looked white and the bright blood covered her neck and face.

Verin slowly shook his head.

Onata wasn't breathing.

Chapter Thirty-One

GREZA KNELT DOWN BESIDE ONATA'S STILL body. She was dead. The bullet had torn through her neck. It had been quick but that was a small consolation.

Alethia ran up and crouched down beside her.

"Can you help her?" Greza managed to say through a tight throat.

Alethia shook her head.

"Why not?"

"I can't bring back the dead. Once the spirit leaves the body, it goes somewhere I can't reach it."

"But ..."

Onata was gone. It had happened so fast. In just one instant, she was dead.

Verin put his hand on her shoulder.

"We have to get inside," Verin said.

"What about her?"

Verin pointed to Tempest.

"Please take care of her."

Tempest nodded. Verin then led her through the palace's main door. Golden guards were rushing around everywhere and nobles and generals were yelling at each other over what had just happened.

Greza had a job to do. She had to protect Verin. She took a deep breath and tried to focus on what was going on around them.

Tears welled in her eyes and she kept looking back as the doors closed behind her.

"Are there any more surprises I should know about?" Verin yelled.

A Dark Elf noble rushed up to him with hands outstretched.

"Please, Lord Verin, do not blame us for this. It was the work of a lone man. We had nothing to do with this."

"How many other lone men do I have to worry about?"

Normally Verin kept his emotions in check when dealing with diplomatic situations, but this time he was furious.

"Find out who that man was and find out who his friends were," Verin said.

She could tell that his anger was growing and would not be satisfied until something was done. Probably something drastic. He would not be appeased by half-hearted attempts.

Then the Princess approached him. The generals and nobles were getting as far from him as possible, but she walked up to him. She moved with careful strides and put her hand on his arm.

"Please, Lord Verin. We're doing everything we can. We all knew this was a risk," The Princess said. "You must understand that many still look on you as the enemy. That won't change quickly or easily."

Her voice was soft and beautiful like a song. She reminded her of a bird in spring time: bright and full of life.

"That wasn't just my bodyguard. That was my friend," Verin said.

"And we will find the cause of this. I promise you. Please, we have important business. The enemy is invading our lands and if we don't act many thousands of innocents will die."

Verin looked the Princess in the eyes and Greza saw his rage subside.

"You are correct. We have business."

As the nobles and generals surrounded Verin to placate him, she took the opportunity to hide behind a pillar and take a few deep breaths. Her eyes were burning and she wanted to cry, yell and punch someone in the face. Anyone.

She looked for Onata for advice and when she realized what she was doing, the pain stabbed at her heart even more.

Greza needed someone: anyone, but everyone was busy as they should be. The fate of the entire Empire was on the line. No one had time for an escaped, slave Ork girl.

She closed her eyes, controlled her breathing and went back out.

The meeting was changed from the throne room to a more secluded, but still impressive room. There was thick crimson carpet with a long oak table. The walls were covered with faded murals of famous battles and the chairs had gilded crests of all the major families of the Empire.

It was a room for the self-congratulation of the nobility.

The Emperor, with a guard on each side, sat at the head of the table. They sat Verin at the other end. Greza stood beside him and the space on his other side felt like a gaping wound.

Alethia stepped up and took the other side. Tempest was still outside dealing with everything else.

Decaron and the other mercenary generals took seats opposite the Imperial officials.

No one looked happy.

Then Duke Trimalius stood up and opened the meeting. He gave a very brief overview of the situation as if no one was exactly aware of what was happening. He then repeated the Emperor's offer of alliance and marriage of his daughter in exchange for leading their armies to victory against the invaders.

Verin accepted without speeches or ceremony. He nodded and signed the treaty they placed in front of him. Then the Emperor stood up and announced the engagement and the new heir to the Empire.

Greza was sure that the history books and paintings would lavish this scene with far more pomp and expressive gestures.

Right after the meeting, the Emperor and the Princess were escorted out and Verin was left to discuss the war. That took most of the day. They gave Verin reports of their forces, equipment and leadership. Verin had to clear half the table to lay down a map and mark where all the Empire's assets were. Red marked military units. Blue marked fortified positions. Yellow marked logistical assets and so on.

They argued and debated about troop movements and training new units well into the night. She wasn't sleepy. She couldn't sleep after everything. Her mind was on Onata and couldn't think of anything else. After the meeting adjourned and Verin was shown his quarters with new guards from his army, she went to find Onata.

Onata's body was in the cellar of the palace where it was cold and dry. It was laid out on a stone slab where bodies were stored while awaiting burial.

She sat on a bench built into the wall and looked at Onata's corpse. It wasn't her anymore. It was obviously not her, just an empty shell. The Onata who understood the world in a way Greza never would, was gone.

Her friend was gone.

$$****$$

WHEN SHE AWOKE, SHE WAS LYING ON THE STONE bench in the cellar. The lantern had gone out and it was pitch dark. She didn't know if it was still night or morning. She wondered if anyone was asking for her and made her way in the dark back to the ground floor of the palace.

Soldiers and guards were everywhere. The energy of people rushing around filled the air. Yes, the war was coming closer and everyone knew it. They could feel it too.

When she walked outside, the bright sunlight hurt her eyes and she had to raise a hand to her brow.

"Greza!" She heard Tempest's voice bellow. "There you are. We've been looking everywhere for you."

"I was with Onata."

Tempest's mouth closed. He then waved for her to follow him and she trailed behind as he took her back inside the palace to the same meeting room as before. Verin was discussing the war with his generals, mercenary and Imperial.

When he saw her come in he stopped everything he was doing and hurried over.

"Greza, are you alright?" He asked.

"I'm fine."

"I looked for you last night. We had a room ready for you. Your stuff's there and everything."

"Doesn't matter. You have work to do."

He grabbed her shoulders and looked her in the face.

"Of course it matters. You matter very much."

"I don't. You have more important things to worry about than me."

Verin looked to Tempest.

"Excuse us for a moment," Verin said and then grabbed her arm and pulled her out into the hall. "Listen to me, Greza, you are very important. I won't sit by while my friend's in pain. I'm hurting too. We'll give Onata a proper funeral because she mattered. You matter."

"Why?"

"That's a stupid question."

He broke away from her and leaned against the wall. He folded his arms and looked her up and down.

"You really have no idea who you are, do you?" He asked.

"Of course I know who I am."

"No, you really don't."

"Then who am I?"

"You're my friend. You're not some body guard. You watch my back because I trust you. You're smarter than me. You're nobler than me and you'll always do what's right, regardless of anything else. I need you with me so I can see what I'm supposed to be."

"My Duke, you … think too highly of me."

"I don't, Grez. In fact, I hate myself for not putting you higher. As of right now, you are no longer my bodyguard. You are now my third advisor."

"I couldn't possibly."

"I already look to you for advice on everything. Why not make it official?"

"Verin, it's too much."

He put a hand on her shoulder and stepped closer.

"It's not nearly enough. Do you accept your new position?"

She hadn't seen this coming. If anything she thought she'd be relegated to some lesser position now that he was surrounded by the best of the Empire. She was an embarrassment to be seen with and he wanted to promote her? It didn't make sense.

If she were smart, she'd refuse. Being near him only hurt her.

She nodded.

"Excellent."

Then they heard footsteps coming down the hall. It was the Princess.

"Princess Ariana, it's a pleasure to see you," Verin said.

The Princess's pink lips parted in a smile and she gave a small curtsey.

"I came to see how the war planning is going."

Verin raised an eyebrow.

"Is that something Imperial princesses usually concern themselves over?"

Her smile faded.

"It's my Empire and my people. I have far more of a concern for it than you do."

He bowed.

"You are, of course, correct."

He waved for the door and followed her. At the door he turned back to Greza.

"Advisor, I need you to advise."

She hurried to follow them. She had a job to do and Verin was relying on her to do it.

****

THEY HAD BEEN THERE FOR OVER A WEEK AND THE ENtire time Verin had been working almost non-stop organizing the Empire's defense. He ate and slept in the planning room. She had overheard Imperial generals whispering how impressed they were with Verin and his dedication. He remembered small but important details without trying. He kept the lo-

255

cation and name of every unit in his head and knew how to move them.

Out in the plains to the west of the capital, divisions of troops were training with a new pike formation Verin had thought of. The pikes were to keep the heavy cavalry from charging while gunners stood behind. They were set up in block formations pointing out on each side, like a game board. The superior maneuverability of enemy cavalry would be meaningless to formations like that.

Greza stepped out of the planning room and walked down to the end of the hall where a set of doors were. She opened them and walked out onto the balcony. From there she could see the city spread out in front of her and the game board formations of the armies training off in the distance.

Then the door opened up behind her and Princess Ariana walked out. Not what she needed. She had managed to avoid her this past week thanks to her duties, but now she was trapped.

"Greza, I'm glad I found you. I've been meaning to speak with you," she said in her soft, musical voice.

Greza didn't know if the kindness in her voice was an act that had been rehearsed since childhood or if she was honestly as caring as she appeared to be.

"Of course, your Highness."

Ariana smiled and leaned against the rails. Today her hair was in an insanely intricate braid with gold ribbons twisting in and out. It must have taken a long time to do. She didn't have to work or do anything useful, so why not?

"You know Verin very well, correct?"

"I suppose so."

"We haven't had time to really meet and talk. All I see of him is his work."

"Well, it's important work."

What did this Princess want? Nobility always wanted something.

"Of course it is. That's not what I'm speaking of. I admire his dedication. Tonight is the formal engagement announcement. We're to feast and it will be my first time speaking to him. What is he like? What should I talk about? What should I avoid?"

She didn't want to help her. She was trying to steal the man she loved.

No, that wasn't correct. Verin wasn't hers and Ariana had no choice. She was doing her duty as was Verin.

"He was kidnapped as a child and sold into slavery. So, don't be sympathetic to slavery."

The Princess's hand went to her mouth before she recovered herself.

"Of course not."

"But don't let that fool you into thinking he's not educated. He's smarter than he lets on. He loves books. Before this war started he was always reading."

"Really? What sort of books?"

"I don't think it matters to him. He reads novels, philosophy, history, poetry, and anything else he can get his hands on."

"I never would have guessed."

"So, when you speak to him tonight, speak to him as you would any other educated man. In fact, I imagine that he'd appreciate the distraction. Start talking about Imperial history and stand back."

Ariana nodded.

"I see. Thank you, Greza. They said you were wise and kind."

"Wise and kind? They must not know me very well."

"Perhaps they knew you better than you realize."

"Not likely."

Ariana laughed and looked back to the door.

"I didn't think I'd be engaged so soon," Ariana said. "I always thought I'd avoid it somehow."

"You don't want to marry?"

"I've never wanted to marry."

"Why is that?"

Ariana sighed and then looked directly at her instead of avoiding eye contact like she usually did. It was what nobles did; they never looked directly at their servants.

"Because it's a dungeon without walls. I'd much rather live how I please, not tied to one person. It's so ... limited. But, I'm sure you have better things to do than listen to a spoiled girl."

Greza bowed as the Princess left.

She still didn't understand the Princess and didn't know if she was someone worthy of respect or just a false-faced noblewoman. She hated not knowing.

Eventually the time for the feast came and she escorted Verin to his quarters where he could freshen up and get ready for the feast.

She was about to excuse herself when he stopped her.

"Come on in, Grez. I need someone to talk to."

"Of course, My Duke."

She followed him in and he closed the door.

His apartments were nicer than any she had ever seen. The wooden floor was polished to almost a mirror shine. There were couches, plotted plants, paintings and a chandelier. Everything in here seemed fit for a prince. Even her masters back in Roristan didn't have any room nearly this expensive.

Her own quarters were nicer than anything she was used to, but were a pig pen in comparison to this.

Verin walked behind a screen and she didn't follow. She turned around and examined one of the paintings. It was a woman holding a bunch of flowers in a forest.

"Greza, what do you think of all this?"

"You have a lovely room."

"I mean the war, this alliance, this ... everything."

"I think you're the man to lead us."

"Does your prophecy say I can lose or am I destined to win no matter what?"

"There's always free will. We're not forced to do anything we don't choose ourselves. Onata chose to save you. She didn't have to."

"So, if I make a wrong decision, I can lose and we're all dead."

"You don't talk to me when you want comforting lies, My Duke."

"I suppose not."

Verin then walked out from behind the screen without a shirt on and Greza quickly looked away. She did not want to see that. Actually, she wanted to see it very much but not like this. Not in a room all alone with him.

"I'm supposed to change into these formal clothes. It's far too expensive for me. You could feed a platoon for a week on the cost of this one stupid outfit."

Greza glanced over to see the black and gold clothing lying on one of the couches.

"You're heir to the Empire now. They believe there's a certain standard of dress."

"But I hate it. I don't want to look like them."

"Might I suggest wearing it now to appease them? We all have to make concessions during an alliance. Once you're Emperor, then you can change what you want. Until then, don't give them reasons to go back on their deal."

Her concession was losing him.

He chuckled behind her.

"You're more devious than you seem."

"Just logical."

"And what is your opinion of Princess Ariana?"

"She seems very nice."

"That's all?"

"I don't know her."

"Yes, but you're an excellent judge of character."

Was she? The prophecy said Verin was going to turn into a scourge and she could see his hidden resentment. She knew he was capable of severe actions. Even through that she knew she loved him.

"She is intelligent but hard to read. She keeps her face hidden behind a mask," Greza said.

"I see. That doesn't give me much to go on and I have to prepare myself for an evening with her. Have you heard any rumors about her? Does she have lovers?"

"Would you want to know?"

"Perhaps not. But I'd still like to know what sort of person she is."

"You won't have long to wait."

"I finally get an evening away from the Planning Room and I have to spend it with the Emperor and his daughter. I'd rather spend it with you."

With her? As comrades in arms or ...

"We can't always get what we want," she said as much to herself as to him.

He was engaged now. There was no possible way she could have him. It wouldn't be right.

Once he was changed into the black and gold clothing, she helped him straighten everything out, and looked him over. He was very impressive in the new clothes and looked like a leader. Maybe the Imperials were correct about the theatrics. He looked like a different man: a powerful man.

"Well?" He asked.

As an answer she guided him to a full-length mirror.

"Not bad," he said.

She then escorted him to the feast. It was in the Great Hall and it was filled with people. Several long tables were put end to end and the amount of food was appalling. She had heard reports of famine in the west due to the war and here they were stuffing their faces.

Verin excused himself and went up to the head of the table and sat next to Ariana. Ariana smiled in a way that seemed too rehearsed.

Greza took a seat that wasn't directly next to anyone. She had no special seat of honor. Alethia detested parties and wasn't there and Tempest was surrounded by three Minotaur women at the other end of the table. No one had time for her. Even Onata would have found new friends and disappeared to do who knows what.

Then a large man came and sat down next to her. At first she thought it was another Minotaur but when she looked she saw the shaved head and scarred face of the giant man.

He nodded at her.

"Relax," he said. "I'm not going to kill you. We're on the same team now, remember?"

He gave a smile that had no humor in it.

She turned back to her food and pretended to ignore him.

"You're Greza."

"I know."

"I've been asking around about you."

"Oh?"

"They say you're the strongest. I think we both know that isn't true."

She didn't answer and kept her eyes forward as she picked at some baked ham.

He leaned toward her. His face was close enough that she could feel his breath.

"Since we can't fight, why don't we go to my room and do something else?"

She almost choked on her food and had to take a quick drink of some tart juice that was sitting in a silver goblet beside her.

He laughed a roaring and unsuppressed laugh.

"Yeah, they said you were locked tighter than a miser's purse. Shame." He leaned in closer until his lips were almost touching her ear. "I could show you a whole new world of pleasure and pain, honey. Maybe next time we fight, I will. I'll keep you alive long enough to experience the ends of both paths."

She wanted to glare at him, to stare him down and show she wasn't afraid. But she was. She looked away so he wouldn't see that fear and didn't move or he'd see her hands shake.

This was a man that not only wanted to kill her; he actually had the power to do so. She couldn't take him in a fight and they both knew it. If it ever came to that, she would lose and then this man would ... she didn't want to think of it.

He laughed and then got up and left.

Greza's evening only got worse. The entire time she watched Verin and

Ariana. She saw her whisper in his ear and he would laugh at whatever vapid thing she said. Their smiles kept growing and their laughter more frequent.

He never laughed like that with her. Ariana was everything she wasn't.

This was torture. She had no one to talk to and had to sit there watching the man she loved fall in love with the most beautiful woman in the Empire. Was this her reward for following the Path of Light?

Perhaps her Path here was at an end. What was her purpose now? The Victor was where he needed to be. He had been protected twice and now only had to win a war and sire a child. Neither of those things required her to be here, though she realized that she now wanted to help with both.

Verin leaned over and whispered in Ariana's ear and she made a laugh that showed all her too white teeth.

"Damn this."

She got up and walked out of the banquet hall. She found a pillar to lean against and closed her eyes. This was too much. Onata, the giant man and now this. Was she being punished for something?

"Greza!" She heard Verin call out.

She opened her eyes and saw Verin jogging down the hall toward her.

"Where are you going?" He asked.

"I'm tired."

"But the feast is just beginning. There are going to be jugglers and dancers and music."

"My head hurts. I just want to lie down."

"Please come back and ... are you alright? You look sick."

"It's a headache. I'll be fine in the morning."

"What's wrong, Grez? I can tell something's wrong."

"Nothing's wrong. Don't mind me. Go back to the feast and enjoy yourself."

She turned around and walked away. He called after her but she didn't answer.

Chapter Thirty-Two

AS THE DAYS PASSED, MORE AND MORE BAT-
tle reports came in. Mostly they were fighting retreats while
evacuees fled to the next city. They were being pushed back
further every day. The fighting retreats were costing them, but it was costing the Horde even more. The ratio was perhaps 2 to 1, but Verin said that
wasn't good enough, not even close.

As the enemy drew closer by the day, Verin fell more and more in love
with Princess Ariana. Greza could see the slow progression. What she didn't
see was a growing affection from Ariana, who continued on being the same
sweet and charming but slightly disinterested self.

Greza was having trouble sleeping again. Memories from the gladiator
fights and the battles kept her up so she went to the Planning Room. Good,
no one was there. She sat down at the table and looked at the map where
painted wooden chips marked the locations of military units of ten thousand. Red was friendly. Black was Horde. There were far more black than red.

Greza paid more attention to the logistics of the matter. Conscription
for commoners and nobles alike was going to be enacted next week and food
was going to be purchased from the Eastern Kingdoms. They needed more
bodies, blades, blankets and beans. If they could keep those things flowing
then they could win.

She heard footsteps running down the hall coming toward the Planning
Room. An Imperial guard rushed in, almost out of breath.

"Is Lord Verin here?" He asked.

"No, I believe he's asleep? What's the matter?"

He pointed down the hall.

"There are messengers. They're from the Horde."

Greza stood up, almost knocking her lantern over.

"A horse-man?"

"Yes, strangest thing I've seen. There's also a bird woman with him."

"I'll wake Verin. We'll be right there."

He nodded and rushed off again.

Greza ran down the hall and reached Verin's door in only a few moments. She was incredibly fast when she wanted to be. She didn't even knock and went right in. The two guards knew better than to stop her.

She found Verin sprawled out on his bed. Shirtless again but she didn't have time to worry about it. She shook him awake.

"Verin! Wake up."

"Huh?"

"There are messengers from the Horde."

"Wait ... what?"

"There is a horse-man and a bird-woman downstairs."

He was instantly awake and up. She helped him with his shirt and coat and dressed him in his armor and gun belt. Once he was ready she led him downstairs to the Great Hall where the throne and their visitors were.

They passed Princess Ariana who was still in her night robe. Verin didn't stop.

"We have messengers from the Horde," was all he said.

Good. He wasn't so far lost to her that he'd delay something as important as this.

They rushed downstairs and into the Grand Hall. There, standing in the middle of the room were the two emissaries of the Horde.

The Horse-man had a human body from the waist up where the horse's neck usually was. He wore dull gray, crude looking armor with an angled breastplate to deflect bullets and carried a long two handed curved sword and a bow on his back. He had long black hair and his goatee fell down to his waist. He was clean and his bare upper arms were covered in thin swirling tattoos.

The Bird-woman was a petite and pretty thing, though stark naked. Instead of arms she had black feathered wings. Her legs weren't like a bird's though. They had feathers and claws, but they were double jointed, forward and back, like a dog's, but decorated like a bird's.

The Bird-woman sat on the Horse-man's back. She also had long black hair and stunning green eyes that seemed to take everything in.

The guards had their weapons drawn and surrounded the two emissaries.

Verin walked in at a controlled pace. He took a moment to look them over like he was judging them.

"We are representatives of the Sintaros and Harrapi Peoples. Are you the one in charge?" The Horse-man said in a thick accent that sounded like he was grunting all his words.

"Give me a reason why I shouldn't just kill you right here," Verin said.

"Because we have much to discuss."

"I can't imagine what. You've killed every messenger we've sent to you so clearly you don't wish to talk."

"But now we do."

"Maybe I don't."

The Horse-man ignored him.

"We've come to demand your total surrender. You have seen what we are capable of. Our forces greatly outnumber yours. We are unstoppable. Our gods lead us while you squabble about which powerless deity you should ignore. You don't have the forces to win and you don't have the conviction. We have no desire for further bloodshed. Surrender and convert to our gods and you will be spared."

Verin looked over to Greza who did her best not to show surprise. They were religious fanatics.

"Why do you wish to conquer us?" Greza asked.

"It was prophesized that at the time of the Three Summers, a leader will rise up in the Eastlands where men walk on two legs. This leader will unite the Eastlands and bring war to our people. We are here to ensure the safety of our lands."

"By destroying ours?" Verin asked.

"Yes."

A leader that would unite the Eastlands. They were here to stop Verin. He was going to unite the Empire and they were here to stop him. Were they here as a result of the prophecy or was the prophecy a result of them?

"Why didn't you come to us asking for a peace treaty instead?" Verin asked.

"Because we know that you would not honor it. Your Empire enslaves its own people. They would enslave us as well."

"I was fighting the Empire to end slavery. We didn't even know about you until you showed up massacring innocent people."

"That is what we are here for: Peace."

"You mean surrender. That's not the same thing."

"It is for us."

Verin stepped closer and looked up at the tall Horse-man.

"Listen to me, Horse-man. We didn't know about you and frankly, wouldn't even care. But you showed up without warning and slaughtered my people for some stupid prophecy from imaginary gods. We will not surrender and there will not be peace.

"But, if you continue and we win this war, and I fully plan on it, I will march my armies into your lands. I will capture your children and send them East where they will learn our ways and laugh at your gods. I will kill anyone who raises a weapon against us. I will tear down your temples and burn your cities. I'll make sure your lands can never wage war against us because they'll be too busy trying not to starve! You'll be less than the dogs and will be scorned by my people until the end of the world. You will get no mercy or talks of peace from me."

The Horse-man nodded his head.

"And this is the answer we expected."

"Take your bird-whore and leave before I decide to kill you for the fun of it."

Verin then turned and left.

"Greza, see them out," he said before disappearing through the door.

"He is the Scourge," the Horse-man whispered to the Bird-woman.

"Wait, what did you say?" Greza asked.

"Nothing that concerns a heathen."

"You called him the scourge. Why?"

The Horse-man and Bird-woman looked to each other.

"She knows something," the Bird-woman said.

"He is the Scourge that, unless stopped, will bring ruin to our lands and create a thousand year tyranny," he said.

"Where did you learn this?" Greza asked.

"It is in the records of our people," he said.

"Who are you?" She asked.

"I am a representative of the Centaur and she is of the Harpy clans. We will not give you our names because names are power and we do not wish to give our enemies power," he said.

"But you, you know something of this prophecy," the Harpy said.

Greza nodded.

"You know the Conqueror must be stopped."

"Your prophecy must be wrong," Greza said.

The Harpy looked at her with her giant green eyes and squinted.

"You don't believe that, do you?"

"Perhaps she will survive the Purging and once she converts, we can talk then," the Centaur said.

With that, they turned and left. She watched them go, unsure of what to think about anything.

****

ALETHIA SPENT HER DAYS TALKING TO THE IMPERIAL sorcerers. They were deep into conversations about the nature of reality bending magic that sounded more like math than magic.

Tempest, when he wasn't barking orders at lesser officers, was spending his time with females. She hardly saw him anymore.

Verin was either planning a desperate campaign against the Horde or having dinner with Ariana. All his free time was spent with her now. She only saw him in the Planning Room.

During her free time she would go to the library where she was always the only person there or wander the palace, seeing how people were dealing with the war. She listened in on conversations to judge the morale and make sure there weren't problems that didn't filter up to Verin's attention.

One morning she was walking through the halls on her way to breakfast. She had a book about the history of the Dark Elves within the Empire.

She heard Verin and Ariana talking up ahead so she ducked to the side and out of the way.

They almost passed her when Ariana turned and saw her.

"Greza! Good morning," Ariana said.

Verin turned and smiled.

"There you are. I hope you're not hiding," he said.

She shook her head.

"Ah, Greza. You really need to stop by my apartment and I'll have my girls do something amazing with your hair. Maybe some new clothes. We should get you up to Imperial Standard. You're one of Verin's officers now."

She looked down at her Chimera uniform. She was a soldier, so what was wrong with looking like one?

"Stop by later today and we'll make you look pretty."

Make me look pretty? Of course the Princess thinks I'm ugly. Anything in comparison to her was.

She almost tore her book in two.

Ariana waved and continued to drag Verin down the hall. He hadn't even stood up for her. He let Ariana condescend to her and didn't say a word. He probably didn't even realize what Ariana said. He was too struck with love to see anything other than his own happiness.

I'm invisible to him.

The problem was that there was a discrepancy between what Verin said and what he did. He said she was important to him but he acted like she didn't exist.

The other problem was that it was growing more painful to watch him with Ariana. She was the Princess from the prophecy so they were meant to be together, but every time they laughed it was like a knife in her chest. Their smiles were slaps to her face.

If she was a greater person, she'd accept it and be happy for Verin. But she wasn't a great person. She was no hero from a prophecy. She was just a normal person trapped by powers greater than herself.

She passed by a large room where the young nobility often spent their evenings. It was a party every night with them.

Normally she avoided them because such things held no interest to her, but this time she peeked in. She had nothing else to do.

There were couples doing strange dances that she had never seen before. They were pressed against each other and it looked almost like it was an imitation of marital acts. As she looked around she saw couples off to the side doing things that only married couples should do, and in front of everyone.

"What is this?" Greza asked a young Satyr woman at the door.

The woman's eyes were sleepy looking and she had a goblet with an odd green liquid in it. Her brown hair was done up in two elaborate buns just behind her horns. Ribbons spiraled up her horns with jewels hanging from the tips.

"This? It's our nightly ball. You never been?" She said in a slow and slurred voice.

"It's always like this?"

"Oh yeah. Definitely. Only ... yeah ... it's kinda slow tonight. Just, boring, you understand?"

Then Greza got an idea and she wouldn't be satisfied until she got the answer.

"Tell me, did Princess Ariana ever come to these balls?"

"Oh yeah. Definitely."

"And she participated in," she waved her hand at the party, "all that?"

"Participated? Ha! She invented most of it. That philly is wild! You should see her when she ... oh, wait. Yeah. Definitely. She's crazy. She's danced in bed with just about everyone here." Then the girl made a big, vacant smile.

No wonder the Princess didn't want to get married. Her idea of a nice evening was degrading herself with every living creature in the palace.

What was she supposed to tell Verin?

She imagined the conversation. She would tell him and he wouldn't believe her. He'd then get angry that she'd accuse his fiancé and kick her out.

Was that a reason to not try?

If Onata was here she'd know what to do. Perhaps it was better if Verin didn't know. Ariana couldn't come to these parties now so maybe they were safe. The past was the past and people changed.

The whole thing confused her and she put as much distance between her and the party as she could. This was how things were in the Empire. She shouldn't be surprised. She had seen it before as a slave. At least these people weren't killing anyone like her old masters.

Still, it was wrong and Verin should at least know.

Greza was about to head to Verin's room when she remembered that he wouldn't believe her anyways.

Instead she found herself walking to the library again. Those Centaurs and Harpies knew them very well so maybe there was a record or some ancient legend about them. If any place in the Empire had such knowledge, it was the Imperial library.

****

SHE SPENT ALL MORNING FLIPPING THROUGH THE most ancient histories and legends and couldn't find anything. If the information was here then it was buried deeper than she had time for.

After lunch she went to the Planning Room where everyone was gathered. The generals gave their reports on how their units were doing. Most here were still in training and only a few had gone out with their armies.

Greza pointed out where some units could be better deployed and worked on compiling a list of non-military assets such as engineers, masons and team drivers. It was the inglorious side of war that never made it into the history books.

At dinner she tried not to look at Verin and Ariana though she could still hear their laughter.

She went back to her room and read while she tried to fall asleep. But memories of killing and death filled her mind again. Maybe it had something to do with the approaching Horde and the bad news that kept poring in.

Maybe Verin was awake. He often stayed up working and he had a way of making her feel better no matter what the situation was.

Greza made her way down the dark hallways, passing only a few guards on late patrol. When she got to Verin's door she saw only one guard. They knew who she was and never questioned her but this time the guard put up his hand.

"Can't go in."

"Nonsense. I'm his advisor."

"No, I mean ... he's currently occupied."

"If he's working then I'm here to help."

She made for the door again and the guard moved his halberd to block the door.

"He's not working but he's too occupied to receive visitors."

"What is he possibly doing that couldn't use my help?"

The guard looked nervous about something. He was looking at his feet fidgeting with his hands.

"He's in there with Princess Ariana. They're occupied."

"Oh."

"Sorry, miss."

She turned and left as numbness spread over her entire body. Of course she knew it would happen eventually. Verin and Ariana were getting married after all. What else would she expect?

She had hoped to have a little more time with him.

She could have had her one night but she had turned it down. Adriana had not turned him down so she got the prize.

I have no one to blame but myself.

The man she loved was making love to another woman and the images wouldn't leave her head. She had lost and there was nothing else to do.

This is my reward for doing good. Since I first met him I loved him. Everything inside me is begging to have him. I want to marry him and have his child. But the thing I want most will never be mine. My reward is to have what I want most paraded in front of me, always out of reach.

As the days passed and the war grew worse, she found herself less and less useful. Verin was so busy talking with generals that actually commanded troops that he seldom if ever asked for her opinion. Some days they didn't speak at all.

The giant man that could kill her would appear every other day or so with a report. Apparently he held some position within the Emperor's Palace Guard, but she could see that he did more than 'guard.' His name was Daran and no one ever questioned him and even the generals stood back when he entered the room.

Her part of the prophecy was over. She had found the Promised Victor and led him to where he needed to be and he was doing it. She hadn't received any impressions or feelings from the Divine Lights in weeks. No matter how hard she prayed, she didn't get any answers. All she got was an increasing desire for Verin and that certainly didn't help.

Her usefulness was at an end to Verin and the Divine Lights. She didn't do any good here. She was a fighter and would serve best if she was out at the front.

Over the next week the idea that she no longer belonged grew within her. At meals she ate alone though she was surrounded by people. Verin and Tempest were becoming strangers and she never saw Alethia anymore. She and her fellow sorcerers were always hidden away doing who knows what.

Then one morning she was in the garden reading a book. It was some Imperial holiday that she had never celebrated as a slave so it didn't matter to her. She was sitting under an apple tree with her book and some dried fruit when she heard Verin and Ariana enter. They were walking along the colonnade that circled the garden. She was hidden behind a hedge of bushes and well out of sight.

"You did not!" Ariana said.

"I certainly did. I jumped off my horse and beat him over the head with the butt of my pistol."

"How barbaric," she said with a laugh in her voice.

"Sometimes the only solution is a barbaric one. Did I tell you about the troll that almost killed me?"

"A troll? No, never."

"It was about a month ago and this armored war troll suddenly appears before me through a spell by one of your Imperial war sorcerers. All I had were pistols which would only make it angrier."

"By the stars," she gasped in feigned interest. "What did you do?"

"I didn't do anything. Greza jumped up off a horse and came down on its head with both fists. Cracked its skull in one blow."

"Impossible."

"No, it's true. Ask Tempest. She single handedly beat a troll to death."

"My, Greza is a little berserker, isn't she? If only she paid attention to her appearance. Tell me, Verin, was she ever your lover? Don't be shy. You can tell me."

"No, she wasn't."

"Not your type?"

"Actually, she turned me down."

"The gall of that woman. How dare she?"

"She's very religious."

"So? Next time I see her I'm going to have words with her."

"Please don't. She's very set in her ways. She still thinks I'm some prophesized hero."

"She's a fanatic. I don't like fanatics. They can't be reasoned with."

When Verin didn't say anything, Ariana went on.

"It's not good to have a fanatic by your side. They won't think clearly and will offer bad advice based solely on their beliefs. It's best to send her away where she can do what she's good at: beating trolls to death."

Ariana continued speaking but her voice faded away as they left the garden and re-entered the palace.

Greza sat there for a long time with the book in her lap. All the thoughts swirled in her head like a whirlpool, preventing her from doing anything.

Was that really how he thought of her: just a mindless fanatic? He now only had ears for Ariana and she was telling him to get rid of her. Assuming he resisted at all, how long would Ariana tolerate her. Even she thought that Greza was wrong to turn Verin down.

They are going to get rid of me.

She didn't want to be anywhere else and she didn't think she could withstand a rejection from Verin. The thought of him sending her away made her eyes burn and chest tighten. Her heart was beating furiously and all she wanted to do at that moment was flee.

She had to leave before she was cast out; something that would be too painful for her to bear. They all thought she was tougher than armor, but none of them knew her, not even Verin.

Chapter Thirty-Three

VERIN LED ARIANA INTO HIS ROOM AND closed the door. She moved like a feather on the wind. He had never seen anything so beautiful or graceful in his life. She was educated but the more and more he talked with her he realized that she didn't care about it. Education to her was a medal to be worn on the chest and nothing more.

More and more he missed the long conversations he'd had with Greza. Greza could talk about anything for hours at an end.

"Will you send away the fanatic or shall I?" Ariana said, falling into a pile of cushions on his bed.

"She's not being sent away. She's the smartest person I know. I need her."

"Do you? I haven't seen you talk to her in a while."

How long had it been since he had actually sat down and talked with her. She was there every day working along side him, but now that he thought about it, they really hadn't spoken.

Verin suddenly felt like a complete jackass. Greza had just lost her best friend and he was spending all his time with Ariana. Yes, he enjoyed her company but really he needed to show the Emperor that he was willing to play along. He needed this to work. Once he became Emperor he would show himself for what he really was and the sniveling nobles wouldn't like it one bit.

"I'm going to see how Greza's doing."

"She's fine. Stay with me. I promise you'll have more fun."

She grabbed his hand and pulled her down onto the bed next to her. That was what Ariana was: a pleasure seeker. Everything she did that seemed noble and virtuous was an act. She was a good actor and even had him fooled for a while, but she was as empty as any tavern wench.

Greza had substance. She was a real person. She was the smartest, most selfless person he had ever met.

"No, I should go see her," he said and started to get up but she pulled him down again and crawled on top.

"The Ork fanatic can wait till morning. I promise you that you'll have a much better time tonight if you stay with me."

Her warm lips on his made him lose his thoughts for a moment. When she broke away he realized that he had a choice. He could go see Greza now and spend a quiet evening talking about anything and everything, or he could wait till morning and spend the night with Ariana.

She began kissing him all over the face and her hands caressed his arms.

It could wait till morning.

****

HE AWOKE TO SUNLIGHT STREAMING THROUGH THE curtains. Ariana was asleep in his bed and even when asleep with tussled hair she was a sight that eased the eyes. His eyes lingered on her bare back until he finally gathered his thoughts and got dressed.

Ariana wanted him to get rid of Greza. That wasn't going to happen. She was someone he trusted and that was a rare thing. A lifetime in the slave mines showed him that trust came very rarely and never easily. But he trusted her.

Also, she was the smartest person he knew and if anyone would let him know that he was making a mistake with the war, it was her. Knowing that she was at his back ready to interject with a correction or alteration gave him the courage he needed to face those generals every day.

He really didn't know what he was doing; he only pretended that he did. He was only guessing. This whole war could go very badly for him and then he'd be blamed and called the greatest failure the Empire ever had. Fortunately, if he failed, there wouldn't be enough time to have to worry about it.

Verin approached Greza's door and knocked.

No answer.

He knocked again.

"Hello? Greza?"

Still no answer.

He saw a guard walk by on his hourly patrol.

"Have you seen Greza today?"

"No, my lord. I've been here for two hours and no one's come in or out."

"Thank you."

He knocked again and when he received no answer he tried the handle. It was open. Verin walked in and saw that the room was empty. The only thing in the room was a black Chimera uniform folded neatly on the bed.

In that instant he knew that she was gone.

No. This can't be real. I need her. She couldn't have just left without telling me.

Verin then ran to Alethia's room. He didn't knock. He threw the door open and found her asleep in bed.

"Wake up!"

Alethia rolled over and squinted at him.

"What?"

"Greza's gone."

"Gone?"

"Gone! All her things are gone. She's left."

"That doesn't make much sense."

Alethia was useless at the moment. It always took her several hours to wake up.

Next he went to Tempest's room. He found him in bed with a Minotaur female. He shouted her out of the room.

"Where's Greza?"

"I don't know." Tempest said, getting out of bed. "I saw her last night though."

"Last night?"

"Yeah. It was late. Maybe two or three in the morning. It was strange. She was crying. Who knew she could?"

"Did she say anything?"

"She gave me a note. Told me to give it to you in the morning."

Tempest pointed to his desk where a single folded piece of paper lay. Verin rushed over and tore it open. It had Greza's beautiful script all over it.

My Duke,

I have decided to leave. I know that I am no longer of any use to you and I would serve our cause more effectively on the front line where I can put my one and only ability to good work. I heard you and Ariana speaking in the garden and it confirmed my suspicions: that you think less of me for rejecting your advances and that I am a joke to you. You see me as only a single minded fanatic that's only good for "beating trolls to death." Perhaps that's deserved. I have always done my best to serve the Divine Path and to serve you but I see that my usefulness is at an end to both. My Path here is done. Thank you for everything you have done for me. You have given me a home and very fond memories. I will always look to you as the man I admire most and will never find your equal if I live to be a thousand. Please remember me once in a while.

Your obedient soldier, Greza

I love you.

Verin stared at the paper in his hands.

This couldn't be possible. She was gone? Why would she leave?

His mind went back to his conversation with Ariana in the garden. She had said those things, not him. But if Greza was listening in, she wouldn't have heard the difference. He hadn't refuted Ariana. At the time he didn't see the point because he didn't want an argument, but if he had known Greza was listening ...

What an idiot I've been. I've ignored her ever since arriving in Torna. Not once did I ever consider it possible to lose her. She was the most loyal soldier I had.

This is my fault. My moronic neglect led her to leave. If I had just paid a little attention to her this would never have happened.

"She left in the early morning. At least a five-hour head start."

"She's gone?" Tempest asked.

"We can still catch her."

"I don't see how unless you know which direction she went."

He didn't. She could have gone anywhere.

His support was gone. The one person he was relying on had left and it was his fault.

Verin grabbed the desk and flipped it over on its back.

"Calm down, Ver," Tempest said.

Instead of calming down he turned and punched Tempest in the jaw.

"Don't tell me to calm down. She's gone!"

And the last line of her letter burned into his mind. "I love you." This entire time she had loved him and he hadn't seen it.

Four months later

GREZA STOOD IN FORMATION AT THE FRONT OF THE unit. The box formation bristled with pikes and gun barrels pointing in every direction. Her square was right at the front, facing the enemy.

It was a gray day showing the beginning of winter. Dark clouds on the horizon promised rain and biting winds.

A half a mile in front of her was a massive Horde army. This was just a minor incursion into the Imperial province, but the rest of the Horde was right behind it. During the summer and fall the Horde had pushed forward without pause. Rumors continued how the Horde was slowly starving and Greza wondered if they'd starve soon enough to do any good.

The Imperial capital was only twenty miles to the east. Victory today would only delay the Horde in reaching the capital city. It was unavoidable at this point.

She could make out the spears and banners of the enemy. Their dull gray armor created a line of jagged stone in the distance.

"Hey, new girl. Just don't drop the pike, alright?" The sergeant said.

She had jumped from unit to unit over the past few months in an effort to not be noticed. She wore scarves, bandages and helmets to remain hidden. Sometimes she spoke with the Ork accent she remembered from childhood and pretended to be a dumb oaf.

Wherever she went, she made sure it was the place that needed her the most. She went from battle to battle and killed as many Horde as she could.

She gripped her pike and felt the hard wood through her gloves. The Centaurs had learned to stop charging them head on and instead came within bow range, fired and then retreated again. They'd do this over and over again all day until a square weakened.

Greza pulled the scarf down so she could breathe easier. In battle she didn't need to hide. No one would be paying attention to her.

"You've seen battle before, right Troka?" The young man to her right said. They were pressed shoulder to shoulder but she hadn't bothered remembering their names and it took a moment to remember that "Troka" was her alias this time.

"Yes. Many times."

"Are we going to make it?"

That was a dumb question. There was so much luck involved that no amount of skill or effort could ever guarantee anything. At any moment a stray arrow could strike someone between the eyes and no amount of training could prevent that.

"If we're lucky," she said. It was the closest thing to an honest answer she could come up with.

Horns began blaring from the Horde. It was their signal. She recognized it. Three long notes followed by drums. They were on the move.

"Here they come," she said.

A kid somewhere behind her was muttering something she didn't understand but the tone was quite clear. He was afraid and he had every right to be.

The wall of gray, armored Centaurs rushed forward and she could feel the ground vibrate beneath her feet. The Harpies over head were circling, ready to attack at the same time the Centaurs did. They'd drop rocks and sometimes bombs though those had been growing far less common. One sign that their logistics was starting to fail: one sign of hope.

She controlled her breathing as the wall of armored Centaurs raced toward her. She could hear the roar from their hooves and feel her bones shaking from their charging.

A cloud of darkness rose up from the Horde.

"Arrows!" Someone shouted and they all lowered their heads. Their helmets had wide brims to cover their faces and necks and their armor was thick in the arms and shoulders.

Arrows rained down on them with two bouncing off her helmet. Others landed at her feet or flew by. Screams from around her told her that other arrows had found their mark.

A second later more arrows came down, wounding other soldiers. Guns barked, blasting white clouds that started to fill her vision. With each volley she saw more Horde go down.

A melon sized rock from a Harpy hit the kid to her right and he crashed to the ground and didn't move. All around her soldiers were being wounded by arrows or rocks.

Their square was weakening. That meant they'd charge soon.

The gunners kept the rate of fire up and pike men from other parts of the square filled the gaps in the front.

The Centaurs were already starting to prepare for a charge. She saw them getting into position.

"They're coming! Get ready!" Greza shouted out.

The Centaurs formed into a spearhead formation and charged forward. Now she could make out their armor clearly. Their armor was composed of segments that offered heavy protection but also freedom of movement. Their helmets were angled to ward off projectiles and they either carried one-handed swords and shields or giant two handed weapons that curved back in a graceful yet aggressive way.

She held her pike and aimed it at the one weak point in their front armor, the area around their horse shoulders.

Her aim was true and the Centaur impaled himself on her pike. She felt the massive weight push the pike back into the ground and the Centaur fell forward. She barely managed to jump out of the way.

Others weren't so lucky and she saw several soldiers crushed to death:

trampled by the charging Horde. They burst into the square like a broken dam. They were inside and the square was destroyed. Their only chance of survival was to make it to a nearby friendly square.

Her pike was now gone. She raised her gauntleted fists and charged for the nearest Centaur. He was hacking away at a gunner who held his rifle up to block the attacks.

Greza jumped up onto the back of the Centaur as if she were about to ride him and reached for his head. In one quick motion she twisted the head and broke the neck. As the Centaur slumped to the ground she jumped off and looked for another target.

She saw one killing a pike man with his sword. She ran over and put all her weight into a single kick that broke the Centaur's right front leg. He bellowed in pain and fell to the ground.

A Centaur saw her and charged at her with his two handed sword leveled at her. She deflected it with her cestus and punched his horse's side where the armor was just leather. She heard ribs crack and he too collapsed to the ground.

Once again she found herself in the middle of battle where she was meant to be. One after another she took Centaurs down. She broke legs, arms and ribs. They were difficult to kill but not impossible.

As the square disintegrated around her she broke one more Centaur's leg and ran to the next square. They let her through and she went into the middle where a medic was taking care of wounded soldiers.

Then the Centaurs retreated and repeated the same process. Arrows and stones until there was an opening and then charge into the breach. It was simple and effective.

As the day wore on the squares began retreating. Artillery from a nearby hill pounded away at the Horde, giving the infantry time to pull back.

The sergeants began barking orders.

"Pack it up! We're moving out in a rush. Get in formation and move! No wasting the Empire's time and no wasting my time. We're heading to Torna!"

They were going to the capital and Verin would be there.

He was married now and she didn't know if she could witness his marital bliss and stomach it. She still thought of him every day.

Now as the army marched toward the capital, she grew closer to Verin with each step. A part of her wanted to run off and find an army somewhere else to fight in, but she knew most armies were coming to Torna.

They passed by burned out farms and evacuated villages. The wells were poisoned and the fields torn up. Half the Empire was now burnt and taken by the Horde. How they were going to feed everyone was something she couldn't imagine.

The army didn't reach Torna until well into the night. Camp fires from thousands of soldiers filled the fields around the city. Rumor was that all civilians were being evacuated as well. Made sense. It was too dangerous and with all the soldiers there was no room for them.

Was this a last stand or was Verin planning something else? If they lost the capital she didn't know if the army's morale could take it. It was already close to shattering. Six months of constant defeat would affect anyone's spirits. The whole purpose of the battles was to slow the Horde down and buy time for them to starve. She wondered if these common soldiers even knew that or if they only saw battle as a way to win.

"Hey! Troka! Where are you?" She heard her sergeant call out her fake name.

"Here, sergeant."

The man with the once polished armor ran up to her.

"You speak Ork, right?"

"Yes."

"They need you up front."

"What's going on?"

"There's a bunch of Orks from the Wild Tribes. No one can understand a damn word they say."

He led her up to the front of the column where the officers were gathered around a group of Orks wearing war paint and crude iron armor. Further away was a large mob of Orks carrying all kinds of primitive weapons.

They shoved her up front and the officer made her translate. She asked what the Orks wanted.

"We want to fight," the Ork chief said and Greza translated.

"You wish to fight the Horde?" The captain asked and Greza translated.

"Yes. They invade our lands. They push us out. Here, softies make stand and fight back. We will join," the chief said.

"They want to fight with us? I've never heard of them cooperating with anyone. What are we supposed to do with them?" A lieutenant with shiny armor asked.

"They're ten times stronger than your best soldier. I'm sure we can find use for them," Greza said.

"Like what? They're uncontrollable barbarians," the lieutenant said.

"Put them in the center of our squares. When the Horde breaks in they'll have a bunch of Ork brutes to deal with," Greza said.

The captain laughed.

"You make a good point. Tell them that they are welcome to join our fight," the captain said. He then turned to her.

"We need you to be our liaison with this Ork tribe. Try to keep them in control. Alright?"

"I'll do my best, sir."

And like that she found herself in charge of a hundred Ork warriors.

The chief walked up to her.

"You're a runt Ork?" He asked. His lower jaw jutted out even further to mark his superiority.

"That's right."

"Why do you fight with them? They're weak. You are weak if you follow them. We will not take orders from you. We want the War Chief of the soft-ies."

"No, you have to listen to me. I speak for the War Chief."

"No. You are weak and we do not listen to the weak."

These Orks only valued strength. The captain put her in charge of them but they'd never do as she said while they thought of her as weak.

"Then fight me."

The chief laughed.

"You are not a fighter. You are a whelp and nothing more."

She banged her gauntlets together.

"Fight me then!" She shouted.

The other Orks laughed.

"Very well. I will fight you. If you lose, then you are a slave to my tribe."

"I won't lose."

"What are you doing?" The captain asked.

"I'm about to fight this Ork so I can lead them."

"You can't possibly fight that beast," the captain said.

"I absolutely can. Whether I win or not is what is in question."

The chief unstrapped an enormous club from his back. It appeared to be made out of an entire baby tree. She had forgotten how incredibly strong Orks could be. It was a massive club with iron bands wrapped around it that no human could ever wield. He was also a good head and shoulder taller.

"No club?" He asked.

"I don't need it."

Without pausing the muscular chief in his leather and iron scrap armor charged forward. He was fast and when he swung his club she barely managed to dodge it. She felt the air rush past her face.

As soon as the club swung past her she bolted towards him. Instead of bringing the club around for another swing, he jabbed at her with the butt. But she saw it coming and ducked beneath it.

She was inside his defenses and with both hands she punched upwards into his gut. Her metal fists connected and knocked the air out of his lungs. The chief staggered back, gasping for air.

Greza didn't hesitate and pressed the attack. She charged forward again and stepped up onto his thigh. With all her strength and momentum she threw one uppercut that connected in the chief's jaw.

It was a blow that would have killed any human and shattered their skull. The chief fell back, unconscious.

She landed on both feet and glared at the other Orks.

The gathered Orks let out a collective gasp.

"My word," the captain said.

She pointed at the Ork tribals.

"Now, you listen to me. Understand? While you're here you will do as I say. No killing. No stealing. No fights. We can't waste a single man. All our energy has to be used against the Horde. Understood?"

The Orks quickly nodded.

"How did you do that?" The captain asked.

"I was lucky."

Chapter Thirty-Four

THE HORDE MOVED INTO THE OUTSKIRTS OF the city. From her position on the city wall she could see the black and gray wave of Centaurs sweeping into Torna. The ancient city wall was the first line of defense. It had to hold because the second and last defense was the palace and not everyone could fit in there and fight effectively.

Greza had four pistols loaded with lit wicks. She had her knife and her cestus and she was ready.

Verin was somewhere in the palace on one of the high towers overlooking the city. He'd be where he could see and direct the city's defense.

She turned away from the approaching Horde that covered the plains and toward the palace. He was up there somewhere. He was in a tower looking over her. She wondered if he ever thought of her and if he ever missed her. A second didn't go by that she didn't feel his loss.

He was on the Path though. Today would determine everyone's fate. He didn't need her. His path was before him.

She no longer had a path though. She was drifting around like a piece of wood on the tide. She floated along with no control over where she went.

Officers were walking along the battlements inspecting their troops and offering words of encouragement.

Down on the ground behind the wall were the reinforcements. Not everyone could fit so most waited down there in the city square and when a man on the wall fell, someone would come up and take their place. Also, if the Centaurs managed to break through then the troops down there would be needed to seal the breach.

The officers had made the strategy clear. Keep Harpies from getting through and getting to the gate. They'll attack anyone on the wall while the Centaurs below try to smash the gates open. There were three main gates so three main points of attack.

Then she saw something odd. In behind the gates they were setting up cannons. But the cannons weren't pointing above the walls, but down at the gates. There were 12 cannons at her gate and rumor spread that it was the same with the other two. Cannons were powerful but even that many weren't going to be enough to stop the enemy if the gates were taken. They'd be able to fire one or two shots before they were overtaken.

The Horde worked its way through the city streets. They moved slowly to make sure they didn't miss any pockets of resistance. The masses of dark shapes in the streets would halt around the churches long enough to set them ablaze.

And all too soon they were at the walls. Centaurs couldn't scale walls like other races, so they'd have to smash through the gates. Down the large boulevards of the city she saw giant wheeled siege machines. Battering rams with fire resistant roofs. Centaurs pushed and pulled the great machine forward. She assumed other rams were being hauled to the other gates.

A Harpy swooped out of nowhere and knocked a soldier off the battlement. He plummeted down into the houses below screaming the whole way down.

"Eyes up!" A sergeant shouted.

Gunners from all over the wall began pouring fire into the Centaurs that moved the siege ram. Arrows flew up to the wall and Harpies swooped in to knock more people off.

A Harpy flew down toward her. She timed her shot and let loose with her fist in time to connect with the Harpy. She heard its bones crunch and it tumbled down to the street below.

She fired her pistols at the Centaurs amassing at the gate and quickly reloaded. It was like the tide coming in. Thousand and thousands of armored Horse-men crashed against the gate. They had their shields up above their head. Her pistols weren't going to do much.

Baskets of rocks were brought up and she threw a few rocks down before they ran out. Boiling oil was poured down and nothing seemed to affect their numbers at all.

The riflemen were doing better. It was their constant volley after volley that was bringing Centaurs down.

If the walls weren't so narrow they could have brought cannons up. That would have kept them from the gates unless they were suicidal.

They were killing the Centaurs that hauled the ram but every time a replacement came up the ram crept a little closer to the gate. The machines were the size of houses and barely fit down the main street of the city.

Then palace guards in gold armor came up carrying barrels full of black sphere bombs. A separate group came with the firebrands to light them. Greza got her hand on two of them and threw them down. The rain of bombs was effective but too short lived.

Three hours passed. They'd haul rocks and occasionally more bombs using a donkey powered elevator and she'd throw them down. The Centaur arrows weren't doing much and the Harpies were more of a nuisance.

Down below she saw thousands of Centaur bodies. They were dying like wheat being cut down by sickles but they had their siege ram against the wall now and she could feel the steady thumping of the ram as it struck the wooden gate.

They were going to break through. That much was unavoidable now. She would do far more good down there than up on the wall.

Greza took off running down the narrow stairs until she reached street level. She hurried over to the cannon crews.

"You better stay back, miss," a lieutenant said. His armor was dinged and dull from too many close calls.

"They're going to break through," Greza said.

"Yeah, we're counting on it."

"Counting on it?"

The Dark Elf male turned to her and smiled.

"We've been planning this for months. We know what we're doing. If you want to help, go grab one of those assault shields and guard us from arrows."

He pointed to a pile of heavy wooden shields. She took one and stood ready to defend the cannon crew.

She watched a crack in the door slowly grow wider. They were breaking through.

"Load cannons!" The lieutenant said.

They opened the crates behind them but there were no cannon balls inside. Inside the crates were chains with wicked barbs.

"Chains?"

"Yeah. Just watch," the lieutenant said.

The cannoneers loaded all the cannons with the vicious chains and readied themselves. Gunners took positions behind assault shields.

What were chains going to do against the thousands of armored Centaurs that were about to pour through the gate?

Then she heard cheering from behind her. Men in brass armor carrying strange metal contraptions walked out into the city square. They were fully enclosed in thick metal and leather and even their eyes were protected by glass. Instead of guns they had long pipes with tubes that went back to brass cylinders on their backs. There were about fifty of them.

"What are those?" Greza asked.

"Our Volcano Guard."

Verin had been busy indeed.

Then there was an ear shattering 'crack' from the gate. It was breached. Two more blows from the ram knocked the gate completely off its hinges causing them to crash down like fallen trees kicking up clouds of dust.

"Ready!" The artillery captain bellowed.

And like a flood, armored Centaurs began racing in through the open gate.

"Team one, fire!"

Two of the cannons fired. It was so quick but Greza saw it. As the chain left the barrel, it whipped around, spreading out in a flying mass of flailing death. The chain whipped through the Centaur horde cutting them to pieces faster than a thousand swords. Blood sprayed out everywhere covering the inside of the gates with splattered gore.

"Team two, fire!"

Two more cannons fired as the first two reloaded.

The chains whipped through even more Centaurs that tried to come through. Over and over again the cannons fired in steady turn. There were enough of them and the reloading was fast enough that the firing never stopped. They had trained for this and knew exactly how many cannons they needed and how fast they needed to be.

A few arrows flew through the gate and she used her shield to block them. They 'thunked' into her wooden shield without harming anyone.

"Halt!" The captain shouted.

No one was trying to come through. The Centaurs were holding back.

The lieutenant laughed.

She heard the distant 'booms' of cannons firing elsewhere.

"Look up!" Someone shouted.

She looked up and saw a cloud of Harpies descending on them. The gunners aimed up and fired.

As the Harpies tried to get to the cannons the Centaurs tried to push through again. She used her shield and fist to fight off the Harpies as they tried to claw at her and the crew. The gunners were dropping them in droves and blood was falling down on her like rain, but they kept coming.

The Centaurs came through the gate. The cannons fired but some managed to escape the whipping chains. A dozen Centaurs charged at the Volcano Troops.

What happened next she could barely believe.

Fire burst out of the Volcano Troops pipes and engulfed the Centaurs in pillars of flame. Next they aimed up and fired at the Harpies. The gouts of flame ignited some causing them to fall like balls of fire. The survivors flew off.

More arrows came through the gate causing the captain to duck. The Human captain was a large man with a neat beard. His helmet had a plume showing that he was nobility. That didn't matter now. They were all equal while they fought for their lives.

This defense was staggering in its effectiveness, but if it halted then the Centaurs would break through and it would be all over. It was effective as long as they kept it going.

More gunners were sent up to the wall.

The Horde sent more and more archers to the open gate in an effort to take out the cannon crews. She stood in front of them until they were ready to fire and as soon as it fired she went right to her position in front of them.

The cannons were getting too hot and soon they'd have to cool down. Young boys with water pails came to cool them down while the Volcano troops stepped forward and put out a wall of flame to block the Centaurs.

This went on all day until night fall. The Horde withdrew only after the sun went down. Masons hurried to the gate to reseal it while crews came out with food and water. Medics were running around everywhere. The crying of the wounded filled the immense plaza where the farmer's market had once been.

"How long do they expect this to go on?" Greza asked.

"Days if we're lucky," the Dark Elf lieutenant said. "They'll break through sooner if we're unlucky."

She sat down on a crate of chains and noticed that there weren't many crates left.

"How much ammo is left?"

"Maybe three more hours worth."

"That's it?"

"That's it."

"What do we do after that?"

"Fight for our lives the old fashioned way."

Lanterns filled the town square by the gate with yellow, dancing light. Workmen continued to try to wall up the open gate. Against that ram it was only buying time.

The cannon crews were already asleep. She didn't blame them. They had had a hard day and another one coming up.

Greza lay down in a pile of cleaning rags and put her hands behind her head. Verin had done everything he could have and more and yet it still didn't look like enough. Once the ammunition for the cannons ran out, they'd be back to pikes and guns to block the breach.

AT DAWN THE BATTLE STARTED AGAIN. THE RHYTHMIC pounding of the siege ram began cracking the stone wall that had been hastily thrown up in the breach. It bought them an hour.

Greza blocked arrows as the cannons fired the last of the chains. The corridor that made up the gate was a river of blood and smoke. The Centaurs that had tried to pass through had been turned into chunks.

It was the worst thing she had ever seen. She never wanted to see it again, but now that the ammunition was gone, she wished it could continue.

"Pike men!" The Captain shouted.

Platoons of pike men and gunners ran up to block the exit. The Volcano troops burnt anyone who tried to enter until their fuel ran out and they retreated. They were on their own now to face the oncoming horde with their hands.

Greza dropped the shield. It was time for her to enter the melee and do what she could.

Once the Centaurs realized the cannons had stopped they charged through in mass. It was a solid wall of armored Horse-men. One crashed into the pike formation, impaling himself on the pikes and the Centaur behind him leapt over his dying comrade.

Greza charged at the Centaur that broke through and swiped her arm, breaking the Centaur's leg. He fell into a pile and Greza waded into the battle. She threw a brick at a Centaur and closed the distance to rip his sword out of his hands and run him through with it.

The pikes and guns in such a narrow area in front of the gate proved effective in bottling the Centaurs but occasionally a few would break free and Greza would smash their ribs or break their legs.

She rested between assaults and even managed to eat a biscuit. The Human, Elf and Satyr soldiers were wearing out and had to be replaced more often.

Then she saw the Ork chieftain approach. He held his club in both hands. "Why didn't you tell us the good fighting was here?"

"I didn't know where you ran off to and I've been busy."

The chieftain grunted and walked away. A few minutes later he and his Orks came in and took over the front position. The noble captain in charge didn't argue. When the next assault came the Orks roared and charged forward with a ferocity the worn out defenders couldn't hope to match.

Their clubs smashed the bones beneath the Centaur's armor and their inhuman strength outclassed the enemy. It was another slaughter. The Orks in the tight confines of the gate were an unstoppable wall like the cannons had been.

Greza was just starting to get tired and she was only a runt Ork. These full bloods fought all day without tiring. In fact, they seemed to relish it. If an Ork fell to a Centaur sword, the rest bellowed and fought even harder. Greza jumped in and fought with them, but in a fight like this, where raw brutality was paramount, they were masters.

At the end of the day the gate was filled with Centaur corpses and created a new barricade that couldn't be rammed through. The enemy would have to climb over a mountain of their own dead.

That night the Orks sat around their own fire and sung awful songs about slaughter and destruction. No one else understood them and for once she wished she was ignorant of the language.

The Orks offered her some of their food and she had to take it. Refusing would have offended them and she needed their good will.

"You fight with the ferocity of a true Ork," The chieftain said in Orkish.

"Thank you. This fight needs ferocity."

"If we'd known this war was going to bring this kind of fight, we would have joined much sooner."

This got a laugh from the other Orks. She had never seen Orks this happy before. Mostly she knew slaves. This was how they were meant to live and they loved it.

She was very glad they weren't fighting a horde of Orks.

"I am Garabak. What's your name?"

She didn't see any reason to lie. They didn't speak Imperial.

"Greza."

"Greza? This is a powerful name. It means 'princess' in our tongue"

"I thought the Orkish word was Gretan."

"No, Greza is ancient word. No Ork would use that name on a common child. When I fought you I knew you were no normal Ork girl."

"I'm no princess."

"Maybe, but you have spirit of princess. Unlike Elfs and Humans, Orks don't pay attention to who our parents are. An Ork rises on his own merits, not blood. What makes an Ork noble is their strength. Maybe your mother was a pig farmer's daughter. Doesn't matter. She knew you'd be strong. She gave you a strong name."

She had never considered why her mother had named her 'Greza.' She had always assumed it was a meaningless Ork name. But now she saw the potential her mother had felt and hoped for and for the first time in a very long time she felt that she had indeed had a mother.

She went to bed with thoughts of her mother instead of thoughts of Verin.

In the morning it started again. The arrows were fewer now. The Horde must be running out. What else were they running out of? Bodies, she hoped.

Around noon she saw a slender figure dressed all in black walk into the square. She was surrounded by six guards in gold armor.

It was Alethia.

She hid behind an Ork warrior and watched as Alethia walked to the gate where most of the Orks were fighting like monsters.

"I need them to clear a path," Alethia called out.

One of the captains called for Greza using her fake name.

It was unavoidable. This battle was too important to lose due to her petty problems.

She ran out to where the captain and Alethia were.

"Here's our interpreter," the captain said.

Alethia looked over and for a moment her face was unreadable. Then recognition dawned on her and her dark eyes went wide.

"Greza?"

"I'm here."

"Where have you been?"

"Fighting the war. We can talk later. What is your plan here?"

She started as if to say something but stopped. She then turned toward the gate.

"I need those Orks to clear the gate so I can reach the bulk of the Centaur army."

"What for?"

"My friends and I have come up with a spell, a very dangerous spell."

"Very powerful?"

"Very."

"But won't that ..."

"It doesn't matter. Even the common soldiers here risk everything. I can't be expected to be exempt from that."

"No, Alethia. How much will you lose?"

"I've written much down."

"I can't let you."

Alethia narrowed her eyes at her and shook her head.

"If you could die to end this war, wouldn't you?"

Of course I would. Without hesitation.

"Listen, Greza. I need to reach the bulk of the Horde. While I perform the spell I need you to protect me."

"Will do."

"Hurry, it's almost time."

Greza shouted the orders to the Orks and they pushed forward, clearing a path out past the gate and into the Centaur army. Alethia followed. Greza kept a Centaur away by shoulder ramming him and then breaking his spine. She also caught an arrow in mid-flight which even surprised herself. It had happened so fast that she hadn't had time to even think about it.

Once they were out past the gate and surrounded by enemy Alethia stopped. Gunners fired between the Orks and the riflemen from up top did their best to cover them.

"This is it," Alethia said. "When I say go, move behind me. All of you."

Greza relayed the order to the Orks and they nodded. They were crude barbarians, but they weren't stupid. Magic was something all cultures respected and feared.

Alethia then turned to Greza.

"He loves you."

"Who?"

"Verin. He hasn't been the same since you left."

"That's impossible."

"It's not and he does."

"But he's married."

"Doesn't change his feelings."

She thought about everything in the moment she had.

"I can't go back," Greza said.

Alethia nodded.

Greza didn't see how it was possible that Verin loved her. She had never seen any signs. How could he love her when he had Ariana? It didn't make sense.

"I understand. Listen," Alethia said and put a hand on her shoulder. "I won't remember any of this. I don't know if I'll even remember you. But know that I thought of you as a friend."

A friend. Just as she was about to lose her, she learned that Alethia was her friend.

"That's not fair," Greza said.

"No, it's not."

Then Alethia raised her arms.

"It's time!" Alethia said.

Everyone rushed behind Alethia and got into a tighter formation.

Blue light surrounded her and suddenly lightning shot out of her hands and eyes. The angry white lightning spread out hitting Centaurs and jumping to the next, branching out and hitting more and more as it went.

The entire Horde in front of her was shaking like they had seizures and she could smell burning hair and flesh.

The lightning continued to spread, jumping from Centaur to Centaur. Greza saw that their metal armor was what drew the lightning to them. Before she knew it, every Centaur she saw was being cooked by the lightning. It spread through the Horde and she witnessed thousands of them dying at once. The smell was unbearable and she gagged.

Then as suddenly as it started, the lightning stopped and Alethia fell to the ground. She was accompanied to the ground by thousands of Centaurs, only they weren't breathing and Alethia was.

Greza rushed over and picked Alethia up.

No Centaur near the gate was left standing. Thousands had just died in the space of a few moments. Smoke from their charred bodies created a foul smelling fog in the air. The further off Centaurs didn't move forward and only stood there, shuffling their hooves as if they didn't know what to do. Thousands of their comrades lay smoldering on the ground.

They hurried back inside and the pike formation closed the entrance again.

Alethia was unconscious. She took her to the captain.

"Is she alive?" The captain asked.

"She is."

But what had Alethia lost to unleash that spell? How much of her memory was left?

A soldier from the wall ran down and came up to the captain. He had a giant smile on his face.

"Sir, half the Horde just fell over dead."

"Half?"

"It seems like it."

"Impossible."

"No, sir. There was a sorcerer at each gate and each one let out that lightning. Damndest thing I ever saw."

"What's the rest of the Horde doing?"

"They've fallen back, sir."

There was no more attack the rest of the day.

Chapter Thirty-Five

AT NIGHT GREZA SNUCK INTO THE PALACE and found Alethia. It was easy. With all the chaos and people running around, no one cared if a soldier wandered into a bedroom.

Alethia was awake and reading a book. She looked up when Greza entered.

"Hello?" Alethia said.

"Alethia? How are you feeling?"

"Fine, thank you."

"That was quite a spell you did out there."

"That's what they tell me."

"Do you remember me?"

Alethia nodded her head.

"Greza. You're a very good fighter if I recall correctly."

"I suppose I am."

"Are you still running messages for Verin?"

"No, not any more."

"Moved on to more important things. Speaking of which, I need to get back to my journal here."

"Okay. Glad you're alright." Alethia was anything but alright. She had forgotten too much. "Oh, and could you do me a favor?"

"I suppose."

"Could you not mention to Verin that I was here?"

"Sure ... I guess."

She left and walked back to the square where soldiers were laughing and joking. She hadn't heard that in a long time.

Alethia was gone now. She was alive but she didn't remember their friendship or belief in Verin.

In the morning she was awakened by shouts from the wall. She threw on her helmet and readied herself for battle.

"They're leaving!" Someone shouted from the wall.

She ran up the long stone stairs to the top of the wall. As the soldier had said, the remains of the Horde were slowly moving away. There seemed so few of them now.

A few soldiers began shouting curses at the fleeing Horde and that started an avalanche where everyone was shouting at them.

As they shouted, cheered and some even danced, word spread that Lord Verin had come to the middle gate. She could barely see the top of the middle gate from where she was and people just looked like specks.

Within the hour the officers were organizing their units to move out.

"Move out?" One bearded human asked.

"Yes. Lord Verin says we're following the Horde all the way to the border. We're going to run them down and kill them."

"But they're horse-men? How're we supposed to run them down?" A soldier asked.

That was a good question. What was Verin thinking? The Horde could move much faster. And there would be nothing for their own armies to forage from. The Western Provinces were a wasteland now. Was this just about revenge or sending a message?

Whatever it was, it couldn't be worth it. Everyone here was exhausted and done with fighting. They had won. Wasn't that enough?

She was not going to go chasing cats and trying to catch an army that couldn't be caught.

As the army gathered supplies and prepared to move out, Greza crept to the main gate and slipped out. She stayed close to the wall until she reached the eastern side where the drainage ditch was covered with bushes and trees. She made her way along the stream until she was a good mile or so away and then started walking a south easterly direction.

Then something caught her eye. Movement behind her. She turned around to see who or what was following her.

The Ork warriors emerged from the shrubbery.

What by the Divine Path did they want?

The Orks, still carrying their clubs in hand approached her and the chieftain stepped forward.

"You go to find more battle?" The chieftain asked.

"I don't know where I'm going."

"Then come with us. Help us reclaim our land."

"But the Horde is retreating. They're gone."

"No, from others. You are clever like Elf, but your heart beats like an Ork."

"You're offering me a job?"

"You will be our War Chief. You will lead our tribe to victory."

She tried not to laugh. What was she supposed to do with a bunch of barbaric Orks?

They towered over her and she saw little resemblance to Elves in their bulky forms, but when she looked closer she saw the angled jaw line and the clear eyes that saw more than people knew.

And then she got to thinking.

These were people, not mindless beasts. They were asking for her help. If she did become their chief, she wouldn't just lead them to victory; she would show them the Path of Light. They would win and attribute their victories to the Gods of Light. She could convert an entire tribe and show them a way to live without fighting.

"Where is the rest of your tribe?" She asked.

"South, in an Empire fort."

"How big is this fort?"

"Small, but full of Orks with no home. The soldiers have guns and stay high on the walls watching us."

"If you had guns you could take the fort and make it a new home for your tribe."

"But we don't know how to use guns."

She smiled because it just so happened that she did.

Two years later

GREZA SAT ON A THRONE MADE OF WHALE BONES wrapped in bear skin. On her head was the Lion Crown, a skull of a lion killed by the great Ork chieftain Darakat when he unified the tribes against the Empire two hundred years ago.

Most of the local tribes were under her leadership now. They stayed away from the Empire's borders. She didn't want them knowing of their growing power. They'd assume that a united Ork nation would be a threat and normally they'd be right.

These Orks she had beat into submission with her armored fists, but once under her rule, she taught them the Divine Path. Ten months ago she had taken the first Ork to the old monk in the monastery and had the first ever Ork priest conferred. She also took the book of prophecies for her own.

Now there were six Ork priests and she was the High Priestess and Queen. They were a people desperate for a leader. They knew they lacked something and without that something, they'd never progress. They saw the nations around them rise up and destroy them time and time again. But in her leadership and the guidance of the Divine Path, they knew their mission. They were a people with a purpose again.

Slowly and carefully they had begun to amass weapons. They bought boats and hired sailors to teach them. With their new navy they captured several islands that few people paid any attention to.

The Empire was entirely too busy prosecuting their war against the Horde. Verin, in what must have been anger fueled madness, had followed the Horde back to their homelands and was invading the West Lands. It was a war that brought no honor, glory or even purpose. It was a waste of life and it was all in vain.

The merchants she sent out to trade in the Imperial towns also gathered information and all the news they could. She wanted to keep track of everything Verin and the Empire did.

Hardly any of it was good news.

After the Emperor died a few months after the victory at the capital, he began seizing the wealth and lands of the nobility. At first the People loved him for it and saw it as justice. But then he raised taxes, imposed harsher laws and declared minor crimes punishable by death. The excuse was that the Empire was in troubled times due to the war and anything, including stealing a loaf of bread during the famine, was considered a crime against the state.

She watched it all from her throne and worried.

"What's next on the schedule?" Greza asked.

Kratz approached from the side. She wore her black robe with the red skull of her tribe on her chest. She fumbled with her papers before finding the right one. Like Greza she was a runt with more dominant Elven features.

Kratz had a thin face with pronounced lower incisors. She was always glaring but that was a defensive mechanism she picked up from being the runt of her family. Her hair was done in the elaborate bun style of the Imperial woman.

"A human sailor wishes to speak with you. He says it's a matter of trade," Kratz said.

"This couldn't be done by Tranax?"

"They said it's a big trade," Kratz said.

"Let's hear him then."

Kratz waved to the guards to bring the human trader in.

The guards, who now carried carbines, ushered in a stocky bearded human with messy brown hair. He wore fine but worn clothing and a large smirk on his face. He was probably used to finer establishments.

Her throne room was an old Imperial fort that they had taken. It was a stone keep with a repaired stone wall around it. Wooden buildings had been added to it for blacksmiths, barracks and stables. It was surprisingly functional but nothing to look at. Orks liked to decorate with the bones of their kills and even the starburst symbol of the Path of Light was displayed in bones above the throne. The Orks considered that a sign of utmost respect.

He walked in and stopped a few paces from the base of her throne's platform. He made a bow that she couldn't tell if it was honest or in jest due to its flamboyancy.

"We thank the Divine Lights for your safety and ask that they watch over us and guide us to be friends," Greza said.

"Thank you for seeing me. Guess it's true what they said. You all really are followers of the Path."

"Indeed we are. What is the nature of your business with us?" Greza asked.

The man raised his eyebrow. This probably wasn't the greeting he had been expecting. He was probably expecting drums and a lot of yelling in Orkish.

"My name is Desmon. I've come with an offer. I've recently acquired two ships. They're old navy ships but have been kept in good repair."

"How much are you asking for them?"

"Fifty thousand each."

Greza laughed.

"Really, Desmon. You take us for idiots. Fifty thousand? I wouldn't pay that for four ships. That's assuming they're actually in good shape."

"Oh, they're in excellent shape."

"I'm sure they are."

Desmon folded his arms and smiled.

"You don't like that offer, then maybe this will be more tempting. I'll give you those two ships for free."

"And?"

"If you purchase an island for two hundred thousand."

"What island?"

He took a map out from his belt and rolled it open. She gave permission to come forward and he approached the throne and showed her the island. It was further east than she would have liked, but there were no islands blocking her territory from it.

"Interesting. I'll have to send my own surveyors and examine this island for myself. But before I do, tell me why the island is so cheap."

"It belongs to the provincial governor, but he offered it for one hundred and fifty thousand to anyone who could clear it of pirates."

So that's what it was. He was offering the ships to help destroy an infestation of pirates. In exchange, he'd get a cut of the profits as the middleman. If she weren't trying to hide her activities, she'd ignore the middleman and go straight to the governor. But if the transaction was done through this man, then no one would notice.

"It will take a day to send a team out and come back. Until then you are my guest, Mr. Desmon."

She indicated a chair to the right at the base of her platform.

"Thank you, your highness."

He sat down. The Ork officers eyed him but didn't seem impressed. Kratz ordered a maid to bring Desmon some fresh juice. There was no alcohol in her court.

"So, tell me Mr. Desmon, what news is there from the Empire?"

"The usual. War in the West Lands. Another provincial rebellion. Said rebellion destroyed with ruthless efficiency. They've taken to calling the Emperor, "the Tyrant" when he's not around."

"This is not cheerful news."

"Oh, but there is a bit of cheerful news!" He smiled and his bushy eyebrows and mustache rose in almost comical exaggeration. "The Empress is pregnant! The sorcerers say it is going to be a boy! Isn't that charming? Now we'll have a second generation of tyrants running around."

Greza remembered the prophecy. The assassin was to come after the Victor had sired a child. A child that she had always wanted. She should have been the mother, but the Path had led her in a different direction.

"How far along is the Empress?"

"Five months."

"How delightful," she said with a forced smile.

"If I may ask, how did you convince your clansmen to take to the ocean? I heard that Orks dislike the water."

"I threw them in."

"You what?"

"I was afraid of water too, but with proper motivation I could overcome my fear. I applied the same logic to them."

"Maritime Orks. I never would have guessed."

"Well, the Empire hasn't left us much room on land."

"May I ask another question?"

"Of course, but I'm under no obligation to answer."

"Where were you educated? No one I've asked knows anything about you."

"And you did much asking, I assume."

"It pays to know as much about a potential partner as possible."

"I've traveled far, Desmon, farther than you'd guess. I've been with important people and important situations."

"Then why are you here? Couldn't you be someplace more promising?"

"More promising? I'm spreading the Light and giving these people hope for a future. What could be more promising than that? Gold? Titles?"

"Well, yes."

Greza looked around the courtroom at her people. They were her people and she could help them. She wasn't their queen, she was their servant.

"I'm right where I belong," she said. "Tell me more about these rebellious provinces."

"Oh, they're the same provinces that rebelled during Verin's first invasion. Maybe it's personal, I don't know."

She thought about Fairfield and the poor people there. What would that depressing place be like now that most of the men were off fighting in the west and Verin had raised their taxes even higher?

Verin had turned into the Scourge.

Chapter Thirty-six

ONCE SHE RETIRED TO HER ROOM SHE PACED instead of sleeping. What was this assassin waiting for? Thousands were dying in a completely pointless war and the people were losing their freedom under the tyrant Verin had become.

He had done everything he said he would do. He had cast out the nobility to the streets. But why the tyranny? From what she could guess, he was so focused on the punitive war that he didn't know or care how the people were doing. He had all attention on the West Lands. Everything else was a distraction.

But where was this Assassin? She hadn't wanted to believe, but the prophecy had been true. Verin was turning into the Scourge. She didn't want to see his legacy burn in the fires of his own cruelty. He deserved better.

Seeing Verin dead was better than seeing him become a monster. He was destroying everything he had fought for.

But where was this Assassin?

There was a familiar soft knock at the door.

"Come in, Kratz," Greza said.

The door opened and Kratz came in. She was holding her tablet with blank sheets of paper. A pouch with all her inks and pens was attached to her belt.

"My Queen? I heard you pacing again. What's the matter? Is it the business with the island?"

Kratz's head cocked to the side like it always did when she awaited an answer. She was a full-blood, but her frame was slender and puny. A runt, an outcast like Greza had been once. Maybe that was why she had taken a liking to Kratz at their first meeting.

"No. We'll send our men to clear the pirates out. That's not a worry."

"Then what?"

"The Emperor."

Kratz squinted and wrinkled her nose.

"You fear he'll learn of us?"

"No. Yes, but that's not it right now."

"Then what?"

Kratz took her usual seat at Greza's desk. It was captured from a pirate vessel and Greza had liked it. It had carved images of dragons and other monstrous beasts. Kratz usually sat there during their late night sessions when Greza couldn't sleep.

"Kratz, remember the prophecies about the Victor?"

"That he'll become the Scourge? It's happening, isn't it?"

"It is."

"Then the Assassin will appear and kill him."

"But why is the Assassin waiting so long? Doesn't he see what's happening? If this continues both the Empire and the West Lands will be destroyed."

"The Emperor is paranoid, they say. He doesn't trust anyone and only his closest advisors get to see him in private. Perhaps this Tempest is the Assassin?"

"No, he's already the Bull. And he's in the West fighting Verin's war for him."

"It's someone he knows well that he would trust."

"Sounds logical."

Greza walked over and poured herself some apple juice. She held the cup without drinking as she continued to pace.

"They say he's one of the best swordsmen in the Empire."

"Decaron is better."

"Decaron? Verin had him executed two months ago."

"What?"

She almost dropped her cup.

"Yes, Decaron lead a coup against him. He failed."

Impossible. Decaron was smart and powerful. He had fought the Empire to see justice and then was killed by the man he had fought for.

Whoever killed him had to be skilled and strong enough to do it. And they had to be trusted.

"Greza?" Kratz asked quietly.

"Hmmm?"

"Greza. I think you already know the answer."

She looked to Kratz. She wasn't moving and was looking directly at her.

Greza then knew the answer in an instant and her heart filled with the burning of the Divine Lights.

It was her. She was the Assassin. Verin trusted her. She could get close. She was strong enough to do it. It wasn't going to be some heartless, faceless assassin. It was going to be a woman who loved him more than anyone else in the world.

"I'm the ..."

"You are."

"I don't want to be, Kratz."

"You do have a choice. You can choose not to and watch him descend into tyranny."

She had taught Kratz too well. Most Orks took a liking to the Path due to its simple cause and effect logic. It made sense to the rational Orks and Kratz had taken to it like few others.

"Kratz, prepare for my departure. I leave in the morning. Turundi is in charge of this island business and the council of Chieftains is in charge with you as the Judge. Understood? Tell the Priests to moderate all things."

"Of course, Greza."

Kratz had helped her write their Constitution after all.

Greza ran to her closet but suddenly stopped.

What was she doing? She was running off to kill Verin?

"I can't kill him," Greza whispered.

"You must."

"I love him, Kratz."

"All the more reason. Don't let him get any more blood on his hands."

This was wrong. It had to be. Maybe he could be saved.

"I have to try to save him."

"If you think you must."

Yes, she would speak with him first and see for herself if there is any hope. If he could be turned back then she would give up everything to see that happen.

"I leave in the morning. Have a horse and supplies prepared."

"Yes, your Highness."

She was going to save Verin. She was the only one who could.

In the morning she went out to the stables and hundreds of her people were there to greet her.

Her people. She had never had people before. Even in the Chimera Company she had been apart from everyone else. She had been an outsider everywhere she had been. But now when she looked across all the green faces she saw her people. She saw where she was supposed to be.

"Brothers and Sisters, I assume you've heard why I must leave."

They silently raised their fists in the air as an affirmative.

"I go to stop the Victor from becoming the Scourge. Follow the Path while I am gone and it will keep you safe. You are a beautiful people and are growing more beautiful as I see the Light shine from your faces."

Kratz came up and handed her a sack.

"I packed some food for you. All your favorites," Kratz said.

"Thank you, Kratz."

She embraced the young woman and Kratz squeezed hard.

"Come back to us!" One of the Ork warriors called out.

She smiled at him.

"Of course I will. I'll be back within the month."

"Take a hundred of us with you. We'll make sure you get there," another warrior said.

"I would welcome your company but I must do this alone."

They all moved in to embrace her and one by one, she embraced them all. This wasn't an empty Imperial show of tradition; this was their honest and real feelings. Orks only showed their feelings to the ones closest to them and she was honored to be allowed to be their friend. The little children crushed her in their embraces and the giant warriors squeezed the breath out of her. They were painful people to love but well worth it.

Then it was time. She mounted up and rode out of their unfinished walled city that was growing by the day.

She rode all day and only stopped at night because her horse needed rest.

For two weeks she rode northward and on the eleventh day she saw the impossibly high towers of the capital rise above the plains. As she rode closer she saw that there were few banners on the towers and the roofs in the city didn't sparkle as they had before.

Dozens of soldiers guarded the gates and searched through every cart, basket and bag. Greza carried no weapons. She wore only her breastplate and gauntlets, no visible weapons.

"What's your business in Torna?" A soldier asked.

"I'm looking for a job as a guard, either with a merchant or a caravan."

"No weapons allowed."

"I have none with me."

The guard didn't believe her and searched every inch of her. His hands lingered on her buttocks but if she said anything she'd have a dozen guards on her. She had to go unnoticed so she ignored it the best she could. They saw her cestus and didn't realize that they were weapons.

Eventually she was cleared and she walked in through the gate she had fought at during the battle of Torna. The city square that greeted her didn't have bright banners and crowds of busy people. The place looked empty and the few people she saw hurried from place to place with their heads down like they were afraid. The trees that lined the streets were withered and dying.

She looked at the spot where the cannons had been and then up on the wall where she had been stationed.

It was only two years ago but if felt like forever. She had changed. The city had changed.

Verin had changed.

Greza continued on to the palace where she would save Verin, one way or another.

The palace had barricades in front of the gates that bristled with guns. Who were they afraid of here? The people?

The guards stopped her and demanded she dismount. She obeyed and held her hands out to the sides to be checked again. They checked her over and went through all her belongings.

"Right, what's your business here?" The main guard asked.

"I'm here to see the Emperor."

One of the guards behind them started laughing.

"See the Emperor? Well, miss Ork. It don't work like that."

"He'll want to see me."

"No he won't."

"Tell him Greza is here to see him."

"I'm not going to waste my time with that. Now piss off."

"He holds court every morning. Anyone can attend," one of the other guards said without looking up from his game of dice.

"Yeah, but its noon now. Got to wait till tomorrow, right," the first guard said.

She turned back and found an inn. Hardly anyone was there and she spent the rest of her day in her room praying for guidance. If there was a way to save Verin, let her find it.

Greza spent the night in a cramped and smelly room at the cheapest inn she could find. Very little laughter filtered up to her from downstairs and she was left alone with her thoughts. She tried to imagine what she'd find tomorrow. Would he be so changed that she wouldn't recognize him or would he be the same, smiling Verin she had always known?

She thought about her new family and thought about the love they openly gave her. Kratz would be worrying about her the entire time.

She was back at the palace before dawn and was the first one in line. There were different guards and they searched her like all the others.

At eight in the morning the doors opened and she and a small crowd entered. The Grand Hall had changed like everything else. The banners that displayed the Noble Family crests were gone and only the Imperial Lion was present.

The throne had a platoon of guards in front of it and the small section for commoners also had guards all around it.

A half hour later trumpets blared and men in full but simple robes entered and after that, Verin.

He wore unadorned battle armor and had a gun on each hip. He wore no crown and held no staff of office. He looked exactly as he had the last time she saw him and for a second all thoughts of him being a tyrant fluttered away into imagination.

"Right, let's get this over with. Bring on the complaints," Verin said without looking out at the people.

A merchant that had a problem about one of the guard commanders stepped forward and presented his case. Halfway through Verin raised a hand and stopped him.

"You say this captain forces you to pay him?" Verin asked.

"That's correct, Your Highness."

"So, you think you should sit back on your fat ass and do nothing while he works his life short to protect you and you can't even give him a few coins? Get out of my sight."

The man was then escorted out without ceremony.

What sort of justice was that? Verin wouldn't let that happen ... but he had. She tried to look into his face and see any change, but he looked the exact same.

"Anyone else?" Verin called out. No one said anything. "Good. I wasted enough time here."

Then Greza raised her hand.

"I would like to speak," she said out loud.

Verin didn't look and only waived his hand for her to come forward.

She stepped between the guards and walked out into the middle of the room where she bowed on both knees.

"My Emperor," she said.

Verin turned his head and when he saw her he froze. She waited on her knees. Then Verin bolted up and stepped down to ground level.

"Greza? Is that you?"

She looked up at him. Their eyes met and in that instant every memory rushed back into her mind and down into her heart, threatening to drown her.

He was beautiful. He was everything she wanted. If the Gods of Light held any compassion towards her, they'd let her be with him, even for just one night.

"It's me, my Emperor."

He pushed past his own guards and ran up to her. He lifted her to her feet and looked her over.

"It is you. You've come back."

"I'm back, My Emperor."

He then turned to the assembled crowd.

"You're all dismissed. Get out of my sight."

Once the crowd cleared out he took her to a back room where there was food and wine. He didn't touch any of it. He leaned back against a table like he always used to do and stared at her.

"Why did you leave?" He asked quietly.

"It was too painful to stay."

"Painful?"

"Every day I'd watch you and the Princess fall in love and I was weak. I wish I had been stronger but I wasn't."

"You loved me once."

She looked to him. Even now, after everything, she still loved him.

"Why are you here? Why now?" He asked.

"I wanted to see you. I have a lot to talk about."

She told her story about everything that happened after she left. She stopped her story when she reached Ork Lands and only said that she was "living with the Orks now."

"But why come back?" He asked.

She didn't have to lie.

"I wanted to see you again."

"Nothing's been the same since you left. Tempest is off fighting in the West. Alethia doesn't remember me and Decaron turned traitor."

"I'm here now."

He nodded and then stood up.

"Follow me."

He led her up some narrow stone stairs that went to his quarters. It was his quarters and there was no sign of the Empress. There were no women's clothes, ornate mirrors or bottles of perfume.

"Where is the Empress?"

"She doesn't live here. She lives in the thirteenth tower away from me. Forget about her. It's only me and you now. Please, have a seat."

They sat down in large, cushioned chairs facing each other.

"I missed you Grez, more than you know."

"And I missed you."

"No one told me that it would be this difficult being Emperor. If I had known I'd never have accepted it."

"But now you are. Verin, why are you waging war in the West?"

He raised an eyebrow.

"Really? You can't figure that out? We have to destroy them now or in a generation there'll be another Horde pouring across our borders only this time they'll have guns. We can't let that happen ever again. We came so close to losing the Empire."

"You mean to wipe them out?"

"Not completely. A few I have sent back for reeducation. Others we leave as workers in their own lands."

"Slaves?"

"Not exactly."

Verin was turning them into slave labor. The man who fought to rid the Empire of slaves was turning a whole race of people into slaves.

"You can't make them into slaves, Verin. Don't you remember why we fought?"

"It's better than they deserve. They should be grateful that I don't wipe them off the face of the world."

This was not the Verin she knew. Verin would never tolerate such things. Ever. What had happened to him?

"I've been gone for a while, Verin, but people say that you're executing people for simple crimes now."

"Of course. Our men and women are in the West Lands, fighting for them and all they can do is steal and murder. We're at war and we need every asset we can get. Every loaf of bread they steal is one less for a soldier that's fighting for their safety. It's treason."

"Please, you must show more mercy."

"I mustn't do anything. I'm Emperor and I do as I please. This land will be punished for centuries of indulgence. They don't deserve to be happy. You of all people should know this."

Greza didn't like this line of conversation so she asked about Alethia.

They spent most of the day talking about everything. They talked about the old days in the Chimera Company. They talked about their battles and their march to the capital. She even told him her story of the battle of Torna in detail.

"You were right there and I didn't even see you. I could have seen you. I could have held you."

"You see me now."

"I do. But do you see me?"

"Of course."

"No, do you see me how you used to see me?"

He reached in his breastplate and pulled out a crumpled piece of paper. He slowly opened it.

"It's your letter. The one you left for me. The last lines say that you loved me. Was that true? Do you still love me?"

She never imagined that she'd have to answer for that in person.

Of course I still love him, but what am I supposed to say?

"I do," slipped out of her lips.

As soon as the words left her lips she knew they were true. A warm feeling spread across her body and a peace she had never felt entered her mind.

Despite her love, she was going to resist him, but then she saw a picture in her head, a brief image like a faded memory. Only this was no memory. It showed her sitting on a beach holding a child. Somehow she knew that child was hers and Verin's.

As quickly as the mental image came, it was gone and she was left with the almost overwhelming feelings of warmth and love.

All her life she had saved herself for the one she would marry. That would not happen. Instead, the Gods were giving her this. This was her path. Maybe it was her reward, maybe it was just her Path.

He got out of his chair and stood before her. Verin reached down and pulled her up until they were face to face. She could feel his warmth and his breath on her face. This is what she had wanted.

"Verin, I ..."

"No, I won't let you go again. You love me. I know you do. Kiss me."

"But I ..."

"Then I'll kiss you."

He leaned in and put his lips on hers. And like that she was kissing him. The one man she had ever desired. This was a dream and for a moment she let herself be swept away by it. She didn't think about the war. She didn't think about the prophecy or the scourge. All she thought about was being wrapped in his arms.

As he kissed her he reached up and unstrapped his armor. Then he unstrapped hers. He pulled her to his bed and lay down with her on top of him.

She had never kissed before and had never imagined it to be so wonderful. It was like being in a warm bath: all her senses were filled with overpowering feeling. She smelled him. She felt him. She tasted him.

As they kissed Verin slowly undressed them until she could feel her skin against his.

For the first time, Greza made love and knew what it was like to be held.

Chapter Thirty-Seven

GREZA LAY NEXT TO VERIN, THEIR LIMBS EN-
tangled in each other's. Nothing in her life had equaled
this, not even close. She felt alive, like pure fire was running
through her veins.

Before it would have been wrong and by all the rules it was, but something was different here. The Path led here and she was doing what she was
supposed to do.

She hadn't known what to expect, but it hadn't been that. At first it was
odd. Wonderful, but odd. But now she was absolutely content like she had
just feasted from the best table.

"Grez? You'll stay and be my advisor."

"I wasn't planning on staying."

"I'm not letting you leave again. You're staying and you're going to be my
advisor like you should have been."

"I don't think you'll like what I have to say."

"And what do you have to say?"

"I'll advise you to end this war and stop the suffering. Release your grip
and let the people live in peace."

"And I'll have to reject your advice. I'm not stopping the war, so don't
even try."

"And the laws?"

"When I feel that the Empire is suitably chastised, then maybe I'll relax
the laws."

"And how long will that take."

"If it happens, not for a long time."

"Innocent people are suffering."

"No innocents are suffering. The Horde aren't innocent. The Imperial
citizens definitely aren't innocent. Tell me, who's innocent?"

"Is there nothing I can do to change your mind?"

She ventured her hand up and caressed his cheek. He responded by pulling her closer.

"Not a thing."

He then kissed her and made love to her again. This time though, his words remained in her head. As pleasurable as this was, his darkness soured everything. He wasn't going to change. He didn't want to change. He wasn't just being neglectful; he was purposefully making the people of both nations suffer.

There had to be hope.

The image of the child. There was a future, she just had to find it.

It was late at night when he finally grew too tired to make love. Her body was alight with the memory sensations but her mind was a troubled sea. Verin fell asleep and she looked at him.

He looked like the same, noble Verin that she remembered, but his heart was twisted. Had it always been this twisted? No, there had to have been hope before. But now she didn't see hope. He wasn't going to change.

She also felt that if she tried to leave, he would use force against her. She could sense a barely held in check violence just below the surface. Even his love making was growing less gentle. It was like his anger was slipping out.

When he finally awoke in the morning she offered him some juice. He took the goblet, sipped it and then threw it to the floor.

"Where's my wine?"

"Verin? Is there a room I can freshen up and maybe get some clean clothes to wear?"

He turned to her and smiled that warm smile of his.

"Of course, Grez."

She was led to a room with a blue marble bath tub where silent servants dressed in yellow robes prepared a bath for her. She washed herself as her mind raced. It was a beautiful room with latticed windows and elegantly curved tables that held scented candles. It was definitely a woman's room.

What was she supposed to do? He wasn't going to change. He was only going to get worse. She was supposed to kill him, but could she really do that? If she snuck out she could make it back to her lands without being caught. She was a good rider.

But then the Empire would still be causing everyone to suffer and eventually they'd find her tiny kingdom by the ocean.

She thought of her people. She remembered their smiles as they bid her 'farewell.'

They deserved to be happy.

Yet here she was, in an Empire of misery. No one else could stop Verin except for her. She had to do it. The Path had led her here and she couldn't deny it.

Verin was the greatest man she had ever known and she would never know his equal. Yet she had to kill him.

"Divine Lights, lend me strength. I can't do this."

She got out of the bath and changed into a red dress that had been laid out for her. She slipped on the black velvet boots and tied her hair up into a bun with two gold pins the length of her hand to keep it in place. They were worth more than any single item in her kingdom. When she got home she'd sell them to finance a new colony on the island they'd take from the pirates.

Then she opened the door to return to Verin and she almost ran into a wall. No, it was a man. She looked up at the towering figure and recognized him. It was Captain Daran. His shaved head covered in scars looked down at her.

"Greza. I was surprised to hear that you've returned."

He stepped inside, pushing her back and closed the door behind him.

She knew he wasn't here to be sociable. He was evil but he was no fool.

"I'm going to ask you a few questions and you're going to answer them truthfully. If I sense that you're lying, I'll break your arm. Lie again and I'll break your neck. Understood?"

"Verin won't stand for this."

"He will when I tell him that you've run off again."

This man meant to harm her. She looked around the room and her gauntlets were on a table by the door, behind Daran.

"What are you doing here?" He asked.

"I came to see Verin."

"Why?"

She needed time to think of something. She couldn't beat this man in a fight. If he moved to hurt her, he would end up doing so.

"I needed to ask why he was waging war in the west."

"What does it matter to you?"

"I don't think it's right."

"You came here to ask him about that? I don't believe it. What aren't you telling me?"

"Nothing."

"Now, that's the first lie you've said. I'm afraid I'm going to have to break your arm now."

He reached for her and she pulled back. He smiled.

They both got into the Tallan Passive Stance. He then shifted into the Shotan Offensive and she shifted into the Reyan Defensive. His form was perfect.

"I was hoping I'd see you again. I've wanted a rematch. It's not that I want to know who's better, I know that already. I just want you to know from experience who's better. You see, there's a difference between knowing and experiencing. When you know something from a book, there's always room for doubt and malleable opinion. But once you experience something, there is no more doubt. And you will experience me, Greza."

She wanted to say that she was going to defeat him because she had a mission to do, but life didn't work like that. If she failed here, she'd fail her mission and Verin would continue being the Scourge.

The problem was, she couldn't beat him. Maybe it was lack of faith, maybe it was her logical mind or her cowardly heart.

He lunged forward and she barely managed to dodge. His hand came within an inch of her nose. Before she could fully recover he was striking for her again. His giant fist flew past her head as she ducked backwards.

Her hand shot out to stop her fall and she lashed out with a kick. It landed on his thigh instead of his knee and only distracted him for a second.

Then he had a hand on her left wrist. His other hand was coming in as a fist to break her arm. With her free arm, she shot it up and tried to deflect the blow. It didn't hit her arm but his hammer fist crashed down on her shoulder, knocking her to the ground.

She sprawled across the ground and got to her feet.

He was smiling.

"I thought you'd put up a fight at least."

She didn't wait and charged in. He blocked her first punch but her second punch got him in the gut.

He didn't even seem to notice and the next thing she knew, his fist was in her face. Everything went white and then black and she found herself on the floor again. She struggled to stand up.

He looked at her with his soulless eyes.

"You're going to die here in this room, Ork. You know this, right?"

He walked toward her. He wasn't in a hurry. He didn't need to be because she wasn't going anywhere.

She landed another punch on his face and a trickle of blood escaped his nose, but in the next instant, he grabbed her right arm and swung her like a club, smashing her against the wall.

The wind was knocked out of her lungs and she gasped for breath.

He had her. There was nothing she could do to escape his grip. If only she had a weapon, a knife maybe.

Then she remembered the long pins.

Before Daran could bring his other arm over and break her arm, she reached up, grabbed her pin and jabbed it in his eye. It sunk in and when he jerked his head back, the pin went with him.

He bellowed and flung her away.

She crashed against the floor and struggled to her feet. He was crouched over in pain but kept his good eye on her.

"Now I will make your death as humiliating and painful as I can," he said. "I'm going to do things to you even the devils in the Ten Hells would hesitate to do."

She grabbed the other pin and her hair tumbled down around her shoulders.

He roared and charged at her. She side stepped and landed a punch on his ribs. She felt one crack. With only one eye his depth perception was gone. His swings fell short or went wide. She landed another punch on his face and sent him back a few steps. With her other hand she jabbed the giant needle in his neck and yanked it out before she lost it again. Blood poured out of the wound but he kept coming.

He reached for her and got a hold of her dress. With both hands she pounded his forearm like hammers and he let go. Then she threw the needle at his face and he ducked away.

As he lost sight of her she moved in to his side and used her full weight to step in onto his knee. His knee cracked and gave way, bending in an unnatural direction.

Daran roared again and fell to his good knee. The ground was not where he wanted to be. He couldn't move fast enough and she rushed behind him.

Greza locked her arms around his neck. He tried to pry her arms free, but they were locked together and weren't going anywhere. He was strong but he was still a human. He had size and weight, but pound for pound, she was stronger.

He struggled as she held tight. She couldn't let him loose for a second. This had to end now or her Path was in danger. The people of the Empire were in danger. The child she had seen was in danger.

As she choked the life out of him he grew weaker and weaker until his movements were like someone who hadn't woken up yet.

Eventually he slumped to the ground.

Once he was there she went to the table and put on her gauntlets.

This man was another monster. He was responsible for unnecessary suffering. He was too strong for anyone else to stop. It was up to her.

With one axe swing of her metal fist, she threw all her strength into one blow and shattered his neck.

Greza stood there, panting and looking at the dead monster. She couldn't believe that she had done it and she then realized that she hadn't thought it possible.

Her body ached and she knew she had bruises all over.

She gathered her things and put them in her backpack and hurried outside. There were no guards anywhere. Apparently he had wanted privacy.

Her feet then led her back towards Verin's quarters where she had no idea what to do. She couldn't kill him. She loved him. But she had also seen the immense suffering he was willingly causing.

He used monsters like Daran and killed good men like Decaron. Hopelessness and fear were written on the faces of the people she saw in the streets.

She reached his door without the hint of an idea of what to do.

Greza knocked on Verin's door and he answered it wearing a smile and nothing else. Though his body held no more mystery, she still blushed and turned away. It was a lot to get used to. She also looked away to hide the fact that she had just fought for her life and was still coming down from the surge of energy in her veins.

He saw her reaction and laughed.

She didn't feel like laughing and his smile was a knife to her gut.

"Verin, what does Captain Daran do?"

"He watches my back and stops threats before they become a worry."

"Was he the one who found out about Decaron?"

"Yes. Without him I'd be blind."

"He's not a good man."

"Good! I don't want a good man to have his job. His work requires a very bad man."

"How can you have him working for you?"

"Because he gets the job done."

"Is that all that matters?"

"Well, yes, actually. Morality is a luxury an emperor can't afford."

She shook her head and moved over to the chair where a tray of sliced fruit awaited her. She placed the tray in her lap and began eating. She didn't taste the fruit.

"Greza, I know you always want to do what's right. I know you want to be nice and merciful to everyone, but that's not how the world works. You're living in a children's story where good is good and bad is bad and good always wins. You need to look at reality."

"Verin, you have to stop this war."

"No, I don't. I don't have to do any such thing. That war will go on until their spirits are crushed or I run out of men. I won't let them live to come back and destroy us in some future generation."

"And your own people? How long are you going to crush them?"

"Until they realize that what I say is law. Until they stop rebelling against me. Until they start doing what's necessary and support the war. You're not about to spout some of your useless philosophy at me are you?"

"Not this time."

"Greza, I want you to see what I'm trying to do here. I'm creating a world that can survive no matter what. I don't want a world where an elite class sits around amusing themselves all day and then when a crisis hits, they're completely useless to do anything about it. I'm making a world that could have stopped me and the Horde. It'll be a stronger world."

He paused and looked down at her. Every word he had said was a punch to her face. With each punch her hope died more and more until all that was left was a dark hole where her heart used to be.

"Isn't that worth fighting for?" He asked.

Greza looked up at him.

"A better world is worth fighting for."

She even managed a smile.

She placed the tray back on the table and stood up. She took his hands and led him to the bed.

There they made love again. Her ecstasies lasted into the night. He joked about missing dinner and talked about the next stages in the war. She tried to smile.

Eventually he fell asleep.

Once he was in deep sleep, she crawled out of bed and put on her traveling clothes again. She carefully packed her new red dress into her backpack along with the pins and a few rings he had lying around and prepared to leave.

The last thing she did was strap on her old cestus. They had been with her almost her entire life and were as much a part of her as her own hands.

As she put them on she knew that she had made her decision.

Greza slowly walked over to where Verin lay asleep and looked down at him. She stared at him for a long time, trying to memorize every curve of his face and body.

"I'm sorry I couldn't save you. I love you more than my own life," she whispered to him.

Then Greza raised her armored fists high into the air and brought them down with all her strength. Her eyes were closed and she felt the skull give way and crack apart. She felt warm liquid spray against her face.

A sob wrenched through her gut and escaped her lips.

Unwilling to look at what she had done, she stumbled blindly to her bag and fell on the floor. She used the tablecloth to wipe as much of the blood off her hands and face as she could.

It was a long time before she was able to stand.

She left the room and didn't look back. She wanted her last image of Verin to be him sleeping peacefully in his bed.

Half blind from tears she ran to the stables. They knew who she was, and that she had the Emperor's special attention.

She saddled her horse and rode out of the palace and the city as fast as she could.

She rode all night and well into the morning. Greza only partially paid attention to where she was but the horse seemed to remember the way.

Once her mind cleared enough to think, she found herself in a hazy fog of the mind where she couldn't feel anything. It was like all her senses were wrapped in a warm blanket.

She led her horse through streams and avoided the road without feeling or seeing much of anything. They'd be after her. After all, she had just killed the Emperor. Or maybe they didn't care.

She had killed Verin. The thought brought the sobs rushing forward again. She threw up.

Greza wasn't sure how long it took but eventually she reached home. It was late at night and only the stable boy was up. He had been reading his scriptures.

"I'm glad you're back safe, Your Highness," he said with a fist to his chest in a salute.

She tousled his hair without thinking and stumbled to her room. A few moments later Kratz came in with a lantern. She had only a thin night robe on and bare feet. She never went anywhere with bare feet.

"Greza, what happened?"

"I did it. I killed him. I smashed his head open with my fists."

Greza sat down in a chair but didn't even feel like taking her boots off.

Kratz knelt down in front of her and slipped her boots off. She helped Greza undress and got her into bed.

"I'm sorry, Greza. I wish it didn't have to be you."

"Me too."

Kratz kissed her forehead and went over to sit in a chair. She did that when she was worried: sit up with her all night.

Over the course of the next week she gradually came back to something approaching normal. At least on the outside. On the inside she wanted to die. She didn't want to live in a world where she killed the only man she had ever loved.

Kratz kept reminding her why she had to do it, but that only helped a little. People knew that something was wrong but didn't ask. They knew what she had done and were kind enough to let her grieve on her own terms.

They were good people. Sometimes they fought too much or shouted too loudly when playing drums, but they were good, simple people who looked to her for help.

Her Orks were barbarians, true, but they were on the Path. They had a long way to go still and they knew it. That didn't deter them, only invigorated them.

A month went by without her lunar cycle. She asked Kratz if she should see their doctor. The old woman was brought in and asked many questions.

"I feel different," Greza said.

"Of course. You're pregnant."

Kratz covered her mouth with her hands and looked down to Greza's belly.

"Pregnant," Greza said, letting the word enter her mind.

She had Verin's unborn child in her womb. She knew it would happen, yet it still excited and terrified her.

✶✶✶✶

TWO MONTHS LATER IT WAS ANNOUNCED THAT THE Empress Ariana had given birth to a boy and named him Kiron. She was now the sole ruler of the Empire and Kiron was her heir. Ariana immediately rescinded all of Verin's laws and began the long process of repairing her broken Empire. No manhunt for the assassin ever took place.

Six months after that, Greza gave birth to a girl she named Veris. Veris was her heir. She would be raised to walk the Path and treat all people as equals. She would be trained to protect and guide them.

Their tiny kingdom grew. It spread over the islands and soon encompassed more than the united Ork tribes, but also humans, satyrs, elves and anyone else who didn't belong. Refugees found their way there, including escaped slaves from the West Lands and lost people from the east.

As Greza held her baby girl in her arms she stood on the roof of the keep looking out over the growing city. The docks were growing larger as they reached out into the harbor and buildings under construction outnumbered finished ones.

She knew that one day the Kingdom of the Free People would come into contact with the Empire. Her daughter, the daughter of Verin would face the son of Verin. Whether it would be in a Great Hall or a battle field, she didn't know. But face each other they would.

She felt it in the center of her soul. The prophecy wasn't over.

Coming soon

The Broken Promise

Book 2 in the Path of Light series

About the Author

Zachary Hill has been making up stories since he could remember. He served two tours in Iraq, taught English in Italy and Japan, graduated from Southern Virginia University and and now resides in Utah with his wife. He loves many nerdy activities including comic books, table top gaming, history and art. You can find him at *Minimumwagehistorian.com*.